PRAISE FOR THE NOVELS
OF SALLIE BISSELL

CALL THE DEVIL BY HIS OLDEST NAME

"Tightly wound, *Call the Devil by His Oldest Name* offers a disturbing look into contemporary Appalachia; very well done." —P.T. Deutermann, bestselling author of *Firefly*

Featured Alternate Selection of The Literary Guild
Alternate Selection of the Mystery Guild

A DARKER JUSTICE

"Another page-turner: A chiller that delivers thrills as fast as it telegraphs them . . . [A] fast-moving story, elegantly told, in which Bissell . . . weaves a palpitating web of sinuously deadly suspense."
—*Los Angeles Times Book Review*

"Bissell's Crow is one of the most intriguing characters in today's mystery genre." —*Tulsa World*

"Bissell's tale gathers a full head of narrative steam that keeps the pages turning. For thriller fans who value action." —*Booklist*

"At the end of this book, I felt I had read a masterpiece." —*Deadly Pleasures*

"I don't think I can say I've been more disappointed when a book ended. . . . The threads of the web came so easily, you didn't know you were caught until you tried to put the book down." —*The Purloined Letter*

"**A carnival ride of pain and terror** that you will feel in your gut . . . it is telling when a new author can make your heart race as if you were climbing a cliff face and your palms sweat as if you were gripping the murder weapon yourself."
—*The Commercial Appeal* (Memphis, Tenn.)

"**A nail-biting debut novel** of psychological terror, survival, and loyalty and friendship."
—*The Purloined Letter*

"The tale compels with its depiction of desperate camaraderie and descriptions of gorgeous mountain scenery." —*Publishers Weekly*

"The charm of Bissell's product is her integration of Cherokee lore into what is otherwise **a gut-wrenching suspense set-up**." —*Asheville Citizen-Times*

"A top-notch thriller . . . the pressure builds steadily in this taut debut." —*People*

"Guaranteed to grab hold of anyone who wanders into its spell. **The author rocks and the novel soars.** Find this book and start reading now."
—*The Rockdale Citizen* (Ga.)

"**A page-turner of the first degree** . . . The author's suspense hangs in the air like the smoky clouds that seep from the earth of the mountains."
—*Southern Scribe*

"Creepy, gruesome, suspenseful."
—*Sunday Oklahoman*

"*In the Forest of Harm* astonishes and impresses through complexity of characters, credibility of plot and terrifying sense of menace. . . . **A story of unrelenting excitement.**"
—*Baton Rouge Magazine*

ALSO BY SALLIE BISSELL

CALL THE DEVIL
BY HIS
OLDEST NAME

Sallie Bissell

A DELL BOOK

CALL THE DEVIL BY HIS OLDEST NAME
A Dell Book / March 2004

Published by Bantam Dell
A Division of Random House, Inc.
New York, New York

Dell is a registered trademark of Random House, Inc., and the
colophon is a trademark of Random House, Inc.

ISBN 0-553-58494-4

Manufactured in the United States of America
Published simultaneously in Canada

OPM   10   9   8   7   6   5   4   3   2   1

For Margaret McLean, my brown-eyed girl

ACKNOWLEDGMENTS

My thanks to the following people:
Alana White and Madeena Nolan,
pals and fellow travelers
Ren White, the most enthusiastic first reader ever
Ramona Davidson, my Trail of Tears guide
Shiela Wood-Navarro, Spanish linguist and tennis
partner extraordinaire
My agent Heide Lange, and her most
capable assistant, Esther Sung
Dolores Dwyer for her superb copyediting
And to Kate Miciak, who devilishly put the last
kink in this rope

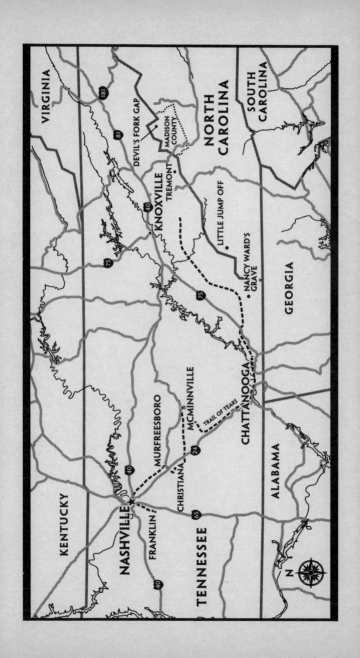

PROLOGUE

HE AWOKE THAT morning to the smell of coffee and salvation. Seeping into his subconscious, the aroma took him back to his mother's kitchen at dawn—coffee hot in his mouth, linoleum cold on his bare feet, eggs crackling in an iron skillet. He listened instinctively for the Farm Report on their scratchy old radio, then he opened his eyes, realizing he was not dreaming of coffee at all—he was smelling it, for real. He lifted one hand to his forehead, then clambered to his feet to peer out of the cave that had, for the past three months, served as home, hospital, and haven from the hunters.

The morning light was razor-sharp, bringing tears to his eyes. A damp mist ghosted up from the creek that gurgled past his slit of a door, and high in a pine tree, the crow he called Charlie gave four raucous caws.

Squinting, he thrust his head into the morning and listened. The creek and the crow he knew well. But if he

turned his head slightly to the left, he could hear a new
sound wafting in on the coffee-tinged breeze. A deep,
not altogether out-of-tune voice, singing.

"*Shall we gather at the ri-ver . . . Where bright angel
feet have trod . . . With its crystal tide forever . . . Flow-
ing from the throne of God . . .*"

He ducked back into the cave, breathing hard. The
hymn recalled a long-ago Sunday when he stood dressed
in a white robe, his arm held tightly by a preacher with
long yellow teeth who thrust his face close and hissed:
Boy, do you surrender your life to Jeeee-sus? Yes, he'd
squeaked like a girl, not caring nearly so much about
Jesus as he did about escaping the old man's sour-milk
breath and cataract-filmy eyes. Without another word
the preacher had pushed him backward into an icy
river, then jerked him out, drenched and sputtering. Afterward his mother had kissed him, and they'd pic-
nicked on fried chicken and deviled eggs on the wide
church lawn. If his father had been pleased, he had not
shown it.

"*Yes, we'll gather at the ri-ver . . . the beautiful,
beautiful ri-ii-ver . . .*"

The voice started up again as the crow flapped its
wings, settling down to watch from a sourwood tree.
Who would be up here singing hymns, this early in the
morning? Not the Feds. Feds always came in groups,
crashing through the bushes like elephants. He'd never
seen any sign of a still up here, and hunting season was
months away. Who could it be? Someone hunting him?
Or someone he might hunt himself?

He sat down to lace up his boots. Mary Crow had
left him with little vision in his left eye and a brain that
sputtered like a faulty electrode, but he'd had the presence of mind, during his long, solitary convalescence, to
exercise his hands and arms with heavy stones he'd
pulled from the creek. Though his legs would never

again move fast or with any kind of grace, his hands could crush bones like pipe straws.

He stuck his head out once more to make sure this wasn't one of his hallucinations. Though the fog was lifting from the creek and Charlie had dropped down to a lower branch of the tree, the voice continued its paean to the Lord.

"Gather with the saints at the ri-ver . . . that flows from the throne of God."

"Okay, buddy," he whispered. "You want a gathering at the river? You got it."

He slipped out of the cave. The singing was coming from downstream, so he turned and limped into the stand of pitch pines that clustered along the creek bank. Walking east, his shuffling footsteps were muffled by a rust-colored carpet of dead needles. He spotted a bright blue kingfisher flying low over the water, then, twenty feet away, he saw the singer. A man. Some hard-shell Baptist, no doubt, tending a small campfire, brewing coffee in a red enameled pot. A tackle box lay on the ground beside him.

Trout fisherman, he decided. And not a very smart one either, making all that racket when the fish were just waking up.

He eased behind a tree to watch. The man appeared to be in his mid-forties, with angular shoulder blades that protruded like plow handles from a green flannel shirt. Though his neck looked creased and sun-worn, it also looked tantalizingly thin, holding the knobby head up like some kind of stem. He considered his odds. If this man had come up here alone, he might have a chance.

His palms began to itch. He rubbed them against his trousers as the man hunkered down to read the creek.

Over there, under that boulder, the fisherman was probably thinking. *That's where the big ones hide. I'll*

*wade out and lay a spinner in there. They'll hit it like
Sunday dinner.*

He watched as the man straightened and drank his
coffee. He saw no second cup, no extra bedroll, no
unaccounted-for fishing rod lying on the ground. All at
once he knew. The Baptist had come alone.

The fisherman put down his coffee and opened his
tackle box. Soon he would have to decide what to do.
Once the fisherman waded out into the middle of the
stream, it would be too late. Right now he stood in the
perfect position, no more than half a dozen yards away.
You once ran the hundred in under thirteen seconds, he
reminded himself. *Surely you can cover twenty feet
without falling down.*

He rubbed his eyes and judged the distance one more
time. Four good strides would get him there; four fast
strides would keep him a surprise.

Opening his mouth, he sucked in a chestful of air,
then he burst from behind the tree. Every step sent pain
jolting up his spine, but he kept his eyes locked on the
man's neck. Though he felt as if he were lumbering
through the woods like a bear, only at the last second
did the man seem to hear him. The fisherman looked
around, startled and wall-eyed, but it was too late. He
grabbed the man's neck with both hands and squeezed.

The fisherman managed a single cry of surprise before he closed off his trachea. The man attempted to
struggle, but he had, as he'd known he would, both mo-
mentum and surprise. As the fisherman writhed vainly
for air, he pushed him facedown into the churning water. The man's neck felt like soft, wet rubber under his
fingers, and when he tightened his grip he felt the soft
pop of vertebrae in his hands. After that, the fisherman
did a quick, frothy little dance of twitches and tics, then,
slowly, he relaxed. First into unconsciousness, then into
death, finally bobbing in the creek lifeless as a hewn log.

Slowly he let go his own breath. *I haven't killed any-*

body like that in forty years, he thought as the Baptist's hair waved like lank seaweed in the creek water. *Still feels the same.* This trout fisherman was no different from the little brown *cá hôi* fisherman he'd offed on a dare, in a soupy little estuary where the Mekong River entered the South China Sea.

He grabbed the man's hair and tugged him over to the bank. Ignoring his vacant eyes and the water that oozed from his open mouth, he dug down deep in the pockets of the man's jeans, pulling out a wallet, the keys to some kind of Ford, and fifty-seven cents in change.

"Okay, buddy," he muttered, pouring himself a cup of the man's coffee while he perused his belongings. "Let's see who the hell you were."

A driver's license revealed the fisherman to have been one Clootie Duncan of Church Hill, Tennessee, a five-foot-ten-inch-tall male with brown (now dead brown) eyes. He'd signed his organ-donor form and was additionally licensed to drive both motorcycles and school busses. He carried no credit cards, but had cash and a paycheck stub from the Hawkins County school system totaling $389.02. His wallet held one photograph—a formally posed picture of himself, suited and bow-tied, grinning behind a sweet-faced old woman in a wheelchair, whose thin white hair wisped up like unpicked cotton. Besides a Sam's Club membership and a coupon from Hardee's, the only other thing in Clootie Duncan's wallet was something called a "Commit Your Life To Jesus" card that enumerated everything you had to do to become a member of Christ's flock. With round, childish handwriting, Clootie had dutifully marked each item with a bright green X and then signed the thing at the bottom, where Jesus had chipped in his part of the deal, promising to "be with you always."

He looked over at the body lying beside him and shook his head. "I don't know, Clootie, but I'd say Jesus took a powder on you this morning."

He finished the rest of Clootie's coffee. He hadn't had a drop of anything hot in over three months, and it tasted like heaven in his mouth. Soon, he decided as he jangled Clootie's car keys, he would be drinking coffee again on a regular basis. Drinking coffee, chewing tobacco, satisfying a craving for chocolate that had nearly driven him mad. Once he returned to civilization, he'd take up a number of his old bad habits again.

He emptied the grounds from the coffeepot, and hoisted the body over his shoulder. Though he'd never seen a soul up here, it was not wise to linger out in the open with a dead man sprawled at your feet. He knew a nearby place where Clootie and Jesus could commune undisturbed for the rest of eternity.

Carrying his burden like a sack of meal, he limped through the trees and eased back into the cave. By memory, he threaded his way into the darkness. Fifty feet in, he put Clootie down and began to crawl, feeling along the floor with his fingers. Within moments, he found what he was seeking. The wide mouth of a hole so deep, he'd never heard a pebble hit the bottom. The air that issued from that hole was warmer than the cave air, and stank like a thousand eggs gone bad. He figured this was as close to hell as he would come, at least in this lifetime.

With sweat beading up on his forehead, he took his own wallet from his pocket. He removed his last remaining thirty dollars and a faded photograph of two teenagers at a dance. Pinned to the credit card section of the wallet was a small gold badge that had "Sheriff" engraved across the top and "Pisgah County" along the bottom. He ran his fingertips over the filigreed surface of the gold badge and sighed. This was all that remained of his life since his last encounter with Mary Crow. Money he couldn't spend, a badge he couldn't wear, and a single photograph that mocked him from forty years past.

"Ball-busting cunt," he whispered as he folded his wallet and stuffed it in the back pocket of Clootie's jeans.

He grabbed the body beneath the armpits and dragged it to the lip of the chasm. When he'd gotten it halfway over the edge, the pressure on the dead man's stomach forced air up through his vocal cords, and the corpse groaned as if he'd come back to life.

"Don't give me any grief about this, Clootie," he scolded, straining to push him on into the pit. "You're dead and that's that. Go and take it up with Jesus now."

Clootie's belt buckle struck a tiny spark of light as it scraped against the cave floor, then the weight of his body shifted forward and he tumbled headfirst into a place where he would never have to worry about Sam's Club bargains or the old woman in the picture again. She would likely die soon, too, he figured. Of grief, no doubt wondering what happened to her sweet boy who had gone out trout fishing and never returned home.

He listened, as always, for any kind of noise, but he heard nothing except the resounding thud of his own heart.

After a moment he inched back from the hole, then walked to the mouth of the cave. As he reentered the bright morning air, Charlie cawed once more.

"Watched the whole thing, didn't you?" Logan looked up at the bird. It flapped up to a higher branch, but still kept a beady black gaze upon him. Logan picked up a rock and considered hurling it at the bird, but decided against it. Though he had a long association with crows, the two-legged ones troubled him far more than the ones with wings. First Martha, now her daughter, Mary. Curious and smart, the women behaved like the birds they were named for. Both pried into secrets that didn't concern them; both had tried to drag him down and peck out his eyes. Mary had almost succeeded. She'd killed his old friend Wurth and turned him into a half-blind beast who'd had to leave his whole life behind him. Today, though, his number had come up on the wheel. First he would get out of here, then he could turn his attention to Mary Crow. Maybe he could bring her back up here and drop her down the same hole he'd just shoved Clootie Duncan in. It would be exactly what she deserved.

Dropping the rock he'd intended for the bird, he began to hum the Baptist's hymn. Like Clootie Duncan, Stump Logan had just been born again. He had a little cash, he apparently had some kind of Ford not too far away, and he had a brand-new identity as Clootie Duncan, solid citizen of Church Hill, Tennessee.

He took out Clootie's wallet, inserted his own photograph and money, and looked at the Commit Your Life To Jesus card again. Not much had ever come of his own commitment to Jesus, but maybe this morning things had changed. Shoot, maybe Jesus Himself had sent him this get-out-of-jail-free card. It was hard to say. All Stump Logan knew was that his salvation would take place, not at the end of that narrow gospel road, but somewhere to the south, along I-85, at whatever exit would deliver him straight to Mary Crow.

1

Deckard County Courthouse
Tuesday, October 8

"CAN YOU SHOW us the Popsicle Man, honey?" Mary Crow sat cross-legged on her office floor, close beside Jasmine Harris, a five-year-old who had lately reverted to the babyish habits of wetting her pants and sucking her thumb. Although the child was of normal height and weight, her huge brown eyes and woeful face reminded Mary of children she'd seen in advertisements beseeching aid for Zimbabwe or Somalia. Jasmine, however, was American. She came from a poor section of Atlanta known as Bankhead and the chief disaster she and a number of other children in her neighborhood had suffered was a forty-one-year-old white male named Dwayne Pugh, aka the Popsicle Man.

"Come on, Jasmine. Don't you stop talkin' now." Danika Lyles, the young attorney who worked as Mary's assistant, spoke more gruffly to the child. "You be doing just fine till we ask you that question."

Jasmine stuck her thumb in her mouth and stared down at the photos of four white men, spread out on the floor. For a long moment she did nothing but noisily work her jaws, then she began to edge one tiny finger up on the corner of the photograph third from the left.

Mary held her breath. For weeks, Child Protective Services had brought Jasmine here to be interviewed; for weeks, they'd come up against this block. The child was bright, answered their questions willingly—until asked to identify Pugh. Then Jasmine would stare at his photograph transfixed, as if the man's very image rendered her speechless with terror. Now, as they neared the end of Pugh's trial, Mary needed Jasmine to do more than just suck her thumb as she gaped at Pugh's picture. Mary needed Jasmine to tell the jury exactly what Pugh had done.

"Look carefully, Jasmine," Mary said. "Are you sure this is the man who gave you all those Popsicles?"

For a moment Jasmine just sucked louder, then she moved her finger away from the corner of the photo and tapped it on the man's right eye.

"Good, baby." Danika knelt down on the floor. "Now tell us what he did. Tell us how he hurt you."

At first Jasmine stared at the photo, then she began to scream. Not weep. Not cry. But *scream,* like a small, helpless animal twisting in some predator's claws. The gooseflesh rose on Mary's skin as she reached instinctively for the terrified child, who scrambled into her arms with a death grip of her own.

"It's okay, Jasmine," she murmured, the odor of feces drifting up as the child helplessly filled her diaper. "He's not going to hurt you anymore. I promise. Never, ever again. I promise."

Jasmine shrieked on. Mary began to rock her back and forth, singing an old Cherokee song about why Possum's tail is bare. As Mary sang, Danika quickly scooped up the photographs and dropped them facedown on Mary's desk. By the time Mary had sung the possum song twice, Jasmine had grown quiet.

"Guess what, Jasmine," whispered Mary. "We sang the bad man away. He's not here anymore. You want to turn around and see?"

"No!" Jasmine howled, vehemently shaking her head.

"Okay." Mary kissed her. "You don't have to. You want to go back to Mrs. Williams?"

"Uh-huh."

"Okay. Here we go." Mary carried her over to Alberta Williams, a sweet, bosomy woman who served as Jasmine's caseworker.

"She's going to need some diaper attention," Mary said softly, handing the child over to Mrs. Williams.

"Don't she always." Mrs. Williams rose from her chair with surprising grace, Jasmine clinging to her neck.

"Thank you for coming, Jasmine," said Mary, resting her hand for a moment on the child's soft cheek. "You did a terrfic job."

When the two left the room, Mary moved to her desk and looked at the photograph Jasmine had finally mustered the courage to touch. A flaccid-faced man with thick lips and receding blond hair, Dwayne T. Pugh had originally been ticketed by the Deckard County cops for vending food without a license. When Officer John Clark climbed into the back of Pugh's ice cream truck and found six tiny pairs of Winnie-the-Poo underpants stuffed among the Eskimo Pies, he grew suspicious. They took Pugh in for questioning and got a warrant to search his home, a pricey condo in upscale Avondale Estates, far beyond the means of most ice-cream vendors. That search turned up only one thing of interest: a key to a small brick bungalow off Ponce DeLeon Avenue. When the officers went there, they walked into two rooms of state-of-the-art servers, then two other rooms full of videotapes so sick, they made even the vice cops queasy. But what had gotten Dwayne T. Pugh remanded to the custody of Deckard County was his basement. A cinder-block room with a rusty drain in the middle of the floor, it held an array of expensive videotaping equipment and two large cages. In one barked a pair of snarling, starved Dobermans; in the other huddled Jasmine, nude and sobbing in her own excrement. Though Dwayne T. Pugh swore that he'd never seen Jasmine, knew nothing about any dogs, and had rented the house for the past three years to a man named Harvey Barrett, the Deckard County detectives were convinced Pugh had earned his posh condo and a seven-figure bank account filming African-American children for an Internet porn business called Chocolate Non-Pareils. Now all Mary had to do was convince a jury of the same thing; for that, she needed Jasmine, the only person who could actually tie Pugh to all of it.

"Don't you think she did better?" Danika asked Mary hopefully.

"Well, she kind of identified Pugh," replied Mary. "She's nowhere near taking the stand."

"You keep on her, she'll quit that screaming. She just needs to toughen up." Danika, who'd dribbled her way out of Jasmine's neighborhood on a basketball scholarship from UCLA, had less sympathy for the little girl, maintaining that the only way to survive the streets was to become tougher than the streets themselves.

"Danika, we're supposed to help the victims of crimes, not traumatize them further."

The tall, stork-like woman snorted. "Better to traumatize one and keep twenty more out of that basement."

Mary started to caution her zealous young colleague again, but the opening strains of the "William Tell Overture" started to erupt from her desk. She reached over and grabbed her new cell phone, a state-of-the-art gizmo that could receive photos as well as text messages. The new DA had passed out a dozen to his senior staff "so we can be in touch at all times."

As she fumbled with the unfamiliar buttons, an instant e-mail message appeared on the screen.

My office. Now. Mott.

Sighing, Mary looked at Danika. "I've got to go see Mott."

"You want me to call Jasmine's mother? Set up another interview?"

"No. Come over to my house tonight. We'll go over the evidence files and see if there's anybody else we can pull out of the hat."

"Seven okay?"

"Seven's good," replied Mary, fighting a deep, sucking feeling of defeat as she headed toward the door.

When Jim Falkner had, on the advice of his cardiologist, retired, Hobson T. Mott, or more correctly, Hobson T. Mott's wife Linda, had completely redone Jim's office, swooping down on the room with a Buckhead decorator and two suitcases full of upholstery samples. Within a week Jim's old red leather armchairs had been replaced by calfskin ergonomic seating systems. The *Georgia Code Annotated* now sat on chrome bookshelves, and where Jim had once sprawled at a battered mahogany desk, Hobson Mott perched behind a glass-topped table that seemed to float in midair. To Mary, going to Mott's office felt like reporting to the bridge of the starship *Enterprise*. Mott, however, was no Captain Kirk. Originally from Indianapolis, Mott had spent his college years playing basketball for the chair-throwing Bobby Knight. He was still obsessed with the game—a crop of gold trophies sprouted from his credenza, and he often referred to court with terms like "a slam-dunk case" and "an air ball defense." Mary had heard that he'd hired Danika not because of her stellar law credentials, but because he needed a good center for the department basketball team.

She tapped on Mott's open door. "You wanted to see me?"

Mott raised his eyebrows. Though he was tall and broad-shouldered, he had an unfortunate cast to his skin that made him look like one of the clay heads over in forensic anthropology.

He motioned her forward. "Come in, Ms. Crow."

Closing the door behind her, she perched on the ergonomic chair that most closely approximated her favorite seat during Falkner's tenure. She repressed a sigh. How they all did miss Jim! Although the Deckard County DA now had a much trendier office, the Deckard Country ADAs had sought justice much more happily when sloppy old Jim was in charge. They could do nothing about that, though. If the voters of Deckard County elected a jackass, you dealt with the jackass or sought employment elsewhere.

"How's the Pugh case going?"

"Okay."

"Virginia Kwan throwing you any curves?"

"Not really. I moved to allow taped testimony, given the age of the witnesses. She objected, saying her client has the right to see his accusers. Judge Cate sided with her."

"You've gone up against Kwan before, haven't you?"

"I've beaten her once." Mary thought of the last time she had faced off against Virginia Kwan, a diminutive woman of Chinese ancestry who wore stiletto heels and blood-red nail polish, and was nicknamed "Dragon Lady" by the denizens of the courthouse. Mary had won, but it had been a hard trial, and the next day Virginia had sent her a dozen yellow roses, with a card that read, "Your greatest foes are your best teachers. Next time! Virginia."

"You know, Ms. Crow, I really feel like this case could set the tone for my administration." Hobson took off his glasses and gave her a square, mah-jongg-tile grin. "A slam-dunk conviction would make the African-American population of Deckard County aware that I'll take their cases just as seriously as Falkner did."

"I may not get a slam-dunk conviction, Hobson." Mary grimaced as she recalled Jasmine's scream of pure terror. "I've got a mighty reluctant witness."

"The Harris kid?"

Mary nodded. She always dreaded cases where she had to put children on the stand. "Danika and I have worked with her for weeks. She still can't look at Pugh and maintain any kind of control."

"Control?" Hobson frowned.

"Bowel control. Jasmine Harris gets diarrhea every time she sees Pugh's photo. I don't know what I'm going to do with her on the stand."

Hobson looked as if he might puke. "But you've built your whole case around that kid's testimony."

"Yes," Mary said, again feeling as if she were being sucked down into a dark hole. "I have."

"Ms. Crow, I don't know if you realize this, but the U.S. Attorney is letting us try this case as a personal favor to me. It's garnered a huge amount of publicity. Right now you should be steamrolling toward a conviction, not wringing your hands over whether your witness can handle the stress of testifying."

"She's five years old, Hobson. Pugh's already traumatized her back into diapers. I'm not going to turn that child into a total basket case for five minutes of testimony. Anyway, child pornography on the Internet is a federal crime. If Richard Johnson thinks he can do better, then let him go for it."

Hobson leaned forward, squinting at her as if he'd

discovered some kind of lesion on her nose. "Ms. Crow, when I came onboard here, you were the number one ADA. Falkner's big three-point shooter. You would have questioned the Devil himself if you thought it would win your case."

"The Devil wouldn't shit his pants, Hobson . . ."

"Doesn't matter." He smirked condescendingly. "Look, I know the last year took a toll on you . . ."

"Are you speaking of Judge Hannah's death?"

"Yes. I know you sought professional help in trying to overcome that trauma."

Mary's cheeks grew hot. Almost a year ago the FBI had asked her help in protecting her friend Irene Hannah from a white supremacist group. She had failed. Ultimately Mary had sought psychiatric help to work through her grief. Never, though, had she allowed it to affect her work. "And your point is?"

"Frankly, I think the pressure of that and this case has combined to affect your judgment." Hobson fondled a brass basketball that served as a paperweight. "I can't believe you would even consider not calling this kid to testify."

"She's a kindergartener, Hobson." Mary stared at him, incredulous. "That's coloring books and *Sesame Street* and—"

"Popsicles?" Hobson interjected.

Mary stiffened. Dwayne Pugh had used Popsicles to lure little Jasmine into his truck. He would use Popsicles to lure more children if she couldn't put him in prison. Maybe Hobson and Danika were right. Maybe she ought to gleefully sacrifice one Jasmine to save twenty of her playmates. "Yes," she admitted, her voice flat. "And Popsicles."

Hobson sat back in his chair, now looking like a triumphant dummy from the forensics lab. "See what I mean, Ms. Crow? I'm beginning to wonder if you have the guts for this job anymore."

"Of course I do."

"Then put Jasmine Harris on the stand, and question her as you would any other witness."

"But—"

"That's an order, Ms. Crow," Mott sliced in. "Jasmine Harris goes on the stand."

Mary looked at him, again longing for the sloppy honor of Jim Falkner's administration. "Anything else?"

He smiled. "Just win my case, Ms. Crow."

"I'll do my best." With a single withering glare, she rose and let herself out of the office, leaving the new Deckard County district attorney counting all the votes he would reap on the back of one five-year-old child.

2

Little Jump Off, North Carolina
October 8

STUMP LOGAN PRESSED himself against the weathered gray logs of the store. He hadn't made this particular climb in almost twenty years, and the effort made each breath sear through his lungs like fire. As he waited for his heart to slow and his legs to stop their shaking, he studied the place that had once been his second home.

Outside, not much had changed. The Little Tennessee River still glittered like a silver ribbon on the other side of the road; the gas pump still cranked out hi-test, though not at the twenty-one-cents-a-gallon price of his youth. Moths still batted against the small blue neon sign in the window, ultimately tumbling dead on the old porch that still remained silent as he hauled his sixty extra pounds across it. He smiled. It was just as if Martha Crow still lived here. His heart began to swell with the memory, then he heard an angry male voice inside the store. He turned and peered in the window.

For an instant he wondered if his brain wasn't short-circuiting again. Jonathan Walkingstick, the best tracker in all the Carolinas, was standing right there, in the prime weeks of hunting season, joggling a baby over his shoulder! He'd shortened his hair from a ponytail into a regular barbershop haircut and he'd exchanged his Army camouflage outfit for a red plaid shirt and blue jeans. Jonathan Walkingstick was looking like a real family man.

"You've pissed off that whole county." The tall Cherokee pointed his finger at a woman who was kneeling on the floor, writing with a black marker on a piece of yellow poster board. "Those men need those jobs. They have families to feed."

"We're not asking that they not build the condos. We're just asking them to build them somewhere else," the woman replied, not looking up from her work. "They've got plenty of other flat land over there."

"Not on that riverbank. And not owned by the governor of Tennessee." Walkingstick paced faster in front of the glowing fireplace. "You'll never stop them. They've got too much money. Too much clout."

"We'll see."

Logan watched, stunned. He hadn't had much luck trying to kill Mary Crow in Atlanta, so he'd come up here hoping that Little Jump Off store might give him some clue as to getting rid of her. Though he'd figured out that Walkingstick and Mary Crow were no longer a couple, he assumed the great hunting guide would mend his broken heart with a new bow or a fishing rod—not a new wife and baby.

"But you've got no business over there." Walkingstick jiggled the baby faster. His hawkish features softened as he nuzzled the child's neck. "They're Tennessee bones."

"Those bones belong to us, Jonathan, just like Tennessee used to."

"Yeah, three hundred years ago." Walkingstick transferred the fretful infant to his other shoulder. "That war's over, Ruth. Andrew Jackson beat us, unfair and unsquare."

"Ruth," Logan whispered, watching as the woman capped her marker and moved over to the rocking chair. With the fire bathing her face in its flickering glow, he could almost see Martha Crow sitting there. They had the same black hair and cinnamon skin. *Ruth.* He looked closer, then caught his breath as she shucked off her sweater. All at once she sat there naked from the waist up, her breasts big as melons. *Jesus,* he thought, feeling a kind of awe inside. Martha had never done that.

Walkingstick handed the baby to his wife. The woman cradled the child in her arms and pressed one dark nipple into its mouth. Logan could not tear his gaze away.

"I don't understand you, Jonathan." Ruth continued their discussion as the baby nursed. "Clarinda's coming to help with Lily. They've given us a VIP campsite. Archaeologists from all over the country will be speaking. You'll have a wonderful time."

"Lily doesn't need to be there. A thousand things could happen."

"Like what?"

"She might get sick. Everybody will want to hold her. Somebody with some weird strain of flu might breathe in her face. Somebody might drop her."

"I'm taking my medicine bag, Jonathan. Lots of sage and comfrey. Granny Broom told me what to do if she gets sick."

"Granny Broom?" Walkingstick frowned at a row of bushy plants that hung from the mantel, drying upside down. "What the hell does that old witch know about children? How much sage should you give an infant? How are you going to get comfrey in a nursing baby?"

"You make a tea, Jonathan. Give her little sips, if she needs it, which she won't." Sighing, Ruth frowned at her husband. "Listen. You've got to lighten up. You can't protect Lily every minute of every day. You'll go crazy before she even starts walking."

Logan watched, mesmerized, as Ruth lifted the baby to her shoulder and patted her on the back. Moments later, she nestled it against her other breast. An ancient anger began to stir inside Stump Logan, like the coals of a long-dead fire rekindling into flame, suddenly glowing orange where they'd long been sooty black. Lately he'd been so caught up in his efforts to rid himself of Mary Crow that he'd forgotten how much he hated Jonathan Walking-stick. The smart-ass bastard had almost torpedoed Martha Crow's murder investigation fourteen years ago, asking questions that could not be answered, proposing murder theories that only frightened people more. He thought he'd gotten rid of Walkingstick when he'd hassled him so badly, he'd joined the Army. But Walkingstick had done his hitch and returned, ever since looking at the sheriff of Pisgah County as if he were some pale, nasty thing that had crawled out from under a rock.

"Have you got permits and toilets and paramedics lined up?" Walkingstick was asking his wife.

"Gabriel Benge took care of all that."

"Ah, yes. How could I forget the University of Tennessee's answer to Indiana Jones." He reached down and propped Ruth's poster up against the wall. "Cherokees! Attend the Save Our Bones Rally," it read. "October 11–13, Tremont, Tennessee."

Logan memorized the poster, then his eyes returned to the nursing mother. His wife's tits had been not much bigger than a boy's, and she'd always recoiled from his touch. Never had he gotten to caress breasts so beautiful. Only when it was over had he touched Martha's at all.

Walkingstick tilted his head at the poster as if looking at a work of modern art.

"What do you think?" Ruth asked as her nipple slipped from the satiated child's small pink mouth.

"Reminds me of Wounded Knee," said Jonathan sourly. "What a treat for Lily."

"Oh, give me a break, Jonathan." Ruth drew the baby closer and kissed the top of her head, all covered with wispy dark hair. "Someday, our Lily will tell her grandchildren that she was there when Indians finally came together and spoke with one voice."

Our Lily. Logan shrank back in the shadows as an idea struck him like a thunderbolt. He'd been going about this all wrong! Three times he'd tried to kill Mary in Atlanta, three times he'd failed. Now he realized that the one fail-proof way to do it was right here, just inside this cabin. *Lily Walkingstick. Walkingstick's child.*

He looked up into the sky and shivered, wondering if he was like one of those old people who won the lottery at ninety—someone whose entire allotment of luck got doled out at the very end of their life. He'd never had any luck when he was young, but ever since he'd taken Clootie Duncan's Jesus card seven months ago, the stars had seemed to align, just for him. He'd gotten out of the cave with Clootie Duncan's IDs. He'd found a job that allowed him time off with money to spend. And tonight he'd just been given the way to rid himself of Mary Crow for good and maybe lay some major pain on Walkingstick as well.

He lingered on the porch a bit longer, watching as the young couple's domestic discord abated. Walkingstick started dancing the baby to Van Morrison's "Brown-Eyed Girl" while his wife put her sweater back on and began another poster. Softly Stump eased his bulk off the porch and back into the dark forest. He had a few more details to work out, but all the basics were right here.

"Lily," he whispered, testing the syllables on his tongue as he shuffled through the trees. What a pretty name. Who would have ever thought that you could set a trap for a crow with a flower?

3

"GO, MARY! GO for the sweet spot!" Mike Czarnowksi gripped the body bag while Mary pummeled it with a flurry of punches. They stood in one corner of the huge Justice Center gym, ignoring the six cops playing half-court basketball behind them. As Mary danced in front of the bag, Mike peeked around from behind. "You have a bad day in court?"

"Court was fine." Mary breathed huskily as she stepped back. "It's everything else that sucks." She took a swipe at the bag with a snappy right cross. "You ever work a case involving little kids?"

Mike shook his head. "Nothing beyond finding a couple of lost ones."

"You're lucky. Cases with kids are the worst."

She lowered her shoulders and attacked the bag's midsection, flailing away both Hobson T. Mott and Dwayne Pugh. Four months ago, Dr. Eileen Bittner had prescribed boxing lessons as part of Mary's therapy. They'd been taught by Mike Czarnowski, a cop Mary knew by reputation only. He was known as "The Closer" around the Deckard County Courthouse—rumor had it that detectives would call Czarnowski in when they had a suspect who was withholding some vital piece of information. They'd take the luckless individual up to the seventh floor and lock him in a small, soundproof room, then bring in Czarnowski. Fifteen minutes later, the door would open. Later, the suspect wouldn't have a mark on him, but he would be wild-eyed and more than willing to tell everything he knew. Although dismayed by Czarnowski's reputation, Mary had never asked him about it. To her, Mike was a supportive boxing coach who told her that to punch someone's lights out, all you had to do was find their sweet spot and hit it. Back then she didn't care about dropping anyone to the canvas; all she wanted to do was punch away the pain of losing Irene Hannah.

"You want to go a couple of rounds with me?" he asked now with an eager grin. "I'll go glove up if you do."

"Sorry, Mike. I've got to get home. Danika Lyles is coming over after supper."

"She that good-looking black chick who played ball in California?"

"That would be Danika." Grinning, Mary held out her gloves, implicitly asking his help in unlacing. "You interested?"

"Nah—I'd have to stand on a chair to kiss her. She's got some awesome moves, though. Beats Mott every time they play."

"Danika beats Hobson?"

"Aw, yeah. She's all over the boards. Mott just stands there like his shoes are nailed to the floor."

Mary laughed as Czarnowski pulled off her right glove. "Thanks, Mike. You just made my day."

She showered in the locker room, relishing the sweet, tingling exhaustion of a hard workout. With her hair still damp, she hurried out of the gym, stashing her good clothes in the minuscule trunk of her black Miata. As she started to pull out of the parking lot, she noticed a familiar gray Mercedes, one that sported the bumper sticker "Practice Random Acts of Kindness and Senseless Beauty."

Mary smiled. Eileen was here, no doubt leading one of her special relaxation-for-cops classes. Although Mary had never taken her class, she imagined Eileen's voice would be just as soft and soothing as it had been the first time Mary walked into her office.

"What brings you here, Mary?" she'd asked, smiling, her golden-brown eyes sympathetic.

"I see dead people," Mary replied, sounding exactly like the kid in the movies. "Or at least I see one particular dead person."

"And who would that be?"

Mary had taken a deep breath, and with the same conviction that other patients must confess that they were Jesus or Napoleon or from the planet Remulac, began to relate the whole story of Stump Logan, former sheriff of Pisgah County, North Carolina. About how Irene Hannah had implicated Logan in Mary's father's death; about how Logan had escaped into the woods after Russell Cave exploded. About how after six months of searching, the FBI had relegated Stump Logan to that lengthy list of suspects they presumed dead simply because they could not find them. Which suited Mary fine . . . except that she kept seeing Logan all over Atlanta. Once at the bookstore in Lenox Mall, once at the deli counter of her grocery, the last time standing in her backyard, staring through the window at her. Although he looked gaunt and filthy, as if he'd just crawled out of his own grave, she'd instantly recognized his face and his hard look of hate.

"Have you called the FBI?" Eileen had asked after Mary came to the end of her story. "Told them your suspicions?"

"Every time," Mary answered. "They took me seriously at first. Now they think I'm nuts. Hell, most of Deckard County thinks I'm nuts."

"Do you think you're nuts?" Eileen tried her best to keep the oh-boy-have-I-got-a-sick-puppy-here tone out of her question.

"No." Mary's voice wobbled as she wondered, for an instant, if she were insane and living in some lost episode of the *Twilight Zone*. "But if Logan's not real, then I sure would like to quit seeing him."

Six months of daily therapy and a refillable prescription for Xanax later, Eileen convinced her that she might be projecting Logan's image as a way of coping with the fate of her friend Irene, and her sightings of him dropped to none. At their last session, Eileen had handed her a business card and said, "All in all, I'd say you're ninety-eight percent healthy."

"And two percent obsessed?" Mary had laughed.

"About that."

"Well, that's not too bad, considering."

Eileen gave her a hug. "You've got my number, honey. Call me if you need me."

"I will, Eileen," Mary promised aloud now as she pulled out of gym parking lot. "I will."

She sped through the early-evening darkness to her grandmother's house. Even though it was only mid-October, tissue-paper ghosts and balloons festooned several stately mailboxes, and some ghoulish wag had stuck a Halloween pumpkin on the spiked iron fence that guarded the lawn of one of Atlanta's poshest estates.

"Looks just like Hobson," Mary murmured, relishing the image of her pompous boss getting stomped on the basketball court.

She pulled her car into the basement garage and made a mental note to pick up some Halloween candy, though she doubted any kids would knock on her door. Unlike her grandmother, who loved wild, sparkling parties visible from the street, Mary spent most of her time in the back of the house, giving the handsome old Tudor a dark, forbidding look. She didn't care. For her, the house was full of ghosts. It wore dark and forbidding well.

She hurried up the kitchen stairs, unlocked the back door, and disabled the alarm system that would, in fifteen seconds, go from annoying screech to full howl and bring a squad car of Atlanta's finest straight to her door. The warning beep stopped, leaving the house bathed in a profound, empty silence. Unconsciously, she paused to listen. Even though her grandmother had been dead over a year, she still waited to hear her light footsteps in the back hall, her reedy voice calling her name in an Atlanta accent so old and soft that you could hear it now only in nursing homes and hospital rooms. She sighed. She would give most anything to hear her grandmother again. But then, she wished that about a number of people.

She dropped her briefcase on the floor and switched on the light. She had less than an hour before Danika was scheduled to arrive. Just enough time to eat and spread Dwayne Pugh's sick files out on the dining room table.

She grabbed a chicken linguini dinner from the freezer, shoved it in the microwave, and poured herself a glass of water. She was tempted by a half-bottle of cold Chardonnay, but tonight was a work night. She'd stick with water. Closing the refrigerator, she stopped to look at her favorite photograph on the door. Herself, holding

Lily Walkingstick in the Little Tennessee River, flanked by Ruth and Jonathan. Jonathan's favorite aunt, Little Tom Murray, was an ardent Methodist who was determined to have Lily christened and someone to serve as godmother. Though Jonathan personally thought it was a bunch of malarkey, he loved his aunt, so he'd called Mary and asked her to serve. At first she'd declined, not wanting to board the roller coaster of emotions she felt toward Jonathan and his new wife. But Jonathan had insisted, and Mary had given in. She drove up to North Carolina early one Sunday morning. Jonathan greeted her with a kiss on the cheek while Ruth Moon welcomed her with a perfunctory hug and a small muslin bag of sassafras tea, fruit of her newfound passion for herbs and native medicines. At eleven o'clock Mary held Lily in her arms in front of a Methodist minister and vowed to fulfill a number of religious duties. Though she'd spoken sincerely, she knew the only promise she'd make good on was that she would love Lily as no other. Absolutely enchanted by her round little eyes and lopsided grin, Mary somehow knew that Lily was as close to a child of her own as she would ever get. It would not be given to her to have children, not in this lifetime. "Guess you'll have to put up with three parents, Lily. Thank God you live where you do," she whispered softly, ignoring a throb of wistfulness as she wiped a speck of dust from the baby's photo. "Your mom, your dad, and crazy old Aunt Mary."

She waited for her dinner to nuke, setting a single place in the little breakfast nook that overlooked the peony bushes where she'd last seen Logan. She'd been baking brownies that afternoon. Turned around and there he was, staring straight in at her. They stayed like that for several frozen seconds, then she whirled to punch the panic button on her alarm. When she looked back, he was gone. The cops pulled up three minutes later, but found no sign of anyone in or around her backyard. She caught the indulgent smirk that had passed between them as they climbed back in their cruiser. The next day she called Eileen Bittner.

"He sure looked real," she murmured now as she drew the blinds, blocking any sight of the spot where he'd stood, or at least where she thought he'd stood. The microwave beeped. She unwrapped the steaming dinner and carried it over to the table. Danika would be here soon, ready to go over those files. No point in rehashing all that Stump Logan nonsense now.

Just as she took her first bite, the phone rang. She was tempted not to answer it, then she decided that it might be Danika, delayed for some reason.

"Is this Mary Crow?"

"Mm-hmm," Mary answered with her mouth full, knowing the next line would be an offer for aluminum siding or switching her long distance carrier.

"Hi, Mary. This is Ruth. Ruth Moon."

"Ruth." Mary swallowed, surprised. "I'm sorry, I didn't recognize your voice."

"Did I interrupt something?"

"Not at all. Just grabbing a quick dinner. How's Lily?"

"She's fine. In fact, she's terrific. Jonathan's right here, singing her theme song."

"Her theme song?"

" 'Brown-Eyed Girl.' That old Van Morrison tune."

"Oh." For a moment Mary felt strange, picturing Jonathan at Little Jump Off, crooning to his little girl.

"I guess you're wondering why I called . . ."

"Well," Mary evaded awkwardly.

"I've got an invitation for you."

"Is Lily having an occasion?" Mary asked, thinking of first steps and first teeth and the thousand other firsts that babies amaze their parents with.

Ruth laughed. "No, nothing like that. This weekend, in Tremont, Tennessee, I'm cochairing the first North

American All-Tribe Rally. Representatives are coming from every tribe in the country."

I should have known, thought Mary. No silly baby celebrations for Ruth. For her, Native America would always come first.

"Mary, we're going to protest the Summerfield Development Company's desecration of an ancient Cherokee burial ground. The governor of Tennessee has interests in this development, so everything's gotten pretty nasty. We're planning a peaceful demonstration of over five thousand people. Two of the national news networks will be there."

"That certainly sounds interesting, Ruth . . ."

"We'd love it if you would come and be one of our speakers. You could talk about what it means to be an Indian woman working in a white man's system."

Mary closed her eyes. *What a weekend! Yammer all day about being Cherokee, and piss off the governor of Tennessee while you're at it.*

"It'll be fun, Mary," Ruth coaxed. "As a featured speaker, you could meet Indian activists from around the country."

This just gets better and better, thought Mary as Ruth talked on, telling her about someone named Benjamin Goodeagle, and how CNN wanted to do an interview with her, and John Black Fox's environmental group was going to have twenty petitions going around—

"Ruth," Mary stopped her in midsentence as she heard a *bing-bong* from the front door. "Thanks so much for thinking of me, but I'm afraid this time I'm going to have to say no. I'm in the middle of a big trial. In fact, the attorney who's helping me is at the door right now."

"A trial?" Ruth sounded as if she'd never put lawyers and courtrooms together.

"Yes. A kiddie-porn case." Mary pushed back from

the table, anxious to let Danika in before the doorbell rang a second time. "I'm sorry, Ruth, but I've really got to run—"

"Oh." Ruth's voice faded to nothing.

"But thanks for asking me. I really appreciate it." Mary paused, hoping that Jonathan might ask to speak to her, but Ruth gave no indication of that.

"Well, if you change your mind and want to take a break, Tremont's only about three hours away from Atlanta."

"Thanks, Ruth. I'll keep it in mind. Give Lily a hug and kiss for me and I'll look for you on TV."

Ruth said good-bye. Mary hung up the phone and hurried to the door, casting a wistful glance at the photo of Jonathan, the man who should have been hers, holding the baby who should have been theirs.

4

Wednesday, October 9
Tender Shepherd Home for Girls
Franklin, Tennessee

STUMP LOGAN EASED back in his chair, pleased with the plans he'd scribbled in his notebook. After he'd talked to the remaining two people he trusted in Carolina, he'd begun reading up on his Cherokee history, spending most of the past twenty-four hours checking maps and historical markers and the various old routes that traveled the length of Tennessee. At first he'd put down words awkwardly, with lots of cross-outs, but now his thoughts flowed smoothly from his head to his fingers, their passage marked only by the scratch of his pencil on paper. It felt calming, in a way, to map out this new plan for Mary Crow. Almost as relaxing as a chocolate bar.

Suddenly, as he bent over his studies, a woman's voice filled the room. *"Duncan? Are you there?"*

Logan's heart fell. His alter ego, Clootie Duncan, would have to put away his plans for now. His employer beckoned, via the intercom that connected her room to his.

"*Duncan?*" the voice warbled again, pitched somewhere between irritation and concern. "*You're not having any trouble, are you?*"

"No," he muttered to himself. "I'm just dandy."

He dropped his notebook in the desk drawer, closed his eyes, and sighed. He supposed he should feel more kindly toward Edwina Templeton. She had hired him without a glance at his made-up references when he had showed up at her door, classifieds in hand, applying for the position of "live-in security guard."

"I pay well, Mr. Duncan," she informed him as they chatted on her porch. "My business requires loyal and extremely discreet protection."

"What business are you in?" he'd asked, wondering what kind of work this dumpy, spavined woman might do.

"I run a home for pregnant girls," Edwina replied, her squint-eyed smile as inscrutable as the statues of Buddha he'd seen in Vietnam.

He'd looked at the freshly painted porch of the old plantation house, set squarely on fifty acres of prime Tennessee farmland, and said, "I didn't know pregnant girls went anywhere anymore."

"The rich and religious do." Edwina brushed a bright red ladybug off the sleeve of her blouse. "That's why I need security."

"For what?"

"Raging hormones can make this a pretty volatile place, Mr. Duncan. I need someone to make sure my girls stay put and that their young bucks don't come visiting. Someone to make especially sure my girls don't change their minds when it comes time to give up their babies."

"So you run an adoption agency?"

Again, that Buddha smile. "I make unwanted babies

disappear, Mr. Duncan. Most of them are adopted. A few meet more controversial fates."

Good God, he thought. *This woman runs a one-stop chop shop for sluts in trouble, probably breaking every law in Tennessee.* He understood, then, Edwina's need for protection and why she was willing to pay five hundred dollars a week, plus room and board. With an inscrutable smile that mirrored her own, he'd offered her his hand and his assurance that security-wise, she need never again draw a troubled breath. Three minutes later, after explaining that he was never to answer her telephone, park in her parking spot, or entertain women in his room, Edwina hired him.

But when she took him inside to show him his accommodations, he regretted not having asked for more money. Outside, the house gave the appearance of an old planter's house. Inside, it looked like a museum. Though he knew nothing about antiques, everything from the crystal chandeliers to the brocade drapes bespoke money, and lots of it. Edwina Templeton craved *things,* he decided as he followed her up a wide staircase carpeted with a red oriental runner. Fancy home furnishings for sure; what else, he had yet to determine.

On the way to his room, he learned that his coworkers were Paz Gonzalez, a diminutive Mexican who did various chores around the farm, and his wife Ruperta, who cleaned the house and cooked. Once inside his room, he saw that Edwina's acquisitiveness did not stop at antiques. She had equipped the room of her security officer with a small arsenal of computers and weaponry. Besides a beautiful old Winchester .70 and a Smith & Wesson 686, she kept an array of Tasers, small devices that looked like remote controls, but which shot electrical darts instead of bullets and reputedly could immobilize anything short of a charging rhinoceros. On an old rolltop desk sat a police scanner, a tuner that broadcast the latest weather information, and a brand-new laptop computer, hooked up to the Net on a DSL connection. He found it amusing. Edwina Templeton seemed to covet the very old and very new, both at the same time.

As she showed him the closet and the bathroom that opened off his bedroom, he fingered Clootie Duncan's Commit Your Life To Jesus card, which he kept like a talisman in his pocket. The only thing he'd committed his life to was killing Mary Crow, yet Jesus again seemed to be helping him out. With Clootie's name and Clootie's wallet, he'd just driven up in Clootie's stupid little Ford Escort and landed a job with a single woman who had guns and a fair amount of cash behind her. Now all he had to do was figure out how to use this old bitch to his advantage.

He'd done that one day in June, shortly after he'd put some newly unpregnant fourteen-year-old back in the car with her parents. As he closed the car door, a headache struck him like a lightning bolt. The world—people, trees, the farmhouse itself, spun with a sickening, neon-lit glow. It hurt so bad, he couldn't move. Not his feet, not his arms, not even his eyeballs. He could do nothing except stand by the driveway, staring as the girl's black Beemer became a dot in the distance. All at once he felt a great clap of thunder, then he hit the ground, hard. His last conscious thought was that he was dying, and that it wasn't nearly as bad as he'd expected.

A few hours later, though, he awoke, alive enough to realize that he lay nude on his bed, with Edwina Templeton gazing down at his nakedness. She examined him for a full five minutes, intensely studying everything from the medal he wore around his neck to the scars on his lame right ankle, bending so close to his penis that he could feel her damp breath upon it. He submitted to her scrutiny without moving, wondering if maybe he was the first male she'd ever seen. Then he remembered seeing her diploma from nursing school. Nobody, he

figured, could go through that without seeing at least
one man without his clothes on. Maybe she'd known
men only in theory, though, and not practice. He hid a
smile. Though the thought of congress with this woman
sickened him, if it helped him get what he wanted, he
would teach Edwina Templeton about the function of
men, as well as their form.

It had been laughably easy, even for a rough-hewn
pawer like himself. A longing smile, a flower plucked
from her own garden, help placing a stupid-looking
chest she'd bought in New Orleans. Women fell for the
most trivial of things, and Edwina was no exception.
He'd risked it all late one night when she came into his
room to ask him some computer question. Pushing
aside his topo maps of downtown Atlanta, he'd chanced
a kiss, full on her mouth. She'd instantly opened her
dressing gown, and moments later they lay in his bed,
squeaking the bedsprings as frantically as any of the
teenagers who camped here to have their babies.

Stupid cow, he thought now, inwardly shivering at
the memory of Edwina's too-wet tongue in his mouth,
her stubby fingers squeezing his scrotum like it was an
overripe tomato.

"*Duncan?*" The intercom squawked again. Any moment she'd appear at his door, coming to see if he had
fallen to the floor, jerking in one of his fits. Though
she'd granted him access to everything—her guns and
her computers and her cars—he hated everything about
her, from the scuff of her house shoes on the bare floor
to the way her fingernails curled up at the ends.

"Five minutes," he stalled her. "I'm in the middle of
something." Five minutes would be all he had, now that
he'd given her a time. Unconsciously rubbing the medal
around his neck, he pulled his Mary Crow list from the
drawer. Guns, camera, and laptop he had. Now he just
had to figure out how to weasel the van and a long
weekend out of Edwina.

"*Duncan!*" Edwina's command blasted through the intercom.

"Coming!" He shoved the list back, pulled out a half-eaten candy bar, and stuffed it in his mouth. The sweet, dark cocoa calmed him, softened the static in his head. *You've done this before,* he reminded himself. *You can do it again.*

With chocolate sweetness filling his head, he headed toward Edwina's bedroom. He hadn't quite decided the best way to approach her. Maybe it would come to him while they attended to what was always their first order of business.

"What were you doing in there?" Sitting up in her big walnut four-poster, with her brown hair loosened from its bun, she looked like some aging Scarlett O'Hara. Several antiques magazines lay open on the bed, and he could see where she'd circled some crazy-looking old bed in an auction catalog.

"Reading," he lied as he swallowed the last of his chocolate.

"About what?"

The next person I need to kill, he thought as he bent to pull off his boots. "Cherokee Indians," he replied, landing somewhere in the vicinity of the truth. "They suffered a lot in Tennessee."

"So? A lot of people have suffered in Tennessee."

He unzipped his fly and removed his trousers. It used to unnerve him, stripping in front of her, but she took a strange pleasure in it, and now he just thought about other things while he did it. If it got him out of her bedroom faster, so much the better.

All at once a bolt of pain shot up behind his left ear. At first he thought his knees would buckle, then oddly, his penis grew hard, straining at the fabric of his shorts.

"Well, look at you, Duncan." Edwina pointed. "You must have missed me while you were gone."

Just like a sore tooth, he thought, then he put that

notion out of his mind. Tonight he needed to give the devil her due. Edwina satiated was far more malleable than Edwina left wanting.

He climbed on top of her, pleasuring her in the ways he knew she liked. He kissed her for what seemed like hours, fondling her lumpy breasts, rubbing the inside of her thighs. Finally he pushed himself into her and began the rut she so loved. Twenty-five, thirty, one stroke for each of his fifty-seven years. When his back began to ache and he feared his head would burst, she arched and sucked in her breath, grabbing the pillow behind her head.

Usually he dressed right after they finished. Tonight he rolled off her and sat on the side of the bed, watching her as she lay with her eyes closed, her upper lip moist with sweat. She opened one eye and gave an earthy cackle.

"What'd you do on that trip of yours, Duncan? Get a scrip for Viagra?"

Despite his disgust, he smiled. He was in no way the man of his youth, but he could still put it to even a saggy old bag of bones like this. "Nah. Nothing like that."

"What then?"

"Visited my brother, mostly." He flashed back to Little Jump Off, the way Walkingstick's wife looked that evening, bare-breasted, nursing her kid.

"Bullshit." Edwina shot the word at him like a knife. She stared at him, the soft repose of her face gone. "What do you want, Duncan?"

"What makes you think I want anything?"

"The way you did what you just did." She sat up and covered herself with her gown. "I'm not a fool."

"Okay," he said, slumping his shoulders slightly, hoping to indicate humility. "I need your help."

"For what?"

"I need to get rid of a baby."

"A baby? Where on earth did you get a baby?"

He feigned embarrassment. "I knocked someone up."

"You?" She spat up a laugh. "When?"

"Before I came here. I didn't know anything about it until I went home."

"You're kidding, I hope."

"No." He sighed deeply. "It's true."

"Doesn't the mother want it?"

"She wants to join the Air Force. Fly planes. Bomb terrorists."

"Then why don't you take it? You're quite the man between the sheets these days."

He faked a slow, sad smile. "I'm almost sixty years old. I have fits and a bum leg. What kind of life could I give a child?"

Edwina narrowed her eyes at him, as if trying to decide how much of this to believe. "What kind of baby is this?"

"A girl. Pretty. Healthy, too."

"How old?"

"Three months, I think." He hoped he was somewhere in the ballpark on this one.

"Is she white?"

"Partly."

"Sorry, Duncan." Edwina flopped back on her pillows. "The market's full of half-black babies."

"She's not half-black," he replied. "She's half-Cherokee."

"What color is that?"

"Like coffee with a lot of cream."

"Is she retarded?"

"No. She's perfect."

Edwina stared up at him. He knew she was mentally rifling through the files she kept on her computer. Did she have anybody who wanted a light brown baby? More important, could she find anybody who would pay money for such a child?

"You say the mother is willing to surrender her?"

"She wants me to come get her in Knoxville this Saturday. I was hoping you'd loan me the van and let Paz ride along to help."

"What for?"

"So I can bring my baby back here, and you can find her a home. It would be an adoption, only without the overhead of a pregnant girl. Pure profit." There. He'd dropped his hook. Now all he could do was wait to see if she took it.

Edwina gazed, unseeing, at the ornate bed she'd circled in the auction catalog. "This baby is three months old?"

"Yes."

"That's past the prime age." She frowned at him. "Plus you'd have to get the mother to sign some papers."

"Not a problem," he assured her.

"I don't know. I'll have to think about it." She gathered up her antiques magazines and plumped up her pillows. "Stop by my office in the morning. I'll let you know then."

"Thank you," he said, pulling up his trousers.

"Don't thank me yet, Duncan," she snapped. "When I do a favor, I expect a lot in return."

Expect all you want, sister, he thought as he hurried toward the door. *Expecting ain't getting, in my neck of the woods.*

5

Friday, October 11
Little Jump Off, North Carolina

THE RASPY, INSISTENT *caaww* of a crow awakened Jonathan Walkingstick. All night he'd slept in the same position, his back turned to his wife, his body stiff with anger. Though Ruth had slept beside him, she lay equally rigid, facing the other side of the bed. The fight that had been simmering between them all week had risen to a boil last night, spilling over and blistering everyone at Little Jump Off with caustic words and bitter accusations. Clarinda, Ruth's newly arrived cousin from Oklahoma, had finally tuned them out by sticking her nose in the latest Danielle Steel novel. Little Lily, however, had no escape from their hostility: long into the night the baby had squalled inconsolably. When they were at last able to silence her, they both lay down in icy silence, both keeping to their own sides of the bed, careful not to let their bodies touch.

Caaawwww. The crow cried again. Jonathan raised

up. In the leaden light he could see most of the parking lot, the highway that curved along beside it, and past that, the river beyond. Wispy tendrils of early morning fog rose from the Little Tee, making it look hot instead of cold. The Styx, Jonathan thought, remembering his old mythology book and the seething stream that bordered the ancient Greek underworld. Maybe that was where they lived now. Some backwoods corner of Hades reserved for people ill-suited to be married to each other.

He sighed as he watched the fog curl wraith-like into the air. Last night they'd fought over a man who'd called and wanted to hire him out as a boar guide. Last week they'd fought over her taking Lily to the rally in Tennessee. Last month they'd fought over Ruth contributing a hundred dollars to a Micmac Indian running for a congressional seat in Maine. Maine! One way or another, it always came down to money. He hoarded dimes like a squirrel hoards nuts; Ruth spent money as if they were rich. He had thought Lily's birth might make his wife more cautious with their dollars, but Ruth had grown worse, throwing money away on the most ridiculous of things. If Lily got sick this winter, he didn't know what they would do. He doubted Ruth's goofy herbal remedies would make much headway against pneumonia or the croup.

A sudden dark movement caught his eye. The crow that had awakened him swooped from the roof and landed in the parking lot. It strutted over and hopped up on the rim of the trash barrel beside the gas pump. With a flick of its sleek black wings, it began to pick through the garbage, expertly perusing the trash for a cast-off french fry or moldy crust of bread.

"*Koga*," he whispered. *Crow*. Though the sleek black birds did not usually remind him of Mary, today he thought of her. What would she be like as a mother? Would Lily's fragility and utter dependence terrify her as much as it did him? Or would Mary have Ruth's blind faith that nature and fate would sort things out? She would be vigilant, he decided. Like him. Life had taught both of them both a lot about taking precautions.

He rolled out from under the blanket. Grabbing his jeans and a T-shirt, he tiptoed to the bathroom and closed the door, wanting to dress without waking anyone up. When he cracked the door back open, neither his wife nor daughter had moved.

He crept over to check on Lily. She slept on her stomach, her head turned toward her mother. Soft, dark hair curled around her shell-like ears, and she was making a sucking motion with her jaws, as if even in sleep she dreamed of eating. He stopped and kissed the soft spot on the top of her head, feeling her pulse throb against his lips. How amazing Lily was! She'd become a fundamental part of him the instant she'd entered the world—no less essential than his heart or his brain. Ruth could leave him, Little Jump Off could fall down around his ears—as long as Lily was safe, everything would be okay.

Smiling, he turned and padded downstairs. The cot in front of the fireplace lay empty, and the scent of brewing coffee wafted through the store. *Damn,* he thought wearily as he walked toward the coffeepot. *Clarinda must be up.*

"Hi Jonathan." Ruth's cousin appeared at his elbow so suddenly, he jumped. "How'd you sleep?"

"Fine," he replied tersely. She must have been in the bathroom, behind the bait cooler. A pretty enough girl with firm breasts and a tight rear end—he'd known a number of Clarindas when he was in the Army. All were like those multicolored drinks you got in fancy bars. You had a hell of a good time while you were drinking them, but the next morning you were hanging your head over the toilet, wishing someone would just come along and put you out of your misery.

Clarinda pressed her hand against the small of his back. "You and Ruth make everything better after you went to bed last night?"

Pouring his coffee, he considered his response. He could lie and say Yes, we went to bed and fucked like monkeys and now everything's just fine; or he could tell the truth and say No, the coldest spot in the nation today continues to be the bedroom of Jonathan and Ruth Walkingstick, of Little Jump Off, North Carolina. That was what irritated him about Clarinda—every question she asked worked on about three different levels, each deeper and more dangerous than the last.

"We slept alright," he finally answered, deciding that he was too tired to play her games. "How about you?"

"Okay." She sighed, massaging a little circle on his back. "But it got pretty cold down here in the middle of the night."

"Sorry," he said, moving away from her hand. "You should have asked for an extra blanket."

He took his coffee over to the front window and stared out into the parking lot. Yesterday a man named Duncan had called, wanting to hire him for the weekend as a boar guide. Jonathan had never taken this Duncan out before, but the man spoke as if he knew the area well, and he was willing to pay top dollar. Though he told Ruth it would mean five hundred extra dollars, she would not hear of him going. *You said you'd go with us to Tennessee*, she cried last night. *You promised.*

Suddenly he heard a piercing wail from upstairs. Miss Lily Bird Walkingstick was greeting the day.

Clarinda heard her, too. "Why don't you take Ruth some coffee?" she suggested, pouring milk and sugar into a cup and topping it off with coffee. "Here. She used to drink it like this in Oklahoma."

He took the cup Clarinda offered and walked upstairs. Ruth was sitting up in bed, Lily plugged into one breast.

"Café Tahlequah." Jonathan handed her the mug. "Compliments of your cousin."

"Thanks," she said, her voice cold.

"Lily okay?" He watched the frowning child pulling at Ruth's breast, her gaze serious and intense upon her mother's face.

"Her appetite is."

"How about you?"

"I'm fine."

"Then I guess you haven't changed your mind about the rally." Jonathan wondered if she'd ever once heard, in the past month, any of his concerns about their shrinking bank account.

Ruth's face immediately locked down into the hard, angry lines of the night before. "No, Jonathan, I haven't changed my mind. I'm going. Lily's going. At last count, you were going, too."

"It'll cost us a almost a thousand dollars."

"How so?"

"It's the peak weekend for tourists. If you stayed here and kept the store open, we might clear three hundred bucks."

Ruth set her coffee cup on the bedside table and lifted Lily to her shoulder. "That's not a thousand by my arithmetic book."

"That guy Duncan. He'll pay me five hundred to take him boar hunting for three days. I'm supposed to meet him in Murphy tomorrow morning."

"Now I get it," Ruth said sarcastically, as Lily started on her other breast. "This is really about you going boar hunting."

He rubbed his forehead in frustration, hating the way she could always box him in with her words. "No, Ruth, it's about making ends meet. We're almost broke."

"Broke? We weren't broke last week when you bought that new fishing reel. Or that chain saw."

Involuntarily his hands curled into fists. "Damn it, Ruth, I spend one dollar to your ten. Fish is what we eat! Wood is how we heat this place! Right now it's mid-October. We have a cold, damp winter coming. If you take Lily to that rally and she gets sick, how are we going to pay for it?"

"Breast-fed babies have immunities, Jonathan," Ruth replied smugly. "They don't get sick like other babies. I'm taking my medicine bag, and anyway, we're only going to Tennessee. It's not like she's going to catch bubonic plague there."

"You don't know what could happen, with Clarinda watching her."

"Jonathan, you have fought me about this rally since day one. Go ahead and go boar hunting if you want. I don't care. Just don't make rude remarks about my cousin and stupid excuses about not having enough money to get poor little Lily through the winter!"

He was so angry, he couldn't focus his eyes. Since Lily had been born, it had been like this every time they argued. He'd say one thing and she'd twist it into something entirely different. For the first time in his life, he wanted to hit a woman. Instead, he turned away and stormed down the stairs, where he found Clarinda perched behind the cash register, eating a carton of strawberry yogurt.

"Is all your stuff packed up?" he asked gruffly, at that moment hating her as much as he did Ruth.

"Right there with yours." With her spoon, Clarinda pointed to the front door. If she heard the fury in his voice, she didn't show it.

Ruth had stacked all the gear she'd packed for the trip—their clothes, Lily's clothes, food, diapers, toys, and a portable playpen—in a pile by the entrance to the store.

Without bothering to put his shoes on, he flung the door open and started hauling everything out. Ruth had already worn out one clutch on her truck in the eighteen months she'd lived in the mountains, and she was fast working on wearing out another. Not wanting to take the chance of the thing going bad on her and Lily, he loaded their gear into the back of his old Chevy. By the time the morning fog lifted, he'd attached the camper to the trailer hitch and filled up the tank. Wiping the sweat from his forehead, he looked at his work. Though the makeshift rig looked like something the Beverly Hillbillies might drive; the brakes worked and the clutch was good. It should make the trip over the mountains to Tennessee without any problems.

He strode back inside to find Ruth settling Lily into her car seat. Lily grinned at him. Ruth looked as if she might spit in his eye.

"All packed?" she asked, her voice like glass.

"You and Lily and Clarinda are."

"What about you?"

He did not take his eyes from her face. "I'm going to earn some money this weekend," he said evenly, knowing that Clarinda was watching from behind the cash register.

Ruth studied him for a moment, her eyes rekindling their vicious blaze. Then she said, "You really are one selfish bastard."

Once again, rage boiled through him. "Well, Ruth, this selfish bastard has just loaded your car, checked your tires, and made sure you had enough Pampers to get to Tennessee. Here." He jerked the car keys from his pocket and tossed them to her. She made no move to catch them, and they clattered to the floor. "And this selfish bastard is giving you his truck. Don't ride the clutch on mine like you do on yours."

"Fine," she said as she stooped over and picked up the keys. "You know where I'll be."

"Have a good time. Make the world safe for the Cherokees."

She snapped Lily into her car seat, then picked it up in her arms and walked past him. Clarinda followed. He watched as they got into his old camper, then he turned back inside the store. Something on the counter caught his eye—the black woolen bag Granny Broom had woven for Ruth. Her medicines! He leaped over and grabbed it, then ran out the door. Ruth had driven to the edge of the parking lot and was about to roll onto the highway.

"Wait!" he called, running toward her. "You forgot this!"

Ruth's brake lights came on as she stopped the truck and rolled down her window.

"Here," he said, loping up. "You might need this."

"Thanks." She took the bag and for once looked at him with soft, pre-Lily eyes. "Sure you won't come with us?"

He considered it: closing the store, losing even more money, then having to bunk in with Clarinda. "No, thanks," he replied.

"Fine," said Ruth, her mouth pinching downward. "Have it your way." She shoved the truck into gear, then pulled onto the road that ran along the river, heading west. He watched until they disappeared around a curve, then he fumbled in his pocket for a slip of paper. *Clootie Duncan*, he'd scrawled on a gum wrapper, along with the time and meeting place. *828-555-9572*.

"Wax up your bowstring, Clootie," he said savagely, turning back toward the store. "I'm taking you out for boar."

6

PAZ LET THE cows into the pasture late. Pushing open the rusty gate at the far end of the paddock, he hopped on the bottom rung and swung forward, over the muddy low place the cows wore a little deeper every afternoon as they waited to be fed.

"*Vamos!*" he said to the spotted brown heifer that was the self-appointed leader of the herd. "I have better things to do than watch you!"

As the beasts ambled into the pasture beyond, he hurried along the fence, back to the barn. When he reached the dim structure, he withdrew the small *cuchillo* he kept in his sock, then slipped inside. Working his way slowly down the center passage, he peered into each of the stalls, paying particular attention to the shadowy places underneath the feed troughs. As he reached the last stall, he let go the breath he'd been holding. This morning, praise the

Blessed Virgin, the stalls stood empty. Yesterday they hadn't been.

He'd been standing at the gate, watching the stupid cows, hungrily anticipating the sausages Ruperta would fry for his breakfast, when he felt something whip around his neck. He tried to grab at his throat, but someone jerked him backward as he felt something else snake between his legs. Struggling like a wild horse, he twisted forward, but whoever was behind him pulled both ends of the rope tight, cutting off his air and cutting into his balls.

"*Madre!*" he choked out, the hot, sick pain in his scrotum making his knees buckle. He knew exactly who and what had him—a Scorpion, making full and abundant use of his trademark weapon, the *riata*, a thin, double-noosed leather rope greatly feared in certain circles south of the Rio Grande. Innocuous-looking to gringo cops, with his *riata* a Scorpion could pinch off a man's *huevos* like those of a bull calf. Paz sucked air into his mouth through gritted teeth, sweat already pouring into his eyes. The Scorpion had him quite literally by the balls, and there wasn't a thing he could do about it.

"*Buenos dias, carnal.*" He felt as much as heard a voice at his right ear; the breath warm and moist, the words enunciated with the Vera Cruz accent Paz had grown up with. He hadn't heard it in so long, it sounded strange. Here, in Tennessee, they spoke the flatter dialects of Chihuahua and Sonora. "It took us a long time to find you."

"What do you want?" Paz wheezed, although he already knew what the man wanted, knew all too well what he would never leave without.

"The money you stole."

"I told you before, I do not have it. Jorge took it." Sweat began to trickle into Paz's eyes.

"That is not what Jorge told us. Jorge swore upon his mother's soul that you had the money."

"He lied."

The Scorpion gave the rope a savage tug. "My friend, I was there when they questioned Jorge. For three days, they kept at him. Believe me, Jorge died a truthful and repentant man."

"Except for one lie." Paz gasped, fearing that he might vomit. "I do not have your money. I never have. Jorge is a liar and a coward."

"So you say."

Paz tensed the muscles of his butt and thighs, waiting for the rope to tighten again, but the pressure on his scrotum unexpectedly eased. He felt the Scorpion shift, then the man reached over his shoulder and held something in front of his face. At first Paz could only see his hand—dark brown, callused, with a string of death's head tattoos encircling the wrist. That identified him as a *perseguidor*, a bounty hunter, one of the Scorpion elite sent out to settle old scores. He had apparently settled a number of them, according to the skulls on his skin.

"Pay attention, *carnal*!" The Scorpion again pulled the cord tight. "Look at what's in my hand, not on my wrist."

Paz felt his heart throbbing in both his neck and his testicles as he tried to focus on what the Scorpion held, a small brown bottle capped with a medicine dropper.

"Remember this?" the Scorpion whispered in his ear.

Paz's mouth dried up like dust. He'd last seen a bottle like that when the Scorpions caught him on the beach near Vera Cruz. It had taken five of them, but they'd ripped his clothes off, held him down on the sand, and dribbled the contents of that bottle on his stomach. It felt as if they had covered him in glowing coals. When he could stop screaming he'd lifted his head to see the outline of a scorpion sizzling into his puckered flesh.

"Our money in three days, my friend." The man palmed the little glass bottle, making it disappear like a magician doing tricks with a coin. "Or your wife." The man licked Paz's ear with a sloppy, wet tongue. "I hear

her *almeja*'s as tight as a virgin's. We will stretch it con-
siderably, then we will put out her eyes. *Comprende?*"

"*Clinga tu madre,*" Paz snarled, curling his hands
into fists.

"Don't concern yourself with my mother, *chilito*.
Your wife's the one you need to watch out for."

The Scorpion gave the *riata* one final, grand jerk that
left him writhing on the ground, then he was gone. When
Paz could look up, he saw only the barn behind and the
rolling fields of the farm, dotted with grazing cows.

"Paz!" Ruperta's voice jarred him back into the present. He looked around, dazed. The cows had already
wandered halfway across the pasture while he'd been
reliving yesterday's nightmare. "Señora wants you!"

"Coming!" he called back, pulling the gate shut,
closing off the entrance to the barn. Though he had not
seen them today, he knew the Scorpions were watching
and waiting. Sometime tomorrow they would show
themselves. Sometime tomorrow they would want their
money.

All night long he'd tried on different plans as
Ruperta might try on shoes. He came up with none.
They had no car to get away in, no gun to kill the Scorpions with. He could, of course, steal either of those
items from Señora, except she watched them like a
hawk and seemed to know what they were doing every
minute of the day. He dared not even call his cousin
Raoul—they were never to talk on Señora's telephone.
Turning themselves in to the police would keep them
safe for a little while, but the police would eventually
send them back to Mexico, and everything would begin
again, only worse. The only thing that held any promise
of success was giving them what they wanted. But how
could he, Paz Carrera Gonzalez, with no gun, no car,
and little English, come up with fifty thousand U.S. dollars by tomorrow afternoon? It was impossible.

You've got to think of something, he urged himself as

he hurried back to the house. *And you've got to think of it fast.*

"What took you so long?" Ruperta looked up, frowning, from one of her most hated duties—polishing Señora Templeton's silver with a smelly pink paste. Ruperta found dusting all of Señora's fancy furniture equally tedious, but she said at least the dust rags didn't stink and the lemony furniture polish wasn't so hard on her hands. Polishing silver, she said, was the worst.

"Señora has been calling."

"Sorry." Paz looked into her eyes and went cold inside, picturing the Scorpions fondling Ruperta's breasts, pushing themselves between her thighs, then dropping acid into her eyes. "The cows sometimes do not like to leave the barn."

"She wants to see you in the study," Ruperta said, rinsing one of the heavy silver trays with warm water. "She and *Gordo*."

"Gordo?" The one named Duncan, whom they called Fatso—*"gordo"* in Spanish—behind his back. What could that crippled bully want with him? "Why?"

"I don't know." Ruperta glanced at him in concern. "Go see. If you don't understand all their words, try to remember and we can look them up in the book."

"Okay, okay," Paz said under his breath as he left Ruperta and hurried down the back hall to Edwina's study. Trying to understand Señora Templeton made him jumpy enough. Who knew what Gordo would add to the mix? *Nothing good,* Paz decided as he raised his hand to tap on the door. *Nothing good at all.*

"Come in," he heard Señora say, her voice brusque. For one who delivered babies, she was terribly impatient. He opened the door. She sat behind the massive carved desk that always reminded him of a coffin, while Gordo rested his fat carcass on one corner. Both eyed him as if he were important in some way he was unaware of. He felt a chill of apprehension crawl up his spine.

"*Sí*, Señora?"

"Come in, Paz. And close the door behind you."

He did as she ordered, sweat already trickling down his armpits. *Oh, Jesus,* he thought. Perhaps she knew about the Scorpion. Perhaps Gordo had seen him and told her. He stood there for what seemed like forever, then Señora spoke.

"Paz, Mr. Duncan is going to pick up a child in the eastern part of the state. I want you to go with him."

He'd been thinking so frantically in Spanish that he had difficulty understanding her English words. "*Por favor?*" he stammered.

"I want you to go to east Tennessee with Mr. Duncan," Señora repeated, her little pig eyes growing smaller as she increased the volume of her voice. "You'll be gone overnight."

Overnight. *Pasar la noche.* The words exploded in Paz's brain. The night before the third day. The night before the Scorpions would return for their money. The last night Ruperta would have her beautiful eyes. *No,* he thought. *I cannot go anywhere. I cannot leave my wife.*

He took a deep breath before he spoke, knowing his refusal could cost them the small safe haven they currently had. "I'm sorry, Señora," he said slowly. "But I cannot."

"You most certainly can," she snapped. "Ruperta and I can take care of things while you're gone."

"No." He shook his head. "I cannot."

"What do you mean you can't?" Gordo scowled at him. "This woman's your boss, boy. You do what she says."

Paz lowered his eyes, gathering the courage to refuse again. Then he had an idea. Gordo must need him very badly, otherwise Señora would never let him leave the cows untended. Perhaps he would agree to go with Gordo—but only if Ruperta could come, too. Then, at some point, they could slip away from both Gordo and the Scorpions, and lose themselves in America once again.

"I would be of no use with a baby, Señora. Ruperta, though, is the eldest of six. She knows much about such things."

"Okay," said Gordo. "Then I'll take Ruperta."

Paz straightened his shoulders. Did this fool not see he was a man? That this was his *esposa* he intended to travel with? "No, Señor," he countered firmly. "I could not allow that."

"Seems to me that you're laying down a mighty lot of rules there, boy." Gordo folded his arms.

"Hang on, Duncan," said Edwina. She scowled at Paz. "You're saying that you'll go if Ruperta can come, too?"

"Sí." Paz held his breath as Ruperta's eyes, his life, the rest of whatever future they had, seemed to hang in a fragile bubble over Señora's ugly desk. The right word would allow it to continue floating; the wrong word would burst it to nothing.

Finally, Señora looked at Gordo and shrugged. "I don't mind. I don't have any girls here right now, and while you're gone I can make some calls about this baby."

"I really only wanted to take one other person," objected Gordo.

"So you get two. You'll only be gone overnight—what does it matter?"

Gordo gave a disgusted sigh, then turned his cold gaze on Paz. "You and Ruperta will have to do exactly as I say," he told Paz. "This ain't gonna be any vacation."

Paz nodded, wanting to laugh. Gordo had no idea how not like a vacation this would be.

"Okay," Gordo said grudgingly. "Can you be ready to go in an hour?"

"*Sí*," Paz answered, backing toward the door before they changed their minds. *Holy Mother*, he thought.

They had been given a way out. Now he just had to figure out how to get Ruperta to pack everything without
letting her know they were leaving this place forever.
She would miss the television in their own room and the
shower that always had hot water, but she would have
her eyesight, and she would never have to polish
Señora's silver again.

7

"AREN'T YOU GOING to call Jasmine? It's almost two-thirty." Danika whispered as Mary watched the red-suited Virginia Kwan try to rattle the computer expert who'd traced a complicated cyber-porn trail back to Dwayne Pugh's personal computer. Judge Cate looked as alert as ever, making notes on the man's testimony, but the jurors were something else. Sleepy from the carbohydrate-laden lunch served up by the jail trustees, and weary after a week's worth of complicated testimony, the panel watched Virginia with drooping eyes, numbers six and eleven even jerking themselves awake from time to time. *Don't ever call anybody important on Friday afternoon,* Irene Hannah had once warned her. *Save your fireworks for Monday morning.* Mary had taken that advice like gospel. She hoped she wasn't going to have to change her ways today.

Keeping half an ear on Virginia, she turned and

looked at the crowded courtroom. Relatives of the abused project kids took up most of the seats—Jasmine's mother and grandmother, Isaiah Reed's parents, Diamond LaForge's husky father and even huskier uncles hulking in their chairs like the defensive line of the Atlanta Falcons. Their eyes were not glazing over from the highly technical testimony, but rather were pinning a fierce look of righteous expectation on Mary. Their children had been molested. All their hopes of redress rested upon her. So far, she felt no better than okay about this prosecution. She'd had to call a lot of snore-inducing technical experts, and she still feared Virginia Kwan's ability to come up with some totally off-the-wall defense that would sink her case like a paper boat in a rainstorm.

A tiny movement caught her eye. She looked toward the far corner of the courtroom. Hobson Mott sat in the back row looking straight at her, his brows lifted in a silent question.

She turned around, enraged. That sorry son of a bitch had come to check up on her. *Put Jasmine Harris on the stand.* Mott was worried about his reputation among the African-Americans; he needed this. His threat was unspoken but clear: *Get me a conviction, Ms. Crow. Or spend the rest of your career prosecuting B&Es.* She didn't want to put that tormented little girl on the stand, didn't want to go against Irene's adage about Friday afternoons, but her boss was in the courtroom, waiting for her to do it. She took a long breath, trying to quell her fury, to clear her head. *Okay, Hobson,* she promised him silently. *You want Jasmine, then you've got her. But we're doing this my way.*

"Ms. Crow?" Judge Cate asked expectantly as Virginia Kwan finished and the computer expert stepped down.

Mary rose from her chair. "I have one more witness, Your Honor." She looked down at her papers, intentionally stretching the moment to give the jurors a chance to wake up. When everyone was sitting a little straighter in their seats, she spoke in a clear, strong voice. "Your Honor, the State calls Jasmine Harris."

A low anticipatory murmur rose from the courtroom as the bailiff opened the door to the witness room. Mary glanced over at the defense table. Virginia had begun scribbling notes on a legal pad, but the sallow color already seemed to be draining from Dwayne Pugh's skin. *Good,* Mary smiled to herself as Jasmine came into the courtroom, clutching the caseworker's hand. *I just surprised both of you.*

Jasmine had come to court in her Sunday best— gleaming Mary Jane shoes with lacy white anklets, a lavender dress with a frilly white pinafore, crinoline petticoats that rustled with every step. A tiny black patent leather purse had slid to the crook of her elbow as she kept the thumb of her free hand firmly planted in her mouth. When they reached the edge of the jury box, the bailiff scooped the child up and carried her to the witness stand, her petticoats a white froth in his arms. Only Mary noticed that the whole time, the child had kept her eyes on the great seal of the State of Georgia behind Judge Cate, her face turned away from Dwayne Pugh.

The courtroom listened in silence as Judge Cate first complimented Jasmine on her pretty outfit, then asked her if she knew the difference between telling the truth and telling a lie.

Jasmine nodded solemnly. "Jesus don't want you to fib."

"That's right, Jasmine. So when we ask you some questions, you aren't going to fib, are you?"

"No, ma'am." Jasmine stuck her thumb back in her mouth.

Judge Cate looked at Mary. "Okay, Ms. Crow. Your witness."

Mary slipped off the jacket of her black suit, revealing a pink silk blouse. She'd donned the most child-friendly item in her closet this morning, and she walked to the witness stand not in her usual crisp way, but strolled over to one side of it, standing close to Jasmine.

"Hi, Jasmine." She smiled as she lowered the microphone. "We're going to have to talk into this thing, so everybody can hear us."

Jasmine looked at her with panicked eyes. *It's okay, honey,* Mary longed to tell her. *If this goes like I've planned, it's going to feel like a shot. It'll hurt a little, but not for long.*

"Can you tell us your name?"

"Jasmine Harris."

"Can you tell us how old you are?"

Jasmine held up one hand, fingers outspread.

"Five?"

She nodded.

"Can you tell us where you live, Jasmine?"

"Sixteen twenty-two Loveless Avenue." Jasmine fidgeted with her purse as she answered the question in a whisper.

"And do you have a lot of friends there?"

"Yes."

"Do you and your friends play outside?"

"Yes."

"Last April did an ice-cream truck come to where you and your friends were playing?"

Jasmine ducked her head lower and stared at the little purse in her lap. "Yes."

"Did a man drive that ice-cream truck?"

A pause. Then: "Yes."

"Did the man who drove the truck ever give you any Popsicles for free?"

Jasmine sat silent. Then two big tears began to roll down her cheeks as she whispered, "Yes."

Mary leaned closer. Here it comes. The one question that Jasmine had never been able to answer. "Jasmine, I want you to look around this room and tell us if you see the man who gave you those free Popsicles."

Jasmine did not move. Mary watched as a tear lingered on her chin, then dripped onto her starched white pinafore.

"Jasmine?" Mary said softly. "Can you show us the Popsicle Man?"

All at once Jasmine raised her head, pointed one chubby finger directly at Dwayne Pugh at the defense table, and began to scream. Beyond hurt, beyond anger, it was a primeval keening that recalled every horror that had ever been visited upon a child. The jurors went rigid in their seats as Jasmine's grandmother answered with a loud wail of her own, and the entire phalanx of LaForge men leapt up with enraged shouts of "He be the one, Your Honor! Just give him to us!"

Judge Cate rapped her gavel. Mary squeezed Jasmine's shoulder as a foul odor filled her nose. She looked down. Brown shit spotted Jasmine's pretty white petticoats, one soupy turd dripping down the little girl's leg onto her lacy white anklets.

"Order!" Judge Cate banged her gavel again and glared at the fierce LaForges. "You people sit down, or I'll clear this courtroom!"

She nodded at the bailiff, who started to move toward the LaForges, but the men sat down. Jasmine screamed, her mouth wide open and square, feces now running down both legs. The jurors sat ashen-faced. Dwayne Pugh looked as if he'd just swallowed vomit. Virginia Kwan stared at Jasmine with icy eyes.

"Let the record indicate that the witness identified the defendant," Judge Cate loudly instructed the court reporter over Jasmine's piercing screams. She banged her gavel again. "We'll recess for fifteen minutes, to let the witness regain control."

Mary smiled at the howling little girl. *It's over, Jasmine,* she wanted to say. *I promise you, you'll never have to do this again.* "I have no further questions of this witness, Your Honor."

Judge Cate glanced at her, surprised, then turned to the defense.

Just as Mary had hoped, Virginia Kwan shot to her feet. Mary knew she wanted this screaming child out of the courtroom, and out of the minds of the jurors who would no doubt relive this moment all weekend. "No questions, Your Honor. Although I reserve the right to recall."

"Mrs. Williams," Judge Cate turned to the case-worker, who was sitting opposite the jury box. "Jasmine is free to go."

Mrs. Williams hurried over to the witness stand. She'd come prepared with a white blanket to wrap around Jasmine's lower half. Just as Mary had instructed, she scooped the weeping child up and exited the courtroom, walking directly in front of the jury box, allowing each juror to see, hear, and smell the effect Dwayne Pugh had on little Jasmine Harris.

After Mrs. Williams and Jasmine left the courtroom, Judge Cate spoke. "This trial stands in recess until nine o'clock, Monday morning. Jurors, please remember not to discuss these proceedings with anyone. Spectators, if you come here Monday, be prepared to show proper respect for this court, whatever may transpire upon the witness stand."

With that, the judge rose and whisked through the door to her office. The jurors filed out. Two bailiffs escorted Dwayne Pugh back to jail. Everyone else stood up—Virginia Kwan gesturing furiously at her young male assistant, Jasmine Harris's mother and grandmother dabbing at wet eyes with crumpled tissues, the LaForge crew talking low with heads close together, as if plotting some act of sedition. Mary looked at the seat where Hobson Mott sat. It was empty.

"That was some piece of prosecuting, girlfriend." Danika walked over to tower above her.

Mary glanced at Virginia Kwan, who was now making a call on her cell phone. "It went well. But Virginia'll come up with something by Monday morning. Never rest your case on one good witness, Danika. You've got to play till the end of the game." Good Lord, she thought with a shudder. She was beginning to sound as silly as Hobson.

"So what should we do?"

"Take tonight off," replied Mary. "Go out with your boyfriend, have a nice meal. Come over to my house tomorrow about three. We'll make our final preparations for our big slam-dunk."

Danika frowned. "Our slam-dunk?"

"The *boss's* instructions," said Mary bitterly, walking over to the prosecutor's table to collect her papers. "A slam-dunk conviction for this trial, Jasmine Harris be damned."

"Think we'll get it?"

Mary opened her briefcase, disgusted with herself for caving in to Mott. "We're sure going to try."

8

❦

"YOU EVER GET sick from these roads?"

Clarinda tightened her seat belt anxiously as her cousin negotiated another hairpin curve. They were driving along the back roads from Little Jump Off, North Carolina, to Tremont, Tennessee, twisting through confetti-bright autumn leaves that swirled down to the highway like rose petals at a wedding.

"When I first came here." Ruth sniffed, her eyes red from crying over Jonathan. "I guess I've gotten used to them."

Clarinda clung to the door handle, giving up on the magazine article she was reading about sixty-four romantic ways to turn men to mush. In Oklahoma, you could read or write or even turn a couple of men to mush while you were driving. Here, she couldn't even look at the fashion ads without getting carsick. When Ruth had invited her to come over, she'd pictured these

Appalachians like the Rockies—sharp and gleaming, a perfect place to meet rich young skiers or fly fishermen with money to burn. Instead, she'd found stoop-shouldered mountains thick with ugly trees, inhabited by slow-talking men whose idea of a hot date included fiddles and moonshine. This trip wasn't turning out like she'd hoped at all. She should have known. Hers and Ruth's ideas of fun had differed since the day they were born. She'd always liked music and parties and having fun. Ruth preferred books and political rallies, and now, brewing up medicinal teas that smelled like rotting fungus and tasted even worse.

"I don't know how you stand this place. It gives me the creeps."

"The creeps?" Ruth steered around another curve. "Why?"

"All these trees. It's like they're closing in on you. Listening to everything you say."

"You're just accustomed to Oklahoma. North Carolina's beautiful when you're with someone you love."

Clarinda snorted. "You sure about that?"

"About what? North Carolina?"

"That you're with somebody you love."

"Why do you say that?" Ruth's voice trembled as if she might start crying again. "Because Jonathan and I had a fight?"

"No. Because you two act just like my mom and dad." Clarinda looked out the window and thought of her sour parents, locked in a thirty-year-long, drunken boil of an argument that ultimately had driven her and both her sisters out of their house before they graduated from high school. She hated her parents. When she was little she used to pray that she would wake up one day and belong to Ruth's folks, who were pleasant and agreeable, and for the most part, sober. Her cousin had all the luck. Always did.

"That's not true, Clarinda," Ruth cried. "We've just been under a lot of stress lately."

"Oh, yeah? Jonathan didn't look too stressed this morning when I came out of the bathroom."

"What do you mean?"

"Oh, nothing. He just gave me that look."

"What look?"

"You know. That look. One beat on your face, two beats on your boobs, a glance at your crotch, then back to your boobs again."

"He did that?"

Clarinda shrugged. "Maybe I got it wrong. Maybe it was just a North Carolina mountain howdy."

"What did he do after that?"

"He went over and got some of those stupid Ding-Dongs. Then Lily woke up." She fumbled in her purse for her cigarettes, taking a curious pleasure at the way Ruth's chin was wobbling. "Look, it was nothing. I shouldn't have even mentioned it."

"No. It doesn't matter," Ruth said, but Clarinda knew she lied.

They drove west, a dazzling blue sky piercing through the golden lacework of leaves overhead. Crossing into Tennessee, they entered the Great Smoky Mountains National Park, with its tidy brown signs pointing out trails and picnic areas and quiet walks along the way. Clarinda had high hopes that Tennessee might prove less oppressive than North Carolina, but the terrain seemed identical—tall mountains covered in trees, the air thick with the smell of cedar and pine. Once again she felt a curious longing for the dusty, dry plains of Oklahoma.

"You ever think about coming home?" she asked, noticing how the ends of Ruth's mouth had begun to pull down in an inverted U.

"You mean move Jonathan and Lily out to Oklahoma?"

Clarinda nodded. "You mom would think she'd died and gone to heaven."

"And Jonathan would think he'd died and gone to hell," Ruth said bitterly. "He'd never move to Oklahoma. These trees, this forest, are too much a part of him." She sighed. "I'm afraid I'm a North Carolina Cherokee now."

They drove out of the park. As they approached a small outpost of civilization, Lily began to whimper. Quickly Ruth made a hard right turn into a McDonald's parking lot.

"Feeding time at the zoo," she explained, parking the camper under a big mottled-bark tree at the far end of the lot. She unbuckled Lily from the car seat, then Clarinda watched as she pulled up her shirt and put the baby to her nipple, smiling as Lily began her earnest sucking.

"What does that feel like?" Clarinda wanted to go out and smoke a cigarette, but the whole breast-feeding process fascinated her. Who'd have thought old bookworm Ruth would ever marry and start whipping out her tits to feed a baby?

"Terrific, when you haven't done it for a while." Ruth brushed back the damp curls around Lily's forehead. "Your breasts get heavy when they get full."

"But does it feel like, you know, *good*? Like when a man does it?"

Ruth smiled. "It feels good, but in a different way."

Clarinda shook her head and went into McDonald's, leaving Ruth to change Lily's diaper. She returned with Big Macs and Cokes for the both of them, and they pulled back on the highway. Though traffic grew a little heavier, it was nowhere near the October gridlock that Jonathan had so direly predicted. *Too bad,* thought Clarinda, her last hopes for a hot weekend fading. *All the cool people must be going somewhere else.*

Ruth echoed her thoughts as they sped toward Tremont. "Wonder where all the tourists are?"

"On the beach in Florida, if they're smart," said Clarinda, thinking maybe she would go there too when this was over. Florida. Or maybe New York. Tall buildings instead of all these stupid trees.

They twisted along a series of turns, then the road straightened and crossed land that was as flat as any she'd known in Oklahoma. The cars ahead of her slowed to a stop, and she felt better. The sun was brighter here, hotter. She could actually see a horizon in the distance, something beyond just trees. Then she jumped as her cousin yelled.

"Look!" Ruth cried. "There it is!"

"What?"

"The dig. That's where your ancestors are buried, Clarinda."

Clarinda looked out Ruth's window. Right by the side of the road spread a huge flat field covered in black plastic tarps. Bulldozers from the Summerfield Development Company sat at one end, held at bay by a grid-work of small stakes that divided the whole thing up like a giant checkerboard. Short, Hispanic-looking guys in hard hats waved protest signs at one end of the field, while clusters of sunburned blond girls worked hunched over the sun-heated tarps, digging up, Clarinda supposed, little chips of dead Cherokees. She sat back in her seat and sighed. Ruth had told her they were going to another Woodstock. This was looking more like a field trip for science club nerds.

They inched onward, passing a sign nailed to a tree that read "SOB One Mile Ahead."

"What's SOB?" Clarinda laughed. "Son of a bitch?"

"Save Our Bones," Ruth snapped, as if she were stupid. "That's what you're part of."

"Speak for yourself," muttered Clarinda. "I just came to baby-sit."

The line of traffic crept on, made up mostly of battered campers and vans with out-of-state license plates.

She sighed again as she saw dream-catchers dangling from rearview mirrors, and ragged bumper stickers that wanted Leonard Peltier freed. Same old shit she saw every day in Oklahoma. If she ever got enough money, she was going to Sweden. Not one Indian would be there, and she could meet lots of rich blond guys who might regard a full-blood Cherokee as something exotic.

"Look at all these people!" Ruth exclaimed as they pulled up behind a rusting VW microbus with New Jersey license plates. "This is actually going to happen!"

Clarinda flopped back in the seat and closed her eyes. She couldn't believe she'd ridden a bus all the way from Oklahoma for this. The next time Ruth called her, she was going to be busy doing something else. She smiled at the idea of telling Ruth *Sorry, cuz, but I'm busy. I'm having a root canal.* Then she jumped and opened her eyes as something hit the hood of the truck.

She peered out the windshield. Two bare-chested guys in hard hats grinned from either side of the truck. On the middle of the hood lay what looked like a steaming pile of cow shit.

"Hey, Pocahontas," called the one standing on Ruth's side of the truck. His face looked like a boiled shrimp, and the hair on his chest had been bleached white by the sun. "You comin' to dig for bones?"

"Who the hell are they?" Clarinda cried, twisting around in her seat.

"I don't know," whispered Ruth, putting a protective hand on Lily's car seat.

"I said, are you coming to dig for bones?" the big man repeated. Clarinda saw that the one near Ruth held a shovel; the one moving toward her carried a sledge. *Shit*, she thought. A ripple of fear threaded through her. These Tennessee guys looked nasty.

"Lookee here," called the one closer to her. "These two ain't half-bad."

Boiled Shrimp leaned down and peered in Ruth's

open window. His eyes were blue and bloodshot, and Clarinda could smell the beer on his breath all the way across the truck. "You two comin' for that protest rally?"

Clarinda's stomach clenched as she stared at the bright green wad of chewing gum that bobbed in one corner of his mouth. What if he hit her with that shovel? What if he hit Ruth? She'd dealt with her own father too many nights not to take angry drunks seriously.

"Yes." Ruth answered him calmly. "We are."

"Thought so." The man slid his gaze over to the manure that graced her truck. "Shit likes shit, sister. Welcome to Nikwase County."

"We're protesting exploitation," Ruth explained, as if the two men had just dropped by to say howdy.

"Exploy-what?" jeered the other man. Clarinda felt his gaze on her chest, eyeing the butterfly tattoo that peeked from the top of her halter.

"Tashun, Smitty," explained Boiled Shrimp. "These gals are coming to protest ex-ploy-tashun."

"Shit." Smitty spat on the ground. "I don't think they're coming to protest nothin'. I think they're coming to get *laid*." He winked at her. "Look at this, Miss Butterfly Tits. I'll give you something to protest about!"

Clarinda watched in horror as he straightened, stepped to the front of the truck, and grasped the sledge with both hands. Swinging as if he held a baseball bat, he slammed the hammer into the right headlight. The inside of the cab rocked as a shower of glass tinkled on the pavement.

"Hey!" Ruth cried. "Knock it off!"

"Knock it off?" called Smitty, moving over to the other headlight. "Okay, bitch. Whatever you say!"

"Holy shit, Ruth! Do something," shrilled Clarinda. "They're going to tear your truck apart!"

Ruth was fumbling for the lug wrench Jonathan kept

under the driver's seat when Clarinda heard a new voice call from behind the truck.

"Yo! Brother! Hold up!"

Clarinda looked in the side-door mirror. A dark-haired man dressed in jeans and a black T-shirt was hurrying toward the two construction workers.

"Who the fuck are you?" Smitty looked up from the headlight, blinking.

"Second-shift framer, brother. The sheriff's about fifty feet behind me, pulling the paddy wagon after him. They're hauling us in on every charge they can think of."

"Are you kidding?" Boiled Shrimp went pale.

"They just put the cuffs on my brother-in-law."

Smitty peered back down the line of traffic. "I don't see nothin' down there."

"Couple of deputies are riding horses. Summerfield says he ain't bailing anybody of out jail, and any man of his who gets arrested can just kiss his job good-bye."

Boiled Shrimp stepped back. "Hold on, Smitty. I can't go to jail. They'll find all them warrants my ex-wife put out on me."

Smitty lifted the sledge. "Aw, come on. This is *fun*. Your ex-wife served you up in Virginia. This here's Tennessee."

"It don't matter. I'm outta here. These two ain't worth it." Boiled Shrimp nodded toward Ruth and Clarinda.

"Don't say I didn't warn you." The dark-haired man hurried on down the line of traffic. Boiled Shrimp hastily followed. Smitty looked longingly at the other headlight, then he, too, turned away from the truck and ran to catch up with his buddy.

Clarinda sat frozen, her heart beating a thousand miles an hour. Ruth looked down at Lily, who, amazingly, had slept through the whole thing.

"Holy shit," Clarinda cried. "These people are fucking furious!"

"I know," said Ruth, leaving the lug wrench under the seat. "I wish Jonathan had come."

Just as the words left Ruth's mouth, the dark-haired man in the black T-shirt reappeared, sauntering up from the other side of the truck in front of them.

"Hi, ladies," he said, grinning. "Sorry you had to meet up with one of Nikwase County's unofficial welcoming committees."

"You aren't one of them?" Ruth stopped, confused, her window half rolled up.

"No. I'm with the rally. We've gotten so many complaints about people being hassled by the construction guys, we decided to keep an eye on the traffic ourselves. Let me see what I can do about that." He gestured at the manure steaming on the car hood.

He walked back down the line of traffic, returning moments later with a small camp shovel. Working gently to avoid scarring the truck's weathered paint job, he scraped the mess off and dumped it on the roadside.

"Thanks," Ruth told him when he came back to her window. "I really didn't want to show up here with cow dung all over my car."

"You shouldn't have anything else to worry about. The gate's about fifty yards ahead and our security's tight from here on in."

"Ask him his name." Clarinda poked Ruth in the ribs. "He's kind of hot."

"Hey, what's your name?" blurted her cousin awkwardly. "So I can thank you officially."

"Gabe Benge," he replied cheerfully. "Coordinator of all this with a lady named Ruth Walkingstick, who I'm hoping will show up pretty soon."

Ruth began to laugh, and rolled her window all the way down. "I'm right here, Gabe," she said, extending her hand. "You just shoveled cow manure off my car."

9

PAZ SAT IN the front seat of the van, the sun hot on his face, Ruperta's gaze hot on the back of his head. "It's a trap, Paz," she'd cried when he told her what they were going to do. "We don't get sent out for babies. Señora must have found out we're *ilegalidads*. She's sending us to the police!"

"No, no." Paz had taken Ruperta in his arms, wishing he could tell her about the Scorpions; yet knowing if he did, she would probably fall to the floor, paralyzed with fear. "Señora just wants us to help Gordo. If she wanted to turn us in, she would not waste her gas taking us to the police. She would just call them to come here."

To his great relief, Ruperta saw the logic of his words. As she resumed folding their clothes into their battered suitcase, he stuffed the money from their mayonnaise jar into his pocket and put his *cuchillo* back down in his sock. Ruperta did not know it yet, but neither of them would ever see this room again.

Now he sat up straight in the van, twisting around every five minutes or so, giving Ruperta a reassuring wink, but also looking to see if anyone followed them. He'd spotted the Scorpion just as they left, leaning against the scraggly tree that grew at the end of the drive. He was tall and wiry, with a thin black mustache that bracketed the corners of his mouth. For an instant their eyes met, then Gordo pulled onto the road, the van's tires throwing up little pebbles that no doubt peppered the man's face. *Please God,* prayed Paz, the sweat breaking out on his forehead. *Today let him be the one blinded.*

Such roads in this country, he told himself as he twisted around again to gaze anxiously out the windshield. No dangerous potholes, no washed-out bridges eternally awaiting repair. Nothing to prevent you from putting hundreds of miles between you and the thing you feared, unless, of course that thing was a Scorpion. He squirmed, remembering the bite of the *riata.* Señora's fancy van and this good road would only buy him time. Eventually they would find him. Not once had they failed.

"We're going to the mountains," Gordo announced, speaking for the first time since they'd pulled out onto the highway. "We're going to save a baby from some bad people."

"What kind of bad people?" Ruperta asked her question with eyes so wide that Paz almost laughed. What kind of bad person could Gordo possibly know who would compare with a Scorpion?

"Gypsies," Gordo explained. "Gypsies that look like Indians."

"Gypsies?"

Paz watched Ruperta dig in her purse for their little

dictionary. *Gypsy* must not be used on her American soap operas, where she'd learned much of her English.

"That's right." Gordo nodded deeply, looking at her in the rearview mirror. "Gypsies act nice to your face, but alone, they beat their babies when they cry. And if they cry a lot, they just leave them in the forest, for the coyotes to eat."

Paz frowned. He'd never heard of any Gypsies who did such things, but this was America, where people gunned down total strangers just for cutting them off in traffic. Anyway, what did he care about Gordo and his Gypsy baby? In a few hours, he and Ruperta would be gone.

"How old is the baby?" Ruperta's voice was soft with concern.

"Three months," replied Gordo. "They call her Lily."

Paz looked back at Ruperta, again secretly checking to see if anyone was following them. Only a Greyhound bus, way in the distance. So far, so good.

"Of course they won't want to give her up," Gordo continued. "So we might have to trick them." His cold gray eyes speared Paz like a fish. *He knows,* thought Paz, panic once again crawling up his throat. He knows all about the Scorpions. All about *before.*

"You and Ruperta need to do exactly as I say. Otherwise, there'll be trouble."

Paz made his face a mask before Logan's hard eyes, but reached down and touched the cool ivory handle of the *cuchillo* in his sock. *Oh, yes, my fat friend,* he responded silently. *Try to keep us from escaping the Scorpions, there will be trouble indeed.*

They stopped for gas, then turned south, toward Atlanta. Paz felt cheered, somehow. In the year they'd spent in America, they'd stayed the longest in Atlanta, where they'd lived with his cousin Raoul. He and Ruperta loved the big, flashy city and wanted to stay, but Raoul had advised him to keep moving north. "You won't be safe here," he warned Paz. "The Scorpions know Atlanta, and even though the American cops now hunt Arabs, eventually they will catch you, too. Here," he said, giving him a slip of paper with a name and an address scrawled on it. "Julio Mendez's cousin has just quit working for this lady in Tennessee. She is very rich, and will now perhaps need someone new. Anyway, it will be safer for you up there." So they took a bus to Nashville, then walked the thirty miles to Señora's grand house. She hadn't wanted to hire them at first, but Ruperta, who didn't mind making a fool of herself with her bad English, convinced her truthfully that she was an excellent maid, and untruthfully that Paz knew all about cattle and farming. Until now, it had worked out well. The cows were easy enough to figure out, and Ruperta kept Señora's fancy furniture and crystal chandeliers free of dust. Though Ruperta missed her friends in Atlanta, she liked having a bedroom all to themselves and a bathroom where roaches did not scatter each time the light came on.

They drove through a smaller town, then out into the country beyond. The land here was flat, but surrounded by tall gold mountains. A sharp breeze scuttled leaves along their route, and by the side of the road, men in overalls sold apples and firewood from the backs of their trucks. They passed campsite after campsite— Smoky Hollow, Whispering Pines, Unaka Creek. At one called Hillbilly Heaven, Paz saw a sign in the shape of an arrow head that read "SaveOurBones." Three cop cars sat opposite the entrance, holding back a crowd of angry, hard-hatted *obreros* waving signs. Two long-haired men wearing red T-shirts stood at the entrance of the campground, their arms crossed against their chests, their faces hard and unforgiving.

"What's going on?" Ruperta leaned forward from the backseat.

Paz fought the tightness in his chest he always felt whenever he saw American cops; he sank down lower in his seat. "Sit down, Ruperta," he told her in Spanish. "And be quiet."

Gordo touched the bill of his cap at the cops who leaned against their patrol cars, then turned into the campground, pulling up beside one of the long-haired men.

"You here for the rally?" The young man leaned against the van. Paz gripped the handle, ready to bolt. This Indian didn't sound like any he'd ever seen in the movies. Maybe Ruperta had been right. Maybe Señora and Gordo had brought them to some kind of camp where the cops rounded up all the *ilegalidads* before they sent them back. Señora would do such a thing for money; Gordo would help her just for a laugh.

"Yep," said Gordo.

"There's a twenty-dollar fee per carload. You with any tribe?"

"Croatan," Gordo replied. When the young man stared at him blankly, he added, "Lumbees, to you young'uns."

The guard checked his clipboard. "Okay. We've got a few of you guys here. Go to the top of the hill and take a right. The Lumbees are down on the far side of the creek."

Paz watched Gordo pull his wallet from his pocket and hand the guard a twenty-dollar bill.

"Thanks." The young man took the money and waved them through. Paz's grip on the door handle loosened as Gordo drove forward and the troopers grew smaller in the van's side mirror. Maybe Gordo wasn't taking them to some kind of internment center, after all. Maybe they had indeed come to a Gypsy camp. It didn't matter to him. For now, he had enough to do keeping an eye on the cops and watching for a singularly tall man with a death-head bracelet tattooed on his wrist.

Two hundred miles to the west, at the old white farmhouse where Paz and Ruperta had begun their journey, Edwina Templeton lay dozing on the only truly comfortable sofa she owned. Located in a mudroom off the kitchen, the sofa sat beneath the west-facing windows of the room where she'd shoved it just for rare moments like this, when she was the only soul in the big house and the afternoon sun made the worn leather upholstery feel like butter on her skin.

"Doc, no!" Edwina cried aloud, her eyes fluttering open, awakened by an edge-of-sleep dream that blurred the lines between reality and somnolent fantasy. She sat up, her ears sharp, wondering if Duncan had prematurely returned. Quickly she rose from the sofa, brushing the wrinkles from the long white lab coat she wore. Never had she been able to stand the thought of anyone watching her sleep.

She walked to the kitchen and looked out the back door. The van was nowhere in sight. The only noise she heard was the comfortable *tock* of her Philadelphia tall case clock in the hall. She started to relax again. She was still alone.

She put a kettle of water on to boil. As she reached in the cabinet for the Lady Grey tea she saved for special occasions, she caught sight of the day's mail resting on the counter, a thick, cream-colored vellum envelope addressed to her in an elegant, sloping hand.

Her heart began to beat fast all over again. Today, just after Duncan's departure, the mailman had delivered an item sought by many but extended to few—an invitation to put her house on the Christmas Tour of Homes.

She stared at the thick envelope, lost in thought. The missive from the society matrons of Williamson County signified, for her, the end of a long journey. She'd had the misfortune to grow up poor in a county of great wealth. Her parents lived in a trailer park just down the road from this very property. Though her mother had real talent as a seamstress and had worked hard to make sure she looked nice, she'd walked to school when others rode, eschewed after-school skating parties to earn money baby-sitting, and prayed to God that none of her classmates would ever drive by to see her father in his undershirt, passed out drunk on their front steps. She'd started the first grade as "Edwina"; she'd finished high school as "Whinny," a name the boys gave her because they said she looked like she should be pulling a plow.

However equine she might have looked, she had brains enough to make herself useful to their general practitioner neighbor, Dr. Skinner. She baby-sat, with admirable patience, his one retarded son and then, when the boy died, she took over the housekeeping as Mrs. Skinner methodically anesthetized herself into oblivion with Seconal and Myers's rum. Edwina was surprised one night when the doctor caressed her thigh as she served him dinner; she took pleasure a few nights later when he squeezed her breasts as she washed the dishes. When he called her into his examination room and pulled her skirt up and her pants down, she realized that she might have lucked into something. What exactly, she wasn't certain, but it sure looked like a way out of the trailer park and into the plusher ranks of the smug people she'd gone to school with.

She'd quickly learned how to please the doctor in ways he'd never imagined: in exchange, she extracted his promise to send her to nursing school. By the time she graduated, Mrs. Skinner had died, and she came back to work for Dr. Skinner as lover, nurse, then co-conspirator, when one of Nashville's wealthiest debs made a secret visit to this house late one night and bled out on the table. The furor over that didn't end until eighteen months later, when Doc walked out to the barn and mainlined enough Thorazine to kill a horse. Edwina wound up with this house, which she'd lived in and turned, over the past forty years, into the mostly legal operation it was today.

The acceptance, however, that she'd sought since high school eluded her. She tried to live like the women she envied: shopping at the right stores, lunching at the right restaurants, generously supporting horse shows and golf tournaments for various charities. She'd been commended for her efforts, too—been given plaques by Planned Parenthood and the Tennessee Adoption League. Yet, for all her good work, as she walked to her car from the eleven o'clock service at St. Phillip's, she sometimes saw the women she'd known as girls giggling among themselves, the name "Whinny" reaching her ears like a long-ago taunt borne on an endless breeze.

"Maybe not anymore, though," she said aloud, taking the now-shrieking kettle off the burner. Maybe that moron Duncan would bring back some kind of baby she could make some money on. Maybe she would be able to buy that antique bed she'd been salivating over in the New Orleans auction catalog. If she could get it shipped here and set up in the downstairs bedroom in time, it would knock the knickers off those Christmas tour bitches. They would be sick with envy. They would finally see her for what she truly was. And they would never dream of calling her "Whinny" again.

10

❦

LOGAN PARKED EDWINA'S van between an Airstream
trailer with Florida plates and an old VW van that was
covered in bumper stickers. A couple of elderly Floridi-
ans puttered around the Airstream, seemingly having
blundered into the rally by mistake. On the other side, a
tattooed man lifted his hand once in greeting, then disappeared with his girlfriend into the van. Shortly thereafter it began rocking, its worn shocks announcing each
pelvic thrust with a loud metallic squeak. Ruperta
pointed out the window and giggled, murmuring the
word *tórtolos*.

Logan walked over to a fiery red maple tree, unwrapped a Hershey bar, and considered the pair he'd
brought with him. He'd always suspected Paz was duck-
ing the cops; now he was certain. Innocent men do not
sink down in their seats when they pass state troopers,
sweat dotting their foreheads. The migrant workers

he'd dealt with in Pisgah County knew the border dance
so well that getting busted provoked nothing more than
resigned irritation, yet Paz had looked at those troopers
like a rabbit cornered by dogs. The INS didn't instill
that kind of terror in anybody. The little bastard must
be in very deep shit down Mexico way.

He took a bite of chocolate, hoping it would calm
the manic thrum inside him. Ruperta, on the other
hand, had surprised him. Though she'd seemed upset
when he'd likened the Indians to Gypsies, she had not
shown the wide-eyed, Hail Mary kind of fear he'd expected. Even now she was chattering to Paz, slyly ap-
praising three strapping male Indians who wore nothing
but deerskin breechclouts between their legs and a
smear of rusty paint across their faces. He sighed. He
would have to keep an eye on these two. Paz for one
reason, Ruperta for quite another.

He finished his candy bar and walked over toward
Paz, letting his old sheriff's gaze impart his meaning.
*I've got you by the short hairs, amigo. And you're
gonna jump when I say so.*

"Come on, you two," he said as Paz pulled Ruperta
closer. "Let's go for a little walk."

He followed behind the Mexican couple as they
strolled through rows of campers, all parked beneath
various tribal totems nailed to the trees. It was happy
hour in Native America. Senecas from New York were
drinking Genessee beer while Alabama Choctaws
nipped from a bottle of Jack Daniel's. Two Rappahan-
nock women decanted a plastic jug of homemade scup-
pernong wine while their husbands argued about the
Redskins football team.

Logan watched the two ahead of him. Ruperta was
clutching Paz's hand, whispering in his ear every time
she spotted someone in native costume. Paz took scant
interest in the feathers and war paint; he scanned the
crowd nervously, as if looking for someone he knew.

They crested the hill of trailers to find a small cove. A stage had been set up at the far end, where hundreds of Indians crowded around a rock band. To Logan it looked like any other rock concert, but when the breeze turned in their direction, he caught the smell of frybread and smoky sage. The mix of aromas sent a sudden wave of nausea through him, and he hurried Paz and Ruperta on up the hill. Puking at strange odors was another little gift from Ms. Crow, one he'd prefer not to exhibit in the middle of a crowd.

As they walked, he noticed other demonstrators were joining the rally. Green-shirted Appalachian ecologists passed out leaflets about the dangerously high ozone levels in the Smoky Mountains, while a group called the Saviors of the Southern Forests tried to torch a dummy made up to look like the congressman from western North Carolina, reputed to be nothing more than a pawn of the timber lobby. As the causes and the numbers of protestors grew, Logan realized that the rally had grown too big for them to just happen upon one woman and a baby. He would have to find another way to locate Walkingstick's wife. He stopped for a moment to let Paz and Ruperta listen to the music, then stepped over to a long-haired man wearing one of the red SOB staff shirts. He hated to leave even a wisp of a trail for the cops to follow, but he had no choice.

"Say, buddy, do you know where I might find some Cherokees named Walkingstick?"

"Let me check." The young man, who had a turquoise stud stuck in one nostril, peered at the clipboard he was carrying. "Cherokees are over by the volleyball court." He pointed to the other side of the cove. "But Ruth Walkingstick's behind the stage. Next to Gabe Benge, according to this."

"Thanks." Logan smiled. He waited until the young man moved farther down the hill, then he eased back over to Paz and Ruperta.

"Come on," he told them. "We need to go this way."

Again he walked behind them, trying to disguise his limp as best he could. If Walkingstick hadn't fallen for his boar-hunt scam, he would recognize his lopsided gait in a heartbeat. Should that happen, the game would be over. Walkingstick would turn him in to the cops for sure—if he didn't just kill him outright.

They picked their way around the crowd, dodging golf carts carrying official SOB staff. They passed a tent with Army cots and a big red cross stitched on the top, then another, smaller tent labeled "Media Information." As they neared the stage, Logan noticed a circle of women gossiping about something, laughing noisily. He recognized the thick Appalachian accents immediately. Cherokees. Though they all looked vaguely familiar, the woman he'd watched remove her blouse at Little Jump Off did not stand among them.

The Walkingsticks must be at their camp, he decided, walking a little faster. Mommy and baby, for sure. If his luck held, Daddy would not be accompanying them.

He directed them onto a path that led off the main road. It meandered through the trees for fifty yards, then bottomed out along a creek. Suddenly he saw it. A secluded campsite with two vehicles parked side-by-side. One was a camper van with an orange University of Tennessee flag dangling from its aerial. The other was a clunky, modified Chevy pickup with North Carolina tags.

He turned to Paz and Ruperta. Paz was eyeing everything—the trees, the creek, even the honeysuckle bushes. Still looking for something, Logan thought. Or for someone.

"Follow me," he whispered to the pair. "Quietly."

This time, he led the way. They followed him without question, crossing the creek on large, flat rocks and slipping into the trees along the other side of the bank. When they reached a rhododendron thicket directly behind Walkingstick's trailer, they stopped. Ruperta started to say something, then hushed: a baby began crying.

"Come on, come on," Logan urged as he peered through the thick green leaves. "Show me who's there."

Then it happened. Almost as if on command, the screen door of the trailer squeaked open and the woman from Little Jump Off stepped out. Walkingstick did not follow; instead, another woman came to the camper door, the baby yowling in her arms.

"All I have to do is announce Benjamin Goodeagle," Walkingstick's wife was telling the other woman. "Then I'll come back and you can go to the party."

"How can I get her to quit crying?" asked her young friend, awkwardly jiggling the child.

"Play the Mozart CD," Walkingstick's wife called over her shoulder. "Or the Hopi flute music. I'll be back in ten minutes."

"Don't lose track of the time," the other woman called. "My party starts at six."

The younger woman watched as Walkingstick's wife headed up the path toward the stage, then she and the wailing baby disappeared into the camper. Logan felt a surge of satisfaction. No Walkingstick. No man. Not any kind of security at all. Just two women, and one of them would rather be partying than baby-sitting that child. Everything was going according to plan.

"You're gonna get your wish, Miss Babysitter," he murmured as strains of soothing classical music began to float from the camper. "This time tomorrow, you can dance the night away. Quieting Lily Walkingstick won't be a problem at all."

At that same moment, another man had Lily Walkingstick on his mind: Jonathan Walkingstick sat on the hood of his truck, watching the sun slide behind the pine trees above him. The dying sky blazed brilliant pink—just the color of the little cap and shawl Aunt Little Tom had knitted for little Lily. What an asshole he'd been, coming down here. He should have just sucked it up and gone with his wife. Even if Ruth had become hard to get along with, at least he could have kept his child safe from the hundred different hands that would beg to hold her, away from the various noxious breaths that would blow their germs in her face.

"Idiot," he chastised himself. "You don't deserve a child like Lily."

After Ruth left, he'd kept the store open until noon, then driven three hours on roads that went from paved to graveled to mud, finally winding up here, at the bottom of a mountain on the banks of Dick's Creek. For two more hours he'd sat, growing cold and impatient, listening to the distant shrill of screech owl and the gurgle of the creek beside him.

Motionless, he gazed into the darkening woods, watching as a fat, hunched-back raccoon crept out of the underbrush toward the creek. The diurnal animals were bedding down for the night, leaving the world to their nocturnal colleagues. Soon owls would begin swooping down on voles and field mice; skunks would leave their burrows to claw grubs from rotten logs. He had done nothing to improve his family's lot this day. In fact, he'd spent this entire afternoon sitting on his butt, waiting for this son-of-a-bitch to show up.

"*Clootie Duncan,*" he read aloud, pulling the gum wrapper from his pocket for the third time. "*Dick's Creek Trail Head, 4:00, Fri. aft.*"

This was the place, and he'd been here since three o'clock. He'd thought it odd from the get-go, driving this deep into the forest this late in the day, but the guy had promised him five hundred dollars for a two-day hunt. Hell, for that much money, he'd have taken him out for snipes at midnight.

"Five more minutes," he muttered, watching the coon dip its paw into the creek, then rub water all over its masked snout. Five more minutes, then Clootie Duncan could hunt frigging boar all by himself. He was going to scramble back up that road and get over to Tremont, Tennessee. If he drove hard, he could make it by midnight. Then Ruth could save all the bones she wanted, Clarinda could get laid, and he could keep his Lily safe again.

Cheered by that thought, he scooted off the hood of the truck humming "Brown-Eyed Girl," the tune that bubbled through his subconscious like a subterranean spring. As the last rays of sunlight disappeared behind the mountains, the cool air grew cold, and he began to feel the damp of the creek deep in his bones. He reached inside the truck and retrieved his jacket, wondering what Lily was doing right now. Probably eating supper, he decided. They will have found their campsite, set up the little pop-up camper. Ruth will have met with that Benge character while Clarinda will be out meeting God knows who. He frowned. He didn't like the idea of Clarinda even touching Lily. Every time she took the child in her arms, he fought the urge to rush Lily upstairs and give her a bath.

He looked up into the sky again. Venus had risen, a dim gold twinkle of light that grew brighter as the minutes passed. It was getting late. "Your five minutes are up, Duncan. I'm calling the game." Shaking his head, he chuckled. For the first time in his hunting guide career, he'd been stood up.

He got back in Ruth's small pickup, glad he'd given her his Chevy. As expertly as Ruth handled breast-feeding and political rallies, when it came to auto maintenance, she sucked. Though she nicknamed her little Toyota "Whirlaway" and always kept it clean, she neglected to change the oil or the water or even fill the gas tank beyond a quarter full. He'd topped off her tank and inflated

the tires before he left Little Jump Off, but the clutch was
living on borrowed time. He'd warned her about it fifty
times, but she couldn't seem to break the habit of riding it
as she tried to get accustomed to the steep grades and
twisting curves of mountain driving.

"Okay, Whirlaway," he said as he started the engine.
"Let's get the hell out of here."

The engine caught like a champ. Shoving the
gearshift into reverse, he backed away from the creek,
his tires slipping a little on the mud. He turned on his
lights to illuminate what the Forest Service laughably
called a road, then he headed back up the mountain. He
drove quickly, trying not to get bogged down in the
mud, until, without warning, Whirlaway balked. Jumping and bucking like a horse, the truck stopped moving.
Though the engine hummed as steadily as before, it
went not an inch farther as a bitter, burning smell
flooded the cab.

"Aw, fuck!" he cried. He opened the door, watching
the truck's rear wheels as he gunned the engine. The
burning-rubber smell grew stronger, but the wheels just
quivered instead of turning. He turned off the motor and
lay his head against the steering wheel, breathing in the
acrid air. Here, in the cold and the dark, in middle of this
sinkhole in the mountains, Whirlaway had given up the
ghost. The clutch that his wife had for months abused
had chosen this particular moment to die.

"Shit!" He thumped the steering wheel with his palm
and tried to figure out what to do. He could wait here
and hope that Clootie Duncan showed up, or he could
get out and walk to the little town of Murphy. Since he
hadn't seen a single car since he'd pulled off Route 129
two hours ago, he doubted any kind of cavalry was going to come to his rescue. Murphy was at least fifteen
miles away. If he left now, he could get there before midnight, but everything would be closed, and he really
didn't want to pay for a motel room. Paying for a new

clutch would be bad enough. Better to stay here, get some rest, and hike out around dawn. That way he'd reach Murphy by the time the parts store opened. He could get his clutch and maybe persuade somebody to give him a lift back here.

"Sorry, Lily," he said aloud, reaching in the back for his cooler of food. "Daddy's coming, but not for a little while."

11

❦

PAZ LAY ON the floor of the van, his arms cradling his head. A bright moon cast shadows upon his face as he listened to the beats of a thudding drum. THUMP-*thump-thump*-THUMP. The Indians had kept at it for hours, unremitting, until he felt as if everything—his heart, Ruperta's heart, the trees outside the van windows, even the Scorpions who followed them—were all locked in the same incessant cadence. He'd tried to cover his ears, but it did no good. *Go, got to Go, got to Go*—all creation seemed to throb with that message.

So far, things had not gone well. He'd hoped for—no, he'd *counted* on—Gordo's unwitting participation—allowing Ruperta and him some privacy, turning his attention away from them for five minutes, perhaps even closing his eyes and nodding off to sleep long enough to allow them to slip away. That had not happened. Gordo had been happy for them to sack out in the back of the van, but he had remained wide awake in the driver's seat, pecking away on Señora's fancy laptop computer, fattening his face further with chocolate candy.

Mierda, thought Paz. Now they had to get away, not only from the Scorpions, but from Gordo too. Gordo was going to steal that baby, and soon. Bad enough that they were *ilegalidads*. But if the American cops caught them and accused them of being *secuestradors* too, then they may as well turn themselves over to the Scorpions.

But what to do? The drums had lulled Ruperta into a deep sleep. He could not leave without her, and even if she were awake, he could not slide open the door of the van without alerting Gordo. Paz squeezed his eyes tight, thinking hard, going over everything he'd heard and seen Gordo do. Then, all at once, the drumming stopped. At exactly the same instant, an idea occurred to him. Though it seemed as ludicrous as one of Ruperta's silly afternoon TV shows, it just might work. . . .

Gordo, like most Americans, spoke only English. If Paz could wake Ruperta up and tell her what to do in Spanish, they just might be able to get away. They would not get to leave with their belongings, but they might at least escape with their lives. It was not what Paz had hoped to do, but it was all he could think of. He took a deep breath in preparation for the worst nightmare of his life to begin.

"*Madre Maria!*" he screamed, batting at some invisible monster over his head. "No, no, no! *Por favor,* NO!"

"Jesus Christ!" Gordo jumped as if someone had stuck him with a pin.

"*Paquito!*" Ruperta bolted upright, blinking. "What is wrong?"

"Ruperta, listen," Paz shrieked in frenzied Spanish. "We've got to get away from Gordo. He's going to steal that baby! Come and calm me down, then say you have to go to the bathroom!"

"What?" Ruperta gaped at him as if he'd gone mad.

"Pretend to wake me from my nightmare!" Paz shrieked at her like a lunatic, though he gazed into her eyes with absolute clarity. "Then say you have to pee!"

She looked puzzled, then, to his great relief, she caught on. "*Calmate, querido,*" she cooed, putting her arms around him. "You're having a dream . . ."

"I'm not kidding," he whispered desperately, burying his head against her shoulder.

"Everything okay back there?" Gordo sounded hesitant, as if Paz's outburst might indicate some serious mental condition.

"*Sí,*" Ruperta answered. "Sometimes, in strange places, Paquito has bad dreams."

"Me, too," muttered Gordo, turning back to his computer. "More often than I'd like."

"Wait one minute," Paz whispered in Ruperta's ear. "Then ask to use the bathroom. Ask in English."

She rocked him in her arms. He pretended to grow fully conscious, wiping the sweat from his forehead.

"Did you have one of your nightmares, Paquito?" she crooned softly.

"One about snakes," he lied. His real nightmares were not of reptiles, but Scorpions. "And babies."

"Are you feeling better now?"

"*Sí.*"

"Good for you." She gave his back a final pat. "But now I have to pee."

"Can't you hold it?" This time he faked his usual irritation with Ruperta's midget-capacity bladder.

"Not till morning."

"Ai-yi-yi." He sighed wearily, winking at his beautiful, clever wife. "Come on. I'll take you to the *baño.*"

They got to their feet, both listening for any protest from Gordo. But he remained focused on the computer screen.

"Señor, Ruperta needs the bathroom," Paz told him. "I'm going to walk with her."

"Scared the piss out of her, did you?" Gordo chuckled, not lifting his gaze from his work.

"I suppose so." *Oh, Holy Sweet Maria,* Paz thought as he slid back the heavy door. *This is going to work.* He hopped from the van, then raised his hand to take Ruperta's. She looked at him with frightened doe eyes, but stepped to the ground beside him.

He turned. The van of the young lovers sat still and quiet, ten feet away. Fifty feet beyond that stood a square wooden structure that held showers and toilets. They would walk in that direction until they passed the van, then they would run up the hill and into the woods. They were small and quick, like jackrabbits. Fat, limping Gordo could never catch them.

"When I say run, run," he whispered in Spanish as he and Ruperta moved toward the latrine. "Up the hill, as fast as you can."

They crept forward, holding their breath, listening for any sound from Señora's van. Nothing. Apparently Gordo was staying at the computer, trusting that they would return. What a fool Fatso was, to think they were stupid just because they spoke English poorly. Soon he would learn how clever they truly were. But not yet, Paz reminded himself as they drew closer to the van. Just get into the shadows. Eight more steps. Then you can congratulate yourself.

Suddenly they heard a noise behind them.

"Paz!" Gordo's voice struck him like a bullet. "Stop!"

Ruperta froze as if she were a soldier under Gordo's command. Paz kept moving forward, tugging her along with him. "Come on," he cried in Spanish, "if we get to the shadows we can beat him up the hill!"

She gazed at him, teary-eyed, not knowing what to do. Behind them, Gordo was moving toward them, brandishing a dark object in his right hand.

"Run, Ruperta!" He tugged her harder. "He's got a gun!"

"A gun?" That terrified her further. Her mouth began moving but no sound came out; she couldn't budge her feet at all.

"Come on!" He tried to pull her with him, but she lost her balance and fell, sprawling, to the ground. Paz stood there staring at her, open-mouthed, as Gordo limped up, pointing a pistol straight at him.

"You're kind of antsy to get to the ladies' room, aren't you, boy?"

"We got mixed up," Paz sputtered, smelling the stink of his own sweat. "We couldn't remember the way."

"Oh, yeah?" Gordo poked the gun into his ribs. "Then how about she just pisses here? And how about you let me have this?" He reached down, lifted Paz's pants leg, and pulled the *cuchillo* from his sock. The blade felt cool sliding against his skin as Gordo withdrew it.

The fat man thrust his face close and spoke in a whisper. "If you think I don't know about you, *mi amigo,* you're mistaken. I know all about you. I know you've got no green card, I know you're running from the cops, I know somebody made your chest look like a salt map of Mexico." Gordo pocketed his knife and gave him a sour grin. "I also know that unless you and your little *esposa* here don't do exactly as I say, I'm going to turn you in. Maybe to Immigration, maybe to those *asesínos* who've been hanging around Señora Templeton's property for the past week. You *comprende, compañero?*"

Paz felt as if he were tumbling into some black pit. What a fool he'd been to assume Gordo did not know Spanish just because he chose not to speak it! All this time they'd called him *Gordo*—Fatso—thinking it was a great joke he did not understand. Numb with fear, he nodded.

"Okay, then," said Gordo. "Ruperta, do your business. Then we're going back to the trailer and talk about what you two are going to do tomorrow."

Paz stood there helpless while his wife lowered her jeans and squatted on the ground. In a moment she stood and pulled her pants up hastily, trying to hide her bare bottom from Gordo's bold stare. When she turned back around, she kept her eyes lowered, her stricken face turned away.

"Let's go, *amigos*." Gordo pointed his gun toward the van. "We have a lot of ground to cover tonight."

By noon the next day, they had covered it. Paz sat in the front seat of the van, wearing a red SOB T-shirt Gordo had stolen and an official-looking identity badge that Gordo had forged on his computer. Ruperta sat hunched on the backseat while Gordo inched the van along with a thick crowd of Indians, all of them heading toward the stage. Most were dressed in T-shirts and jeans, but a few wore tribal outfits, resplendent in buckskin and feathers. The tall, muscular ones who wore mostly nothing were there, too, raising angry fists to the encouraging cheers of their friends. Drums again beat their insistent tattoo, occasionally drowned out by the *whump* of the police helicopters overhead.

"Remember what you're going to say?" Gordo prodded as they crested the hill.

"I'm Joe Little Bear," Paz repeated for the thousandth time, his mouth dry as a cracker. "A Navajo from New Mexico. I served with Johnny in the Army."

"Jonathan," Gordo corrected.

"Jonathan. Ruth wants me to bring the baby Lily to her. To be with her on TV."

"And?"

"And I'll bring her back in just a few minutes."

Gordo eyed him suspiciously. "That's good. Think you can remember it?"

Paz nodded, numb. What choice did he have? This man had Ruperta and his knife. His great escape plan had failed, like everything else he'd tried in this miserable country.

They rolled past the stage and up another, smaller hill. Gordo pulled off the road and turned off the engine. Despite the drums and the helicopters, Paz could hear only a great whirring wind that seemed to rush like a gale through his ears.

"Okay." Gordo looked around. "Get going. Hurry, but don't run. Ruperta and I will wait for you here."

"Sí." Paz's voice came out in a raspy whisper. He turned to look back at Ruperta, wishing he could kiss her, wishing he could tell her how much he loved her, how sorry he was for all this.

"Paz . . ." she began, her dark eyes mirroring his own fear. She said something else, but Paz opened the door and jumped out of the van hastily, slamming the door and shutting her words out behind him. There was no point in talking now. He should have pushed her into the darkness last night and tried to slash Gordo's throat. At least one of them might have gotten away. Now they had to do what Gordo wanted. *Later,* he promised himself. *If I don't get killed stealing this baby, I will make sure that Ruperta goes free.*

On rubbery legs, he followed the path down to the creek. The water sizzled like grease in a skillet, while high in the pine trees a blue jay scolded him.

Holy Mother, Paz prayed, knowing the bird was announcing his intrusion to everyone within earshot. *Please don't let these people kill me before I can save my Ruperta.*

With his head down and his hands stuffed deep in the pockets of his jeans, he walked past the first, newer trailer and on to the second. He saw no one, but frenetic guitar music seeped from inside. Wiping the sweat from his forehead, he said a silent *Ave Maria* and stepped up to the weathered screen door.

"Hello?" he called, trying to sound Southern, like the people back at Señora's. "Anybody home?"

"In here," answered a gruff voice.

He peered through the screen. In the dim light he saw the woman he'd seen the night before sitting on one of the two cots inside the trailer. A tall man with a ponytail sat on a little stool at her feet, his hands clutching the waistband of her jeans. Both looked annoyed, as if he'd interrupted them.

"Hi." Paz smiled broadly, hoping their music might conceal his accent. For a moment he could not speak; the words he was supposed to say were zooming around his head like gnats. "I'm Joe Little Bear," he finally blurted, his voice reedy and high. "I was in the service with Jonny-than."

"He ain't here." The man on the stool was looking at him with a flat, hostile stare.

Mother of God, thought Paz. *Now what?* He plunged ahead, repeating what he could remember of Gordo's words. "Ruth sent me down here for Lily. Ruth wants her to be on TV."

"Ruth's going to be on TV?" The girl's eyes glittered, envious. "Then maybe I'll take the baby down there myself."

Paz shook his head, near panic. This girl was not part of the plan, and Gordo had not covered this contingency. He clenched his fists and willed himself to speak with more coherence. "I think she wants only the child."

"She would," the girl replied sullenly. "Ruth always has all the fun."

Grinning, the ponytailed man slid his hands down her thighs. "You go wrap that kid in a blanket, honey, and I'll show you more fun than you've ever dreamed of."

The girl looked at him a long moment, as if trying to decide between him and the possibility of being on television. Finally she gave a small sigh and moved over to the baby's crib. As she began to bundle the child up, the man turned back to Paz.

"Where'd you say you were from, buddy?" The man's eyes bored into him.

"New Mexico." Again, Paz repeated what Gordo told him. "I'm Navajo."

"You sound more like you're from old Mexico."

Smiling, Paz shrugged again, praying that the girl would hurry up with the baby and this man would ask him nothing more. As he stood there he heard more drumming from the rally, then the sound of many people cheering. At last, she lifted a pink bundle from the crib, as Ponytail held open the wobbly screen door. "Walk slow," she ordered, thrusting the sleeping child at him. "If you're real lucky, she might not wake up."

Paz took the baby in his arms. She felt much heavier than the newborns he occasionally carried at Señora's. He held his breath as the baby nestled against him, then he looked up at the couple and nodded. "I'll bring her back soon."

"Take your time, Joe," said the man, winking as he wrapped his arms around the girl. "We ain't going anywhere. Knock first, though, if the blinds are pulled down."

"Okay." Paz kept his smile frozen on his face as he turned from the camper. Although overhead the sun was bright and warm and a more sedate cardinal had replaced the raucous jay, he felt as if the earth were breaking in two. He, Paz Carrera Gonzalez, the pride of his parents, of the good Sisters and Father Ramon, had just stolen a baby away from her mother. He was committing the worst of crimes; he was beyond redemption. He should stop now. If he were any kind of man at all, he would give the baby back and just tell Gordo he would not do it. But he kept hurrying along the path, the word *destino* echoing mockingly in his head, pulling him back to Gordo and the van. He realized then that he and Ruperta were truly no better off than the child in his arms; their fates were inextricably bound one to the other. Whatever harm befell this child would surely befall them, too.

12

❦

IT WAS THE kind of Saturday that wanted a child, or at least a dog. The white haze of pollution that usually hung caul-like over Atlanta dissipated, revealing a startling blue sky, empty of everything except an occasional vee of geese winging steadily toward Florida. The wind gusted in from the north, cool and carrying the rich, indefinable mixture of smells that signaled autumn. Mary knew as she watched the little boys next door tumbling like puppies in a pile of fallen leaves that Atlanta would play outdoors this weekend—cool, sparkling days like this had become a rarity in the urban South, no less special than a January morning that presented three inches of glistening snow.

She'd allowed herself to sleep till noon, then she dressed in jeans and an old Emory sweatshirt and sipped her morning coffee on her grandmother's back patio. A seedless birdfeeder swung reproachfully from a low

branch of a redbud tree while weeds grew thick in the
peony beds. Though she paid to have her two acres of
sprawling lawn regularly cut and trimmed, she kept up
with the rest of the yard only as her work allowed. The
place reflected her neglect. The goldfish pond, long
empty of goldfish, was choked with dead leaves, and the
crape myrtles that her grandmother had kept so nicely
trimmed now looked like a cluster of old women with
wildly frazzled hair.

"You really have no business here," she scolded herself aloud, thinking that she ought to take the advice of
her friend Alex and move to some upscale condo where
she might meet more single people her own age. Four
thousand square feet of space for one childless woman
was ridiculous, but the old place had been her refuge
ever since her mother had died, fourteen years ago. Her
grandmother had come roaring up to Little Jump Off in
her white Cadillac the instant she heard the news, and
the morning after Martha Crow's funeral she loaded
Mary and her one suitcase in the car and whisked her to
Atlanta. Although it was worlds away from the little
mountain cabin she and her mother had shared, over
the years Mary had grown to love its odd nooks and
pantries. Her great-grandfather Bennefield had built the
place in the twenties, and she felt as if the walls still held
secrets she had yet to discover.

"Someday I'm going to sell you and move to a
condo," she told the old house, sounding like a mother
issuing a threat she had no real intention of carrying
out. "But not anytime soon."

She finished her coffee, then started in resolutely on
the peony beds. Five hours later, with the peonies looking only marginally better, her gloves and garden snips
lay on the ground. Mary was inside, letting the glorious
day die without her. Once again she'd succumbed to the
house's siren call; once again the ghosts had lured her
upstairs.

She sat in her favorite room of all. Though the furniture was all ancient Bennefield antique, the decor was all America, circa 1965. Photos of a skinny blond teenager in various team uniforms lined the walls, interspersed with posters of the Beatles and Jimi Hendrix. A bright red electric guitar stood in one corner, surrounded by stacks of old record albums. An archaic stereo system, complete with tape deck and bulbous headphones, covered one wall. She twisted around in her chair and turned on the tape. It sputtered for a moment, as if troubled by some electrical short, then the unmistakable rhythm of an electric guitar playing rockabilly came on. A young man's voice filled the room, singing Elvis Presley's "That's All Right, Mama." Though the pitch and timbre were not those of the King's, it was a pleasing voice, filled with such energy that shivers went down her spine. Beyond a few snapshots, the voice and this room were the closest experience of her father that she would ever have.

As she listened, she sat at her father's old desk, a long mahogany affair pushed beneath a bank of picture windows. Spread out all over it were stacks of thirty-five-year-old letters, all addressed to her grandmother. On one end were yellowing business-sized envelopes with a Fort Bragg return address. At the other end lay smaller and dirtier envelopes sent from Vietnam, bordered in red, white, and blue with "FREE" printed where a stamp should be. Between the letters, a laptop computer sat on a large desk calendar that had names, dates, and times all connected with intersecting lines.

She looked at the calendar and read the notes she'd made months ago, feeling like a long-dry alcoholic who'd just succumbed to a bottle of whiskey. Right here lay her dirty little secret, the obsession that always shadowed her. She was determined to figure out the puzzle of the relationship between her parents and Stump Logan. That Logan had killed her father was a given; that he had murdered her mother was highly likely as well. What Mary Crow didn't know was the *why*, and that was what tortured her.

She'd pieced together as much as she could from her father's correspondence. Jack Bennefield had referred to a "Logan" in three of his letters to his mother, then his mail to her dribbled off, as his new bride Martha became his chief correspondent. Mary's mother had not been one to keep old letters, and her grandmother Eugenia could not speak of that time without starting to cry all over again, the death of her only child like a wound that would not heal. As much as she wanted to ask her about it, Mary could not bear to cause Eugenia pain, so she'd let the matter drop. Now everybody who knew the truth was dead—with the exception of Stump Logan.

"And he's dead, too," Mary told herself, getting up from the desk as her father's song ended. "Eileen says so, and so does the FBI." She moved to the door and turned off the light. She'd gone over every line of correspondence at least a hundred times. Her father's room simply wasn't going to reveal anything more. Her time would have been better spent in the peony beds. "Get over it, kiddo. There are some secrets you just aren't going to ever find out."

Downstairs, she slid another chicken dinner in the microwave. As she once again set a place in the little breakfast nook, she turned on the TV, hoping to catch the weather report. If tomorrow was pretty, she'd finish the peony beds early and ask Alex to meet her at the Emory tennis courts.

The national news came on, something about anti-American demonstrations in France, then the anchorman segued into another story.

"Tremont, Tennessee, was the site of a different kind

of demonstration today," he began. *"Native Americans from all over the country joined together in . . ."*

Mary looked up, surprised. It was Ruth's Indian rally. She'd forgotten all about it. She watched the screen as video clearly shot from a helicopter scrolled over a mass of people gathered in front of a small stage. The camera panned on hundreds of angry Indians raising their fists, shouting. Drums thudded. Placards waved. Finally the camera cut to a nearly nude man in war paint tossing a pie in the face of the governor of Tennessee.

"I'll be damned!" Mary laughed at the sputtering, crème-covered politician. "Ruth wasn't kidding!"

The Indian yelled something about "the Red Nation's fight against ecological criminals" as the cops carried him away, then Ruth's face filled the screen. Compared to the raving pie-tosser, she looked like a poster girl for Native America—flawless skin, high cheekbones, a beautiful, almost movie-star smile.

"What we're protesting here is the fact that the governor of Tennessee thinks he has the right to desecrate our burial grounds just so he and his friends can build a new condo development," Ruth was saying, her voice calm and articulate. *"We regard this ground as holy as nonnative Americans regard the Arlington National Cemetery."*

Mary watched, astonished, as Ruth went on, fielding questions with the polish of a pro. When the tape ended and the program went to a commercial, Mary shook her head. That's Ruth, alright. Hitting them with her best shot.

The microwave beeped; she took her dinner from the oven and put it on a plate. The phone rang. Mary decided to let the machine get it, then, impulsively, she scooped it up, on the outside chance it might be Danika.

"Hello?"

"Mary?" A high, frantic voice came through waves of static.

"This is Mary. Who's this?"

"Ruth. Ruth Moon."

"Ruth?" Mary couldn't believe the coincidence. "I just saw you on television!"

"Mary, you've got to come! They've taken Lily!"

"What?" Mary reached over and turned off the TV. "What did you say?"

"They've taken Lily, Mary! And they don't believe me! You've got to come up here and help me out!"

Mary felt as if she'd been suddenly dropped from some great height. "Who's taken Lily, Ruth? And who doesn't believe you?"

"I don't know. The police won't believe me. They say it's a tribal matter." Ruth's voice was quivering on the edge of hysteria.

"Where's Jonathan?" Mary asked urgently.

"I don't know that either!" With that, Ruth's voice dissolved in sobs.

"Ruth? Ruth, try not to cry right now. I need to know—" A wave of static assaulted Mary's ear. She heard a loud crash, then a male voice came on the line.

"Hello?"

"Yes, hello. I was speaking with Ruth Moon . . ." Mary felt as if she were trying to connect with someone in Baghdad or Kabul.

"Is this Mary Crow?"

"Yes."

"Mary, I'm Gabriel Benge—a colleague of Ruth's. Something terrible has happened." The man sounded calm, but she heard the deep concern in his tone.

"Lily's been abducted?"

"It looks like that. We're having some difficulty convincing the authorities that it's not a publicity stunt. Ruth is frantic. She was wondering if you might drive up here and help her sort things out."

"Isn't Jonathan there?"

"Uh, he opted not to come to this rally."

Mary frowned. What the hell was going on? Ruth was hysterical, Lily had vanished, and Jonathan was missing in action? "Has anyone tried to contact him?" she asked Gabriel Benge.

"Ruth has, but he's taken someone on a hunting trip." The man paused. "Ruth's in bad shape, Ms. Crow. She seems to think you've got some kind of in with the police."

"I'm an assistant DA in Deckard County, Georgia, Mr. Benge," Mary explained. "I'm not a cop."

"Ms. Crow, Ruth believes you can make the police believe her. Is there any possible way you could help us out?"

Mary glanced at the Pugh files heaped on her kitchen table. She was in the middle of a trial, but this was Lily . . . this was her goddaughter, Jonathan's baby!

"Where exactly are you, Mr. Benge?" she asked the man on the phone.

"Hillbilly Heaven campground. On Route 321, east of Tremont, Tennessee."

"I'll be there by midnight," she said, scribbling the directions on the back of her phone bill. "Tell Ruth I'm on my way."

13

MARY CHANGED INTO clean jeans, threw a couple of sweaters into a small overnight bag and jumped in her car. *Someone's taken Lily!* Ruth's panicked words had sounded like those of the mothers, mothers she sometimes interviewed at precinct houses, wildly venting their rage and heartbreak over what somebody had done to their child.

"It's probably just a huge mix-up," she told herself, trying to warm away the cold, sick lump of fear in the pit of her stomach. She'd been to powwows before where child care had been a communal effort, with babies passed from person to person. Somebody had probably taken Lily to hold and then just lost track of the time. By the time she got there, Lily would be back in Ruth's arms, sound asleep.

She tried hard to cling to that belief as she sped

toward Tennessee, her speedometer seldom dipping below ninety. At eleven P.M. she turned east, passing campground signs that invited people to "come play in the foothills of the Smokies." She exited the intereate, then crested a hill to discover a line of Tennessee state trooper cars pulled off the side of the road, their flashing blue lights slicing the darkness.

Her stomach twisted, but she ignored it. They're here because their boss just got smacked with a pie, she reminded herself, recalling the comical scene on television. "They have nothing to do with Ruth at all."

She slowed to a crawl, pulling out her identification both as a Georgia driver and as an officer of the Deckard County Court, but the troopers made no move to stop her. They leaned against their cars as she passed, regarding her with cold cop eyes. When she came to the entrance of Hillbilly Heaven campground, she pulled in.

A long-haired man wearing jeans and a red T-shirt leaned out of a small information booth.

"Hi," he told her, keeping a cautious eye on the fleet of police cars lighting up his campground like a carnival midway. "Twenty dollars, please. Rally starts at eight tomorrow."

"I haven't come for the rally," Mary answered him. "I've come to see Ruth Moon Walkingstick."

"You and everybody else." He pulled out a clipboard. "Name?"

"Mary Crow."

He shook his head as he scanned the yellow sheet. "I don't see your name. Are you police?"

"No," Mary replied. "I'm law."

"Law?" He glanced over at the cruisers again, as if suspicious the cops were trying to sneak her in as a spy.

"Never mind." She pulled a twenty-dollar bill from her purse. "Just tell me where I can find Ruth."

"Piney Grove campsite. Straight ahead, behind the stage." He pointed into the darkness behind him.

Mary drove into Hillbilly Heaven, following the road as the guard directed. Knots of people gathered at the small fires burning between the campsites, and she could hear the low, insistent beating of drums. An eeriness hung in the air, and she felt as if she'd somehow driven back in time, when red men gathered to fight the white eyes once again.

She crested another, higher hill. To her left, tall lights illuminated an empty stage. A bank of amplifiers lined the back of it, while three microphones awaiting their next speakers stood like skinny stalks of corn.

Driving on, she finally came to a sign that pointed to the Piney Grove campsite. The road twisted through tall trees, then bottomed out beside a creek where three vehicles were parked. One was a police car, one a sleek new camper van, the third a familiar pop-up camper. The last time she'd been in it, Jonathan had given her such a fierce orgasm she wondered if she might not die from the pleasure of it. "But that was a long time ago," she whispered, feeling a single, sharp stab of sadness.

She nosed her Miata in front of Jonathan's truck and turned off the engine. Only when she got out of the car did she realize that she'd been gripping the steering wheel so tightly that her fingers had gone numb.

She scuffed through the dead leaves to the camper door and peered inside. Although both mattresses looked rumpled, nobody was home. Furious voices rose abruptly from the nearby van, where two men stood outside its open door.

"Mr. Bench, we've searched every trailer in this campground. I've put out an APB in North Carolina, Tennessee, and the better part of Georgia." The short, bald man's khaki uniform had more gold braid than most four-star generals. "I'm holding both Miss Wachacha's boyfriend and John Black Fox in jail, along with every Mexican construction worker I could run down. Just what else do you figure I should do?"

"It's Benge, not Bench, Sheriff Dula. Like binge drinking. I don't understand why you haven't called the FBI." The second man towered over the sheriff. He wore jeans with the ubiquitous red T-shirt, and had a face more intelligent than handsome. Short, dark hair curled around his forehead, making him look younger than the thirty-something Mary guessed him to be.

"I'm fully prepared to call the Feds, Mr. Benge. But not for twenty-four hours. And not until I'm totally convinced a crime has been committed here."

"What do you mean? Lily's been gone since this afternoon!" Ruth Moon's voice, coming from within the van was tearful. Mary's heart sank. This was not some oversight in communal baby-sitting. Lily Walkingstick had indeed gone missing.

She stepped forward. "Excuse me," she called. "Is Ruth Moon in there?"

Both men turned, surprised.

"Who wants her?" asked the sheriff.

"My name is Mary Crow. I've just driven up from Atlanta."

"Mary." Immediately the taller man smiled and held out his hand. "I'm Gabe Benge. This is Sheriff George Dula. Thanks for coming."

Mary shook Benge's hand, then looked inside the van. Ruth Moon sat in the turned-around driver's seat. Another, slightly younger woman sat beside her. Both wore jeans and the red SOB shirts, but where Ruth's friend had the bright nervousness of a frightened squirrel, Ruth looked as if she had just washed up on some shore in hell.

Mary stepped inside and knelt in front of her. "Hi, honey. How are you doing?"

Ruth's eyes were red and haunted. "I didn't think you would come . . ."

"Of course I came." Mary hugged her close, catching

the aroma of cigarette smoke and nervous sweat. "I'm Lily's godmother. Remember?"

"Jonathan warned me." Ruth shook her head. "He said something bad would happen . . ."

"Doesn't matter," Mary whispered, smoothing back her hair. "We're all going to help you." She smiled at Ruth, trying to impart as much hope as she could, then she turned to the men.

"What happened?"

The sheriff rested one booted foot up on the edge of the van and pulled a little notebook from his back pocket. "First why don't you tell me who you are."

"I'm a friend of the Walkingsticks," Mary explained. I'm also an ADA for Deckard County, Georgia. Mrs. Walkingstick called me to come here. I dropped everything and here I am." She dug her ID from her purse and passed it to the sheriff. She knew it would zoom her to the top of his shit list, but she didn't care. Predictably, Dula took his time in studying her credentials, then handed them back with a disdainful sneer.

"Aren't you a little far from your jurisdiction?"

"I'm the baby's godmother." She looked directly into his eyes, refusing to back off. "Now would you please tell me what has happened?"

The sheriff turned to the young woman who sat beside Ruth. "Miss Wachacha, why don't you tell Ms. Crow the story?" He flipped back several pages in his pad. "I'll go over my notes again while you talk."

Ruth's companion gave a disgusted sigh, but began a tale she'd obviously told more than once, about how she and her new friend Bobby Puckett were sitting in the pop-up when a man named Joe Little Bear appeared, claiming to be an old Army buddy of Jonathan's who'd been sent to fetch the baby to be on TV with Ruth.

"What Army outfit was your husband in?" Sheriff Dula interrupted, looking at Ruth.

Ruth shrugged. "I don't know . . . Jonathan doesn't talk much about it."

"Eighty-second Airborne," Mary answered quietly. "He was a medic in the Gulf War."

Dula raised an eyebrow, but said nothing as he jotted something down on his pad. Mary had her own question for Miss Wachacha. "Had you ever seen this Joe Little Bear before?"

"No."

"Did your friend Bobby Puckett know this man?" Mary instinctively fell into the rhythm of the courtroom. Gabe Benge leaned against the door, his face rapt with attention.

"No."

"So you're telling us that you just handed Lily over to a man you'd never seen before merely because he claimed to know Jonathan?"

The woman's mouth curled downward, sneering. "He *knew* Jonathan. He said Ruth was going to be on TV. It sounded okay."

Mary looked at the sheriff. "Why haven't you put her in jail?" she asked, not bothering to hide her disgust. "For child endangerment."

"I had her loaded up in my squad car," Dula replied coldly. "But Mrs. Walkingstick here threw such a fit that I let her out."

"For God's sake, she's my cousin," Ruth snapped. "She came here from Oklahoma to baby-sit Lily, not steal her!"

Mary bit back a cruel response: there was no point in questioning Ruth's choice of baby-sitters now. At this moment Lily was the only one who was important, and every second counted. "Does anyone know what this Little Bear looked like?"

"Here." Gabe Benge handed her a piece of lined notebook paper. "Puckett drew this."

Mary looked at the drawing. Bobby Puckett had

drawn a surprisingly detailed drawing of a man in his mid-twenties. The man's eyes looked scared more than hostile, and he sported the scraggly mustache popular with southwestern tribes.

"He wore a rally badge and said he was Navajo," Clarinda added helpfully.

"All the official badges are photo badges." Gabe Benge lifted his own for Mary to see. "And none of the Navajos here have ever heard of a Joe Little Bear."

"Have you searched the campground?" Mary asked the sheriff.

Benge answered. "Our security teams did an immediate camper-to-camper search. Sheriff Dula closed off the campground about three hours later."

"Son, my boys have searched every car that's left this place since we first got the call." Dula thrust out his lower jaw like a bulldog. "Most of my men have been busy trying to keep a lid on John Black Fox's boys."

Mary frowned. "Who's John Black Fox?"

"President of the Red Nation," Dula told her. "Runs around in makeup and a diaper. Assaulted the governor this afternoon."

"John Black Fox is a radical environmentalist," Gabe Benge explained further. "Believes we are truly in the eleventh hour, ecologically speaking, and any action to save the planet is morally supportable. Today he gave the governor a pie in the face."

Mary repressed a smile. "I saw that on television. Sheriff, you believe the pie thrower also took this baby?"

"Could have. Any one of a number of people could have. Environmentalists out to air their griefs, construction workers out of a job, a few locals who don't care for outsiders coming in and making trouble. Hell, I'm not sure that Mrs. Walkingstick's husband didn't do it."

Mary blinked, stunned. "Jonathan?"

Sheriff Dula turned to Ruth. "Why don't you fill her in on the rest of the story?"

The heartbroken woman lowered her face like a beaten dog. "Jonathan never did want us to come here. We argued about it all day Thursday, and yesterday, as we were getting ready to leave, he decided to take some man hunting instead."

"Is that why he threw his car keys at you?" Dula needled.

"He *tossed* the keys to me, Sheriff. Nobody threw anything."

"Miss Wachacha here claims he got pretty mad."

"Miss Wachacha hands babies over to total strangers, Sheriff," Mary reminded him. "Believe me, Jonathan Walkingstick would never throw anything at his wife."

Dula turned his chill gaze on her. "Miss Crow, for someone who lives two hundred miles away in Atlanta, you seem to know an awful lot about Mrs. Walkingstick's husband. You two don't have any little secret sweet thing going on, do you?"

Mary's throat grew tight. *Once we did*, she wanted to say. *Very secret and far sweeter than you can imagine.* "I've known Jonathan Walkingstick all my life, Sheriff," she replied steadily, keeping her eyes away from Ruth. "I can absolutely assure you that he would not kidnap his own child. Has anybody even tried to get in touch with him?"

"We've notified the Pisgah County sheriff and the Cherokee tribal Police," Dula said. "They haven't found him yet."

"Gabe loaned me this." Ruth raised a cell phone. "I've called the store every fifteen minutes, but he's not there. He's still out with his hunting party."

"Did he say who he was taking with him? Where they were going?"

Ruth shook her head. "Out for boar is all he said."

"That's probably Cherokee County," said Mary. "Southwest Carolina."

"You hunt boar, too, Ms. Crow?" Dula smirked.

"No. But I grew up there."

"Okay, folks," the sheriff said, putting his pad back in his pocket. "That's it for tonight."

"What are you going to do?" Mary asked him.

"I've got some boys coming over at first light with their bloodhounds. Those dogs can find most anything, living or dead."

Ruth covered her face with her hands. Mary noticed two huge wet spots on her T-shirt, directly over her breasts. Then she realized that even though her baby was gone, Ruth was still a nursing mother.

"I'll see you folks first thing tomorrow," Dula threw over his shoulder as he walked, toward his cruiser. "Get some sleep."

They stood in stunned silence after Dula left, then Ruth began to weep.

"I'm so sorry . . ." Her apology came out in wrenching sobs. "Jonathan was right. I never should have come here . . ."

As Ruth wept, Mary sat numbly, unable to comfort her. Once again, Jasmine Harris's scream echoed in her head, this time joined by a newer, smaller voice, both crying for help, both turning dark, imploring eyes directly at her.

14

MARY LAY IN Jonathan's camper, trying to tamp down the panic she felt in closed-in, cave-like places. Before Russell Cave exploded, small spaces had not bothered her. Now she hated airplanes, walked up the six flights of stairs to her office, and had only recently begun turning off her light to go to sleep. The camper was low-ceilinged and close, and every time she closed her eyes she saw Irene Hannah's face swimming up at her through the darkness.

They'd gone to bed after Sheriff Dula left. Ruth had finally introduced the pouty Miss Wachacha as Clarinda, her cousin from Oklahoma, then proceeded to darken the young woman's mood further by telling her that she had to surrender her bed to Mary. Before they doused the lantern, Mary had offered Ruth one of her Xanax, thinking it might help her get through this horror of a night, but Ruth brewed a cup of tea with some leaves she fished out of the medicine bag she now carried. By the time Mary got back from brushing her teeth at the nearby bath house, Ruth was stretched out on the mattress, snoring.

"What did she take?" Mary asked Clarinda, who appeared to be medicating herself with a bottle of Jack Daniel's.

"Beats me," Clarinda replied sourly. "You Carolina people are the ones into this herb shit."

Mary took off her shoes and collapsed on top of Clarinda's bed. The insistent rhythm of the rally drum had finally stopped; only the gurgle of the nearby creek broke the nighttime silence. She lay staring into the darkness, her claustrophobia forgotten as she tried to figure out who might have stolen this baby. Ruth had apparently made some serious enemies: both the construction workers and John Black Fox's militant environmental group seemed to have reason to hate her. Though Indians were not above stealing cars and TV sets and other people's wives, babies were rarely included in their criminal repertory, and most hard-hatted construction workers were more likely to take a lead pipe to someone's skull than to snatch an infant. As Mary stared into the shadows, the only other possibilities she could think of were an obsessed childless woman who might take a baby to raise as her own or a pedophile who stole infants for pleasure and profit.

Dwayne Pugh. The thought struck her so hard, she felt as if she'd been slammed with a brick. She'd blindsided him in court Friday with Jasmine Harris, stunned him with that child's testimony against him. Could this be his sick idea of revenge? Her mind raced. Pugh was easily capable of something like this—he had the money and the smarts, and his kiddie-porn network consisted of a bunch of self-aggrieved perverts who would rejoice at sticking it to someone with an office in the courthouse. But how could Pugh have connected Lily with her? No public record existed that linked her with any of the Walkingsticks, and the friends to whom she'd shown off Lily's picture certainly wouldn't have told Dwayne Pugh about her.

"Don't be so self-centered," she whispered, forcing herself to breathe more slowly. "You prosecute criminals in a courthouse hundreds of miles away from Ruth and Jonathan. Not all the dots connect to you."

Satisfied that Pugh's trial and Lily's abduction were just a miserable coincidence, she tried to sort through all the other people Ruth had likely pissed off. Finally she fell into a dream where Dwayne Pugh held a shrieking baby bear in his arms as Stump Logan chased her like Frankenstein through a mine shaft, his footsteps reverberating like gunshots in her ears.

She jumped as if she were falling, then her eyes flew open. The dream seemed so real, the footsteps so loud that she sat up in bed, her heart thumping. Then she realized that the banging *was* real—someone was pounding against the side of the camper.

"Mrs. Walkingstick! Wake up!"

Mary rolled off the mattress and shot to the door. Dula and Benge stood outside, their faces grim. *Dear God*, Mary thought. *They've found Lily. And she's dead.*

"What is it?" she asked, dreading their reply.

"The search-and-rescue boys are here," Dula informed her. "They'll need to get a scent from the baby's clothes."

"Give us a minute, Sheriff," Mary answered, limp with relief. "Mrs. Walkingstick's still asleep." She glanced at her watch: 5:02 A.M. The sleep that had felt like a ten-minute nap had lasted four hours. She put her shoes on, then shook Ruth and her cousin awake. Moments later, they stepped from the camper. Ruth carried one of Lily's little jumpsuits and a bright pink blanket.

Four men in coveralls stood quietly by Gabe Benge's van, accustomed, Mary supposed, to meeting at odd places at even odder times of day. Coffee steamed from the paper cups in their hands, and four sad-looking bloodhounds lay at their feet, thumping the ground with their tails as the three women walked toward them.

Dula pushed forward. "Have you got something with the baby's scent on it?"

"These." Ruth held out the clothes and the blanket. Her whole body shook as if she'd been marched at gunpoint in the endless hours since Lily's abduction, she managed to keep her voice clear and steady.

"That'll do," said one of the trackers. He took the little jumpsuit and stooped to hold it to his dog's nose. The rangy hound sniffed it noisily, then scrambled to his feet, pulling his master toward Ruth's camper. "Come on, Moe," the tracker urged. "Let's go find her."

His companions did the same thing with their own dogs. In moments, all the teams had dispersed, dogs with noses to the earth, men following them, leather leads in hand. Mary wondered if the dogs would bay like Plott hounds or beagles, but Moe and his companions worked without a sound, as if mindful of the sorrow of their task, graceful as ghosts through the trees.

"What do we do now?" Ruth pitifully asked Sheriff Dula as the last team disappeared into the shadows.

"Nothing," he replied glumly, running a hand over his hairless head. "Except wait."

Fifty miles across the mountains, Jonathan Walkingstick lay staring into the darkness, listening to the quivering cry of a screech owl. He'd drunk the six-pack of beer he'd brought and spread his bedroll in the back of the broken-down truck, curling up with an old Stephen King novel he'd found stuffed under the seat. He'd slept fitfully, waking for good when the owl began calling close to the camper, as if protesting his intrusion into its hunting grounds.

Yawning, he sat up, reflexively uttering the Cherokee word for screech owl, *"Wahuhu."* Though he heard screech owls most every day, he hadn't spoken that particular word in years. Why had it floated to the top of his subconscious today?

"Wahuhu," he repeated, the syllables sounding strange to his ears. Mostly he was happy to leave the Cherokee speaking to Ruth. He thought it pointless to become fluent in a language that no more than a few hundred people still spoke, but sometimes the old words came to him. *Wahuhu. Ahwe. Atsadi.* Owl, deer, fish. Ruth, of course, would claim he was channeling some long-dead Cherokee hunter. He chalked it up to too much beer and too little sleep. Still, it would be fun to teach Lily a few words of his own someday. Let Ruth instruct her in Granny Broom's goofy herbal remedies and political nonsense. He, her father, her *ehdoda,* would teach her about real things. *His* things.

All that, however, was years away. Right now Lily was asleep across the mountains in Tennessee and he had a fifteen-mile hike ahead of him and a clutch to replace.

He scooted out of the back of the truck, grabbing a package of Ding-Dongs and the thermos of coffee that amazingly, he'd remembered to bring with him. Though it was still dark, he knew by the soft, feathery fluttering in the trees that the birds had awakened, the sun would soon rise. Sitting in the driver's seat of the truck, he ate the cupcakes and drank a cup of the still-steaming coffee and wondered how his family was doing. Probably just fine, he decided. As long as Lily has Ruth, she's happy. As long as Ruth has a scratching post to sharpen her claws on, then she's happy. If they lived close to a competent mechanic, they could probably exist perfectly well without any help from him at all. Still, he was going to join them. *He* needed *them,* even if they didn't need him.

He popped the last bite of Ding-Dong into his mouth and washed it down the rest of his coffee. He'd better get going if he wanted to make it to Tennessee by tonight.

Without bothering to lock the truck, he shoved his wallet and car keys in his back pocket and began to make his way up the road in the darkness, walking in the long, silent strides that had carried his ancestors up and down the Appalachian mountains for the past two thousand years. He and Mary Crow used to walk like that for hours when they were children, and he could still cover more ground at a walk than most white men could jogging.

Two hours later, he reached the paved road. Fifteen miles to go, he told himself. Unless somebody comes along and gives me a ride.

"Fucking bastard." Aloud, he cursed the stupidity of his plight, the time and money lost on this wild-goose chase. If he ever saw that Duncan character, he was going to beat his five hundred dollars out of him. If he ever saw Ruth again, he was going to show her the proper way to drive a manual transmission in the mountains.

He stopped abruptly, surprised. What did he mean *if* he ever saw Ruth again? Of course he would see Ruth again. Tonight, if he had any luck with the clutch. Tomorrow, at the latest. What was he thinking about, never seeing Ruth again?

Clarinda, he decided, attributing his subconscious slip to his wife's cousin. He'd known that girl was trouble the minute she'd walked in their door. Clarinda, the adored cousin. Clarinda, the small bent twig on the much-missed family tree in Oklahoma. Clarinda, the secret spoiler, who would happily sow the seeds of discontent just to see what might grow.

"Fuck," he muttered, quickening his pace, his footsteps echoing on the blacktop. He should have gone to that rally, regardless of how angry he was with Ruth. Now Clarinda would have her ear, unimpeded until he got there. *But Ruth*, he could just hear her say, her voice soft as down yet lethal as a whiff of cyanide. *North Carolina's so green and strange. You're so far away from home. Everybody misses you so. You don't want Lily to grow up without knowing your own family, do you?*

All that, Jonathan knew, was true. He and Ruth had talked about it, and although she missed her parents horribly, she also realized that their life was here. But he knew the kind of spin Clarinda could put on it. *Why won't Jonathan let you come home? Why does he hate the causes you believe in? Why is he so anal about Lily? Pretty soon, he'll be making you stay at home, too.*

All at once he grew aware of his footsteps. Rapid, hard, *urgent*. He was almost running. He stopped and looked at his hands. They were clenched into fists. He was out here in the middle of a forest, ten miles from the nearest human being, spoiling for a fight. He shook his head. What was he thinking of? Ruth loved him and and Lily and the store. He loved her. Sure, they had been at odds with each other since Lily's birth, but what couples didn't fight? And what man wouldn't balk at having his baby daughter cared for by someone who thinks piña coladas are a food group and Buffalo wings are haute cuisine?

"You should bring Ruth some strawberries," he told himself, remembering the old Cherokee legend of how when the first man and woman quarreled, the man brought the woman strawberries as a peace offering. He chuckled. How many repentant Tsalagi husbands had, in centuries past, relied upon the sweet red berries to assuage the wrath of their wives?

"It's probably worth a shot," he decided, remembering how Ruth smiled when he would revert to some old tribal custom that most people no longer remembered.

As the day dawned clear and bright, the autumn foliage burned like fire in the trees overhead. Maybe some tourist would come along. Maybe he could hitch a ride with some family who would be thrilled to give a full-blooded Cherokee Indian a lift to Murphy, North Carolina. Once he got to Tennessee, Clarinda could get back to Oklahoma, and he and Ruth and Lily could get back to normal.

15

❦

HE KNEW IT had gone too smoothly—Paz walking up through those pine trees carrying the baby, the still-sleeping child snuggling into Ruperta's bosom, the ease with which they had simply rolled back through the campground and onto the highway beyond. At first he thought Clootie's Commit Your Life To Jesus card might be making his luck hold, but as soon as he merged onto I-75, Jesus bailed out. The baby woke up and started to shriek. Ruperta opened a bottle of the formula he'd bought, but the damn kid didn't seem to know what to do with it. The baby'd take the rubber nipple in her mouth, then spit it out as if it were something nasty. The more Ruperta offered it, the angrier the brat grew, balling up her little fists and yowling like some bear cub separated from its mother.

The racket continued for hours—the baby screaming,

Ruperta jabbering in Spanish, Paz alternately swearing
and crossing himself.

Finally, when the hard, bright tongue of a headache
began to lick around his eyes, Stump Logan turned,
worn-out, into a Kmart parking lot, understanding fully
why some parents beat their babies to death. They must
do it with great joy, relishing each blow as payback for
all their suffering. Even Paz looked grateful as Stump
ordered him to leave Ruperta and the squalling kid in
the van. For an hour he and the little wetback strolled
up and down the aisles, tossing items in their cart. By
the time they returned, both Ruperta and the baby had
fallen into an exhausted sleep, Ruperta's dark hair
damp with sweat, the baby's diaper oozing with shit.

Now they were in Chattanooga in room 114 of a
ratty cinder-block motel called the Taj Mahal, rented
from an Indian woman in an orange sari who wanted
five dollars extra to supply them with a phone. Paz
snored from one of the lumpy beds, while Ruperta and
the baby slept in the other. Logan sat in a chair propped
up against the door, studying a map of Tennessee and
praying the baby would not wake up and cry again. The
throbbing in his head had just begun to ease. If she
woke up and brought it back to full flower, he'd have to
kill her.

He leaned over and lifted one corner of the water-
stained curtains. Though it was still dark, the truck-
driving couple he'd listened to farting and fucking all
night were climbing back into the J.B. Hunt cab they'd
driven up in. He checked his watch: 4:33. Almost time
to get up. They had a lot to do today.

He hobbled to the bathroom, then crept over and
touched Paz on the shoulder.

"*Sí?*" The little man jumped, instantly awake, alert
as a fireman.

"Get Ruperta up," Stump ordered softly. "But don't
wake that damn baby!"

Nodding, Paz leaned over his sleeping wife and put his hand on her shoulder. Ruperta shot up, rubbing her eyes, then immediately turned to the child.

"Don't wake her up!" Paz cautioned in a whisper. "She'll give Gordo another headache."

"*Sí,*" Ruperta replied. She smiled down at the infant, then rose and hurried into the bathroom, locking the door behind her.

Stump looked at Walkingstick's kid. The little brat slept on her stomach, her legs tucked under her, her butt high in the air. His timing was perfect.

Grabbing one of his Kmart sacks, he sat down beside her. She flinched at the sudden bouncing of the bed, but didn't awake. From the sack he withdrew a pair of small, sharply pointed scissors.

"Señor?" Paz's eyes widened.

"Hold her still," Stump ordered. "Let's get this done before Ruperta gets out of the john."

Trembling, Paz did as he was told. Stump grabbed the dark fringe that curled around the back of the baby's neck, then began to cut the hair that Lily Walkingstick had come into the world with, smiling as the locks fell into his palm, feathery as corn silk.

"*Madre . . .*" Paz whispered in horror as he watched the gleaming point of the scissors snipping around the child's tender neck.

Stump snipped just above her ears, dropping the dark hair on the sheet beside her. She began to stir and squirm when he started trimming the crown of her head. He cut on. Minutes later he stopped and smiled. Not one hair on the little girl's head was now longer than half an inch. Edwina wouldn't consider her much of a prize, but who cared what that old heifer thought?

The bathroom door opened. "*Madre de Díos!*" Ruperta screamed as Lily began to cry. "What are you doing?"

"Shut up!" Stump commanded. "These walls are like paper. Do you want the police to come?"

"*Silencio,* Ruperta!" Paz pleaded with his wife. "He isn't hurting her."

"Just watch." Stump grinned at the terrified Mexicans. "You'll like this."

With Lily awake and squalling, he flipped her over, unsnapped her dirty white jumpsuit and tugged it off. The cold air on her warm skin enraged the baby further, and she flailed at him with her fists and legs. Digging down into his sack again, he pulled out a new jumpsuit, this one blue with a tiny cowboy stitched on the front. By the time he'd stuffed her legs and arms into the garment and snapped it shut, Lily's mouth was square with rage, her cheeks bright red. As tears rolled down the sides of her face and into her stubby hair, he scooped her up.

"There," he said proudly, showing her to the stunned Mexicans. "Lily Walkingstick has just become Willy Gonzalez. Meet your new parents, young man!"

He thrust the screaming baby at Ruperta. She held Lily close, jiggling her on her shoulder until her shrill cries gradually faded into hiccuping sobs. Then she laid the little girl gently back down on the bed and started to unsnap the outfit he'd just put on her.

"What are you doing?" Stump roared. Surely this chattering parrot of a woman wasn't going to give him any grief.

Ruperta shot him a dark look. "She needs her diaper changed, Señor."

Muttering to herself in Spanish, she lifted the child's bottom and peeled away her diaper, revealing skin blistered with rosy bumps.

"Did she have that yesterday?" Logan frowned at the angry rash.

Paz shook his head. "Ruperta says nothing you bought the baby agrees with her. Not the milk, not the diapers, not the ointment for her bottom."

Stump shrugged. "Life sucks. She'll just have to deal with it."

When Ruperta had the child buttoned back up, she tried to feed her another bottle of formula. As the baby began to twist her head away from the nipple all over again, Stump could tell her opinion of it had not changed. Feeling a fresh rivet of pain above his left eyebrow, he let himself out of the motel room. The Taj Mahal's parking lot was empty, except for their van. He walked over and unlocked the driver's door. He needed a smoke. He needed chocolate. Mostly he needed not to have that kid shrieking at him all day. He would try it as they'd planned, then, if Ruperta couldn't keep that brat quiet, he would send her and Paz out to get some food and just mash a pillow down on her noisy little face. When they returned he'd tell them she'd had some kind of fit and died. Edwina would be furious at losing something she could turn into ready cash, but Edwina could go fuck herself. Right now all he cared about was getting his trap line out for Mary Crow. For that, dead bait would work just as well as live.

16

❧

THE BLOODHOUNDS FOUND nothing. Though they sniffed along the ground for the better part of two hours, all the scents led them in a large circle around the last place Lily had been seen—Ruth's camper.

"That's because everybody carried her everywhere," said one of the trackers as he loaded his weary dog back in his pickup truck. "If she'd been old enough to walk, she would have laid her own scent down. Moe could've followed that." He looked at Ruth with mournful eyes that mirrored those of his canine friend. "I'm mighty sorry, ma'am."

"Thank you." Ruth shook his hand and forced a smile. "Thank you for trying."

The trackers drove off, just as the radio in Dula's squad car began to squawk. Dula scurried over to catch the call. A static-filled dispatch crackled through the campsite. Finally Dula signed off and walked toward them like a man with a pipe bomb up his ass.

"Okay, folks. Here's the deal. Quite a scrap broke out down by the condo site. John Black Fox's boys set a couple of bulldozers on fire and the construction workers are retaliating by tearing up the campground. Two men were assaulted, and I just got word that the governor has officially expressed a lack of confidence in our local authorities. He's sending in the National Guard to keep order. It might be better for everyone involved, Mrs. Walkingstick, if you just went home."

"Go home?" cried Ruth. "What about Lily?"

"Your husband has your child, Mrs. Walkingstick. Go home and wait for him. He'll cool off and come back."

"Why can't you understand?" Ruth shook her head wildly. "Jonathan would not do that. Joe Little Bear stole Lily! You've got to find her! I'm an American citizen. It's my right to demand that—"

"Okay, okay." Dula held up one hand, as if a crazed woman was one problem more than he could tolerate. "Go down to my office in town. You can set up your camper in my parking lot, at least until your baby shows up. Otherwise, I can't assure your safety. Those construction boys are mad as hell and they're lookin' to crack some heads."

"But you'll keep searching for her?" Ruth asked frantically.

"As long as I can, Mrs. Walkingstick."

Mary helped Ruth and Clarinda pack up the camper, then she followed them, along with Gabe Benge, down to Sheriff Dula's office in Tremont. They parked at the back of the lot, underneath some tulip trees whose yellow leaves were big as dinner plates. As Mary got out of her Miata, Clarinda was already striding toward Gabe Benge's van, her spike heels clicking across the pavement. Ruth paced around Jonathan's truck in a tight circle, as if motion of any kind was preferable to standing still.

Mary went over and put an arm around her shoulders. "Come on, Ruth. Let's go sit down."

They joined Clarinda inside Benge's van. They all crowded around the tiny dinette, their knees bumping.

"When did you last call about Jonathan?" Mary asked Ruth.

"I called Aunt Little Tom, the state troopers, the tribal cops, and the Forest Service about fifteen minutes ago."

"Anybody seen him?"

"Not a soul." Fighting back tears, Ruth fingered the buttons on the cell phone. "They promised to send him here, though, if they do. Aunt Little Tom said she would call all the ladies in her canasta club and organize a prayer circle."

"Ruth, is there anybody else you can think of who might have any reason at all to take Lily?" Mary asked.

"Nobody." As she gripped Mary's hand, tears rolled down Ruth's cheeks. "Isn't there anything else we can do? If I have to sit here and make cell phone calls all day, I'll go crazy."

Mary knew she was right. They needed jobs. Busy fingers kept worried minds from wandering into territories that were simply too terrible to consider. Her gaze fell on the photocopied sketch of Joe Little Bear that was lying on top of Benge's tiny refrigerator. She smiled. She'd just thought of something they could all do.

Half an hour later, Benge returned to the camper with thirty more copies of the Joe Little Bear sketch. Mary, Gabe, and Ruth divided them up and set out in three different directions, leaving Clarinda in the van with instructions to call Little Jump Off every fifteen minutes. Ruth and Benge headed to the big Baptist church on the edge of the square, figuring that most of this little town would be there on Sunday morning.

Mary covered the religious recalcitrants, electing to go from house to house along Mountain View Drive. Most of Tremont was indeed in church, but she did get a few responses—two young mothers home with sick children, who clutched them tighter when she showed them her picture; a retired Army colonel who swore he'd shoot Joe Little Bear on sight, no questions asked.

"No, sir," Mary protested, terrified that this man might, indeed, kill some innocent stranger. "If you see this man, just call nine-one-one. Please."

Assured of the colonel's cooperation, she worked her way down the rest of the street, then hurried back to Dula's office. On the way she met Benge, headed back from the other end of town.

"I thought you and Ruth were at the Baptist church," she said as he fell into step beside her.

"We split up. Ruth took the Baptists. I canvassed the Methodists at the other end of town."

"Any luck?"

He shook his head. "People are pretty upset about us coming to protest. I got the feeling no one wants to have anything more to do with any Native American problems."

Traffic was heavy for Sunday morning in a small mountain town; Indians seemed intent on reaching the SOB rally, tourists seemed equally intent on getting away from the demonstrations. Benge stopped at a little café called the Green Trout Grill. "Let's go in here. We can show them our sketch and maybe get a cup of coffee."

The place was empty, except for a teenage boy who slumped behind the cash register, playing a game on the restaurant's computer. Reluctantly he looked up from the screen. "Table or booth?"

"Booth," said Gabe.

He handed them menus. "Order anything. We're serving both breakfast and lunch."

"Bring us two cups of coffee now, please," Gabe told him. "And keep it coming."

They sat at a booth beneath the front window. Once the boy brought them mugs of hot coffee, they ordered ham sandwiches, two for here, two more to go. The boy shuffled back to the kitchen; they sat in exhausted silence, watching the line of campers and cars that crawled past the window.

The coffee was hot and strong and reminded Mary of the stuff Jim Falkner used to brew in his office, when they worked late and needed an extra jolt of caffeine to keep going. She smiled at the memory; she loved and sorely missed her old boss. The thought of him brought back the office; the thought of the office brought back Dwayne Pugh. In less than twenty-four hours, his trial would resume. Although she felt reasonably confident about wrangling with Virginia Kwan again, she knew that unless either Lily or Jonathan turned up soon, she was going to have to stay here. She couldn't leave Ruth alone, in the care of her nitwit cousin and a sheriff who didn't seem at all convinced Lily had been abducted. She would give it a couple more hours, then she'd call Danika and instruct her to ask for a continuance. Mott would be pissed beyond all reason, but who cared? Lily Walkingstick was missing. Mary opened her purse and pulled out her phone to get Danika up to speed when she noticed that the e-mail icon was blinking. Odd, she thought. She'd deleted all her work mail yesterday afternoon, and no one ever sent anything from Deckard on Sunday mornings.

Must be Danika, she decided as she punched the READ option. Already working at the office. But when she saw the message on the little screen, her heart turned to ice.

"Good God," she whispered. "I've got an e-mail."

Benge gave her an odd glance. "So?"

She turned the phone so he could see it. "It's a picture of Lily Walkingstick!"

17

"WHAT THE HELL?" Benge stared at the tiny screen, un-comprehending.

She fumbled with the phone, uncertain about all its features. She'd never received a picture on the thing before, and though the tiny image looked out of focus and bizarre, she knew it was definitely Lily Walkingstick.

"Where is she?"

"I can't tell." Why hadn't she paid more attention when Hobson handed these phones out? "The screen's so small, it's hard to see the details—"

Just then the boy sauntered back to the table with their sandwiches. "Y'all want any dessert or anything?" he asked, eager to slap their ticket on the table and re-turn to his computer.

"Are you hooked up to the Net over there?" Benge asked him.

"America Online."

"You got a printer attached?"

The boy shrugged. "An old one. Prints about one page an hour."

Benge pulled out his wallet and handed the boy a twenty-dollar bill. "Ten of that is for lunch. The rest is yours if you can get us online and give us ten minutes of time."

The kid's pudgy face lit up. "Sure. Come on over."

Behind the counter, he shut down a game called "Saracen Assassin" and logged on. As the pleasant male voice bid them welcome, the boy relinquished his chair. Gabe Benge held it out for Mary.

"Go to your server at work," he instructed her. "Download the image from there. The graphics might be better."

Mary navigated quickly to the Deckard County server, typing her password in at the prompt. Instantly a larger version of her e-mail filled the screen. The computer warned her not to open the attached file unless she knew who sent it, but she ignored the warning. If she crashed this kid's computer, she'd see that he got it fixed.

Drumming her fingers on the counter, she waited. A blurred image finally appeared on the screen. As she realized what it was, she felt as if she'd been flash-frozen from the inside out.

A picture of Lily Walkingstick swam into focus on the larger screen. But not the happy, healthy Lily she'd held in her arms six weeks ago. This Lily looked as if she'd been left out for wolves. She lay naked on her back, crying, tears rolling from tightly closed eyes. Her little hands were balled into fists and her feet looked blurred, as if she were trying to kick her kidnapper away even as the photo was snapped. She lay behind some kind of iron fence at the base of a pile of rocks. What Mary's eyes could not get past were the words that blazed across the bottom of the picture. *Mary, we need you. Jonathan.*

"Holy shit!" Gabe Benge leaned so close, she could feel his breath on the top of her head. "That's Nancy Ward's grave!"

"Nancy who?"

"Nancy Ward. You know, Chief Attakullakulla's niece. The *ghighau.*"

Ghighau. Most Honored Woman, Mary translated, her Cherokee coming back with painful slowness as she tried to recall her history. Nancy Ward had been a Cherokee woman who'd counseled peace with the whites, way back in the eighteenth century, when North Carolina still belonged to George III. But what had that to do with Lily? And who had sent this picture to her?

"Where is this grave?" she asked Benge urgently.

"North of Chattanooga. I take my undergraduate classes to dig along the river there. It's mostly dug out, but it's a great place to learn technique."

Suddenly he wheeled her chair around, his eyes snapping with a dark fire. "Look, if the sheriff guessed right about you and Walkingstick, then you need to come clean right now."

"What the hell are you talking about?" She met his hard look with one of her own.

"I watched you last night. You defended Jonathan Walkingstick like someone who was much more than a friend."

"At one time we were more than friends, Mr. Benge. That is no longer the case."

"Then why is this e-mail addressed to you?"

"I don't know. All I can tell you is that Jonathan Walkingstick would not kidnap his own child. Nor would I be involved with any man who could."

For an eternity Benge's eyes bored into hers, then he nodded. "Good," he said. "I'm glad to hear that."

"I'm printing two copies of this." She turned back to

the computer. "One for Ruth and one for Dula. The Feds can track these address lines and figure out where this was sent from."

Gabe gave the boy five more bucks for two prints of the photo, then they left the café, only to find that in the course of a ham sandwich and a cup of coffee, the Tennessee National Guard had invaded the town. Soldiers in combat gear patrolled the streets, while hulking troop carriers squatted next to the curbs. As they picked their way through the tangled traffic, Mary felt as if she'd been dropped by mistake into someone else's nightmare. She was certain Jonathan would never kidnap Lily, however furious he might be with Ruth. But who else could have sent her that message with his name at the bottom? Who else could both link her with Lily and Jonathan and access her through the Deckard County server?

And then, as she and Gabe Benge crossed Main Street, she realized exactly who could. Stump Logan. Logan knew her, he knew Jonathan, and as a former sheriff, he knew how to reach her through the back door, so to speak. Logan could have found out about Lily easily. No doubt he still had pals in Pisgah County who told him everything that was going on.

Stop it, she scolded herself. *Logan is dead. The Atlanta cops say so, the FBI says so, Dr. Bittner says so. It can't be Stump Logan. It must be Dwayne Pugh.*

"I think I know who might have done this," she said, as if giving voice to the words might increase their veracity.

Gabe Benge scrambled to avoid a guardsman lugging a huge bottle of water. "Who?"

"Dwayne Pugh. A man I'm currently prosecuting for child pornography."

"Where is he?"

"He's been locked up in the Deckard County jail for months. We're in the middle of trial right now."

Benge frowned. "If Pugh's locked up in an Atlanta jail, how could he have stolen Ruth's baby?"

"He's got brains and money and friends. The kiddie pornographers are like a brotherhood of roaches."

"Okay. Say Pugh did this. What do we do?"

"Here." Mary handed one of the prints to him. "Take this over to Dula. Tell him he needs to get the Feds tracing this. I'll give this one to Ruth. As hard as this is to look at, at least she can see that Lily's still alive."

They pushed through the crowded sidewalk. When they reached the sheriff's parking lot, Gabe headed into his office while Mary hurried to the van. She looked in the door to find Clarinda sitting cross-legged on the sofa, filing her nails, a fashion magazine open on her lap.

Mary asked her, "Have you gotten in touch with Jonathan yet?"

"Nope."

"Where's Ruth?"

"Putting up posters." Clarinda looked up from her nails as if Mary had interrupted something vital to her existence. "Did you find out anything?"

"A little," Mary replied. "I really need to talk to Ruth."

"Here I am," came a voice over her shoulder.

Mary turned. Ruth hurried toward her, clutching her last copy of Puckett's drawing and a roll of masking tape. "I've been putting these up all over town. Has something happened?"

"Kind of. Someone sent me this through my office e-mail."

"Oh, my God!" Ruth cried. "It's Lily!" She covered her face with the picture, as if needing to inhale the image, then drew back and studied it intently. "But where is she?" she asked, just beginning to fully comprehend

the horror of the image. "And why did they take off all
her clothes?"

"And what does *'Mary, we need you, Jonathan'*
mean?" Clarinda's query dripped with suspicion.

Mary put a hand on Ruth's arm. "Honey, I'm in the
middle of prosecuting a child pornographer named
Pugh. He's wealthy and clever and mean." She winced
as she saw the new hope in Ruth's face begin to flicker
and die. "I think Pugh could have had Lily kidnapped
and somehow have put me together with Jonathan."

"Oh, God. My poor little girl!"

"Ruth, as awful as this is, try to see the positive side
of it."

"Like what?" huffed Clarinda. "That her kid's been
snatched by some perv who takes pictures of her naked?
That doesn't sound so positive to me."

"Lily's alive." Mary ignored Clarinda and tried to
connect with Ruth's stricken eyes. "She's not lying dead
somewhere. I've got some leverage here, now. Because
of this, I can get the Atlanta cops onboard."

Gabe Benge walked up. Reading his tight-lipped
frown, she asked, "You couldn't find Dula, could you?"

"The National Guard has commandeered his office.
I left a message with one of his deputies to tell him to
come see Mrs. Walkingstick immediately." He brushed
past the three women and stepped into the van. A few
moments later he came back out, a thick red book in his
hand. He handed it to Mary. "Doesn't this photo look a
lot like where the baby is lying?"

The women clustered around him. The grave in the
e-mailed photo did look startlingly similar to the one on
the printed page. A pyramid of rounded stones, surrounded by an iron picket fence. In the middle of the
stones in Gabe's photo was a plaque erected by the
DAR, memorializing the site of Nancy Ward's grave.

Ruth looked at Gabe. "Is this *the* Nancy Ward
grave?"

He nodded. "It's just north of Chattanooga."

"Then let's go!" she cried. "Chattanooga isn't far—"

"Hang on, Ruth," cautioned Mary. "I'm not sure that's the best thing to do."

"Why not? If Lily's there . . ."

"Ruth, we don't know when this picture was taken. Lily's probably not there anymore. And if you leave Dula's jurisdiction now, he'll be even more certain this kidnapping is some kind of domestic squabble between you and Jonathan and he'll drop the search like yesterday's news. As long as you stay in his county, he's got an open case on the books. He'll have to work it."

"So we just have to sit here?" Clarinda stuck out her lower lip.

"No," said Mary. "Go park yourselves in the Sheriff's office. Convince Dula that Jonathan had nothing to do with this. If you don't get to talk to him within the next hour, call the FBI yourself."

"I can do that?" asked Ruth.

"Yes, you can. The Feds may opt not to get involved at this time, but at least you will have lodged a formal complaint."

"What are you going to do?" demanded Clarinda suspiciously.

"First I'm going to call Atlanta, then I'm going to go pay my respects to Nancy Ward, the Most Honored Woman of the Cherokees."

18

❦

WHILE GABE AND Clarinda helped Ruth set up the camper, Mary walked beneath the bright yellow trees. She still could not imagine how Dwayne Pugh could have put her, Lily, and Jonathan together, but he had to have done it. There was simply no one else. No one alive and walking the earth, anyway. She needed to have Pugh questioned, and questioned hard. She could call Sanford and Maestra, the two vice detectives who'd worked the case, but that would go in the official log books. If it got back to Virginia Kwan that Mary was having her client interrogated about a kidnapping that occurred two hundred miles away in Tennessee, Kwan would have one of her famed fire-breathing dragon fits. Mott would find out and probably declare Mary mentally unfit to prosecute anybody. Until she could tie Pugh's threats to the missing Lily, she needed to proceed quietly. Inadvertently she shivered. She knew exactly who could help her.

She pressed one of the preprogrammed numbers on her cell phone. The phone rang twice, then a man answered.

"Justice Center gym."

"Mike Czarnowski, please."

"Hang on."

She waited, listening to the muffled shouts of what sounded like a fairly rowdy basketball game. Then a male voice came on the line.

"Czarnowski."

"Mike? This is Mary Crow."

"Hey, Killer." The gruff voice softened instantly. "You coming down this afternoon?"

"Not today, Mike."

"So what's up?"

"Mike, I need a favor."

"You name it."

"Remember Dwayne Pugh?"

"That asswipe you're prosecuting?"

"Exactly. Look, Mike, I've got a situation here. I'm up in Tennessee. Someone abducted the baby of some friends of mine."

Czarnowski gave a low whistle. "Stole a baby? Jeez, Mary."

"Listen, I know this sounds paranoid as hell, but I'm wondering if Pugh set this up somehow."

"From jail?" She could hear the same incredulity in Mike's voice that she'd heard earlier in Benge's.

"He could do it."

"You want me to find out?"

Mary hesitated. Never had she thought she would ask for such a thing, yet never had she dreamed anyone would steal little Lily Walkingstick. It was time to take the gloves off and play outside the rules. "Yes, Mike. I do."

"Give me some particulars."

"The victim's a three-month-old Cherokee female.

Black hair, brown eyes, light tan complexion." *My god-child*, she thought. *The closest thing to family I've got left.* "Her name is Lily Walkingstick. She was abducted from the Hillbilly Heaven campsite in Tremont, Tennessee, sometime Saturday afternoon. Sheriff's got an APB out in Tennessee and Carolina."

"Feds involved?"

"Not to my knowledge," Mary replied. "Hopefully, they soon will be."

"Okay, Killer. Don't worry. I'll find out something."

Mary switched off the phone. She knew cops beat confessions out of people every day, but she'd never dreamed she'd call and order one up like a take-out pizza. *Cracked ribs and bruised kidneys, please, but for God's sake, no black eyes!*

But there was nothing she could do about that now. She rejoined Gabe Benge back at his van, and minutes later they were edging into the line of traffic heading west.

"So how far away is Nancy Ward's grave?" she asked him.

"A couple of hours," he replied. "Take a nap, if you want. I'll wake you when we get there."

"Thanks, but I'm okay." She didn't want to nap: a short sleep would only make the great mound of fatigue inside her heavier to bear. Still, as the bright autumn landscape flashed by, Gabe's invitation began working like a subliminal suggestion, and she found her eyelids drooping. Sitting up straighter in the seat, she turned her attention to him.

"So how come you know so much about Cherokee history?"

He shrugged. "My dad got me interested when I was a kid."

"Really? Is your father into Indian lore, too?"

He glanced at her. "You don't know the villainous name of Benge?"

She shook her head.

"I'm a descendant of Bob Benge. He was a Cherokee outlaw who terrorized the pioneers in southwest Virginia."

"Wow. FBI criminal, huh?"

"FBI?"

"Full-blood Indian."

He chuckled. "He was. I'm not. Benge's descendants intermarried with the Scotch-Irish Virginians pretty fast. I'm a half-breed, at best."

"Join the club."

"You're not full-blood?"

"My mom grew up in Snowbird, my dad was from Atlanta."

"Zalagish hewonishgi?" he asked eagerly.

Hearing the soft, musical speech of her childhood, Mary smiled "Some. *Gado dejado? Hadlu hinel?*"

"I can't believe I've finally found somebody to speak Kituwah with!" He grinned, then remembered to answer her question. "Gabriel Fergus Benge. University of Tennessee, most years."

"Most years?"

"This year I'm on sabbatical. I had planned to go dig up mummies in Peru."

"And now?"

His smile faded. "I don't know Ruth Moon well, but I'm the one who persuaded her to get involved in this rally. I'm not leaving until her daughter's been found."

Mary studied him, impressed with the way he shouldered that responsibility. Though she'd never seen or heard of Gabriel Benge until last night, something about him felt comfortably familiar, as if they were old friends resuming a long-interrupted conversation without a beat of hesitation. Pondering that, she leaned back and turned her gaze out the window. A herd of Black Angus cows dotted a green hillside like black ink drops spilled from a pen. *Me, Lily, and Jonathan,* she wondered. *How could Pugh have tied us together?*

"Mary?"

She jumped. "What?" she croaked, for an instant unable to place herself. Time and distance seemed to have passed without her notice.

"We're here."

She looked out the window. The van had stopped in a paved parking lot at the base of a hill. A Tennessee state historical marker rose directly in front of them. Slowly it all came back to her. Gabe Benge was driving her to Nancy Ward's grave, to look for Lily. Somewhere between the Black Angus cattle and here, she'd fallen asleep.

"Okay," she said, willing the muzziness out of her brain. "Let's go look around."

They climbed out of the truck. On one side of the lot, a dirt path led to a canoe launch on the Ocoee River. On the other side, a paved, landscaped pathway curved around a small hill. They walked up the hill, looking for anything that might indicate Lily had been there. Yellow chrysanthemums bloomed tightly on either side of the trail, the grass grew to a sedate half inch, and someone had swept the walk free of dead leaves. It was the cleanest public park Mary had ever visited, but there was no sign of Lily. As they neared the hilltop, she saw a mound of stones surrounded by a tall iron fence. Gabe pulled the photograph from his jacket.

"This looks like the place. The kidnapper must have jumped that fence, set the baby down at the base of the grave, and snapped the photo. Judging by the shadows, I'd say they did it early this morning."

Mary eyed the fence. It stood well above her head, the iron spikes sharp and pointed. "There must be at least two kidnappers, then. Nobody could jump that fence with a baby in their arms."

Gabe nodded. "I hadn't thought of that, but you're right."

They walked clockwise around the fence, which was studded with various items people had left to honor Nancy Ward. Bedraggled eagle feathers dangled in the breeze, mixed in with faded dream-catchers and scraps of bright red yarn. As they circled the enclosure they found a mud-encrusted Lookout Valley High School ring from the class of '99, an empty champagne bottle, an upturned horseshoe spray-painted gold. Nothing, though, remotely to do with either Lily or her. If Pugh had left some clue here to taunt her, she and Gabe were both missing it.

A hundred yards away, across the highway, stood the beginnings of a new subdivision. The main road looked like a deep orange scar in the earth, and three houses rose in various stages of completion. Tomorrow, construction workers would return and resume their work on the site. Today, Sunday, the subdivision looked as deserted as this grave.

"Nobody would have been working over there this morning," she told Gabe Benge. "Nobody would have seen anything going on up here." Suddenly she felt the frustration of cops. By the time she got cases, most of the loose ends had been tied up. Out here, in the world beyond the Deckard County Courthouse, trails went cold fast.

Her phone beeped. Quickly she dug it out of her pocket. Any news, at this point, would sound good.

"Hello?"

"Hey, Killer. Mike here."

She fought the urge to turn away from Gabe and whisper. "Did you talk to Pugh?"

"Yes, ma'am, I did." Czarnowski sounded smug. "I talked for a good while. Old Dwayne listened pretty good, too."

"And?"

"He's not your boy, Mary." Czarnowksi's voice went flat.

"What?" She couldn't believe this. Pugh had to be the one.

"He didn't do it. By the end of our conversation he wished he had, but he didn't."

"But how can you be so sure? He's a sociopath and a liar. And he's smart, and he's—"

"Mary, men lie to me only once. When they learn what that lie costs them, they always come up with the truth. Trust me on this, darling: Pugh's a slimy wad of snot, but he didn't have anything to do with your little Cherokee baby."

"Mike, are you positive?"

"Yes. Absolutely."

Mary closed her eyes. She'd engaged in junta tactics, and for what? Nothing, except for inflicting some well-deserved pain on Dwayne Pugh. She felt sick inside.

"Thanks, Mike," she said sadly, knowing she would never again walk into the Deckard County Courthouse in quite the same way. "I appreciate your trying."

"I'm sorry, Mary. I wish I could have done more."

She dropped the phone back in her purse just as a mockingbird landed on top of Nancy Ward's gravestone. The gray-feathered bird perched with its long tail at a rakish angle, its throat throbbing with song. Although it sounded beautiful, all she could hear was Lily, crying on that grave.

Gabe touched her shoulder. "I take it you did not get good news?"

She turned and faced him, straight on, feeling as if she were confessing a sin. "For the first time in my career, I just had a man questioned by an officer famous for encouraging reluctant criminals to own up to their deeds."

"In other words, you had the shit beat out of him."

"Right."

"And?"

"And he couldn't get Pugh to cop to any of this." Miserable, Mary shook her head. "My wonderful theory just crashed and burned."

"You're absolutely convinced that it isn't Walkingstick?"

"Without a doubt," she answered firmly. She stared at Nancy Ward's tombstone a moment, then switched her cell phone back on. "I'm calling Ruth," she told Gabe. "Maybe she's gotten some news from Dula or Jonathan."

"What if she hasn't?"

"Then I'm calling my assistant in Atlanta. To tell her to ask for a continuance."

She pushed the buttons that would connect her with Danika when, just as before, a blinking e-mail icon materialized on her screen. Once again, she'd received a picture; once again, the image was of Lily Walkingstick.

19

❦

"HOLY SHIT!" CRIED Gabe. "Another one!"

"Come on," Mary said, staring at the tiny picture on the phone. "Let's get to a computer where we can print off a clearer image."

They raced back to the van. While Mary called a stunned Danika, explaining the situation and telling her to ask for a continuance, Gabe drove south, catching I-75 to Chattanooga. "There's a fair-sized college there," he explained to Mary. "We can log on to the Internet at the library."

They reached Chattanooga just after sundown. On the way to the college they saw a Kinko's, and pulled in. The clerk behind the counter took an imprint of Mary's credit card and gave her a swipe card that served as an electronic key. They hurried into the computer room, to the first PC they came to. When the welcome screen came on, Mary logged on to the Deckard County server.

Twenty new messages appeared, but only one had a .jpg file attached. She clicked the mouse; the file opened.

It was Lily. This time she lay in front of a weather-beaten tombstone that had a long-eroded lamb carved at its top. The child wore nothing but a disposable diaper clumsily fastened around her legs. Although she still stared at the camera with defiant little eyes, she no longer exhibited the squalling rage of the first picture. Her fists were not clenched, nor was she flailing her feet at the photographer. To Mary, she seemed to be drooping, like prisoners of war who still had the will but not the strength to fight back. Mary moved the cursor down to the lower margin of the picture, where a new message appeared. *Please, Mary. Come now. I need you. Jonathan.*

Without thinking, she touched the computer screen. She knew Jonathan Walkingstick better than anyone else on earth. Every thread of her being told her that he was incapable of this, yet here was a picture of his baby with a message clearly addressed to her. Of course she would come if he needed her. Without question and without fail. And Jonathan knew that.

She glanced up. Gabe was watching her. His face was like stone.

"I know how this looks," she said defensively. "But believe me, Jonathan is not responsible for this."

"You wouldn't kid a kidder, would you?" Gabe's smile was mirthless.

"No," she answered quietly, noticing that his eyes were not brown like she'd thought, but a blue so deep they almost looked black. "I would not."

Once again he studied her; once again his face softened. "Okay, then. Let's make some copies of that and get back to the van."

Ten minutes later they sat in his camper, comparing the two photos of Lily.

"Look," said Gabe. "This is still a Hotmail account,

still Lily Walkingstick's name, but the address lines at the top have changed."

"He's moving around," Mary said.

Gabe shrugged. "Maybe. He's at least using different computers."

"Do you recognize this tombstone?" Mary almost laughed at her own question. What made her think Gabe Benge had intimate knowledge of every old cemetery in Tennessee?

"No, but if he's sticking with the Cherokee thing, then it could be the Shellsford Baptist Church." He turned to pull a book down from the shelf behind him.

"Is that some archaeological site?"

"No. It's one of the few places east of the Mississippi where nineteenth-century Cherokees were buried like whites. Here." He pointed to a black-and-white photo. "That's the Shellsford cemetery."

To Mary it looked like a thousand other old graveyards, tombstones broken and listing at odd angles, as if the dead rose up to dance when no one was looking and then hastily scooted back into their graves. "I don't know. I don't see that particular grave there."

"Wait!" Gabe exclaimed. "I just thought of something. If this picture was taken at Shellsford, then the kidnapper could be following the Trail of Tears."

Mary blinked. She well knew about Andrew Jackson's brutal, forced removal of the Cherokees to Oklahoma in 1838. In fact, right after Lily's baptism, Jonathan's Aunt Little Tom had put a personal spin on that tragic history.

"*When my grandmother's mother was a girl, soldiers from Georgia marched down this very road we're standing on,*" the old woman had told them. "*Came to this cabin where my great-grandmother's family was eating bean bread and squirrel stew. The soldiers stuck rifles in their faces. Made them get up and leave right then. They left kettles on the fire, supper on the table.*

They were terrified that the soldiers were going to kill them. The soldiers marched them hard, into country they did not know. Finally one night, my great-grandmother's father sneaked his family away from the soldiers. They hid deep in the woods, and finally made their way back here!" Aunt Little Tom had spoken with such passion that Mary almost looked over her shoulder to make sure the Army wasn't coming down the road to again force-march them off to places unknown.

Now she refocused on the matters at hand. Gabe had retrieved a pen and a tattered map of Tennessee from his glove box. He spread it out on the dinette.

"Look. The first photo was taken here at Nancy Ward's grave." He made an X on the map. "If the second one was taken there"—he made a second X at Shellsford—"then whoever's got Lily is following the northern route of the Trail of Tears."

Mary frowned. "Where does it go from Shellsford?"

Gabe traced the route with his finger. "Northwest to Nashville, then up to Hopkinsville, Kentucky."

"Then on to Missouri and Arkansas and Oklahoma." Mary's heart sank. Somehow she knew that Lily would never see that part of the trail. The baby looked so much worse than she had in the first photo, taken only hours earlier. At this rate, she wouldn't make it out of Tennessee alive. And for what reason? The whole thing made less sense by the minute.

"But why?" she asked Gabe. "Why Lily? Why Cherokee graves along the Trail of Tears? And why are these photos being sent to me?"

"If we assume Walkingstick's not the kidnapper," he replied logically, "I'd say somebody's after you or Ruth Moon."

"A fair number of people want me dead," Mary told him, "but Mike Czarnowski eliminated the most likely suspect." She frowned at Gabe. "That leaves Ruth. How does John Black Fox feel about her? And that construction company?"

"John's as radical as any of the old Black Panthers, but he has a lot of respect for Ruth. And as bad as Summerfield stinks as a corporation, I can't see them having a child kidnapped." He rubbed his chin thoughtfully, his eyes on the map. "And neither Fox nor Summerfield knows you. Who could put the Walkingsticks, you, and the SOB rally all together?"

Again she thought of Stump Logan, but the mental image of him hoisting babies over six-foot fences was almost ludicrous. Logan was old and lame, plus he'd always acted alone. *And don't forget he's dead,* she almost blurted aloud.

"I'm going to call Ruth and tell her what's going on," she said. "If she's gotten the FBI involved, they should have these new address headers."

"And if she hasn't?"

"Then I'm going to call the Feds myself while you drive us to this Shellsford Baptist Cemetery. We've got another grave to visit."

At that same moment, someone else was tracking a different trail. Sitting at Clootie Duncan's desk, Edwina Templeton scowled as she heard the Philadelphia clock downstairs strike eight. Duncan had left at noon on Friday, vowing to return with his baby the next day. Now Sunday was fast turning into Monday, and Duncan had yet to reappear.

"Where the hell has he gone?" Edwina muttered peevishly as she rifled through Duncan's papers. Among an extraordinary number of crumpled candy wrappers she found a half-dozen books on the history of the Cherokee Indians, three detailed maps of Tennessee, a pamphlet from her own office entitled "Basic Baby

Care," and a receipt for four boxes of .300 Magnum rifle shells.

Edwina gave a low whistle. "Looks like daddy's gone a-hunting. But what on earth for?"

She hurried over to the cabinet where she kept her weapons. Opening the door, she stepped back, stunned. Two of her Tasers were gone. So were the old Winchester .70 she used to shoot four-legged skunks and the Smith & Wesson automatic she kept for the two-legged variety.

"Good Lord," she cried. "All this to get one baby?"

She wondered if Duncan might be one of those jealous types who would take both his baby and his girlfriend and shoot them both, in some weird kind of hillbilly revenge. Probably not, she decided as she returned to the desk. He'd shown little real emotion when he'd talked about the child. But she knew he was up to something. Any man who would woo her as if she were a teenager had to be a little suspect. She had eyes and mirrors enough to know that her breasts sagged and her butt looked like a bag of loosely packed oranges. Men did not feign love for women her age without some deeper motive.

"But what could it be?" Up until a minute ago she'd figured Duncan's impetus had been fairly straightforward. Relieve an old girlfriend of a love child she didn't want, and maybe make a buck or two on the side. Now, she wondered. With that Winchester and four hundred rounds of long-range ammunition, Duncan could do some serious damage. Could he have gone off his nut and be planning some kind of sniper attack? If so, what would happen to Paz and Ruperta? And her van?

"Damn," she snarled, finding nothing more incriminating than chocolate candy stashed in his desk drawers. She should have known better than to trust Duncan with anything. Better to have left Paz and Ruperta in charge here and gone with him herself. But, oh, how she loved it here alone, when the big old house stood empty of staff and clients! Then its gleaming floors and moiré-papered walls became truly hers, and it took on the sheen of a real home—her real home.

"Just think a minute," she said, closing the drawer as she tried to rein in the skittery fear that was rising inside her. "Duncan might be crazy, but he isn't a fool."

She could, she supposed, call the police and report him for stealing her van and kidnapping her two servants. But she knew from experience that police tended to linger, asking hard, tricky questions. The last thing she wanted was for any of the Christmas-tour women to drive past and see a squad car parked in front of her house. She had no close friends she could call, nor did she keep company with her neighbors. No, there was nothing she could do except wait and hope that Duncan returned. If he didn't, the worst thing she would be out of would be that antique bed. The van and the two Mexicans would be easy enough to replace.

"Just go on as you'd planned," she told herself. "Then if he does show up, you'll be ready."

Hurrying into her bedroom, she climbed up on her bed with the auction-house catalog and her address book. Although it was an odd time to conduct business, she needed to call one of her colleagues in Florida. Her boobs and her butt may have sunk to ruin, but she still had a memory like a ticker tape when it came to the adoption market.

She looked up the number and punched it in her phone. It rang once, twice, then, on the third, a high nasal voice answered gruffly, as if awakened from sleep.

"Hello?"

"Myrtle? This is Edwina Templeton."

"Who?"

Edwina heard a commercial for Burger King blaring in the background. She raised her voice. "Edwina

Templeton. Calling from Tender Shepherd Home, in Tennessee."

"Oh, Edwina, of course! I'm sorry. I just walked in the door." The commercial ceased abruptly.

"Listen, Myrtle. The last time we talked, didn't you say you had a couple who was looking for a half-Arab child?"

"Yes." Myrtle's voice sharpened.

"Are they still looking for a child?"

"I haven't talked to them in a month or so, but I assume they are. Why? Have you got one?"

"I might be getting one," Edwina replied cautiously. "Do you think your couple might be interested?"

"I'd have to call them. The man was pretty particular. He's from some old Middle Eastern family. Very proud, those people." Myrtle coughed. "What kind of baby have you got?"

"All I know for sure is that it's a girl." Edwina looked at a picture of the bed in the auction catalog. If she played her cards right, she might be able to get the bed and something else, as well. Some little antique Christmas doodad to show off on the tour.

"Is it half-Iranian?" Myrtle wanted to know. "That's the key with these people."

"Oh, yes," Edwina lied. "That's why I thought of you right off the bat. Why don't you find out if your couple's still interested and then give me a call? Maybe we can work something out for everybody concerned."

Myrtle chuckled. "And that something would entail a number with zeroes behind it that we can put in the bank?"

"That would be correct, Myrtle," replied Edwina. "A number with lots of zeroes after it. I just hope your clients are as full of money as they are of ethnic pride."

"Not a problem," said Myrtle. "For the right baby, they'll dig down deep."

20

"MARY JUST GOT another e-mail." Ruth put the cell phone down and looked at her cousin, who sat playing solitaire on her cot.

"What was it?" Clarinda looked up, the four of spades poised in her hand.

"Lily again. In another cemetery."

"Oh, gross." Clarinda grimaced. "What are they going to do?"

"They're driving to someplace called Shellsford."

"So Mary knew where the second picture was taken?"

"Gabe did. He thinks whoever's got Lily is taking her along the Trail of Tears."

"The Trail of Tears? Why?"

"I don't know. But I'm going to find Dula. I'll make him get the FBI involved."

"Ruth, we've gone over to his office thirty times. He's never there."

"Then I'll wait," Ruth declared as she rose and reached for her denim jacket. "Stay here and play cards if you want. I'll go by myself."

"Never mind." Clarinda wearily tossed her last card down on the mattress. "I'll come too."

The two women stepped out of the camper. Where earlier the streets had been lined with tourists, National Guardsmen now walked regular patrols, their cadenced footsteps thudding ominously on the pavement.

Clarinda shivered in the crisp mountain air. "I wish we'd never come here."

You and me both, thought Ruth, walking slump-shouldered to keep her breasts from chafing against her bra. Lily had missed six or seven feedings, and though her milk let down and drenched her blouse with every unanswered phone call to Little Jump Off, her breasts were engorged with excess milk, her nipples hot and sore to the touch. *I'll take some squaw root after I see Dula,* she promised herself. She felt a feverish heat, as if Lily's absence were some kind of sickness spreading outward from her breasts, soon to engulf her whole body.

At the sheriff's office, a half-dozen exhausted-looking men sat at various desks around the open room. Three wore Nikwase County deputy uniforms, the others were National Guardsmen. In the middle stood Dula, coffee cup in hand. Ruth gasped involuntarily at the sheriff's appearance. His once snappy trousers were splattered with thick orange mud, while his shirt looked stiff with dirt and sweat. Even his badge had lost its glitter. His face looked like a raccoon's in reverse, dark soot outlining the white skin around where he'd worn his sunglasses. Dula seemed to wobble as he stood there, as if the tiniest breath of air might blow him over. He looked up as they entered the room.

"Hello, ladies." He nodded without much enthusiasm. "I understand you've been looking for me."

"We need to talk to you." Ruth tried to sound as confident and forceful as Mary Crow always did.

"In here." He beckoned them forward perfunctorily, unimpressed by her tone.

They followed him to an office that overlooked Main Street. He switched on the lights before he took his place behind his desk. "Have a seat," he told them. "Update me on that baby of yours. Hubby shown up yet?"

Ruth frowned. "Have your deputies not told you anything?"

Dula gave a thin smile. "They said you'd gotten some kind of e-mail."

Ruth handed him the print of the photo Mary had given her, then went on to explain that Mary had received a second photo, just hours ago.

"I've got the address headers right here. Mary says the FBI can trace them."

"Where's Mary Crow now?" asked Dula, studying the photo.

"She and Gabe Benge just left Chattanooga, heading to someplace called Shellsford. They think whoever's got Lily is taking her along the old Trail of Tears."

Dula sipped his coffee and looked up at her with weary eyes. "Mrs. Walkingstick, I've been on this job over twenty years. In that amount of time, you learn how to read signs that other people might not see. To pick up on emotions that aren't exactly on the surface, you know?"

Ruth nodded, wondering where Dula was going.

"Honey, if anybody had kidnapped your baby, we would have found some trace of it. I called the FBI early this morning, right after the bloodhounds left."

"So are they working on it?" Her voice swelled with hope.

"No. The Bureau's opted not to override my jurisdiction. But the TBI's got it on their desks, and the APBs are still out in Tennessee and Carolina."

"But—"

"Mrs. Walkingstick, I'm happy to investigate this. That's your right as a citizen and my duty as an officer of the law. But I firmly believe your baby's fine. It's your marriage that's in serious trouble."

Ruth felt a tingling in her breasts. Her milk was letting down. Soon her shirt would be drenched. "You still think my husband stole our child?" she asked in anger and disbelief.

"It took me about two seconds to see that your pal Mary has a real case on your husband. You yourself told me that she and your husband were 'old friends.' Which, I've come to learn, most always means old lovers." He glanced at Clarinda. "Others confirmed that he was opposed to your coming here, and in fact, you argued quite violently about it."

"But I'm the one who called Mary up here," protested Ruth. "And if Jonathan had planned to steal Lily, why didn't he just do it at home?"

"Actually, he could have stolen the child anywhere," Dula pointed out reasonably. "Mary Crow the same thing—coming up here, pretending to help out." He put down his coffee and rifled through some papers. "I ran a check on her, too. She's not the straightest arrow in the quiver."

"Mary Crow?" Ruth asked, astonished.

Dula found the paper he was looking for. "She got hurt in an explosion over in Carolina about a year ago. Hasn't been the same since, according to her boss. She was even under the care of a psychiatrist for several months, for post-traumatic stress disorder." He chuckled. "I got the idea some folks down in Atlanta wouldn't mind a bit if Ms. Crow did run off with your husband."

"But Gabe was the one who knew where Nancy Ward's grave was," Ruth cried. "If Mary and Jonathan had planned this, why would she involve Gabriel Benge?"

"Benge was just a stroke of good luck. Helped them

cover their tracks even better. Believe me, honey, I've seen this stuff too many times before. People get randy as billy goats over each other, they do things they normally wouldn't dream of."

Ruth wanted to stand up and scream. *Jonathan and Mary would not do this! Never in a million years!* But her legs would not move, her mouth couldn't form the words. All she could do was sit there, humiliated.

The sheriff dug out a tissue from the bottom drawer of his desk and wiped the soot from his face. "Mrs. Walkingstick, this is a case where two and two don't exactly make four, but they come damn close."

"So you're not going to do *anything*?" She didn't want to believe this, but Dula spoke with such assurance, and Clarinda was sitting there smug and nodding, as if she'd known it all along.

"Honey, I've done everything I can. Unless I get further evidence that your husband did not take your child, no. I'm not."

"So what should I do?"

"If I were you, I'd go home. Wait it out. A love nest with a squalling baby might not turn out to be as cozy as they figured. He and the young'un may come crawling back. At the very least, they'll know where to get in touch with you, if you go home."

Ruth gazed around the office, blinking back stinging tears. Her eyes settled on the bronze nameplate on Dula's desk. She realized then, with a pain that felt like a spike through her heart, that she'd just joined the ranks of the damned—the women who were condemned to wait for their lost children to return home. Although she'd seen such women countless times on television and always felt genuine sympathy for them, it had always been a faraway, distant compassion. Never had she dreamed she would one day be initiated into their pitiful club.

Fighting despair, she looked at Dula. "Could I stay here a little longer? Maybe pass out some more sketches?

Talk to some people?" She could not go back to Little Jump Off and just wait. She'd rather sooner throw herself off some mountain and be done with her life altogether.

Dula gave her a reluctant nod. "Just stay out of the Guard's way."

"Thanks. I appreciate all you've done."

"I'm sorry this had to happen, honey, but it ain't nothing new. Your man might smarten up and come home. If he doesn't, then you're better off without him."

No, I'm not, thought Ruth as she turned and stumbled blindly toward the door, her breasts oozing milk for a child she could not nurse, her heart breaking over a man she could not find.

Miles away, Jonathan was trying to find his number seventeen metric wrench. By the time the parts store in Murphy found the right clutch and he'd hiked all the way back to his truck, it had been too dark to work, so he'd curled up to sleep yet another night in Whirlaway. At first light that morning, he woke up and started the operation. It had not gone smoothly. He'd pushed the truck to the most level bit of ground he could find, then wedged four big creek stones behind the wheels so the thing wouldn't roll over him and break his neck. Slowly he'd dropped the drive shaft, then removed the bell housing and gearbox, Whirlaway dripping oil on his face and bits of road grit in his eyes. By noon he'd pulled the old clutch assembly; two hours later he was using the special alignment tool the guy at the parts store had talked him into buying. By sunset he had the bell housing, gearbox, and driveshaft back in place. At dusk he finally rolled out from under the truck. His face was smeared with grease and dirt, his fingernails looked as if he'd been digging potatoes with his bare hands. He climbed in the truck and started the engine, pushing the shift gingerly into first gear. Holding his breath, he eased off the clutch and pressed on the gas. To his amazement, Whirlaway began to move up the hill.

"Damn!" he said aloud, proud of himself. "If the hunting guide business ever dries up, maybe I'll just start turning wrenches for a living."

He killed the engine and climbed out of the truck. He wanted to wash the muck off of him before he went back to civilization. Stripping to his waist, he leaned belly-down over the creek and scrubbed off with the free sample of orange degreaser soap he'd picked up at the parts store. Though the icy water stung like nettles on his skin, when he finally grabbed his shirt to dry off, his hands and fingernails were clean to the point of pinkness.

"At least Lily won't think I'm the monster Ulagu," he said, laughing.

He put his clothes back on and gathered up his tools. Soon the little truck was chugging up the gravel road. He'd worked off his rage at his no-show boar hunter. Now he was simply glad to have the truck working more, glad to be close to seeing his little girl once again. Unconsciously he began humming "Brown-Eyed Girl."

Ten miles later he pulled into a store called Red's Mountain Supplies. He'd eaten the last of his food early that morning, and he wanted to call Little Jump Off, to see if perhaps Ruth had brought Lily home from the rally early.

That would be nice, he thought as he walked up the steps to the store. That would mean the rally would be over, Clarinda would be heading back to Oklahoma, and maybe Ruth would return to her less caustic pre-Lily personality. He pushed open the door and heard the cowbell on the transom above jiggle.

"Evenin'," a heavyset bearded man in a green plaid shirt called from behind the counter. "Help you with anything?"

"Just something to eat." Jonathan grabbed a package of Ding-Dongs and a premade tuna sandwich, then he began searching for his gift of atonement for Ruth. "Been up in the woods for a couple of days."

"You ain't been over in Tennessee, have you?"

"No." Jonathan picked up a jar of Smucker's strawberry preserves, noting that the man had an accent that would have sent Clarinda into hysterics. "Why?"

"That poor state's goin' to hell in a handbasket."

"Why? What happened?"

"Ain't you heard? Some Indian smacked the governor in the face with a pie. Now everybody's fightin' everybody else. They done called out the Guard."

"Where in Tennessee?" Jonathan stood motionless, the jar of preserves like lead in his hand.

"Lookee here." The man turned a tiny TV set around, eager to share the catastrophe. "It's on every channel."

Jonathan watched as a shot of ragged, weeping Indians filled the little screen. A nervous-looking reporter came on, saying something about "Tremont, Tennessee, and the Save Our Bones rally," then the scene shifted to one of violence, as war-painted men screamed and flung rocks and bottles into a line of National Guardsmen. A crowd pushed over a car, while men grappled with each other on the ground. Above it all rose the wail of sirens and the whoop of police cars.

Jonathan looked up from the TV. "When was this?"

"Started last night," the man replied. "They're in a mess of trouble over there."

Without another word, Jonathan dug in his pocket. He pulled out a ten-dollar bill and dropped it on the counter. Gathering everything he bought up in his arms, he turned and raced for the parking lot.

"Hey, wait," the shopkeeper protested. "You got some change coming!"

"Keep it," called Jonathan. "My wife's over there in Tennessee."

"Take the long way up from Georgia, then. They've closed the roads heading west from here."

I knew it, thought Jonathan, leaving a spray of gravel as he raced away from the little grocery and pointed Whirlaway south, toward Georgia. His instincts had proved right; this rally hadn't felt good to him since the first day Ruth started talking about it. That didn't matter now, though. All that mattered now was getting his wife and child away from harm and home, where they belonged.

21

W

"CHIP? ARE YOU there? I know it's early, but don't hang up on me."

Special Agent Chip Clifford rolled away from the naked brunette who lay sleeping beside him and peered at his alarm clock: 6:11 A.M. *Monday,* he thought. *On or about October 14.* He closed his eyes and sighed, recognizing both the caller and the nature of her call.

"Hi, Mary," he answered, trying hard to sound pleasant. "What can I do for you?"

He stared up at the ceiling as she talked. Although he knew the players in her story well, this time her plot had taken a much wilder turn. Now she thought Stump Logan had stolen a friend of hers' baby from that Indian riot in Tennessee, in some effort to lure her along the Trail of Tears. She sounded so reasonable that he would have believed her immediately, had he not heard a variation of this crackpot story half a dozen times before.

Usually she thought Logan was lurking around Atlanta, waiting to kill her. This was the first time she'd put him out of state, with a third party involved. Chip felt bad, listening to such a beautiful, intelligent woman self-destruct like this, but he just let her rattle on. Logan was dead. Mary Crow was being victimized by a ghost of her own making.

"Uh-huh. How do you figure that?" he asked, having this routine down so pat that he knew when to ask just the right questions at just the right places. He hated to chum Mary along like this, but he was stuck. After 9-11, the bureau had sent his best friend Daniel Safer deep into Uzbekistan. Safer had left him with a fierce Russian bear hug and the stern request that he "watch out for Mary Crow." That he'd done. Hadn't he called a full alert the first couple of times Mary thought she'd spotted Logan? When all her sightings turned up nothing, everyone at the office had started snickering each time she called. Chip Clifford had gotten the message— if he wanted to keep his career on an upward spiral, he'd best not initiate any more searches for a stiff.

Still, even though no one had heard a word from Safer since November of 2001, Chip intended to keep his promise to his friend as best he could. Daniel Safer was one hell of a guy.

"What exactly do you want me to do?" He fumbled for the pen and pad he kept on his bedside table. He wrote down what Mary told him, or at least he thought he got most of it. Take down some address headers. Locate where a particular e-mail was sent from. He repeated it back to her, with only one correction.

"Okay, Mary. It may take a while, but I'll see what I can find out. Thanks for calling. Bye."

He turned off the cell phone, then flopped back down in bed. Thank God he hadn't told her he'd call her back. For now, he was off the hook. What he couldn't understand, though, was how the woman could practice law so brilliantly by day and obsess about a dead man in her off hours. It was like Mary Crow put on her sanity every morning when she went to work, and then threw it in the back of her closet when she got home. He was trying to figure that one out when the woman beside him groaned.

"Who was that, honey?" She reached for him without opening her eyes, her voice thick with sleep.

"Just a minor nut case," he answered, nuzzling into the warmth of her soft hair, knowing she was nowhere near the beauty that Mary Crow was, but feeling himself grow hard, nonetheless. "Nobody we need to be concerned with."

Mary switched off her phone. She could tell by the tone of Chip Clifford's voice that he didn't think much of her latest theory about Logan. Still, he'd promised to look into it, and since he was a friend of Safer's, she would take him at his word. Sighing, she looked out the window above Gabe's bed. Low gray clouds scumbled through the sky as a brisk wind stripped dull orange leaves from an old oak. After they'd arrived at the Shellsford cemetery late last night, Gabe had transformed the seats of the dinette into a double bed for her, the passenger seat up front into a single for him. Wired from driving and fighting the feeling of being in such tight quarters, she'd pulled the *History of the Trail of Tears* from his little book collection after they went to bed, intending to read herself to sleep. But the stories had not been the calmative she'd sought. Between October 1838 and March of 1839 fourteen thousand docile Cherokees had been rousted out of their North Carolina homes and marched a circuitous twelve-hundred-mile route to Oklahoma. Few had been as lucky as Aunt Little Tom's grandfather. Those who straggled into Oklahoma suffered from malnutrition and exposure; along

the way three thousand died, most of them children.
Mary finally had to quit reading when she began putting
Lily into every page of the book. Lily hungry, Lily
cold, Lily being dumped in some unmarked grave as
her parents were shoved westward, at the point of a
bayonet.

She turned away from the window and looked at the
wall next to her bed. Gabe had taped two photographs
to it. One showed a teenage Gabe grinning in triumph
as he pulled some kind of pot shard from the ground.
The other pictured Gabe in full Marine Corps dress,
kissing a pretty blond girl in a wedding dress.

Mary felt an unexpected stab of disappointment.
Not that he had been a Marine, but that he was married. For some reason she'd assumed that there was no
Mrs. Benge. Though they'd looked at each other in the
slightly feral way all men and women use to size each
other up, she'd felt something more with Benge. A kind
of kinship as they began to work together, as if they'd
been important to each other in another life.

"Must have been my imagination," she whispered as
she looked at the photograph and wondered why the bride
wasn't here in this camper, sleeping with her husband.

She took her overnight bag into the cleverly designed
bathroom, washed, topped her jeans with her favorite
blue sweater, then stepped down into the main part of
the van. Gabe lay sprawled on the passenger-seat-
turned-bed, flat on his back, a yellow thermal blanket
covering him from the hips down. Sleeping, he looked
almost sculpted, as if he were a cast in a life-drawing
class. Though he may have ditched the Marine Corps
uniform, she could see that he'd kept the Marine Corps
physique. His arms were far more muscular than she'd
imagined, tapering down to strong hands that rested on
his stomach. The morning light made his skin glow like
marble. Feeling a sharp jolt of desire, she had to stop
herself from reaching down and tracing the curves of his

neck and shoulders. It had been a long time since she'd held her body against someone else's—a long time since she'd even wanted to. Guiltily she remembered the beaming bride in Gabe's photograph. She turned to look out the window, where fat robins hopped among the graves, tugging up breakfast worms.

"Lieutenant Benge," she called softly. "Rise and shine."

"What?" He sat up, instantly alert but sleepy-eyed. "What did you say?"

"I said wake up," she repeated, embarrassed that he'd found her standing so close to him.

"You must have seen my photos." He yawned. "Nobody's called me 'Lieutenant' in years."

"When were you in the Marines?"

"Right after undergraduate school."

"Why were you in the Marines? Did they need combat-ready archaeologists?"

"It's a family thing," he replied through another yawn. "My dad, my granddad were all Marines." He chuckled. "I think we're subconsciously trying to compensate for being the progeny of outlaw Bob. I keep a pistol over the kitchen sink."

"You've got a gun in here?" For some reason, Mary was surprised.

"An old Glock nine." He yawned again, then smiled. "In case I'm ever attacked by murderous archaeologists."

Making no mention of his wife, he pushed his blanket off and stood up. She wondered, for an instant, if she was going to see him nude, but he'd slept in baggy white boxer shorts. As he walked to the bathroom she watched the muscles in his back flex, then turned hastily away, lest he catch her frank appraisal of his body.

"Want some coffee?" he asked.

"If you've got some to make," she replied.

"That I do," he answered cheerfully, stepping across the van to the minuscule galley. "Coming right up, ma'am."

Mary folded up his blanket. As the scent of coffee began to warm the air, she gazed at the lopsided gravestones outside and wondered about the Cherokees who'd been driven through here, so many years ago. They'd stopped to bury someone in this churchyard, according to Gabe. Had it been a child?

She hoped not, longing to rewrite history into something more palatable. She hoped it had been someone old, someone who would have died soon anyway. But the book said most who died on the 1838 march were children. And Lily now faced the same fate. . . . Her cell phone beeped. She grabbed it, her heart beating like a drum.

"Mary?" A familiar voice crackled through the phone. Danika. Have you found the baby yet?"

"No, Danika, we haven't. We're following a trail of sorts, in Tennessee."

"Well, listen. Virginia Kwan just called. They want to plead."

"You're kidding!"

"Nope. Kwan says if you'll drop kidnapping, child endangerment, and lewd acts with a minor, they'll cop to one count of kiddie porn."

"Thank God!" Mary wanted to weep with joy. One thing, at least, had worked out. Over the long weekend, little Jasmine's terror had worked its magic. Virginia Kwan knew the jury was ready to hang everything on Pugh, and had advised him to make a deal.

"Should I take it?" Pressed Danika. "And call Mott in for his slam-dunk?"

Probably, Mary thought. That would certainly make Mott's day. But why let him have it? Mott had done nothing but whine about how important this case was while she and Danika had put in the long, hard hours—

why not let Danika close it? A Bankhead girl bringing justice to people who were usually given the short end of the law. Winning this case would be a nice feather in Danika's cap. For Mott, it would simply be another photo op.

"If they'll agree to serve the sentence in state prison, you take it and you close it, Danika," Mary said firmly. "But it's twenty years for Pugh. In general population, not some federal pen."

"Those Bankhead folks will want him drawn and quartered."

"Talk to them in my office, without any reporters. Explain that Pugh won't last six months in general pop. Someone will put a shank between his shoulder blades before he gets his jumpsuit zipped."

"Mott isn't going to like this," warned Danika.

"Just tell him you followed my orders," replied Mary steadily.

"Okay . . . but," Danika sounded worried.

"Congratulations, Danika. You've just become one of the few who've beaten Virginia Kwan."

"Everything okay?" Gabe asked as she disconnected from the phone call.

Mary took the coffee he offered. "For once. My kid-die pornographer wants to plead."

"Hey, congratulations." Gabe grabbed his jacket and retrieved the latest photo they'd received of Lily Walkingstick. "Now let's go see if they did take this pic-ture here."

Gulping her coffee, she followed him outside. The morning sky hung wispy—gossamer fingers of mist plucked at the earth. They walked past the neat red brick building of the Shellsford Baptist Church, deserted on a Monday morning, and entered the cemetery behind it. The first rank of headstones consisted of the plain granite markers favored by the twentieth-century dead. Behind those rose the taller, more elaborate Victorian monuments, while beyond those, poking up from a thick carpet of fallen leaves, a dozen stubby, worn-down stones marked the graves of the early pioneers.

They threaded their way toward them. Two centuries of wind and weather had worn the inscriptions down to runes—almost legible, but not quite. Nonetheless, they searched each ancient headstone, deciphering part of a name here, half a date there. Finally, in the farthest corner of the cemetery, they found what they sought: a tombstone with a carved lamb resting atop the marker. Mary held up the print of the .jpg file. They matched perfectly. Not so very long ago, Lily Walkingstick had lain in the shadow of this stone.

"Two for two," she murmured, recalling the sad pages she'd read last night. The Trail of Tears indeed. She brushed away a leaf that had fallen on the old marker. "Damn. What does it mean?"

"Beats me." Gabe had just begun to compare the first print of Lily—the one taken at Nancy Ward's grave—with the one taken here, when Mary's cell phone shattered the silence of the cemetery.

She pulled it from her pocket. To her great relief there were no new e-mails, just an old-fashioned phone call. Maybe it was Chip Clifford, with news of Logan. She held it to her ear and said, "Hello?"

"Mary? Danika again."

"Hey, Danika. What did you guys work out?"

"The good news is that we've basically got a deal. Kwan insisted that Pugh be given the possibility of parole, and I said the state would recommend it."

"Okay," said Mary. "Then the bad news must be that Jasmine's parents are pissed?"

"No, Mary. It's a whole lot worse than that." Danika sounded as if she might cry.

"What, then?" Mary couldn't imagine Virginia Kwan putting up a stink, since the offer to settle had come from her side of the table.

"It's Mott."

Mary laughed. "Didn't get his picture in the paper, huh? Don't worry, he'll get over it."

"Mary, he just gathered us all together in his office, then sent out an official memo. As of ten minutes ago, you are no longer associated with the Deckard County Department of Justice. Mary—Mott fired you."

22

STUMP LOGAN'S HEADACHE burst into full bloom on Highway 70, just east of Murfreesboro, Tennessee. The baby had pitched such a fit after he'd snapped her last picture that he'd finally given up driving and pulled up at a Waffle House. Sugar and caffeine sometimes helped his head, and the Waffle House served plenty of both. He parked the van, commanded Ruperta to watch the baby, and with Paz in tow, walked in and sat at the counter.

"Coffee?" asked a blond waitress with a shiner going purple on her left eye.

Logan nodded. "Two. Black."

She plunked down two cups in front of them, then moved on to another customer. For late Monday morning, the Waffle House was doing a brisk business. Truckers, mostly, and three men in brown uniforms who looked like shift workers hulked over their plates, shoveling food in their mouths.

After cooling his coffee with some milk, Logan pulled a bottle of extra-strength Excedrin from his pocket. He shook four tablets out and washed them down with the coffee. Though the combination would make his heart race like a hamster in a wheel, it would be worth it if it dammed up the sick river that raged through his head.

"What can I get for you fellas?" The blonde with the black eye returned, order pad in hand.

"We'll have scrambled eggs, sausage, and grits," Stump told her, ordering for Paz. "With another order of the same to go. And add a couple of waffles to mine."

"You got it."

She freshened their coffee and yelled out their order to the cook. Trying to keep his head as motionless as he could, Stump sipped his coffee and turned his gaze to the TV anchored above the counter. A news show flickered from the screen. A pretty white girl and a handsome black man were laughing, trying, under the guidance of a trained professional, to carve a Halloween pumpkin. A commercial for an appliance store came on, then the local news. A reporter appeared and the screen cut to images of National Guardsmen throwing tear gas canisters at war-painted Indians. Stump leaned closer to listen.

"*A political rally turned unexpectedly violent yesterday as National Guard troops were called in to keep order in the mountain town of Tremont, Tennessee,*" the newscaster reported.

"*Over three thousand people gathered in Tremont over the weekend to protest dangerously high ozone levels in the Smoky Mountains and the construction of condominiums over an ancient Cherokee burial site. Governor Campbell, who has business interests in the site, called up two units of the National Guard after a*

protestor flung a pie in his face and rioting broke out
over what Native Americans are calling the illegal incar-
ceration of six of their leaders. Several injuries have been
reported, and National Guard troops are trying to maintain order as tourists flee the area, seeking a quieter place
to enjoy the fall foliage. Officials are asking everyone to
stay clear of this part of the Smoky Mountains. . . ."

Another commercial blared forth, then the football
scores, the local announcer gleefully celebrating yesterday's victory of the Tennessee Titans over the Oakland
Raiders. Logan gawked at the screen, unable to believe
his luck. Everybody at that campsite had gone nuts! The
local sheriff wouldn't give a shit about one baby after all
that! That poor bastard would be working his county
like a field marshal, trying to keep the Indians from
killing the wetbacks, at the same time kissing the governor's ass while he wiped pie off his face!

As Blondie clattered his plate down in front of him,
Logan started to laugh. It was all too perfect. First finding Clootie Duncan, then Walkingstick's troubled little
family. Now a pie-throwing redskin inciting a riot. For
once the universe was expanding in his direction.

With tears of laughter in his eyes, he doused his eggs
with ketchup and his waffles with syrup. Now if his
headache would just go away, he would be God's own
boy . . .

He ate greedily, inhaling the sweet maple syrup
aroma that rose from his waffle, letting its warm, but-
tery sweetness fill his head. Paz, he noticed, picked at his
food as if it were poison, taking tiny bites of egg and
holding his sausage delicately between his fingers.
Stump wasn't worried. His two Mexicans had served
their purpose. Paz and his little tamale of a wife were as
expendable as that squalling brat back in the van. Any
more grief from any of them and he would slit all their
throats, Edwina be damned. This was his last chance to

cut himself loose. No one was going to stand in his way this time.

After he swiped his plate clean with a crust of waffle, he left the waitress an extra dollar and handed Paz the to-go order. When they reached the van, he was smiling. His headache had eased up, and both Ruperta and the baby were stretched across the backseat, sound asleep.

"Let's not wake them, okay?" Stump told Paz as he slid into the driver's seat. "Let's just roll down the highway in *silencio*."

"Okay." Paz glanced back uncertainly at his wife.

"Good man."

Logan stepped on the gas and headed toward Murfreesboro. Half an hour later he turned in at a shopping center just off the main drag. He'd been looking for the library, but nestled in a new strip mall, close to a Starbuck's coffee shop, he spotted a Kinko's.

"We stop here?" Paz blinked at the shopping center, puzzled as if they'd just landed on Mars.

"For a minute." Stump turned into a parking space. "You come with me. We'll let Ruperta and the kid sleep."

He pulled his cap down low over his forehead and grabbed Edwina's camera. Paz looked at him oddly, but followed him without protest.

Except for two groggy-eyed college boys who looked as if they'd just pulled an all-nighter, the computers at Kinko's were deserted. Logan and Paz walked to the counter, where two young men in light blue shirts were binding some kind of booklet.

"Help you?"

"I need some computer time."

"Mac or PC?"

"PC."

"PC's are on the right wall, in the corner."

Four Apple computers lined one side of the wall, while four PCs lined the other. Stump looked at each

one. The first two were too old, but the last two had the
USB ports he needed. Choosing the one closest to the
window, he sat down and stuck his card into the slot.

The machine booted up quickly, ready to do whatever he wanted. *Good,* he thought, retrieving his camera
from his pocket. This would be a piece of cake.

He clicked on the picture icon, then attached the
camera to the computer with a cable. Seconds later, four
new shots of Lily Walkingstick appeared on the screen.
After studying them for a moment, Stump chose the
third one. Anyone with any knowledge of Lily would
know the child. Anyone with a substantial knowledge
of Cherokee history would know the site. Logan was
certain Mary Crow knew Lily Walkingstick. How
quickly she would figure out the route would depend
upon how closely she'd paid attention in history class.

Smiling, he logged onto Hotmail and began to write
an e-mail. Addressing it to mcrow@deckardcty.gov, he
typed in: *Mary, we're waiting for you. Jonathan.* Then
he attached Lily's photo as a .jpg file. He typed "Lily
Walkingstick" as the sender and clicked the SEND button. The file uploaded. Seconds later, the YOUR MAIL HAS
BEEN SENT screen came on.

"Another clue, Nancy Drew," he said softly, deleting
the photos from the computer's hard drive and discon-
necting the USB cable. "Come and catch me if you can."

23

AS THEY PULLED away from the Shellsford Baptist Church, Mary clicked on Hobson Mott's e-mail message. It was a blanket memo to everyone in the court house—judges, attorneys, police officers, maybe even the janitorial crews, for all she knew.

> Please be advised that as of Monday, October 14, Assistant District Attorney Mary Crow is no longer associated with the Deckard County Justice Department. Ms. Crow's cases will be reassigned immediately.
>
> Hobson T. Mott, AG

The terse message seemed to dance, sneering, before her eyes. She felt as if she were trying to breathe through cotton. For the first time in ten years, she was without the one thing that had saved her first, when Jonathan left, then later, when Irene Hannah died. For the first time since law school, she was without her job.

She sat there, stunned. She had never lost a case in her career, yet here she was, sacked like some bottom-of-the-class graduate of a third-rate law school. Her cheeks flamed with humiliation. How could Hobson do this? How she wished she could spit in his eye!

"*Jahyosiha?*" Gabe's halting Cherokee broke the silence that, she now realized, had stretched for miles. He had asked if she was hungry.

"I don't think so," she replied, too sad to launch into a language that she couldn't half speak, anyway. They were driving along a two-lane highway, through farmland that had grown more rolling than mountainous. She swallowed hard. "I've just been fired."

"Fired?" He turned to her so quickly, he nearly ran off the road. "Why? I thought you just won your big case."

"I did." Mary felt her throat thicken. "Guess I didn't win it the way they wanted it won."

Gabe looked at her, his eyes sympathetic. "There's a little restaurant up the road that serves a terrific lunch. Sometimes things don't look quite so bad on a full stomach."

"That's fine," she said absently, slumping back in her seat, not wanting food or comfort or anything except Lily Walkingstick and her old job back.

An hour later they sat in Christiana, Tennessee, at Miller's Grocery, a restaurant housed in an old-timey grocery store, that now served the Southern cuisine of her grandmother's day—fried chicken, butter beans, black-eyed peas, and the ubiquitous frozen fruit salad that had been a staple of Southern ladies' lunches ever since refrigeration had gone electric. She looked across the table at Gabe and wondered if he held her grandmother's opinion that a warm, crumbly wedge of corn bread could cure most anything. *I wish,* she thought, eyeing the menu, wondering how much she would have to consume to make all her troubles disappear.

"How come you know this place so well?" she asked as Gabe waved genially to the woman who stood behind the cash register at the back of the converted store.

"I used to teach here, a few years back."

"They have a college here?" As far as she could see, the town of Christiana seemed to be a post office, a tiny gift shop, and this restaurant, all sprouting up in the middle of Tennessee's version of nowhere.

He smiled. "There's a state university in Murfreesboro, up the road a bit."

She sat back in her chair, the clatter of lunch swirling around her. Two white-haired women at the next table gossiped about someone they'd seen in church yesterday; two other women behind them planned a baby shower for a friend. A busboy scooped dirty dishes carelessly into a plastic tub while a waitress refilled their iced tea. How odd it all seemed. Her godchild was missing and she'd just lost her job, yet people were laughing with their friends, eating chess pie for dessert, figuring up how much to leave for a tip. Lily had been stolen. She could not find her. Jasmine Harris had been abused. And she'd just been fired for sending her abuser up for twenty years in prison.

All at once, she needed to get away. The world made no sense today; none of the rules she lived by applied anymore. She grabbed her cell phone and got up from the table, knocking over her chair. Other diners looked up, startled, as she hurried to the door. She made no apologies but rushed outside, into the warm autumn afternoon.

To her right stood the post office, in front of her nothing but a road and a railroad track. She ran toward the tracks mindlessly, stopping only when she stood on a cross tie between the long iron rails. As she gazed down the tracks, the view looked like a perspective exercise in drawing class. Two arrow-straight lines converged into a vanishing point, stretching through acres of land to link Chicago with Mobile, the North to the South, Canada to the Gulf of Mexico. And here she stood, in the center of it all, unable to find one three-month-old baby and hang on to her job at the same time.

She lifted her hand to shield her eyes from the sun when a sign caught her eye. Nearly covered by a sprawling trumpet vine, it stood tilted next to the tracks, its black letters peeling.

"Abandoning animals is unlawful," she read aloud, and suddenly, without warning, everything—Lily, Mott, Jonathan, and Ruth—all crashed down upon her. She sat down in the middle of the railroad track and started to cry. She didn't care if a train came along. In fact, she wished one would.

She wept until she heard footsteps crunching through the gravel. She looked up. Gabe stood there, holding their lunches on a tray. He looked ridiculous but somehow noble, too.

"I figured today might be a good day for takeout." He said, smiling.

She lowered her head, embarrassed. Gabe had been nothing but kind and helpful ever since she met him. She'd no reason to run out of the restaurant as if he'd insulted her.

"I'm sorry," she murmured. "You deserve better."

"Don't worry about it. I'd be a little hot too, if I were you."

"If you were me?"

"In the past forty-eight hours I've seen you lose your godchild, face off with a small-town sheriff, comfort the woman who married a man you still love, and lose your job. I'd say you've got a right to be a little cranky."

She stared at him, speechless. Who was this man? He'd known her less than two days, yet he seemed to read and accept the troubled terrain of her heart as readily as Jonathan. The smile she gave Gabe was wobbly, but genuine.

"Whoa," he murmured, leaning down to touch the corner of her mouth. "That's something you ought to do more often."

"Let's eat," she said, getting to her feet. "I'm done feeling sorry for myself."

They moved from the railroad track to the broad, gold field that stretched beside it. Gabe brought a blanket from the van and they spread their food out and ate, picnic-style. He'd ordered them both fried chicken and corn nuggets, turnip greens and pecan pie. Though Mary would have sworn she had no appetite, she soon had an impressive pile of bare chicken bones on her plate.

"Pretty good, huh?" Gabe lay back on the grass, his arms cradling his head.

"Delicious." Mary looked over at the restaurant. "Don't they want their dishes back?"

"I'll return them in a few minutes." He turned over to face her. "You feeling better?"

She nodded. Maybe her grandmother had been on to something after all. Maybe corn bread and butter beans did make things seem not quite so bad.

"It's always hard to lose something you love." Gabe's face grew suddenly sad.

"Something or somebody?"

"Either, I guess. I've never lost much of anything, but I once lost somebody."

"Your dad?" Mary offered the only person she'd heard him mention.

"My wife."

"You lost your wife?"

"You saw our wedding photo."

"I did. She's gorgeous."

"Yes, she was. Her name was Becca. She was a graduate fellow in archaeology at UT."

"What happened?" She didn't want to pry, but he seemed to want to talk.

"We were in Washington, at an archaeological conference. I wanted to drive over to Baltimore, to watch Cal Ripken break Gehrig's game record. Becca didn't even like baseball, but she went, just to please me. We watched the game, watched Ripken take a victory lap around the field. She wanted to leave; I wanted to stay to see the whole post-game show. On the way home a drunk driver T-boned our car. I came out okay. She didn't." He studied the blanket as if it could reveal the secrets of the universe.

"That's awful, Gabe," Mary said softly. "I'm so sorry."

"It happened eight years ago. Every day I still wonder what would have happened if I hadn't acted like such a jerk—if we'd left that stadium when she wanted to." He glanced up at her. "You know what I mean?"

She nodded as the faraway whistle of an approaching train broke the warm silence of the meadow. The sad wail seemed to echo both the grief Gabe had just given voice to and the older grief that resounded in her own battered heart. How well she knew how he felt! She'd relived her own actions the day her mother died a million times. However fervently she wished she'd done things differently, the end result always came out the same. You lived your life in ignorance, thinking what harm can there be in lingering at a baseball game, or making love to someone you deeply desired? Only later did you learn the consequences of your acts, when the people you most loved lay dead and the only thing left for you to do was sit beside them and weep.

24

"COME ON, YOU sunuvabitch. Get that damn crate out of the road!" Jonathan gripped the steering wheel, wishing it were the neck of the driver in front of him. For the past hour he'd tailgated an old Ford pickup that had wobbled around the curves with maddening slowness, due either to woefully misaligned tires or a woefully inebriated driver. Every time the two lanes widened to allow passing, the Ford sped up and shot to the middle of the road. When the road climbed the mountains through narrow switchbacks, the ancient truck slowed to the point that Jonathan had to brake to keep from running into it. Finally, at a town called Madisonville, the battered truck turned east. Jonathan blasted his horn, just for spite. As the truck wobbled on toward Sweetwater, a gnarled hand appeared from the driver's window and gave him the finger.

The detour Jonathan had taken from Carolina had

led him hours out of his way. He'd driven mountain roads that had neither name nor number, causing him to take a wrong turn and wind up almost on the other side of Lookout Mountain. Now, after a trip to Wal-Mart for a road atlas, he was nearing Tremont, Tennessee. He'd stopped at several pay phones and tried to get in touch with Ruth, punching in Little Jump Off's number but getting no reply. He'd called both the Tennessee Highway Patrol and the Nikwase County sheriff's office. At the THP he'd gotten a voice menu. The Nikwase County sheriff's line rang busy. With a coldness in his gut, he pushed the repaired Whirlaway north.

"One more hour," he said softly. The guy at that store said people had been hurt at these demonstrations, but he hadn't said how. Had the cops taken clubs to them? Tear gas? Could they have been trampled in the chaos of a violent crowd?

"Don't go there," he snapped aloud, wishing Whirlaway had a radio so he could turn on the news for more information. "Ruth is a good mother. She would have gotten Lily out of there at the first sign of trouble."

But if she did that, then where is she? She isn't back at Little Jump Off. Could Clarinda have talked her into driving out to Oklahoma? On TV he'd seen the governor of Tennessee furious, wiping pie off his face, and the equally furious demonstrators confronting cops and soldiers with rocks and spittle. What had started as an Indian remonstration over a field of bones had grown into a fierce protest of government policies about everything from logging rights in national forests to the ecological impact of gas-burning cars. A goodly number of Americans were acting out their sub-basement opinion of the nation's leaders. It made him sick to think of Lily and Ruth caught up in such anguish.

When he turned toward Tremont, he truly thought he might vomit. National Guard trucks lined his side of the highway, while the westbound lane away from town was littered with all the crap people had ditched as they fled: paper cups, fast-food wrappers, lumpy bags of garbage lay strewn along the road. He swallowed against the sudden tightness in his throat. It looked as if somebody had dropped a bomb on Tremont, Tennessee.

National Guard troops had erected makeshift bivouacs in a strip-mall parking lot. Kids from town loitered, curious and sullen at the lot's edge.

He turned down a side street to find a parking space in front of a Baptist church. The sign in front of the church advertised a "Prayer Vigil to Heal Our Wounds." As he strode back to the main drag of the town, it occurred to him that maybe he shouldn't wait for the vigil. Maybe he should start praying right now, all by himself. Where had his wife and child gone?

People crowded the street, giving the little town the uneasy feel of a kettle on simmer. Civil libertarians, war protestors, and radical ecological groups had flocked to the support of the Native Americans, while the construction workers were aided by flag-waving veterans and sour-looking men who wore heavy boots and carried signs provided by the local brotherhood of teamsters.

"Can you tell me where to find the Save Our Bones people?" Jonathan called to a Guardsman directing traffic.

"The who?" The helmeted soldier looked no more than eighteen. Beads of sweat dotted his upper lip.

"Save Our Bones," Jonathan repeated. "The Indians."

"I can't give out that information, sir," the kid replied. "You'll have to check with Command."

"Where's that?" Jonathan yelled over a jeep that badly needed a new muffler.

"Courthouse. That way." The Guardsman pointed north.

"Thanks."

He hurried up the street, dodging more Guardsmen and nearly stumbling over a thick fire hose that was refilling a pumper truck. Finally he saw a redbrick building with a clock tower on top: "Nikwase County" was engraved across its granite facade.

He started to run, pushing his way through the thickening crowd, not caring whose toes he stepped on. He needed to see his wife. He needed to hold his child.

An Army tent was pitched on the courthouse lawn. He hurried toward it. Inside, another soldier sat at a collapsible table, drinking coffee in a cup. His hair had been shaved so close that his pale scalp was visible, and he had a tattoo of an eagle on his right forearm.

"Sergeant." Jonathan recognized the man's rank from his own days in the Army. "Do you know where the injured are?"

"Most are at the hospital. A couple have made the morgue." The man scowled up at Jonathan. "Who are you looking for?"

"My wife." Jonathan's mouth felt like dry ice. "She came to the Indian rally."

"One of them Bone people?"

Jonathan nodded.

"Bunch of them folks got thrown into jail. I'd check the sheriff's office, if I were you."

"Where's that?"

"Brick building on the side of the courthouse."

The coldness spread inside Jonathan. What if Ruth and Lily were the two in the morgue? What if they'd been beaten to death by those construction goons? What would he do if that had happened?

Suddenly he heard someone call his name. "Jonathan?"

He stopped.

"Jonathan?"

A woman ran toward him. For an instant he thought it was Mary Crow, then he saw the shorter hair, the smudged face and dirty clothes. Her heavy breasts swayed as she ran. She flung herself in his arms, burying her face in his chest. His wife, Ruth. She pressed herself into him desperately, as if he and he alone could save her from some unimaginable fate.

He held her for what seemed like years. People swept in and out of the sheriff's office around them, indulgent of the two young lovers who had found each other in all the chaos. Now all they needed to do was get Lily, and get out of here. Go back to the mountains of Carolina, where they belonged.

He loosened his embrace and looked down at her, brushing the hair away from her eyes. "Where's Lily?"

"Come on," Ruth said, grabbing his hand. "I need you to talk to the sheriff."

"The sheriff? What for?"

"Come on, Jonathan." She was tugging him into the building. "We need to talk to the sheriff."

"Where is Lily?" he demanded, his heart jumping like something caught in a trap.

Ruth's face crumpled like paper. "She's gone, Jonathan," she sobbed. "Somebody stole our baby!"

25

❦

THE THIRD .JPG file arrived along with a rush of hot, oil-tinged air and a din of clacking wheels and squeaking ties. Mary checked her cell phone as a locomotive thundered by, finding the e-mail icon blinking; the sender, Lily Walkingstick. She showed it to Gabe and they waited impatiently, unable to cross the tracks as car after car of Alabama pine rolled north to become condos in Kentucky, apartments in Illinois. Finally the last car passed and they raced to the van, speeding away from Christiana to the nearest Kinko's—this one close to Gabe's old college in Murfreesboro.

"Here it comes," said Gabe, rolling his chair closer to Mary's.

As the tiny pixels of color came on the screen, Mary felt as if she were looking at some transmission from outer space—a cold mosaic of digitized color that represented an infant human being.

Without question, it was Lily. This time she lay not on top of a grave, but at the foot of a highway marker that read "Waverly" and "The Trail of Tears." Someone had cut her hair and dressed her in a little blue jumpsuit with a cowboy stitched on the front. Her eyes were closed, and she exhibited none of the blurred, angry motions of the other pictures. She might have been sound asleep. She also might have been dead.

"We passed that marker on the way to Miller's," Gabe said decisively. "It's not twenty miles away."

"You're kidding!"

"I could drive you there in fifteen minutes."

Mary clicked on the PRINT command. "Give me a minute, then we'll go."

After the printer churned out their copies, they hurried up to the checkout desk. Two blue-shirted young men stood talking behind the counter.

"Hi, fellas," Mary said, digging in her purse for her wallet. "Have you two been working here all day?"

"Since noon," said a thin African-American boy whose tightly braided hair sprouted from his head like sprays of millet.

"Have you sold computer time to anybody with a digital camera?"

The boy glanced cautiously at his partner. "Who wants to know?"

Mary feigned a look of deep hurt. "My best friend's husband is posting some weird shots of her on the Internet. A divorce thing, you know? Can you think back on who's been on the computer this morning?"

"Let's see." The boy gazed up at the acoustic tile ceiling as if he might read the answer up there. "I had you two, before that I had some kid from the college, before that a crazy old lady doin' her family tree." He shook his millet-locks. "Nobody else been in here today."

"Don't forget that old white motherfucker," his shorter coworker said under his breath.

"What old white motherfucker?" Mary leaned closer.

"Old dude in a baseball cap. Came in just before lunch. Had a little Mexican guy with him."

"Oh, yeah." The first kid's face brightened. "He did have a camera, didn't he? He wasn't in here long, though."

"What time was it?"

"Maybe eleven-thirty. Before lunch, anyway." The boy shrugged.

The headers at the top of their latest print indicated that the file had been sent to her at 11:42. Ninety minutes ago. "Did this guy happen to pay with a credit card?" Mary asked.

"Nah. He paid cash. Had a big old wad of money."

She pulled out two twenties from her own wallet and pushed one toward each of the boys. "Okay, guys. Think back and tell me absolutely everything you remember about this man."

"Which one?"

"Either one."

The boys looked at each other. "Old dude's about this high," the tall one began, indicating a height of around six feet. "Fat. Gray beard. Wore a blue Braves cap pulled way low. Had dirty pants."

"Dirty pants?"

"Khakis, but he done spilled somethin' all over the front. Somethin' brown and nasty."

"What kind of shirt did he wear?"

"A sweatshirt. Brown, gray, something dark," offered the shorter one. "Dirty."

"What about the Mexican?"

"Short, skinny. Wore jeans. Looked a lot cleaner than the old guy."

"Did he have a mustache?"

"I don't know. I didn't look at his mouth."

"Did you see what kind of car they drove away in?"

"I wasn't paying any attention," said the shorter boy. "Didn't even see them leave."

Mary sighed. After the thousand or so witnesses she'd interviewed, her instinct told her these boys were telling the truth, as best they could remember it. An old white guy in dirty clothes. More likely sending candids of his grandchildren than clues to Lily Walkingstick's whereabouts. The Mexican could have been a friend, a neighbor, an employee. "Thanks, fellas," she said. "I appreciate it."

She gave a nod to Gabe, and they started walking toward the door. Suddenly the tall boy's voice rang out.

"Yo! Miss Dee-tective!"

"Yeah?" Mary turned.

"One more thing. That old dude with the cap? He had a bad limp. Walked like he had a couple of joints missing."

The smile froze on Mary's face. She knew only one person who knew both her and Jonathan, and walked with a noticeable limp. The only problem with him was that he was dead.

"His name is Stump Logan," Mary explained moments later, feeling as if someone had run an ice cube down her spine. "He knows me and Jonathan, walks with a limp, and he could have a head injury which he might try to conceal with a baseball cap."

Gabe steered around a pothole. "Did you convict him of something?"

"No, but he's a known conspirator against the U.S. government and is suspected of at least two murders."

"So why aren't we calling Dula or the Feds?"

She remembered FBI Agent Chip Clifford's polite, but distinctly unenthusiastic, response. "I have. I don't think they'll do anything."

"Why not?"

"Because everybody but me believes he's dead."

Gabe looked at her seriously, without the laugh or the smirk that she usually got from everybody else. "Tell me about it."

She was silent a moment, knowing that she was once again going down the slippery slope of telling someone the truth and having them think she was crazy. Nonetheless, she gave Gabe the capsule summary, telling him how the FBI had scoured the mountains for Logan after Russell Cave exploded ten months ago, how they had decided that the man must have died of his injuries in some remote mountain hideout. The problem was, she then started seeing him in Atlanta. She'd called the cops and the Feds, but no one else had seen any sign of him. When the FBI started shunting her calls to a receptionist, she'd sought psychiatric treatment. Though the sightings stopped shortly thereafter, somehow she knew that Logan was still alive.

"Okay," said Gabe without missing a beat, when she'd finished. "Let's assume Logan's not dead. Why do you think he wants to kill you?"

"I'd love to ask him that myself," said Mary.

They pulled up at the last place Lily had her picture taken, a state historical marker that stood, literally, at a wide spot in the road. Parking the van, they looked around, but found nothing but the bits of trash people had tossed from their cars—cigarette butts, a flattened can of diet soda. That did not surprise Mary. If, indeed, this limping computer user was Sheriff Stump Logan, he would leave only the clues he chose to leave.

Gabe stood beside the marker and gazed down the empty two-lane highway. "He probably drove along the old Trail of Tears route, pulled off to take the picture here, then went to Murfreesboro, to send it from there."

"And the Trail goes to Nashville next?"

"Nashville, then Hopkinsville, Kentucky. After that Missouri, Arkansas, Oklahoma."

Mary glanced at the sun, just beginning to slide toward the western hills. Somehow, she didn't think Logan would go west. A mountain boy, he'd be way out of his element in the flat lands of Arkansas, the oil-derricked plains of Oklahoma.

"What do you want to do?" Gabe asked her.

"First, I need to call Ruth. Then I'll try the Feds again."

Overnight parking was forbidden at the Waverly historical marker, so while Gabe drove back to Christiana, Mary called Ruth, trying to talk over a sputtering connection that allowed her to hear only about every third word Ruth uttered. She had better luck with Chip Clifford. Though he did not answer his phone, she left a voice mail on his machine. "I'm not imagining this, Chip," she added to her message. "This time I'm absolutely certain it's Logan."

She switched off her phone as Gabe pulled up and parked beside the railroad track. With Miller's grocery closed for the day, the three-building town looked like a movie set, minus cast and crew. As she gazed at the deserted post office, she wondered who else she could bring in on this.

"Mary?"

She jumped. Gabe stood at the dinette, the little table set with a bottle of wine and a plate of cheese and crackers.

"I'm afraid I don't know the Cherokee word for wine," he said apologetically. "But I thought you might like some."

The glass he offered was a full-bodied Shiraz, fragrant and heady. They sipped their wine and watched as the sun turned the sky a brilliant, glittering pink. He finally broke the silence that had sprung up between them. "Can I ask you a personal question?"

She gave a weary smile. "You can ask. I may not

answer." For her, personal questions usually carried a lot of pain.

"Earlier you said that this Logan character was the only link between you and Jonathan Walkingstick. What does that mean?"

She held up her wine. It glowed ruby in the fading sun, and as she gazed into the deep red liquid, she felt as if her entire history floated somewhere in its depths. She hadn't told this story in years, had never told it to a stranger. Softly she began to speak.

"One afternoon in the spring of my senior year, I came home from school, to the little country store where my mother worked." Her throat tightened. "I called her name, but she didn't answer. I found her on the floor, lying by the window, dead. She'd been raped and strangled.

"Stump Logan was our sheriff. He conducted an intensive search for her killer, which turned up nothing. Last year I found some odd letters of my mother's in Judge Irene Hannah's files. When I mentioned them to Irene, we began to piece together a puzzle."

"And?" Gabe didn't take his eyes from her face.

"My father served with Logan in Vietnam. Years after his death, my mother had written to the Army, asking that they investigate Logan. She believed he'd killed my father." Mary swirled the wine in her glass. "And I think he may have killed my mother too."

Gabe gave a low whistle. "But why would Logan murder your dad? And where does Walkingstick come in?"

Mary took a shaky breath. Here came the hardest part. "I would give anything to know why Logan killed my father. What I do know is that at the moment my mother was murdered, I was lying in a little grove of dogwood trees, making love for the first time. With Jonathan Walkingstick."

She avoided Gabe's eyes as she continued. "Because Jonathan would not tell what we'd been doing, Sheriff

Logan made him murder suspect number one. He started rumors that Jonathan and my mother had quarreled, that my mother disapproved of him. Where were you when Martha Crow was killed? Let's hear your alibi, Cherokee boy!"

"And what did Jonathan say?"

"Nothing. Jonathan would have cut out his tongue before he'd have revealed anything about us. Logan knew that. That's what made Jonathan the perfect fall guy."

"So what happened?"

"After my mother's funeral, my grandmother Bennefield brought me to live with her in Atlanta. Logan put so much pressure on Jonathan that he turned down a scholarship to college and joined the Army. To this day, no one knows who murdered my mother." Mary raised her head, not bothering to hide her tears. "Now kids up there scare each other with the ghost of Martha Crow." She gave a bitter laugh. "Do you know what it feels like to have your mother turned into slumber party entertainment?"

Gabe rose and sat down beside her, and took her in his arms. He tilted her face toward his, then kissed her. First like a friend, then more passionately. The desire she'd felt when she'd seen him asleep crackled to life again, and she pulled him close, hungry for the feel of his lips on hers, the smell of him in her head. And then the image of Lily flashed through her mind, and her desire flickered, like a small kindled flame overcome by too much air. She pulled away, shaking her head. "I can't do this now."

"I understand," he replied, leaning back but still holding her in his arms. "Later."

They sat like that for a long time, listening as a another train whistled its approach and wondering what weird, fluke of the universe, had left them here, together, in Christiana, Tennessee.

26

JONATHAN FELT ENCLOSED in a kind of bubble. Though he stood outside the police station in a throng of police and Guardsmen, he saw only Ruth, heard only her voice and the urgent thudding of his own heart.

Somebody took Lily. Saturday afternoon. The syllables rang in his head, but the words didn't form any stream of logic he could comprehend. Now Ruth was talking on a cell phone, almost screaming into the tiny receiver. He watched her mouth moving, noticed the redness of her eyes, the small fever blister beginning to swell on her upper lip. *Somebody took Lily. Saturday afternoon.* While he'd been at the parts store, buying a new clutch.

She closed the phone. "That was Mary. She got another picture of Lily. In Christiana, Tennessee."

"What?" he said, the bubble bursting, all the noise suddenly crashing around them like breaking glass.

Men were shouting to each other, jeeps roared by on the street, choppers flew overhead. "Who?"

"Come on." Ruth grabbed his arm. "We're going to see Dula, whether he wants us to or not."

She dragged him into a building, into a large duty room where men in various uniforms milled about. Standing beside an open door, talking to an EMT, was a man with gold braid on his shirt. Ruth pushed her way through the crowd, pulling Jonathan after her.

"Sheriff Dula!"

The short man glanced at Ruth wearily, then straightened when he saw Jonathan behind her.

"Sheriff, this is my husband." Ruth shoved Jonathan forward. "He does not have our baby. And Mary Crow just got another e-mail!"

Dula sent the EMT on his way, then beckoned them into his office. "Come in. Have a seat."

Jonathan felt as if he'd driven into some kind of bizarre movie. Although the characters looked familiar, their lines were all wrong, the plot racing somewhere he couldn't comprehend. First Ruth had jabbered a tale about Lily, now this sheriff was whining about this being the worst three days of his career. Where was his baby? What had happened to his child?

"Where's Lily?" he demanded of both Ruth and Dula, as if they were conspiring against him.

"That's what I'd like to ask you, Mr. Walkingstick," Dula replied evenly. "What have you been doing these past three days?"

"You tell me what happened to my child." Jonathan's voice came out like a growl.

"Since I wear this," Dula tapped the badge on his chest, "you go first."

Jonathan felt his temper flare, but played it Dula's way. He knew all too well the power of small-town sheriffs. Lily's survival could depend upon having this man on their side.

"Friday morning I drove down to Cherokee County, North Carolina, to meet a man named Clootie Duncan, who'd hired me as a hunting guide. I drove to the Dick's Creek trailhead, but Duncan never showed up. I waited till dark on Friday, then decided to drive here and meet my wife. I didn't make it out of the trailhead." He shot an accusing glance at Ruth. "The clutch on her truck gave out. Saturday I hiked fifteen miles to Murphy, North Carolina, where I persuaded a guy to keep his store open long enough to sell me a new clutch. Then I hiked back. Spent all day Sunday replacing it. I drove out late last night, went to get some food at a place called Red's Market. There I heard about the rioting and that they'd closed off the interstate. I took a wrong turn on the detour and wound up down in Georgia. It took me a while, but I drove straight here."

"Anybody see you do any of this?"

"I've got a receipt from Blue Ridge Auto Parts in Murphy," said Jonathan, remembering how the clerk had been eager to close so he could head off to Disney World with his kids. "And the clerk at Red's Market saw me last night."

"Nobody else?"

Jonathan shook his head.

"You a full-time guide?"

"During hunting season."

"Are your parties often no-shows?"

"First time. Usually I ask for a pretty big deposit. This guy called Wednesday, at the last minute, so I told him I'd need my whole fee up front."

"You get his name and address?"

Jonathan pulled a scrap of paper from his wallet and tossed it on the man's desk. "That's his number."

While Dula paused to reload more questions, Jonathan took his turn. "Tell me what happened to Lily."

"At two-seventeen Saturday afternoon, a call came in to this office that a Native American female, three months old, had gone missing. Officers Finch and Green took the call and did a search of the immediate vicinity. When the baby did not turn up, I took over. I arrived on the scene at four-oh-five P.M. I interviewed your wife, Clarinda Wachacha, Gabriel Benge, Bobby Puckett, and fourteen other members of the Save Our Bones organizing committee. Then I—"

"Wait," Jonathan interrupted. "You're telling me what you did. You're not telling me what *happened*."

"NBC news was interviewing me, Jonathan," Ruth explained. "I left Lily with Clarinda, in the camper. She was talking with Bobby Puckett when a man named Joe Little Bear appeared. He was wearing a rally badge and he told Clarinda that I had sent him to get Lily, to be on television with me."

"Who's Bobby Puckett?"

"Someone Clarinda met."

"And Clarinda and this Bobby just handed Lily over?" Jonathan could just imagine the conversation Clarinda had been having. Puckett probably had his pants to his knees and his dick shoved down her throat when Joe Little Bear showed up. Small wonder she'd handed Lily over.

"This Joe Little Bear said he was a friend of yours," Ruth went on. "Said he'd served with you in the Gulf."

"I didn't serve with any Indians over there."

"Well, that's what he told Clarinda. So she figured it was okay. It wasn't until I finished my interview and came back to nurse Lily that we realized something terrible had happened."

Jonathan felt a hot, helpless rage begin to seethe inside him. To keep from yelling at Ruth, he turned back to Dula. "So have you searched all the campers? Called the FBI?"

"We searched the entire campground. Puckett voluntarily took and passed a polygraph. I called the FBI Sunday morning, filling them in on the situation. They opted not to get involved."

"Why the hell not?" Jonathan wanted to thrash Dula, Ruth, Clarinda, that fucker Bobby Puckett, everybody in this miserable county.

"Because they weren't convinced we had a case. To be frank, neither was I. You and your wife had quite a little spat before you came over here. Your ex-girlfriend is already knee-deep in this case, and other than a receipt from a parts store, you can't really account for any part of your weekend."

"My ex-girlfriend? What the hell are you talking about?"

Ruth put her hand on his arm. "I couldn't think of anything else to do, Jonathan. When I couldn't reach you, I called Mary Crow. She drove up right away." Ruth swallowed as if her next words were painful. "Sheriff Dula thinks you two planned this all along."

"That's bullshit. Where's Mary now?"

"I just told you. She and Gabe Benge have tracked Lily to Tennessee. Mary started getting these on her office e-mail, right after Lily disappeared." Ruth pulled a sheet of paper from her purse.

The image made him sick inside. His Lily, lying on the ground, naked and screaming. Some son of a bitch had stolen his baby and this pissant sheriff thought he and Mary Crow had planned it. He strode around the desk, and jerked Dula up by the front of his shirt. Holding him by the collar, he snapped the images of Lily in front of his face, ignoring Ruth's shriek of protest. "*What's the matter with you,* you sawed-off little jackass? You honestly think I would steal my own child, then send pictures like *this*?"

"Jenkins!" Dula gurgled. "Green!"

Two big Nikwase County deputies burst through the doorway. Jonathan dropped Dula, but too late. The second after he let him go, deputy number one pinioned his arms behind his back, turned Jonathan around as if he was a feather pillow, and kicked his legs apart. Jonathan saw it coming, but there was nothing he could do to protect himself. His breath snagged as the end of a nightstick slammed into his stomach, once, then once more, then once again. Distantly, he heard Ruth screaming, then his knees crumpled as Dula bellowed about how nobody can tell him how to run an investigation, and his own voice crying the only name that really mattered—*Lily*.

27

❦

FOUR HOURS LATER, Jonathan sat on the floor of Nikwase County's single jail cell, in between a dreadlocked black man named Happy Lavalais and a tattered old white man who lay sleeping off what smelled like a mixture of baked beans and Thunderbird wine. The air seemed to shimmer around the old guy's threadbare body, and every minute or so he would fart, and fill the cell with the stench of decomposing alcohol and poorly digested food.

"You could probably light that old fucker off, eh?" Happy Lavalais waved his hand in front of his nose. "He'd go up like a pine tree."

"How long's he been in here?" asked Jonathan.

"They threw him in Sunday, the day after they grabbed me." Lavalais spoke English with an odd French lilt. Jonathan figured him for Jamaican, or perhaps Martiniquais. Apparently Ruth's protest had grown to international proportions.

"What are you in for?"

"Ganja. Cops banged on my trailer looking for some baby just as I lit up the bong."

"A baby?"

"So they say." Lavalais wiped his nose on his sleeve. "Me, I think they just wanted to roust some people. They leaned on some construction workers pretty hard, and a bunch of Indians, too. Then they got bailed out and the political shit started. Place has gone nuts ever since. They're keeping everybody they arrest now over in the next county, at a bigger jail. I haven't seen a real deputy here in days. A tall guy who looks like Abe Lincoln brings coffee every morning, and some old lady wheels in lunch and dinner. Pork chops and iced tea and hot biscuits. She serves it up, then talks to us about Jesus while we eat. Says the jail is her ministry."

"What does *he* do?" Jonathan eyed the drunk, who let fly with another juicy-sounding fart.

"Drinks the tea, but won't touch the food." Lavalais laughed. "She prays especially hard over him."

Jonathan pulled himself to his feet, holding his left side as his breath zinged a knife-like pain all the way around his chest. Two, maybe three broken ribs, he figured. Considering how those deputies had laid into him, he was lucky not to have a ruptured spleen as well. He walked gingerly to the single window of the cell. The day had faded to dusk, the lights of houses were beginning to spark on the mountainside. People were coming home, turning on their televisions, getting ready to eat supper and watch Monday night football.

"What time does that old woman come?"

Lavalais shrugged. "Whatever time she gets the chops done, I guess. Why?"

"Just wondered."

Lavalais's mouth twisted in a gap-toothed smile. "You aren't thinking of checking out of here early, are you?"

Jonathan made no reply.

"Look, my friend, a snootful of dope isn't worth ten years in some hillbilly jail. You got a plan, you cut me in, eh?"

Again, Jonathan remained silent.

He stared out the window, trying to find a position where some part of his chest didn't hurt. This day, which had begun so full of hope, had turned into such a nightmare that he still couldn't wrap his brain around it. Why would anybody have stolen Lily? He and Ruth had less than eight hundred dollars in their checking account. Nobody wanting big bucks would have kidnapped his child. He watched a yellow cat slink around the trash Dumpster behind the courthouse, then trot off down an alley. No, whoever had taken Lily had done it for something other than money. Either Ruth had pissed somebody off big-time, or someone wanted Lily for their own. Damn Ruth! He had warned her not to come here—why just this once could she not have listened?

He turned away impatiently from the window. Where was that old woman with the food? Why was she not coming? He needed to get out of here. He needed to find Lily.

With Lavalais' hard gaze upon him, he made six circuits of the cell—ten steps down, four steps across, ten steps back. Finally he heard a doorknob rattle. He looked out through the bars. Just as Lavalais said, a man who looked remarkably like Abraham Lincoln opened the door from the outer office. He wore canvas pants and a blue work shirt and entered the room with a pearl-handled Colt revolver protruding from a holster. A white-haired lady in a blue pantsuit shuffled behind him, wheeling in dinner on a cart, smiling like everyone's grandmother.

"Good evening, gentlemen," the old woman said as Abe Lincoln unlocked their cell. She nodded at Jonathan, but bid him no special welcome as the newest guest of Nikwase County. "Everyone all right?"

"Just fine," said Happy Lavalais, ogling the food cart.

"Mrs. Lunsford cooked meat loaf tonight, and Mrs. Fortney sent cheese grits." The old lady beamed at them. "First, though, let's all bow our heads for a word of thanks."

Jonathan bowed his head, but kept one eye open. The old lady stood just inside the cell while Abe Lincoln leaned against the wall, head bowed, his right hand resting lightly on the revolver. If he's not real fast, Jonathan calculated, this might work. If he is real fast, then Lily would likely grow up never knowing her true father. *You pays your money,* his old sergeant's words rang in his head, *you takes your chances.*

As the old lady continued to thank God for a laundry list of blessings, Jonathan took a step toward the open door. He meant to dart, quick as an otter, but a sudden, swift pain shot up his left side and made him stumble. Before he could recover his footing, Abe Lincoln had his revolver drawn, the hammer cocked all the way back.

"You of a mind to go somewhere, boy?" The man snarled low, like a junkyard dog.

Jonathan shook his head, realizing escape was impossible. "I just got dizzy."

Abe drew a bead on the middle of Jonathan's chest. "Then maybe you'd best get down on your knees and pray for better balance."

Realizing the man's words were more than a mere suggestion, Jonathan sank to his knees and bowed his head. Finally the old lady ended her prayer with a plea for comfort, especially for those newly arrived in these circumstances. After she said "Amen" and the drunk gave another fart, she began to serve dinner.

"You two move apart." Abe Lincoln pointed his revolver at Jonathan and Lavalais. "Eat by yourselves."

Lavalais shuffled to the far corner of the cell. Jonathan scooted over to lean against the thick iron bars. The old lady gave him a paper plateful of food and a single plastic spoon to eat with. As she handed him a cup of tea, she said, "Have some dinner, young man. We'll talk in a few minutes."

She rolled her cart toward the other men. Though the food looked good and smelled delicious, Jonathan had no appetite. All he could think about was Lily— where she might be and how he was going to get out of here so he could find her. As he took a perfunctory sip of the cold, sweet tea, the old lady returned, carrying a small folding stool and a thick black Bible with gold letters.

"You want to talk, young man?" she asked sweetly, setting down her stool in front of him. "Jesus is always ready to listen."

Jonathan closed his eyes, not knowing whether to laugh or scream. His baby had vanished. His wife was frantic. He was stuck in jail with an aging wino and a Rastafarian dopehead. Right now he needed Jesus to do a lot more than listen.

"What's the matter, son?" The woman touched his shoulder as if he were some kind of wounded animal. "How can I help?"

Jonathan looked up at her. "Somebody stole my baby," he rasped.

"Your girlfriend?"

"No. My daughter. She's only three months old."

The woman's eyes widened behind her glasses. "The little Indian baby?"

He nodded. "I'm her father."

"But they said you were the one who took her. That you got mad at your wife."

Jonathan gave a bitter smile at the quasi-efficiency of small-town gossip. "I did get mad at my wife. But I did not steal my little girl."

The old lady frowned. "Then why are you in here?"

"Let's just say I expressed my opinion of Sheriff

Dula's investigation." Jonathan, winced as he touched his shattered ribs. "And he expressed me right in here."

The woman pursed her lips, then said, "I've known George Dula since he was five. He's not a bad man, but sometimes he acts first and thinks later. Is there anything I can do to help you?"

"Can you get me out of here?" Jonathan asked, hoping maybe she was Dula's old Sunday school teacher, and still had clout with the bald-pated sheriff.

She shook her head. "I'm afraid not. But I'd be happy to call someone for you. A lawyer, perhaps? Or a friend?"

Jonathan considered her offer. He'd never been in jail before, but he knew getting released entailed lawyers and judges and bail bondsmen. What he needed was to get out fast, so he could go search for Lily. "Could you get my wife over here?"

She smiled, her eyes crinkling in a sunburst of wrinkles. "That, young man, I think I could arrange."

An hour later Abe Lincoln escorted Ruth into the room. Though he kept his weapon holstered, he gave Jonathan a look that let him know he would have no problem drawing it, should the need arise. Holding Ruth by her elbow, Abe steered her over to the cell. "You got five minutes," the deputy said as he backed away to keep watch at the door. "Don't try anything stupid."

Jonathan rose to his feet. Ruth stood on tiptoe and kissed him through the bars, smelling of soured milk and cigarette smoke and something else he could not name.

"Honey, how are you?" she whispered.

"Just a few busted ribs," he replied tersely. "Nothing to worry about."

"I was so scared!" Tears choked her voice. "I thought they were going to kill you!"

"I said don't worry, Ruth." He brushed off her concern, not wanting to waste their five minutes talking about his stupid ribs. He reached through the bars and lifted her chin. "Look—you've got to get me out of here."

"I've been trying to get you a lawyer. They only have three in this whole town. One's had a heart attack, one took his family to Florida when the riots broke out. The third one's supposed to call me back tomorrow afternoon."

"I can't stay here till tomorrow afternoon!"

She shrugged helplessly. "The only other thing I can think of is drive to the next county and try to find a lawyer there."

"No, that will take even longer." He squeezed the bars of the cell, wishing he could, like the biblical Samson, simply tear the building down. Why had he grabbed Dula? Why had he acted like such a fool?

"Have you heard any more from Mary?" he asked, desperate to think of something they could do.

Ruth shook her head. "Not since this afternoon."

"But you know where she is?"

"Christiana, Tennessee. A little town near Nashville I think." Ruth tried to twine her fingers in his. He pressed his forehead against the bars. Lily was beyond his grasp now, but gaining speed and racing farther away as the hours passed. And there was nothing—*nothing*—he could do to stop it. If he wound up losing his child because he'd gotten himself thrown in jail, he would go mad. Suddenly he had an idea. He couldn't help find Lily, but maybe Ruth could. He raised his head.

"Listen, honey. I want you to go to Christiana. Find Mary. Help her find Lily."

Ruth gave a little gasp, as if he'd asked her to do something repugnant. "But Mary told me to stay here,"

she objected. "She said I needed to stay in Dula's jurisdiction, to keep the case open."

"I can keep the case plenty open right here in this
cell," he told her. "Right now Mary needs all the help
she can get!"

Ruth let go of his hands and wiped her eyes, brushing away tears she didn't want him to see. "But don't
you want me to stay here with you?" She sounded like a
hurt child. "If I leave, they might beat you up again."

"I'll be fine, Ruth," he promised firmly. "They won't
beat me up anymore. You need to go help Mary. Right
now, as soon as you walk out of here. Buy a map. Find
Christiana. Make Clarinda drive while you get some
sleep."

"But—"

"Ruth," he said, looking deeply into her eyes, trying
hard not to remember that if she'd only listened to him
in the first place, they'd all be back at Little Jump Off,
safe in front of their fireplace. "If we both stay here and
do nothing while Lily's out there lost, we'll never get
over it—not for the rest of our lives. One of us needs to
go find Lily. I can't, but you can."

She gazed into his eyes, as if searching for some different version of himself that his words had not con-
veyed. He didn't know if she found it; all he knew was
that a moment later, she gave a deep sigh and straightened her shoulders.

"Alright," she said, brusquely. "If that's what you
want."

"That's what I want." He leaned forward and kissed
her, then Abe Lincoln called out that their five minutes
were up.

"Go now, Ruth," Jonathan called as she began backing toward the door. "Go get us our old life back."

"Our old life back." She gave him a crooked smile as
Abe Lincoln unlocked the door. "Okay, Jonathan. I'll do
my best."

28

"JESUS CHRIST, CAN'T you shut that kid up?" Stump Logan bore down hard on the gas pedal as the baby's shrieks tightened the screws inside his head.

"We've done all we can, Señor," explained Paz, twisting around in the passenger seat. "She is clean, she is medicated with the rash ointment, we have tried to feed her."

"Then why the hell is she still crying?"

"Ruperta says she wants her mama."

"Well, tell her she's getting a new mama," Logan snapped. "Tell her by tomorrow she'll have a brand-new set of parents."

Paz looked back at the screaming baby, her small fists waving in the air. "I do not think a new mama is what this baby wants."

Logan chuckled. "Everybody in America wants a

new mother, Paz. Tell her she's just getting the jump on everyone else."

He needed to shut out the child's crying so he could concentrate on the road ahead. In a few minutes they would pull into Edwina's driveway and he'd be done with this little shitting, puking mess. Edwina could clean her up and shut her up, and he could get on with his plan. He unwrapped a chocolate bar, trying to clear the static from his head. It wouldn't be long now. Soon everything would turn out okay.

Nine miles later, he pulled into Edwina's long, winding driveway. As he neared her house, he saw that the upper story was dark, but lights blazed from the lower rooms. *Good,* he thought, *she hasn't let any new girls come.* Grinning, he pulled up in front of the door and planted his fist on the horn. The stupid baby started screeching again, but Logan didn't care as Edwina came hustling out the door, eager, no doubt, to see her latest little chunk of change.

"I've been waiting for you since Saturday, Duncan," she snarled as Paz helped Ruperta and the baby out of the van. "It's Monday night. What happened? Why didn't you call? My van looks like a trash pit."

"Sorry," he muttered, feeling as if he were sixteen again and making excuses to his mother. "Everything just took longer than I expected."

Edwina glanced at the child in Ruperta's arms. "I can't accept this baby if you didn't get your girlfriend's signature on that parental rights form."

"Calm down." He patted his back pocket, the repository for all the documents he'd forged for this little adventure. "I got it."

Edwina scowled at him, then turned to Ruperta. "Okay. Take her inside. Let's have a look at what the cat's dragged in."

Ruperta carried the screaming child into a small bedroom in the back part of the house that Edwina used as a treatment room for her pregnant girls. An examination table stood under a big arc light in the center of the room. Edwina flipped on the light as they entered, then rolled a fresh sheet of paper down over the surface of the table. She nodded at Ruperta, who put the baby on the table and began removing her clothes. When the child lay clad in only her diaper, Edwina stepped forward, putting a stethoscope around her neck. "Bring me my notebook, Ruperta. I'll need to write this down."

She examined Lily Walkingstick thoroughly, peering into her eyes with an ophthalmoscope, poking a tongue depressor into her little mouth, jotting down notes as she went along. "A female infant, roughly three months old, posterior fontanel closing nicely. Pupils are equal, reactive, with no strabismus. Lungs are clear, no audible heart murmurs, abdomen normal . . ."

Edwina removed the child's diaper, spreading her legs apart. "External genitalia are normal although she does have a mighty case of diaper rash. Don't you know better than to let a child get like this?" She glared at Ruperta.

"The formula does not agree with her, Señora. I kept her as clean as I could."

Edwina snorted, then turned the baby on her stomach and eased a thermometer into her rectum. "How long has she had this fever?"

"I sponged her off all day yesterday. Señor Duncan said you would give her medicine when we got here."

Edwina withdrew the thermometer. "One hundred and four," she said, taping the diaper back on and once again taking up the ophthalmoscope. She peered into the baby's right ear. "Have you given her any water?"

"I tried, Señora. She will not take anything from the bottle."

Edwina turned to Duncan, her eyes blazing. "Don't tell me your girlfriend was *nursing* this child."

He shrugged. "She might have been. What's the big deal?"

"Unless your girlfriend's on bromocriptine, she's probably got a breast infection. Her baby has otitis media—and diaper dermatitis—and I bet she hasn't taken three ounces of milk since her mother turned her over. Next time you want to enter the adoption market, Duncan, try the dog pound. Their clients can suffer your abuse a little better."

"Will she be okay?" Logan tried to look worried, though this little squawker could die of diaper dermatitis for all he cared.

"Fortunately for the human race, most children survive the care of their parents." She handed the baby to Ruperta. "Give her a tepid—*tibio*—bath and put her in some clean clothes. I'll give her some amoxicillin and aspirin. If she won't take Pedialyte from a preemie bottle, we'll have to start an IV. With luck, she should be okay by the time the parents start coming."

Logan perked up. "You already found her some parents?"

"I've got three different couples lined up and waiting. Any one of them will do better by this little girl than you."

"When are they coming?"

"As soon as I call them." She fished out a bottle containing an inch of pink powder from the medicine chest and poured distilled water in it. "But first I need those papers from you. I can't do a thing without them."

He pulled the forged birth certificate and parental surrender forms from his pocket as she shook up what now looked like a bottle of Pepto-Bismol. He dropped the pages on the examination table. "See you in a couple of days."

"Where are you going now?" she asked in astonishment.

"You said I could have the van for a couple more days after I brought the baby."

"You're leaving right away?"

"I need to finish a deal. I'm running on a timetable."

"I hope you run on that one better than you ran on this one."

He forced himself to smile. "I'll be back later."

"You be back Wednesday, Duncan," ordered Edwina. "I'm tired of your nonsense. And clean out my van before you bring it back."

Go fuck yourself, you old bitch, he thought as he headed toward the door.

"Don't you want to kiss your little girl good-bye? She'll probably be gone by the time you get back."

"You kiss her for me, Edwina," Duncan called over his shoulder. "Just tell her Daddy says to have a nice life."

Miles to the east, the child's real mother was speeding down I-40 in a pickup, sipping from a thermos of herbal tea. After Ruth had left Jonathan, she'd hurried back to the camper, waking Clarinda, who'd fallen asleep over the latest issue of *Cosmo.*

"Wake up," Ruth had said. "We're leaving."

Clarinda blinked. "But where are we going? Did Mary find the baby?"

"Not that I know of," replied Ruth, rolling up her sleeping bag. "We're going to find Mary. Then we're going to help her find Lily."

Clarinda didn't budge from her cot. "I thought Gabe Benge was giving her plenty of help."

"I thought so, too," said Ruth. "Apparently, that's not enough."

Clarinda rolled her eyes, but got up and began stuffing her clothes into her backpack. Twenty minutes later, both women were packed and ready to go.

"Here." Ruth tossed her cousin the keys. "You drive. I need to get some sleep."

"I just took six aspirin," Clarinda whined. "You know what these trees do to my sinuses."

"Okay, okay," muttered Ruth impatiently, grabbing the keys and climbing into the driver's seat. "Just get in. I'll try to stay awake."

They pulled out of Dula's parking lot and stopped at a gas station before they merged onto I-40. Clarinda used the bathroom and stocked up on cigarettes; Ruth bought a map and had her thermos filled with hot water.

"What are you brewing tonight?" Clarinda's nose wrinkled as they finally rolled up the access ramp to the highway.

"Something to keep me awake," Ruth said acidly. "According to this map, it's about five hours to Christiana."

"That far? Hey, I'll try not to doze off," Clarinda said, crumpling up against the passenger door. Ten minutes later, she was snoring.

Sipping her tea, Ruth sped on through the night. At first she drove erratically, nearly nodding off from sheer exhaustion, but as the herbal mixture she'd learned from Granny Broom worked its magic, she began to feel almost giddy with energy, as if she'd downed a pot of powerful coffee. Suddenly in tune with every nuance of the highway, she drafted behind a log-toting semi through Knoxville, then zoomed solo past the smaller towns of Lenoir City and Harriman. As the night wore on traffic thinned out, and she was able to catch brief glances at the huge black bowl of sky overhead. She tried to spot Polaris, the star that had once betokened such good things for her and Jonathan. At Little Jump Off she could find it easily, shining directly over a notch in Hemming Ridge. Here, traveling west through unfamiliar country, she had no idea where it was. *Just like Lily,* she thought, bitterly.

As she drove on through the night she began to see everything, from the lines on the highway to her whole life, with amazing acuity. Lily and Jonathan; Mary and Clarinda.

"Some of them are true helpers," she whispered, Jonathan's words ringing in her head. "Others are simply clutter."

All at once an idea occurred to her. If she would just shake her life out like a quilt, all the clutter would vanish, and leave only what was important to her. Only that way would she get her family back. Only that way would her old life return.

Amazed at the simplicity of the solution, she looked over at Clarinda. She was snoring loudly, slack-jawed from her six aspirin. Clutter, decided Ruth. Clutter of the worst kind. Abruptly she stepped on the brake and steered the truck over to the shoulder of the road. They lurched along the rough pavement, finally stopping just beneath a sign for the next exit. As Clarinda struggled up from sleep, Ruth reached over and opened the passenger door. Laughing, she grabbed her cousin's backpack and threw it into the darkness.

"What's going on?" cried the woozy Clarinda, shivering as cold night air poured in the open door. "Did we have a flat?"

"Get out," said Ruth.

Clarinda frowned as if trying to square reality with whatever she'd been dreaming. "Huh?"

"I said get out. I don't want you in my truck anymore."

Blinking, Clarinda looked around to see nothing but a deserted highway and a sign indicating that the exit for some place named Crossville was one mile ahead. "Have you gone nuts? This is the middle of the night! We're in the middle of nowhere!"

"And it's the perfect place for you." Ruth looked at

Clarinda's shocked expression and started laughing all over again.

"If this is your idea of payback, Ruth, it really sucks. I didn't mean to give Lily away. I've told you a million times I made a fucking *mistake*!"

"Your parents are the ones who made a fucking mistake, Clarinda. It turned out to be you." Ruth pulled Jonathan's lug wrench from beneath the driver's seat and pointed at her cousin. "Now get the bloody hell out of my truck!"

The last vestige of sleep fled from Clarinda's face. She scrambled out the door like a dog accustomed to dodging the furious kicks of its master. When she reached the ground she turned back toward Ruth, her arms spread in supplication.

"Okay, Ruth," she called, as if she'd just indulged her cousin in some bizarre game of revenge. "I'm out here alone, in the dead of night. I've got twenty-two dollars in my purse and no idea of where the hell I am. Does that even the score between us? Do you feel better now?"

Ruth looked down at the woman who'd handed her baby to a total stranger—a piece of pure, unadulterated clutter if there ever was one. "Not quite yet, Clarinda," she said sourly. "But twenty more miles down the road, I'll probably feel just fine."

Reaching over, she slammed the door shut and gunned the engine, jamming the truck back onto the highway. She watched in the rearview mirror, as her little piece of clutter cousin stomped her foot and waved her arms like a puppet and then disappeared into the darkness, just another piece of litter you'd pass on the highway without a second thought.

29

"HI, GABE. I'VE come to help!"

Mary looked up from the dinette, stunned. It was past midnight and she'd just finished her absolute last sip of wine when someone had tapped lightly on the door. Gabe opened it to reveal Ruth Moon standing there, an odd grin on her face. Though she wore the same clothes as when Mary had last seen her, her demeanor had changed. Where before she'd moved leadenly, as if burdened with sorrow, now Ruth darted about like a sparrow, her eyes bright and feverish. *She's lost it,* Mary thought, her heart aching for the stricken woman. *This has driven her out of her mind.*

"You two working hard?" Ruth eyed the empty wine bottle on the table. "Jonathan said I needed to come here and help you out."

Mary frowned. "Jonathan told you to come here?"

"Yes. He said since he couldn't come help you out, I would have to."

"Where's Jonathan now?" asked Gabe.

"In jail," Ruth replied. "Black eye, broken ribs." She cast a sharp glance at Mary. "Broken heart, for all I know."

Oooooh, boy, thought Mary. *This just gets worse and worse.* "Come sit down and tell us about it, Ruth. I bet Gabe will make us a pot of coffee."

"Oh, I've got tea that works much better than coffee."

"Let's do coffee first." Mary looked conspiratorially at Gabe. "Some decaf. Then if we're still thirsty, we'll do tea."

While Gabe fished the decaffeinated coffee from his cabinet, Mary made room for Ruth at the dinette. In a moment she was telling them everything—that Jonathan had finally arrived in Tremont, but had gotten into same kind of fight with Sheriff Dula and was now in the Nikwase County jail.

"He told me to go and find you," Ruth said, her hard edge vanishing. "He said you would need my help."

"What kind of fight did Jonathan have?" Mary knew Jonathan's temper well—slow to boil, but once it did, it could be explosive.

"I was telling him about everything that happened. Then I showed him that first picture of Lily, and he went crazy." Ruth gave a loud sniff. "He grabbed the sheriff by the neck and lifted him up off the floor."

Mary closed her eyes, filling in the rest of the blanks. Dula's deputies had no doubt come to their boss's aid, fists clenched, nightsticks drawn. "How badly was Jonathan hurt?" she asked softly.

"Like I said, he's got some broken ribs." Ruth twisted the hem of her sour, milk-stained T-shirt. "It was horrible."

While Ruth stirred milk into her coffee, Mary gathered all the photos of Lily they'd received and spread them out on the table. As Ruth looked at them, the woman who'd just moments ago burst in like a firecracker seemed to grow smaller by the minute, as if the grotesque images on paper were leaching her very life away.

Mary pointed to the last picture. "Remember when I last called you and we had such a bad connection?"

Ruth nodded, lifting her coffee cup with shaking hands.

"What I was trying to tell you was that Gabe and I may have found the place where this last photo was sent from."

"Where?"

"Murfreesboro. A larger town, just up the road." Mary wondered how she was going to explain this and not set Ruth off on some emotional nosedive again. "Ruth, I think I know who's doing this."

"Not the porno guy in Atlanta?"

"No. Somebody else. Someone who's using Lily to set a trap for me."

Ruth almost dropped her coffee. "A trap for you? But why?"

Mary took Ruth's hand. How much should she tell of this to make it plausible? How much should she leave out, so as not to cause Ruth pain? She considered her options, then told much the same story she'd told Gabe, leaving out only the fact that she and Jonathan were making love when this whole horror had begun.

"But why do you think this Logan is after you?" asked Ruth when Mary reached the end of her tale.

"I don't know. But I think it must be about something that happened a long time ago, something between him and my father."

"Did you tell Sheriff Dula about this?"

"No. I left a detailed message with Chip Clifford, from the FBI."

"Do you think they'll come in on the case now?"

"All we've got is my conjecture. That's not much to convince them that someone they think is dead might be alive."

Mesmerized, Ruth stared at the photos of Lily. Finally Gabe spoke. "Hey, what happened to your cousin? Did she ever get back to Oklahoma?"

"I don't know." Ruth looked up at him, her eyes regaining their feverish gleam. "She might be in Oklahoma. She might still be in Tennessee." She gave an evil little chortle. "She might be dead, for all I know."

"What do you mean, Ruth?" Mary asked, amazed. The woman had just cycled through three totally different personalities in the last twenty minutes.

"On the way over here I finally figured out what was wrong with my life." Ruth leaned over the table and whispered, as if letting them in on a major secret of the universe. "It's clutter. You know? All the extraneous shit that just gets in your way. I was driving along and I started thinking about all the things and people I could do without and I looked over in the truck and there sat Clarinda, this living, breathing piece of clutter. So I just pulled over to the side of the road and got rid of her."

Mary flashed another look at Gabe. "What did you do, Ruth?"

"I put her out," Ruth replied triumphantly. "Threw her and her stupid backpack out of the truck."

"On the side of the interstate? In the middle of the night?" Mary was appalled.

"Oh, she was just a mile from some town. You should have seen her. She came running after the truck yelling, waving her arms. I just gunned the motor and kept on going." Ruth started to giggle, then her gaze fell on the photos of Lily. "If it hadn't been for that sorry piece of clutter," she muttered brokenly, her laughter turning abruptly to tears, "none of this would have happened."

Mary pulled Ruth close to her. She could feel her

trembling beneath her filthy clothes. The last few days had taken a brutal toll on the woman.

"Honey, would you like to take a nice hot shower? I can give you a clean T-shirt to put on afterward. It'll make you feel a whole lot better."

"You think so?"

Mary nodded.

"Okay." Ruth wiped her eyes, suddenly childlike. "If you say so."

"Come on, then. Gabe will get you going."

Gabe turned on the tiny shower and gave Ruth soap and a clean towel. As she bathed, he sat down across from Mary, his face pinched with concern.

"Whoa," he said softly. "Have we just gotten a glimpse of the new, improved Ruth?"

Mary shrugged. "I've seen distraught mothers before, but nothing like this. I don't much blame her for ditching Clarinda, though. Too bad somebody didn't put her out before she ever got to Tennessee."

"But don't you think we ought to call somebody? The cops or the Highway Patrol?"

Mary thought for a moment. Though her instincts told her Clarinda could probably survive a nuclear blast with nothing worse than a broken nail, Ruth had left her cousin in a potentially dangerous situation. "Of course we should," she conceded. "I'll call the state troopers and let them know there's a wildcat loose on I-40."

Just as she reached for her phone, however, she heard the distinctive ring of the "William Tell Overture." With a sinking heart, she read the screen.

"Get Ruth out of the shower," she told Gabe. "We've got another e-mail from Lily!"

Forty-five minutes later, they stood back in the Kinko's computer room, waiting for their new photo to come out of the printer. With her hair still damp from the shower, Ruth wore one of Mary's T-shirts and a more rational demeanor. Both her crazed, frantic look and her zombie non look were gone from her eyes, and she seemed her old herself again—intelligent, capable, and totally focused on finding her child.

"Can you see Lily yet?" she asked Gabe, who was standing closest to the printer.

"Hang on," said Gabe. "It's coming."

They waited the last agonizing seconds for the printer to finish. Finally Gabe grabbed the sheet of paper and held it up. This time Lily lay not in front of a gravestone, but at the base of a statue, where a naked youth cast in what appeared to be bronze, held two horses rearing over his shoulders. A tall obelisk rose behind him, with an angel gazing down on the trio from above. Lily lay wrapped in a blanket at the bottom of the structure, where someone had propped up a crudely lettered cardboard sign that read "Greetings from Nashville, Tennessee."

"Oh my God!" wailed Ruth. "My baby!"

Mary turned to Gabe. "Do you recognize this statue?"

"No. But if it's Nashville, he's still on the Trail of Tears."

"How far is Nashville from here?" asked Mary.

"About forty miles."

"Come on!" Ruth pulled them frantically toward the door. "Lily might still be there!"

An hour later, they stood at the base of Nashville's memorial to the Civil War. Ruth had followed them in her truck, and they'd stopped only to buy a city map at a local gas station. When they realized that it failed to list any points of interest, Gabe had asked directions from a cabby working the graveyard shift for the Music City Cab Company.

"That's on Granny White Pike." The taxi driver pointed at the map.

"Granny White Pike?" Gabe repeated the odd name.

"Yeah," said the cabbie. "Go to downtown Nashville, get on Broadway. Go south on Twelfth Avenue. It's about three miles down the road, on the right. Spooky as hell at night."

The cab driver had been right. The statue stood in a small park at the edge of a residential area, soaring up into the night sky, the tall obelisk glowing white in the darkness. The bronze youth and his two horses scowled down upon them, huge and menacing, making Mary dizzy every time she looked up. An eerie silence hovered over the place, as if the Confederate dead still kept watch. The spot where Lily had lain was empty, as were the other three sides of the monument's base.

"Come on," said Ruth, after they'd made a wide circle of the statue. "Let's go closer."

Mary grabbed her arm. "Not now, Ruth. We need to wait till the sun comes up."

"But why? They might have left some clues—"

"Which we could overlook or trample in the dark," Gabe interrupted, "Mary's right, Ruth. We need to do this when we can see."

"So now you're now an expert on finding stolen children, huh?" Ruth's voice was caustic.

Gabe gave an edgy laugh. "I'm not an expert on anything, Ruth. I just happen to agree with Mary."

"I know, I know. Everybody always agrees with Mary." Ruth walked in a tight little circle. "Look, I'm sorry. I didn't mean to say that. I think I just need something to eat. Or maybe to drink."

"Come back to the van, honey," said Mary. "I'll fix you something to eat."

Ruth hesitated a moment, then agreed. "Let me fix us a pot of sassafras tea. It'll make us all feel better."

"Okay." Mary didn't want any tea, but she thought it best to tread lightly, given Ruth's mercurial temperament. "We'll fix sandwiches. You bring us some tea."

A little while later they sat at the dinette. Ruth had handed them individual cups of tea, while they had fixed her a grilled cheese sandwich. Mary smiled as the tea took her back to her childhood, when her mother would serve cold sassafras tea in the summertime, with little sprigs of mint in each glass.

"This tastes great, Ruth," Gabe told her, sipping from the cup she'd poured for him.

"The old Cherokees regarded it as a curative," she replied, once again her old self. "It does kind of make the world seem a little better." She gazed out the window toward the statue. "Sometimes, anyway."

"We'll go out at first light." Mary glanced at her watch. It was ten past four. "Now, let's at least get a couple of hours of sleep."

Ruth turned from the window and gave Mary the saddest look she'd ever seen. "Do you really think we'll ever see her again?"

"I don't know, Ruth," Mary answered honestly. "But I promise you that neither you nor I nor Jonathan will ever stop looking for her, for as long as we live."

30

SOME THIRTY MILES away, in an antique-studded bedroom at the Tender Shepherd Home, Edwina Templeton lay propped against six down pillows, sipping a predawn cup of Earl Grey tea. A laptop computer lay across her thighs, and her fingernails clacked on the keys as she fabricated a completely new biography for her newest client. Though she'd always had a flair for drama and a small talent with words, turning Logan's little misbegotten offspring into a half-Iranian princess had taken some real creativity. First she'd had difficulty finding an Iranian website written in English, then, when she'd finally navigated to a collection of baby names, she'd had trouble picking one out. "Meshia" was a pretty name that would fit so pretty a child, but it meant "butter made of sheep's milk." "Fojan," which meant "loud voice," suited Logan's baby in a different way, but it sounded like something you'd name a German shepherd. Finally, after hours of searching, she found the perfect name. It was both pleasing to the ear and represented all her hopes for this child. Logan's baby, who had arrived nameless, would hereafter be called "Behbaha," which meant "best price."

With the rest of the family history, Edwina was less obsessive. She named the fictional mother "Mahvash Ankasa," simply because the names were Iranian and she liked the way the syllables flowed together. She made Mahvash a twenty-five-year-old naturalized citizen from Tehran, a bright, progressive young woman who had eschewed the black *chador* in favor of a white nurse's cap.

The father, she decided, should be from Tennessee, mostly because she had a friend up in Nashville who could cover for her if the adopting couple looked at this too closely. *John*, she wrote on the line below Mahvash. *John Winston McIntosh*. She put him down as being born in the county of her own birth, Sullivan, and made him twenty-four years old, the same age as her own father when she was born. She stopped typing for a moment as an odd little thrill of power swept through her. She could give this baby any kind of parents she wanted. Ones like her own—an overworked doormat for a mother, and a father who too often fell over drunk on the supper table. Or ones like the parents of the little girls who'd grown up to command the Christmas Tour of Homes—mothers who led Girl Scout troops, fathers who wore silk neckties and drove their children to school in shiny cars.

"I could go either way here," she said, staring at the computer screen, energized as if she were beginning a novel. For a moment she was tempted, just to spite Duncan, to give his daughter a sordid background of drunkenness and shame. Then she remembered that paying parents preferred children with untroubled histories—babies of nice girls who'd made a single, egregious, nine-month-long error in judgment. And smart. *Very* smart. Above all else, the biological parents had to be smart. Nobody wanted a dull child.

"Let's see, Behbaha," she muttered, beginning a new paragraph. "Your mother was a nurse, a pretty little thing who drowned, two months after you were born. A Labor Day picnic turned tragic. She got in a canoe with friends to paddle across a lake. The canoe capsized halfway across. She could not swim. Your father tried desperately to save her, but the poor thing sank like a stone. He tried to keep things together, but with little money, two more years of medical school, and a tour in the Navy ahead of him, he decided that the best thing would be to find someone who could give you a better home."

She filled up a whole page, adding the little details that brought poor, bereaved Dr. McIntosh and the doomed Mahvash to life. When she finished, she studied the screen and smiled, pleased and not unmoved by her work. It would surely bring a tear to the driest of eyes, move the coldest of hearts.

"Okay, Behbaha Jane McIntosh," she said, saving her file. "You've had a tough beginning, but things are beginning to look up. In no time at all, you're going to get new parents, I'm going to get a big fat check, and we're both going to sleep better than we've ever slept before—you in a comfy new crib, me on my new forty-eight-thousand-dollar bed."

Downstairs, in far less opulent quarters, Paz lay on his own bed, listening to the darkness outside the window. Last night, when he stepped back into this room he thought he'd never see again, he felt as if some priest had granted him sanctuary. For the first time in days, he was not speeding down a highway, trying to mollify Ruperta, Gordo, or a screaming infant. When he finally lay down here upon his cool, clean sheets, he'd longed to take Ruperta in his arms and explain why he'd acted like such a *maniático*. She, however, would have none of it. She'd put Gordo's baby in a little crib in the corner of their room and turned her back to him in bed, without so much as bidding him good-night. Now, though his eyes burned with exhaustion, he could not sleep. He knew that outside his room, Scorpions waited. Soon they would come. Perhaps even now they stood, hiding in the shadows, tossing their little brown bottles up like coins, in wait for his wife.

"Ruperta!" Paz whispered, blowing softly on the back of her neck. He must explain all this to her before Señora awoke. Perhaps together they could work out same kind of plan. All by himself, he was coming up dry. "Ruperta, wake up!"

She mumbled two words in Spanish and yanked the sheet up to her ear.

"Ruperta!" he whispered urgently. "I have to tell you something!" He reached over and squeezed her breast, rubbing her nipple until he felt it grow hard. He felt a corresponding ripple of desire deep in the pit of his stomach, but he ignored it. As much as he wanted to thrust himself deep inside her, he had to tell her about the Scorpions. "Ruperta!"

"What is it?" She turned all of a sudden, wide awake, her voice angry.

"I need to talk to you—" The words stuck in his throat.

"About what, Paz? It's the middle of the night."

"We have to make a plan, Ruperta," he said sternly, trying to sound as if he always pondered life-altering decisions long into the night. "And we have to make it now."

"A plan for what? More little babies to steal from their mothers? More candy-eating monsters to tour America with?"

He sat up and ran the back of his hand along her face. The soft hair on her cheek felt like down. "I have but one monster, Ruperta," he whispered. "It does not want candy, but it will eat your eyes."

"Eat my eyes? What are you talking about?"

He drew a shaky breath, wondering if he dared repeat the Scorpions' threat. As obscene as it felt to give voice to such a thing, not to let Ruperta know would be far worse.

"The Scorpions came last week, Ruperta. They still think I have their money."

For a moment she said nothing, then she sat up and pulled her knees up under her chin. "How many came?"

"I saw only one. More, of course, were hiding."

"Did you explain that you never had their money? That Jorge lied?"

"I did. The Scorpion did not believe me."

"What did he say?"

Paz swallowed. "He said if I did not give them their money in three days, they would put acid in your eyes."

She looked at him in stunned silence, then, to his horror, she began to cry, hastily covering her mouth lest her sobs wake the baby. Her tears broke his heart. "It's Tuesday morning," she sobbed. "How could you have kept this from me for so long?"

"I had not wanted to tell you at all," he said. "I thought Gordo could be our escape! We could slip away from him and go someplace the Scorpions could not find, then all this baby business began."

"Oh, Pacito!"

She collapsed against him, weeping. He held her, miserable, as her body trembled against his. What a wretched husband he was! Unable to protect his wife from such monsters! He wished they were here now, every one, in this room. He would kill them, one by one, with his bare hands.

"Sshhhh!" He held her tight, burying his face in her hair. Soft and freshly washed, it smelled like flowers in early spring. "Don't cry! I won't let them do it!"

"But how can you stop them? We thought we escaped them in Nogales, then in Atlanta. Always, they show up."

"I will stop them, Ruperta," he vowed, covering her wet face with kisses. "I swear before God I will." He slipped his hand down the front of her gown, then gently laid her back on the bed and pushed her nightgown up.

He lay on top of her. "You are my wife," he whispered, his lips against hers. "As long as I live, no Scorpion will harm you."

"Oh, Paz," she wept, threading her fingers through his hair, pulling him closer. He kissed her until she squirmed with pleasure, then thrust himself inside. *You will have this many more times to pleasure your wife,* he seemed to hear a voice whisper inside his head. *This many and no more.* As he felt himself dissolve into her he tried to disregard the voice, wishing that he could stay in this little room forever, looking into the dark liquid stars of Ruperta's eyes.

They lay like that for a long time, her breathing comforting him like the soft, low *swuush* of the waves at Vera Cruz. Finally she stirred beneath him.

"Paz?"

"*Sí?*"

"What are we going to do?"

He rolled off of her, his stomach once again a hard knot of fear. "I don't know."

She nestled against his chest. "You know what we did is wrong, don't you?"

"Running from the Scorpions?"

"No. What we did with Gordo."

"You mean taking the baby."

She nodded. "Do you know what Señora is going to do with her?"

Paz glanced at the little crib in the corner. It and its contents loomed like yet another hurdle to clear before they could escape the Scorpions. "Give her to rich people with no children of their own."

"She's going to sell her, Paz. Señora does not *give* anything away. Señora sells. Señora is a *comerciante*."

"That is not our problem, Ruperta. It's between Gordo and Señora."

For a while Ruperta lightly stroked the scar on his stomach. Then she raised up on one elbow. "Paz, we cannot let that happen."

"What?"

"The baby being sold like a goat or a parrot. She has a mother who loves her. We must return her."

"Ruperta, are you crazy? We have no car, no money, no way of even finding again the place we took the baby from. Even if we could take her back, the American cops would arrest us for being *secuestradors*! And for what? To return a child to a woman who ran off and left her in the care of a *puta*?"

"Paz, we've committed a great sin. We must make it right."

"It's a sin to interfere with things that are not your business! You will bring down even worse trouble than the Scorpions! I am your husband! You must do as I say!"

Suddenly they heard a noise. Paz leapt to his feet, at first thinking the Scorpions were at the door, but then he realized it was only the hoarse *clack* Señora's great clock made just before it struck the hour. Still, Ruperta got up in a swirl of sheets and nightgowns and hurried over to the crib. She scooped the baby up before the first whimper left her lips and held her close.

"Put her down, Ruperta," Paz commanded. "You need to be concerned for us, now. Gordo's baby will have a happy life with rich parents who will buy her everything."

But Ruperta stood there in her nightgown, her beautiful eyes bright and defiant. "What this child needs is her own life back, Paz. With her own mother. Even a dog deserves that!"

31

❦

EDWINA TEMPLETON SWIRLED her last crust of toast
through the remaining egg yolk on her plate and popped
it into her mouth. Washing it down with a slurp of coffee, she removed the white wicker tray Ruperta had
brought in and placed it on the floor next to her desk.
Ruperta could pick it up later, she decided, provided
Ruperta could tear herself away from that baby.

She looked at her watch: 5:25 here in Tennessee,
6:25 in Florida. Five more minutes and she would call
Myrtle Hatcher. Six-thirty was an indecent hour to call
to most people, but adoption counselors were accustomed to phone calls in the middle of the night from distraught parents, sobbing girls. Even to wait until dawn
was a true act of kindness.

She swiveled in her chair and looked out the window. The cows had left the shelter of the barn and were
standing in the little paddock, waiting for Paz to let

them out into the fields to graze. Her eyes narrowed as
she saw a tall, thin figure skulking past them, up toward
the tree line at the end of her property. From this distance the figure looked male, but it was too tall for Paz
and way too skinny for Duncan. Probably some juiced-
up hunter, she decided. All she needed was some idiot
mistaking one of her cows for a deer.

"I'll send Duncan up there to check it out," she muttered, watching as the figure vanished into the trees.
Then she remembered that Duncan had taken all her
guns and was still off completing whatever business he
had and wouldn't be back until tomorrow. *Oh, well,* she
thought. If she heard any gunshots, she'd either send
Paz or call the sheriff. As far as she was concerned, with
all the money she'd make from his baby, Duncan could
take six months off. She would miss him only in her
bedroom, and she already had several personal appli-
ances that could accomplish most of what Duncan
could.

She put the hunter and Duncan out of her mind and
turned back to her desk. Her watch now said 6:30. She
flipped through her Rolodex and punched in the area
code for south Florida.

Several rings later, Myrtle Hatcher mumbled hello,
sounding as if she'd been brought unwillingly out of a
coma.

"Myrtle?" Edwina spoke loudly, hoping to jar the
woman into sensibility. "This is Edwina Templeton,
calling from Tennessee."

"Edwina, how are you?" In six syllables Myrtle's
voice rose from groggy Brooklyn fishwife to alert
Florida businesswoman.

"Fine, Myrtle. I know it's early, but if your Iranian
couple is still interested, I've got the most beautiful little
girl in the world here." Though Edwina pretended that
this deal was still up in the air, she knew quite well that
Myrtle's couple was still interested—Myrtle had fool-

ishly blathered on for most of Sunday afternoon about their "stringent requirements," tipping her hand that the number of acceptable babies was quite narrow.

Myrtle hedged. "Of course they're interested, but they're also considering other children. Tell me more about this baby."

"She's very healthy," Edwina said, impatiently tapping a pencil at Myrtle's bullshit. "Thirteen pounds, eleven ounces, three months and fourteen days old." She went on, telling Myrtle all about her normal development and extraordinary intelligence, deftly omitting the fact that the child came in with diaper rash, an ear infection, and hair that looked as if it had been cut with a chain saw. Silly to point out the minor flaws when so much else was perfect.

"Is she cute? Intelligent? Does she look Iranian?"

"She's beautiful," Edwina answered truthfully. "Lovely dark eyes—straight, black hair."

"What about her skin?" Myrtle lowered her voice, as if someone might be eavesdropping. "She's not real dark, is she?"

Edwina smiled at the true question—*She's not part Negro, is she?*—but she knew she had to be truthful here, too. It would serve none of them to try to pass off a black baby. "Her skin is very light olive. I think she would blend in with your couple nicely. How about I e-mail you a photo?"

"That would be good." Myrtle sounded somewhat mollified. "Let's say this works out, Edwina—how much is your part of this?"

Edwina frowned. Myrtle had let it slip early on that her couple was well-to-do. Of course, all couples who got babies like this had to come up with at least fifty grand, but it was more of a struggle for some than others. Still, for Myrtle to indicate that these people had deep pockets meant that there was a lot more money to be had. Edwina stilled her pencil and took the plunge.

"I'll need seventy-five thousand, Myrtle. You can add whatever you want on top of that."

"Seventy-five?" Myrtle gave a sharp little gasp, as if someone had pinched her bottom. "Good grief, Edwina, do you think these people are made of gold?"

No, thought Edwina. *I think they're made of oil, which is even better*. "Just free market economics, Myrtle. Stringent requirements mean higher prices. This baby is bright, beautiful, and exactly what they want. I doubt there's another child on the market who comes anywhere close."

"Well, we'll have to see about that," sputtered Myrtle. "E-mail that photo and I'll give them a call."

"Right away." Edwina tightened the screw on Myrtle one final time. "But I need to know by noon. I've got another couple in Chicago, all lined up and waiting."

"Okay." Myrtle sounded flat as an old tire. "I'll call you back. Don't forget that e-mail, okay?"

"You'll have it in just a few minutes."

Smiling, Edwina hung up the phone. She had already concocted a perfect background story for this child. Now if she could just figure out how to get the baby looking well long enough to snap her picture, this deal would be in the bag.

Half an hour later, the phone rang in a bright yellow bedroom in Fort Lauderdale, Florida. Kimberly Khatar, dreaming a curious dream about dolphins and electric-powered cars, reached for her husband Bijan. When she felt nothing but rumpled sheets and an empty pillow, she raised up on one elbow. She heard the phone ringing, the shower running in the bathroom, and Bijan singing something that sounded vaguely like an old Rolling Stones tune. Kimberly shook her blond hair away from her face, then stretched across the bed to answer the call.

"Hello?" she said, her voice rusty with sleep.

"Kimberly? Myrtle Hatcher calling. Can you get on line without hanging up your phone?"

Still woozy from her dream, Kim blinked over at Bijan's desk. The green light of the computer glowed as it hummed softly in the far corner of the bedroom. "Yes, Myrtle. I can do that."

"Then log on and check your e-mail. You've got a big surprise waiting!"

"Just a minute. I'll have to put the phone down."

She dropped the receiver on the bed and walked over to the computer. As Bijan cranked his Mick Jagger imitation up to full volume, she keyed in her password and logged on. The usual male voice said, "Welcome," then, "You've got mail!" She clicked on her mailbox, then on the message from "Hatcherlings" with a file attached. As she scanned the text, her heart began to pound. Myrtle had a healthy baby girl, of mixed white/Middle Eastern descent, available today. Holding her breath, Kimberly downloaded the file, watching eagerly as the image resolved on the screen. An amazingly beautiful child stared into the camera. Although her short hair was straight and stuck out from her head in kind of a punk-rock do, her dark eyes were huge and limpid and she had a little cupid's bow of a mouth. The child gazed at the camera not with the wariness Kimberly had seen on other babies up for adoption, but with a real presence; a knowing kind of curiosity, as if she could see way down into your soul. Kimberly stared, transfixed, for a full minute before she remembered that Myrtle was waiting.

Clicking the PRINT command, she raced back over to the phone. "Myrtle? Are you there?"

"Of course I'm here. What do you think?"

"I think she's the most beautiful thing I've ever seen!" Kimberly felt both hot and cold. "What can you

tell me about her?" she blurted out, as if the child were
applying for some position at her insurance agency.

"Her father is a twenty-four-year-old white medical
student, her mother a twenty-five-year-old Iranian
nurse. This couple had been married just two years
when the poor mother drowned in a boating accident.
The father tried to make a go of it, but with med school
and military service, he decided to give the child up."

"How old is she?" Kimberly stretched the phone
cord out as far as she could, trying to grab the picture
from the printer.

"Three months," replied Myrtle. "The perfect age.
They're just beginning to really sit up and take notice of
everything around them."

"She's absolutely beautiful, Myrtle. I don't know
what to say."

"Say you'll take her!" Myrtle laughed. "Children
like this come along once in a lifetime."

"Bijan's in the shower right now." Kimberly held the
picture of the child as if it were the petal of a rose. "I'll
have to talk to him, of course, but . . ."

"There are some things you should know before you
show him this picture, Kimberly," Myrtle told her.
"This adoption is being arranged by a colleague of mine
in Tennessee, so the cost is somewhat higher."

"How much?" Kimberly couldn't pull her gaze away
from the child's liquid eyes.

"One hundred thousand dollars."

"One hundred thousand? That's over twice as much
as we had discussed!"

"I know, dear. But like I said, children of this quality
and background almost never become available. Your
own search has certainly shown you that."

The photo trembled in Kimberly's hand. What
would Bijan say when he found out the cost had more
than doubled? Surely he would not let mere money
stand between them and this precious child. She would

sell her business, if need be. Flip burgers at Mickey D's, if it came to that.

"And I'll need to know your decision as soon as possible. There's another couple who've committed, but I managed to get you and Bijan first refusal. . . ." Myrtle paused. "Is this a problem, dear? Do I need to call my colleague and tell her the folks in Chicago can come and pick up their child?"

"No, don't do that," Kimberly said hastily. "I'll go talk to Bijan right now. We'll call you back in ten minutes."

"Don't dillydally," warned Myrtle. "These things are like contracts on houses. Miss your chance, and the baby goes to the next one waiting."

"Okay, Myrtle. I'll let Bijan know that." Kim hung up the phone, her hand shaking. She sat down on the bed, scarcely able to believe her good fortune. Ten minutes ago, she'd been a woman without a child. Now she held the first picture of her daughter in her hand. *Her daughter.* A little girl who mirrored them exactly— Bijan's beautiful dark eyes and hair, her own fair skin and delicate features. She knew without question that this was the one.

"My sweet, sweet little girl," she whispered, tracing the outline of the baby's face. "Come on." She took the sheet of paper into the steamy bathroom. "I want to show you to your dad."

32

MARY WOKE TO the too-familiar strains of "William Tell." She'd slept with her cell phone under her pillow, on the bed Gabe made up for her. Groggy, she made a grab for it before it could wake him. Her muscles tightened with apprehension as she read the screen, then she relaxed. It was just a phone call. Nothing new from Lily.

"Hello?" she whispered.

"Mary?" Danika's voice resounded in her ear. "Have you found the baby?"

"No. Not yet."

"Where are you?"

"I'm in a friend's trailer," Mary explained, keeping her voice low. "We keep getting these e-mails. We think whoever stole Lily is taking her along the old Cherokee Trail of Tears."

"Oh, dear Lord," said Danika. "Is there anything I can do to help?"

"I don't think so, but thanks. I'll let you know if something comes up. Any more from Mott?"

"We played basketball last night. The bastard acted as if nothing had happened."

"That's Mott for you." Mary gave a bitter laugh. "Everything's got to be his way or the highway." Gabe was beginning to stir in his passenger-seat-turned-bed. "Look, I've got to go. Thanks for calling. I'll talk to you later."

She switched off the phone and waited a moment. Gabe moaned once, then grew silent. *Sleep a little longer, Semper Fi*, she bade him silently as she tiptoed into the bathroom. *You need all the rest you can get. We all do.* It had been a long three days, and who knew how much farther this madman was going to chum them along with Lily?

She washed in the sink and used Gabe's clove toothpaste to brush her teeth, emerging to find him still asleep. She crossed over to the trailer door and opened the louvered window. Outside, the sun had climbed well past the horizon, and the statue and the park around it glistened in clear morning light. She glanced to her right, then jumped with surprise. Ruth sat on the hood of Jonathan's truck, again dressed in her filthy red T-shirt, staring at the van door. Though she'd supposedly returned to the truck to sleep, she looked as if she'd sat there all night, just waiting for them to awaken and start searching the monument for clues.

"This is driving her mad," Mary whispered, comparing the beautiful, clear-eyed poster girl on television with the dirty, erratic husk of a woman who now eyed their camper like a hungry vulture. "It's got to end soon."

She turned away from the door and stepped over to Gabe. "I hate to wake you, Semper Fi," she whispered, brushing her lips against his cheek. "But it's almost nine A.M. We need to get up and get busy."

Twenty minutes later they stood at the base of the

statue, dressed and ready to go. Mary's eyes felt grainy from lack of sleep and Gabe mentioned feeling queasy, but Ruth had returned to her hyperdrive, her movements fast and jerky, like a puppet dancing on a string.

"What should we look for? Where should we start? Should we spread out or stay together?"

"Why don't we form a line and do a sweep around the statue?" asked Gabe. "If we stand six feet apart and walk slowly, we shouldn't miss anything."

"Good idea," Mary said, grateful to have the former Marine's calm logic counterbalancing Ruth's frenzy.

They did as he suggested, making a careful sweep of the perimeter of the monument. When the first pass revealed nothing, they spread out farther and repeated the process. For the next half hour they combed the area around the statue. Gabe picked up two beer cans to recycle; Mary found two used condoms that she opted to leave alone. Beyond that, nothing. The grass around the monument looked as if it had been swept with a rake. Morning commuters made a northbound traffic line into Nashville along the quaintly named Granny White Pike, while joggers and dog walkers made their way south along the pretty tree-lined street. A tall woman with two ebullient boxers waved at them as she let her dogs off-leash to romp in the little park that surrounded the monument. Leaving Gabe and Ruth to make another sweep, Mary trotted toward her.

"You guys lose something?" the woman called as Mary approached. She was attractive, prematurely gray, and she smiled as if not too much would surprise her.

"Kind of," replied Mary as both boxers bounded up to her, wagging their stubby tails. "You haven't seen anybody taking pictures of a baby around here, have you?"

"At the statue?"

Mary nodded, trying to pet both dogs without getting flattened by the affectionate pair. "A little baby. Wrapped in a blanket."

"I saw one last week," the woman answered thoughtfully. "She'd just started to walk. I had to keep Sophie and Charlie on their leashes. I was afraid they'd knock her down."

"No, this would be a much younger child," said Mary. "An infant."

The woman thought a moment, then she looked over Mary's shoulder, frowning in concern. "Hey, I don't want to worry you, but I think last night might be catching up to one of your friends."

"Excuse me?"

"Up there." The woman pointed. "Somebody looks pretty sick."

Mary turned. While Ruth stood reading the inscription on the monument, Gabe was on his knees in the grass, clutching his stomach.

"Oh, gosh!" cried Mary.

"Give him a little vodka and tomato juice," the woman said with a laugh. "Hair of the dog, and all that."

Except he hasn't been drinking, Mary thought as she thanked the woman and hurried back to Gabe.

"Gabe?" She knelt beside him as he retched miserably. "What's wrong?"

"I don't know," he replied, his voice hoarse. "I was doing okay, then all of a sudden, I got really sick."

"Come on," she said, helping him to his feet. "Let's get you back in the van. Logan didn't leave any clues here."

He did not protest as they walked back to the trailer. In fact, he leaned heavily against her as if his legs could barely support him. Mary put him in the bigger bed, and covered him with a blanket. Moments later, Ruth appeared at the door.

"Where did everybody go?"

"Gabe got sick," explained Mary.

"Sick?" Ruth climbed into the camper and looked down at him. "What's wrong?"

Teeth chattering, he said, "I don't know."

"Let's just let him rest now," said Mary, gently nudging Ruth away from Gabe. "I'm going to call Chip Clifford again. Why don't you call Sheriff Dula?"

With the trailer configured for both beds, they had no room to sit down, so Mary pulled another blanket over the shivering Gabe and stepped back into the bright morning, Ruth following. They made their respective calls—Mary leaving another detailed entreaty on Agent Clifford's answering machine, Ruth talking to a clearly uninterested Sheriff.

"That went well," Ruth said sarcastically as she clicked off her phone. "All Dula can talk about is the charges he's filing against Jonathan. Lily's dropped off his list of priorities altogether."

"I imagine Jonathan will put her back at the top," said Mary. "He can be pretty persistent when he wants to."

"That he can." Ruth cast a sidelong glance at Mary. "How did you do with the Feds?"

Mary shrugged. "I left a message. I just hope Chip will act on it."

"So what do we do now?" Ruth started plucking at the hem of her T-shirt.

"We've done everything we can do," Mary told her. "Now we just wait for the next call. It'll either be Chip Clifford or—"

"Another picture of Lily." Ruth finished her sentence.

"Come on." Mary locked arms with Ruth. "Let's go check on Gabe."

Inside the van, Gabe lay trembling like a man with malaria, his pillow soaked with sweat. Mary was shocked at how much worse he'd grown in just the time it had taken them to make their phone calls.

"Gabe?" She put a hand on his forehead. It felt cold and clammy. "How are you feeling?"

"Not so great," he answered sluggishly, his pupils wide as a crackhead's. "Tired . . ."

"How about some ginger tea?" Ruth chirped.

"I don't think so, Ruth." Mary spoke gently, but she was growing irritated at Ruth's total belief in the powers of herbal medicine. "By the way, what was in the tea you gave us last night? That was the last thing he drank."

"Just sassafras and ginseng," Ruth replied huffily. "Totally harmless. We all drank it, and neither of us is sick."

Mary saw Ruth's point, then she realized, too, that she and Gabe had consumed virtually the same food and drink for the past two days, yet he lay prostrate and sweating while she felt fine. And he'd gotten sick so quickly. He must have caught some weird germ, she decided. Probably at that godforsaken rally.

"Come on," she told Ruth. "Let's fold the other bed back up. That way we can stay in here and keep an eye on him."

Mary brewed a pot of coffee while Ruth scampered back to her truck for more tea. With the sun warming the dashboard of the van, they sat waiting for Mary's cell phone to ring, and checking on Gabe. At ten o'clock he said he felt better, but at eleven she could not rouse him from his sleep.

"Gabe?" Mary whispered, growing truly alarmed. She grabbed his hand. It felt like ice. "Gabe, can you talk to me?"

He made no response; not even his eyelids moved at the sound of his name.

"Hand me my phone, Ruth." Mary tried to keep her voice even. "I'm calling nine-one-one."

"Over a stomach virus?" Ruth looked at her as if she'd gone insane.

"Yes." Mary snatched the phone from her hand. "Over a stomach virus."

———

Fifteen minutes later, two burly EMTs bent over Gabe—one taking a history, the other checking his temperature and blood pressure.

"You guys been doing any nose candy?" the history-taking EMT asked.

"No," said Mary. "Not at all."

"Any loaded brownies? Peyote buttons?"

"No."

"It's okay if you have." The medic's tone was calm, but grave. "Something's really doing a number on this guy. If you know what it is, you need to tell me, now."

"We haven't taken any drugs." Mary fought back a rising panic. "He and I have been together for the past two days. Eaten the same food, drunk the same drinks."

"And you feel okay?" The man looked at her with new concern.

"Yes. Fine."

He wrote something down on his chart, then glanced at his partner.

"We need to get him to the ER," the other medic said as he slipped his stethoscope from his ears. "His pressure's going south, fast."

Mary watched as the first EMT grabbed his clipboard and followed his partner out of the van. A moment later they were back, strapping Gabe onto an aluminum stretcher. She felt as if she were in the middle of a sudden tornado, with everything swirling out of control around her. "Where are you taking him?"

"Vanderbilt Emergency."

As they lifted Gabe up to maneuver him out the door, Mary leaned over to kiss his cheek. "Don't worry, Semper Fi," she whispered. "Everything's going to be okay." She squeezed his hand, hoping to fill him with her own warmth and strength, then the medics carried him out the door.

"Hey," she called as they loaded him in the back of the ambulance. "How do I get to Vanderbilt?"

"Just follow us," called the EMT. "It's only five minutes away."

"Thank God," said Mary, buckling herself into the driver's seat of Gabe's van, praying that the hopeful words she whispered to him would turn out to be true.

33

"ISN'T SHE THE most beautiful little thing you've ever seen?"

Kimberly Khatar's teaspoon pinged against the side of her glass as she stirred a pink packet of no-cal sweetener into her coffee. She and Bijan sat in the food court of the Atlanta airport, eating a hurried breakfast before starting the second leg of their flight to Nashville. It had been an extraordinary morning. Three hours earlier, they had been dressing for an ordinary day at work. Then their lives had done a complete U-turn, and now they were at the midpoint of the most important journey they would ever make. They'd managed to make last-minute airline reservations, had dressed frantically and thrown extra clothes in a carry-on bag. Bijan had grabbed his briefcase and checkbook, and here they sat, staring at the picture of the little girl who might well become their daughter.

"She really is pretty." Bijan pulled his chair closer to his wife's and smoothed the photo they'd examined a hundred times in the past three hours. "Too bad you can't see her eyes anymore."

"What?"

"You've unfolded the paper so much, you've almost lost her eyes in the crease."

"Oh, Bijan." Laughing, Kimberly leaned her head against his shoulder and looked down into the little girl's dark, knowing eyes. "What do you think we should name her?"

"Kimberly, we don't even know if we'll like this child. And we have no real reason to think we'll get her, even if we do."

"But we're first in line this time, honey. Mrs. Hatcher said so. Come on, Bijan. Play the name game. Just for fun."

Bijan took off his glasses and studied the photo. "My folks will want Jannat or Atiyeh," he told her solemnly. "Your folks will go for Stephanie or Megan."

"What do you want?"

"Something cool." He watched a woman sit down at the next table and release a tiny white dog from a blue nylon pet-tote. "How about Britney Teagarden? Or Xena the Warrior Princess?"

"Xena the Warrior Princess Khatar." Kimberly nodded as the waiter put a plate of bacon and eggs down in front of her. "I like that. Has a nice ring to it."

Bijan waited until the waiter left his lox and bagel, then he spoke more seriously. "You know, Kim, if this should work out, I don't care what we call her, as long as it's something American. Anything else, and they'll think she's a terrorist."

Kimberly's smile faded. Her husband had told her about the hard time he'd had when he arrived in the states as a twelve-year-old with little English. His classmates had called him everything from Bichon to Be-Jesus and accused him of being a spy for the Ayatollah Khomeini. Only after he developed a sharp bilingual sense of humor and a deadly accurate fastball for his high school baseball team did his classmates call him by his proper name.

"I understand how you feel, Bijan. But I hate for her name not to reflect her heritage."

"She'll have a hard enough time with her heritage as it is."

"But Iranian names are beautiful. And we can't just pretend that she's an all-American girl."

He shrugged. "Maybe an Iranian middle name, then. But nothing long or hard to pronounce. I don't want kids making fun of her on the first day of school."

"Then choose one."

He looked at the photograph again, then smiled. "How about Aziz? Jennifer Aziz Khatar. We'll call her Jenny."

"Bijan, that's perfect!" Kimberly felt her eyes filling with tears, as they had numerous times this strange and wonderful morning. "I love that name."

"I may not be able to make babies," he remarked cheerfully, taking a bite of his bagel. "But I can name the hell out of them."

Kimberly poked at her eggs. It was God or Allah's own irony that of all the people in the world, they had found each other—she congenitally with only half a uterus, he rendered sterile when his cousin Amir, an Iranian med student, had mistakenly treated his swollen glands for mono instead of mumps. Years later they met on the beach at Fort Lauderdale, both sophomores at the University of Miami. They married the day after they graduated, and for the past twelve years, they'd been happy. Bijan had taken over the management of his father's real estate holdings, and she had earned an MBA, starting an insurance company that sold tailor-made plans to small businesses. Children, or the lack thereof, had not been an issue until Bijan's father suffered a stroke and started repeating the word *bace*—baby—every time they set foot in his condo. While most stroke patients obsessed about fresh water or itchy catheters, Farzam Khatar, beachfront real estate king, wanted a grandchild. Soon Kimberly caught the obsession like a virulent germ and she, too, started to long for a child. Bijan, who wanted to please both his father and his wife, was agreeable to adoption, but so inflexible in his requirements that over the past three years only two children had become even remote possibilities.

"We want an olive-skinned, beautiful, intelligent baby with almond eyes," she remembered him informing Mrs. Hatcher. "Our child must reflect ourselves."

At first she assumed Bijan would want only a male child, but she had misjudged him. He'd considered the other little girl they'd had a shot at as carefully as the little boy. But other couples had been ahead of them. Adopting healthy children, Kimberly had learned painfully, was a fiercely competitive venture. Those who got the call first were the ones who carried off the child.

"Heads up." Bijan nudged her back into the present. "Here comes Mrs. Hatcher."

She looked to where he pointed. A bosomy woman wearing a bright yellow pantsuit hurried toward them. She blinked, as if she couldn't remember where they'd been sitting, then she caught sight of them and waved something in a brown paper sack.

"Look what I found at the newsstand!" she called in a loud singsongy voice that made other travelers turn and look at her. "A book! *What to Expect in the First Year of Life*!"

"Dear God," said Bijan, moving his briefcase out of Mrs. Hatcher's chair. "I guess this is for real."

Kimberly put her fork down. She would remember this moment for the rest of her life. She and her beloved Bijan eating breakfast at the Atlanta airport, goofy Mrs.

Hatcher hurrying to help them meet the child who might become their own. When next her parents held their family reunion, she, Kimberly Susan Khatar, might be there with her own child, a dark-haired little girl who would bloom among her sisters' fair-haired progeny. She smiled as she put her arms around her husband.

"Whatever happens, Bijan, I've never loved you more in my life than I do right now."

He looked at her with dark eyes that held mystery and promise and just as much unspoken hope as her own. "Me, too, my love. Me, too."

Miles to the north, in a cheap motel room in Franklin, Tennessee, Stump Logan sat on a lumpy mattress, sighting down the barrel of an old Winchester .70, drawing a bead on a small dog that was trotting across the parking lot of the motel.

He had not hunted anything four-legged since he was kid. Back then it was deer, with his father, a raw-boned mountain farmer who'd spent most of his days digging rocks out of his sticky clay soil by hand. They'd hunted out of necessity rather than sport, and the old man had once slapped him hard when he'd been so awed by a young doe bounding over a six-foot fence that he'd forgotten to lift his rifle to his shoulder. He'd never seen anything so utterly graceful, nor did he again until years later, when Jack Bennefield rose like a gazelle over a verdant green field in Vietnam, trying to snag a football intentionally thrown too far and too high.

Jack Bennefield, Stump thought, following the dog as he raised up on his hind legs to smell the intriguing aromas of the garbage Dumpster. His old buddy. Mary Crow's father. How differently things might have worked out, had he and Bennefield never met. He might well be sitting comfortably on his own front porch, carving whistles for his grandchildren. A cat would be curled up at his feet and his wife would be in the kitchen, pulling a blackberry cobbler from the oven. He would be happy. He would be content. He would be living the life he'd always wanted.

But no. He'd met Jack Bennefield, and that lanky, grinning boy had cast a blight upon his life that he felt to this day. Like an apple tree permanently damaged by a killing frost, his post-Bennefield years had passed stunted and fallow, bearing only the small, bitter fruit of hatred and desire.

"Don't think about it," he told himself, watching as the dog tugged a discarded McDonald's sack from the trash. He'd worked hard. He'd *planned* hard—everything from the getting the proper ordnance together to switching the license plate on Edwina's van. Right now he had only to make one more phone call. Then everything would start. If Clootie Duncan's "Jesus" card held out, he would soon be pushing Mary Crow down that same bottomless hole. How good that would feel. He could almost taste his revenge.

"Pow!" he whispered softly, smiling as he mentally blew the dog to bits. He put the rifle down and returned to the stale honey bun he'd gotten from the vending machine outside his room. That Mary Crow would come, he was certain. Though he knew she was swift and smart as a real crow, he also knew she would be unable to resist the bright lure he'd chummed her along with: Walkingstick's baby. The irony of that made him smile. He almost hoped Walkingstick would come with her. He would push both of them down that hole and they could rot for all eternity, together forever.

He looked at all of the weapons spread out on the bed. The Winchester for long range, a Smith & Wesson automatic for up close. Two Tasers that Edwina kept to calm down the young bucks who sometimes came rutting after their knocked-up girlfriends. Looking like TV remote controls but packing a mighty electrical charge, the Tasers had been new to him. He'd tested them out, outright electrocuting one of Edwina's barn cats and bringing a young bull calf jerking to his knees. He picked up one of them and smiled. Who would have thought a dopey little weapon that ran on CD batteries could coil a man up like a fetus for the better part of an hour?

He had five hundred .375 H&H Magnums for the rifle, a hundred dumdums for the automatic. Target practicing in the calm of Edwina's farm, he'd nailed a beer can from four-hundred yards away. Handicapping himself a hundred yards for nerves and the trees, he figured he could still drop anybody long before they could shoot him. If all his plans failed, he could always take the time-honored route of all rogue cops and fix himself an S&W sandwich. One way or the other, he would have the last laugh. If Mary Crow outfoxed him here, at this juncture, she would have to live the rest of her life wondering what in the hell happened to little Lily Walkingstick. It would not be the ultimate revenge he'd planned for the daughter of Jack Bennefield, but it would do.

34

❦

THE AMBULANCE PULLED away, red lights flashing. Just as Mary was preparing to follow in Gabe's van, her cell phone rang.

"Damn!" she cried, slamming on the brakes. She grabbed for the phone, which she'd stashed in Gabe's drink holder, and checked the screen. To her great relief, it was not an e-mail, but another call. Quickly she put the phone to her ear.

"Mary Crow." She answered in her brusque Deckard County voice.

For a second she heard nothing. Then, to her horror, she heard the sound of an infant, crying. Loud, inconsolable cries that connoted pain or hunger, or something worse.

"Lily?" she blurted before she could stop herself. "Is that you?"

Ruth, who was sitting beside her, jumped as if she'd

been jolted with electricity. "Lily? What do you mean, Lily?"

Before Mary could answer, Ruth lunged for the phone. Mary tried to dodge her clawing fingers and listen to the call at the same time, but Ruth wrenched the phone from her grasp. It fell, bouncing off the dashboard, finally clattering somewhere underneath the gas pedal.

"Damn it, Ruth!" cried Mary. "What's the matter with you?"

"I want to hear my baby!" Ruth screamed.

Unbuckling her seat belt, Mary ducked under the steering wheel. She groped frantically for the phone, but it slipped through her fingers, sidling over beneath the clutch. As precious seconds passed, she finally grabbed it and held it to her ear. The baby's crying had gone, replaced by a male voice with a thick mountain accent, already in mid sentence.

". . . photography studio. Cool Springs mall, at noon."

"Wait!" Mary cried. "I didn't hear you."

"Sure you did," the voice snarled.

"No, wait, we dropped—" Mary began, but the line went dead.

She sat back in the driver's seat, gasping, feeling as if some lizard had touched her with its tongue. She'd guessed right—it really *was* Stump Logan. She'd recognize his voice anywhere.

"Give me the phone!" cried Ruth. "I want to hear Lily!"

"Here." Mary tossed the phone in Ruth's lap. "Be my guest."

Wide-eyed, Ruth clutched the thing to her ear. "I don't hear anything! Where did she go?"

"By the time I picked it back up, Logan was on the line. All I heard was photography studio, Cool Springs mall at noon."

"Oh, my God!" Ruth clasped her hands together, as

if her prayers had been answered. "He must be taking Lily there! He must want to give her back!"

"He doesn't want to give her back, Ruth. He's trying to set a trap for me."

"For you?" Ruth's lips curled. "Mary, did you ever think that maybe just once something isn't about you? That this might be about Lily? My child?"

"I did at first," Mary answered patiently. "But I don't anymore." She looked for the ambulance, but it had disappeared from sight. She took the phone from Ruth and started to punch in 911.

"Why are you calling the cops?" asked Ruth.

Mary gaped at the woman, incredulous. "Because Stump Logan is a murderer who's kidnapped your baby. When things like that happen, you call the cops."

"No!" Again Ruth lunged for the phone. This time, as she grabbed it, her nails left three long scratches down Mary's right cheek.

"Have you gone totally nuts?" Mary cried, her eyes tearing from the sudden biting pain.

"Just what makes you think the Nashville police will do any more than Dula? Or your precious FBI?" Saliva spewed from Ruth's lips. "The cops haven't given a shit about Lily since day one—what makes you think this time's going to be any different?"

With one hand on her cheek, Mary stared at Jonathan's wife. Though Ruth was currently spinning into and out of her mind like someone caught in a revolving door, her words held some truth. Dula had not acted fast enough, and the Feds had chosen not to act at all. Would the Nashville cops really roll out over an unidentified baby's crying and a half-heard sentence? No.

Ruth scooped the Nashville map from the dashboard. "You do what you want, Mary. If there's any chance at all that Lily's going to be at that mall at noon, then I'm sure as hell going to be there, too." She left the phone on the dashboard and scrambled out of the van, slamming the door behind her.

Mary listened to Ruth's staccato footsteps as she strode to her truck. If Ruth went to that mall, anything could happen. Logan could lure her anywhere on the promise that Lily was there, waiting. Then both mother and child would be gone, and both would be her fault. *Damn,* she cursed, her hands tightening around the steering wheel. Logan had rigged his trap as cleverly as any spider; now she was fully ensnared, with no way out.

"Hang on, Ruth," she called wearily. "I'm coming with you."

The vast commercial sprawl of Cool Springs Galleria lay twenty minutes south of Nashville. It reminded Mary of Atlanta, where huge shopping malls spread like metastasizing cancers over rolling hills where cattle had once grazed and corn had been the major cash crop. Ruth had driven down I-65 like a madwoman, changing lanes to zoom past slower drivers, finally skidding to a stop in front of JC Penney.

"Come on," she said, hustling out of the truck. "We've only got ten minutes."

"Just a second, Ruth." Before Mary had locked Gabe's keys in his van, she'd found his pistol and a box of bullets in the cabinet over the sink. Unsurprisingly, Gabe kept the gun clean, oiled, and in perfect Marine Corps condition. Now she stuffed the old Glock in the waistband of her jeans and pulled her loose cotton sweater over it. It didn't hide it much, but if she wore her shoulder bag slightly in front of her left hip, she looked a little less like Annie Oakley at a shooting match. "Okay," she said, wondering offhand how many local laws she was breaking by going into a shopping mall with a loaded weapon. "Let's go."

Inside, the mall was crowded with people. A group

called the "Tennessee Artisans" jammed the already cluttered concourse, selling handmade merchandise from portable displays while a country singer who looked like Clint Black serenaded the shoppers from a small stage. Mary scanned all the storefronts she could see—a photography studio was not among them.

"We need to find a directory," she told Ruth, squeezing past two men dressed in blue Tennessee Titans football jerseys.

They hurried past a maze of quilt displays, an old hot rod that was the prize in a charity raffle, a man vending something called "Roasted German Nuts." Mary checked her watch. Five minutes to noon. She looked around, frantic to find a directory, when she spotted a triangular backlit sign that read "Locate Your Favorite Merchant Here."

They raced over. Every store was listed and located on a diagram. Mary's heart sank when they found three entries under the photography category—Wolfe Camera, the Sears Portrait Studio, and something called KidShotz.

"Which one did he mean?" Ruth asked, twisting the front of her T-shirt.

"Wolfe Camera is just film and equipment," said Mary, recognizing the store from her shopping trips in Atlanta. "That leaves either Sears or KidShotz. We're going to have to split up. Which one do you want?"

"KidShotz," said Ruth. "Lily will be there. I just know it."

"Then I'll take Sears. I'll wait there five minutes, then I'll meet you at KidShotz." She looked at the woman who so desperately wanted to find her child. "If you get there and someone says they know something about Lily, get inside the store and call a security guard."

"What if somebody has Lily there?"

"Then grab her and make as much commotion as you can. Yell, scream, do anything to get someone to come help you. I'll be doing the same thing at Sears."

"Okay."

They raced to their respective stores, Ruth hustling up a flight of stairs, Mary hauling to the far end of the mall. At 12:00 she stepped into Sears sportswear department; by 12:01 she stood breathless in front of the portrait studio. Just as she feared, no one was there. She knew then she'd picked the wrong horse; Logan and Lily must be at KidShotz. She turned and raced back out to the mall, fighting her way up an escalator crowded with toddlers dressed in Halloween costumes, ready to take part in some kind of mall activity. As she rode up the moving steps, snugged in between a six-year-old ballerina and a pint-sized GI Joe, she scanned the crowd of people gazing down on them from the upper level of the shopping center. She noticed no men with beards, no eyes staring into hers; no face with that singular hard look of hatred and disgust.

Damn, Mary thought as the escalator finally deposited her next to the food court. *What the hell is he trying to do?*

She turned the corner, almost running into an adult dressed as Spider-Man. In between the mothers and their wildly dressed children, she caught sight of the KidShotz storefront. She thought she saw a small crowd gathering in front of the store, then she realized it was a small crowd of people avoiding the front of the store. She pushed her way closer, then gasped. Ruth was on her knees in the entrance to the store, surrounded by security officers, clutching something to her chest and keening in a high, loud pitch that only meant despair.

Oh, my God, Mary thought, struggling to reach her friend. All at once she heard her cell phone, its silly ring issuing from her purse. As she ran toward Ruth, she fished it out and held it to her ear.

"You blew it, Mary." The male Appalachian voice rumbled on. "You didn't pay attention to my directions. Damned if you aren't as dumb a fuck as your dad."

35

❦

KIMBERLY KHATAR SQUEEZED her husband's hand as the plane began its final descent toward the Nashville International Airport. Bijan had booked them in adjoining seats on the same flight from Atlanta, and now they sat, three peas in a pod, strapped in a Boeing 757. Kimberly capped off her morning by splurging on three inflight phone calls—one to her parents and one to each of her two sisters. Though everyone had sounded stunned by the news, all had squealed with joy over the prospect of welcoming Jennifer Aziz Khatar into their family. Kimberly's parents had immediately started packing for a trip down from St. Pete, while her sisters began planning a baby shower.

"Are you sure you don't want to call your folks?" She waggled the phone at Bijan.

He turned from the window, then shook his head as if he'd had too much to drink. "I'll surprise them. My mother hasn't boarded a plane in twenty years. She probably wouldn't get past the fact that I was calling her from midair."

"Just think of how happy you're going to make them, honey." Kimberly hugged Bijan's arm.

"You're going to love Edwina Templeton," Mrs. Hatcher brayed from the seat beside Kimberly's. "She's had amazing luck at finding just the right baby for the right parents."

Kimberly nodded at Mrs. Hatcher as the plane's landing gear dropped into position. Actually, she didn't give two hoots about Edwina Templeton. All she cared about was wrapping her arms around the baby who would become her new little girl.

After they landed, Mrs. Hatcher told them that Edwina's place was too far out of town for a taxi, so Bijan went to the Hertz desk and came back twirling the keys to a Lincoln Town Car.

"Why did you get such a big car?" asked Kimberly as they walked toward the huge white sedan. "You usually get Toyotas."

He shrugged, embarrassed. "More protection in case we have a wreck. You know, precious cargo and all."

Kimberly smiled. In the course of a three-hour flight, Bijan had already begun to make the change from carefree husband into responsible family man.

Mrs. Hatcher directed them to the small town of Franklin, twenty miles south of Nashville. After exiting the highway and driving through a blur of fast-food restaurants, gas stations, and car dealerships, they turned down a road that led through miles of rolling pastures dotted with grazing cows. They crossed a narrow creek on a bumpy, two-lane bridge, then arrived at a graveled driveway that led to a white antebellum mansion with a wide front porch and silvery tin roof.

"This is Edwina's," announced Mrs. Hatcher from the backseat. "Looks like Tara, doesn't it?"

Bijan pulled the car up in front of the house. Kimberly hopped out and hurried up to the wide porch, trembling with excitement. When she next rode in that car, she might be holding her own baby in her arms.

The top half of the front door was leaded glass; the doorbell was an old-fashioned twist kind. After waiting for Bijan and Mrs. Hatcher to join her, Kimberly twisted the bell three times. She cringed as its coarse ring echoed through the house, not wishing to awaken any napping babies. For a moment, nothing happened, then she saw a blur of movement on the other side of the glass. The door opened, revealing a young Hispanic woman exactly her height. Like many of the *sirvientas* who worked for the affluent of Fort Lauderdale, the woman wore a gray uniform that gave her the look of a nurse-in-training.

"*Buenos días.*" Kimberly shifted into the Floridian Spanish that had, over the years, become her second language. "*Es la casa de la Señora Edwina Templeton?*"

"*Sí, Señorita.*" The young woman smiled, no doubt pleased to address a stranger in her native tongue.

"*Es un huerfano?*"

The woman shook her head. "*Un hospital de maternidad.*"

"*Me llamo Kimberly Khatar, de Fort Lauderdale, Florida. Mi esposo y yo estamos aquí para ver a la nena.*"

"*La nena? No lo entiendo.*"

"*La nena para adopción . . .*"

The woman shook her head again. She was about to close the door when an older, harsher voice sliced through the air.

"Ruperta? Is that Mrs. Hatcher?"

The young housemaid's eyes grew wide as she tried to formulate her reply.

"Ruperta, who is it?" the harsh voice demanded brusquely.

A short, dumpy woman appeared behind the *sirvienta*.

She wore a camel-colored suit over a creamy silk blouse; impressive diamonds twinkled from her ears. Although the clothes were obviously expensive, they fit the woman too tightly, and made her look as if she'd been thrown fully dressed into a washing machine and dried at too hot a setting. She peered past Kimberly, then smiled. "Myrtle? Is that you?"

"Yes, Edwina. We're here!"

"Come in, come in," the woman said, then dismissed the *sirvienta* with a toss of her head. "I'm Edwina Templeton. Welcome."

Kimberly and Bijan stepped into a spacious foyer where a graceful staircase curved up to the second floor. As the housemaid disappeared down a back hall, Edwina Templeton led them into a large sitting room that looked like a cover of *Architectural Digest*. Papered in an eye-popping red silk moiré, the room was stuffed with the kind of antiques sold at Sotheby's to people with bottomless pocketbooks. Mrs. Templeton had expensive taste, Kimberly decided as she gazed at the opulent furnishings. But then, at a hundred thousand dollars a child, Mrs. Templeton could afford to.

"Introduce me to your couple, dear," Mrs. Templeton demanded after the two older women shared a perfunctory hug and kiss.

Mrs. Hatcher beamed. "Edwina Templeton, this is Kimberly and Bijan Khatar."

"How do you do." Bijan nodded stiffly. Kimberly could tell he was nervous. Her palms grew sweaty, too, as Edwina Templeton appraised them carefully, as someone might look over a yearling racehorse that showed some speed. Kimberly prayed that Mrs. Templeton's sharp eyes would not find some invisible flaw and discard them in favor of the couple from Chicago.

But the older woman was nodding. "Come sit down. We'll chat in here. Ruperta's bringing tea."

In the living room, Kimberly, Bijan, and Mrs. Hatcher

perched on an ornate sofa like birds on a wire. Edwina Templeton took the wing chair opposite them. Soundlessly the uniformed girl returned, bearing a silver tray with a china tea service. As Mrs. Templeton poured them all tea, the girl brought in a tray full of cookies and triangular-shaped sandwiches. Kimberly took a cucumber-and-cream-cheese while Bijan opted for tea alone, the cup rattling softly as he took it from the tray.

"There's no need to be nervous," Mrs. Templeton said, smiling. Her voice was husky and she spoke with a drawl so thick, it sounded almost like Hollywood's idea of a Southern accent. "If this one doesn't work out, there'll be others."

Not for us, Kimberly thought, remembering all of Bijan's requirements. *We're not your average family, by a long shot*.

"How shall we proceed, Edwina?" Mrs. Hatcher set her tea down on the table and snatched a chocolate cookie off the tray. "I know these two young people are eager—"

"I like to bring the baby out and watch how the prospective parents interact with it," Edwina interrupted. "I can tell pretty fast if there's going to be a bond there."

"Are you the sole judge of that?" Bijan spoke for the first time. Kimberly winced at his unintended arrogance, but Mrs. Templeton's smile did not falter.

"Yes, Mr. Khatar, I am. As a private adoption counselor, I'm afraid I do have the last word in cases like this."

"I see." Bijan stared into his tea cup, humbled.

"Why don't you tell me a little about yourselves? What kind of business are you in?"

"Kimberly is an insurance broker. She started her own company five years ago," Bijan said proudly. "I manage business properties for my father."

Edwina Templeton's gaze flickered over the Bulgari

watch on Bijan's wrist. "So I assume you don't find the cost of raising a child today daunting?"

"Mrs. Hatcher has all our financial information," Bijan replied. "But no, money is not a problem. We've worked hard and we've been lucky. Our child will have a comfortable home and an excellent education."

Mrs. Hatcher gave a hen-like cackle. "I can vouch for that, Edwina."

"Is religion an issue between you?" asked Mrs. Templeton, ignoring her colleague.

This time Kimberly spoke. "I was raised Catholic, Bijan is Muslim. We've attended the Unitarian Church ever since we married. We intend to raise any child we adopt in that faith."

"A nice compromise." Mrs. Templeton's smile broadened. "Rational. Respectful." She studied them a moment longer, then she set her teacup down on the tray. "Would you like to see the baby now?"

"Oh, yes," said Kimberly quickly. She didn't know how much more of this she could take. Already she wanted to leap up from the sofa and scream with impatience.

"Good. I'll have Ruperta bring her in." Mrs. Templeton rang a small silver bell. They waited. An antique clock in the hall ticked off seconds that seemed like hours, then the *sirvienta* reappeared at the door. Looking as if she wanted to weep, she now carried a baby wrapped in a soft white blanket. From the couch, Kimberly could see only the top of the infant's head, a dark patch of straight hair.

Edwina Templeton got to her feet. "Mr. And Mrs. Khatar, meet the child who was born Behbaha Jane McIntosh." She prodded the housemaid with a chill nod. "Give her to them, Ruperta."

Ruperta obediently crossed the room and held the bundle out to Kimberly. The latter took the child in her arms, astonished at how light and insignificant human infants feel. As she settled the child against her chest, she moved the blanket away from the small face it swaddled. The little girl did not doze, but lay wide awake and very composed, looking up at her with dark eyes that seemed to stare into some part of her that Kimberly didn't know existed.

"Oh, my God," Kimberly breathed. "She's beautiful."

The baby continued to stare at Kimberly, working her little cheeks, blowing a plump bubble of saliva on her lips. Kimberly fought an urge to undress her, to see if she had the proper number of fingers and toes. But even if she didn't, who cared? Who could look into those eyes and not fall instantly in love?

She tore her gaze away from the baby and turned to Bijan. "What do you think?"

He didn't reply. Instead, he reached around her and touched the baby's hand with his forefinger. Instantly the infant grasped it, and held on tight. "Hello, baby girl," he said softly.

The baby squirmed in Kimberly's arms, then her eyes found Bijan's. She studied him with her strange, old-soul gaze, then she flung her arms up and gave a little squeal of glee, as if Bijan was the most utterly delightful being in creation.

Everyone laughed. Bijan tentatively put one finger against her tummy and the baby laughed again, sending funny little bird chirps into the air. Kimberly laughed, fighting tears even as she did so. For her, there was no doubt. Taking a shaky breath, she lifted her face to Bijan.

"Well, honey?" she asked. "What do you think?"

She felt his kiss on the top of her head, then she felt his breath against her ear. "Kim, I think you and I have just become parents."

36

"THIS IS WHO I am and this is what I've got." Mary dug all her ID cards from her wallet and laid them on the desk. Then she pulled Gabe's pistol from her jeans, removed the ammo clip, and laid it beside the pile of IDs. She and Ruth sat in a small, unused office of Cool Springs Galleria Security, where they had been given bad coffee, a moment to calm down, and a much longer moment to explain the situation to the Franklin, Tennessee, cops.

Detective Jane Frey fanned Mary's IDs like a deck of cards, reading and discarding her driver's license, her handgun license, then the card that identified her as an assistant district attorney for Deckard County, Georgia.

"You always shop with a Glock nine?" Frey asked as she slipped a pack of Marlboros from her purse. "I just carry Visa." A tiny woman with bright blue eyes and bright red hair, she wore tight jeans and a green sweater under a rumpled Burberry trench coat. Mary liked her immediately.

"The gun is not mine. It belongs to Gabriel Benge, a professor at the University of Tennessee," Mary explained.

"In Knoxville?" asked Detective Frey, one pencil-thin brow lifting.

Mary nodded.

"And how did you come by Mr. Benge's weapon?"

"I borrowed it from him. Gabe's undergoing treatment at Vanderbilt Hospital."

"For what?" Frey lit a cigarette, then contorted her mouth around in an amazing curl to avoid blowing smoke in Mary's face.

"The paramedics didn't know," replied Mary. "We were at a Civil War monument in Nashville—he got sick there."

Frey stared at the array of items, taking long drags on her smoke, then she scooped up all the IDs and the gun and stepped into another office. Mary knew that she was running her numbers through a computer, checking to see if Mary's credentials checked out in cyberspace. Minutes later Frey returned, her cigarette gone, but her blue eyes sharp as ever.

"Okay, Ms. Crow," she said, returning the gun and IDs. "You checked out, and there is a Gabriel Benge registered at Vandy." She sat back down and pulled a pen and notepad from her purse. "Now give me the details of all this once again. Slowly."

Mary was tempted, for an instant, to tell Jane Frey the whole story—about Logan and her belief that this was really all about her rather than Lily. Then she realized that she would have to further explain that everyone else in law enforcement thought Logan was long dead. At that point Frey would probably close her notebook and discount her as a lunatic DA up from Georgia on a tear. Better to just repeat what the local police could verify, and keep her true suspicions to herself. Anyway, Lily was the important one, and she and Ruth needed all the help they could get in finding her.

So she began with Saturday, when Ruth had called her from Tremont, and ended with the events of an hour ago, when she'd found Ruth in front of KidShotz, crying like someone tortured by demons. What had upset her so was a strip of photo-booth pictures taped to the front window of the store. The pictures had been of Lily, sullen and short-haired, held by a woman who wore a pale blue T-shirt, a small, filigreed crucifix, and turquoise earrings. Whoever had arranged the subjects had made sure the woman's face did not appear in any of the four photos, rendering her basically unidentifiable. Still, mall security had swung into action at Mary's insistence, questioning all the merchants around the photo booth. Nobody remembered seeing any woman and child resembling this pair.

"That's quite a story, Ms. Crow." Frey scribbled with her right hand, fumbled for another cigarette with her left.

"Yes, it is," Mary answered. "Sheriff George Dula, of Nikwase County, can corroborate everything."

Frey lit up a smoke. "Just tell me this. You of all people should know procedure—why didn't you call us when you got the phone call this morning?"

"I tried. But the baby's mother was convinced Lily was going to be here at noon. We had less than half an hour to get here, and she was absolutely determined to come. Considering the amount of stress she's been under, and the cops' lack of enthusiasm for this case, my coming with her seemed to be the better choice."

As if to underscore Mary's remarks, Ruth's voice grew suddenly shrill. Mary and Jane Frey looked across the room to see her wildly gesticulating to the other detective. "I just want my baby!" she screamed, banging a table with both fists. "I just want my child!"

With a telling glance at Jane Frey, Mary got up and went over to Ruth, wrapping an arm around her shoulders, pressing her cheek against the top of her head. Though Ruth could well have blown their best chance of capturing both Logan and Lily, she found it hard to remain angry with her. She couldn't even imagine what it had been like for Ruth, to rush up to KidShotz hoping to see Lily and finding a mocking photo strip instead. "Be strong, honey," she whispered. "Just stay focused on the fact that Lily's still alive."

"Okay, ladies." Frey stood up and motioned for her partner. "You two stay here while we work out a few details. We'll be back as soon as we can."

Leaving them in the care of mall security, the two detectives left the office, closing the door firmly behind them.

Ruth looked up at Mary with red-rimmed eyes. "What are they going to do?"

"If they work anything like the cops in Atlanta, they'll talk to Dula, then run things by their captain. If he or she says it's a go, they'll join the case."

"And if the captain says no?"

Mary patted Ruth's shoulder. "Then we'll go on, by ourselves."

The mall security secretary brought them Cokes and cheese pizza from the food court. Though the pizza tasted wonderful to Mary, Ruth just picked at hers. For some reason, she wanted to go back to the truck.

"We can't go anywhere until the detectives come back," Mary told her, practically pulling her back down in her chair. "Why don't you call about Jonathan? I'm going to call the hospital about Gabe."

Mollified by that suggestion, Ruth dug her cell phone from her purse and punched in the number she now knew by heart. Mary looked up the number for Vanderbilt Hospital in the security office phone book. Within moments she'd learned that Gabriel Benge had been admitted to the hospital from the emergency room, his condition listed as serious.

"How serious?" Mary asked. "What was he diagnosed with?"

"I don't have that information, ma'am. You'll have to speak to the physician in charge."

"Who is the doctor in charge?"

"I don't have that information, ma'am," the clerk repeated without emotion.

"Thank you." Mary clicked off her phone, realizing that she was going to get only the most minimal information about Gabe over the phone. *But that's okay*, she thought. *At least he's still alive.*

She sat with Ruth until the detectives reentered the room, Frey leading the way. They pulled up two chairs and sat in front of Ruth and Mary.

"Okay, ladies," said Frey. "We talked to Nikwase County. I know you think the sheriff there has blown you off, but he's gone pretty much by the book. Mrs. Walkingstick, your daughter's picture and vital information are now on the National Center for Missing and Exploited Children website, as well as in the FBI database."

"Then why don't I have my baby?" demanded Ruth.

"Do you know how many children go missing each year, ma'am?" Frey's blue eyes sparked cold fire. "I can assure you, we're all trying as hard as we can. Ms. Crow, we've put out an APB for both the woman and the baby in the photo strip, although we really don't have much to go on. I'm guessing from her jewelry, and her visible skin tone that she's of Hispanic descent. We have a growing Mexican population in this county and up in Nashville, as well."

"And?" Mary asked.

"We'll check out a section of town affectionately known as Margaritaville," Frey replied. "If this woman is a local and has shown up with a baby without being pregnant, word'll be out on the street."

"What if she's not a local?" asked Ruth. Her voice shook.

"How about we cross that bridge when we come to it?" answered Frey. "For now, we'll follow up on these photos. You two have a copy of them, don't you?"

Mary nodded. "The secretary made us one."

"Okay. Then we'll get going. I'll keep in touch. Here's my card. If you get any more crying baby calls, call me immediately."

"Thank you." Mary shook the detectives hand. "We really appreciate it."

"Take it as easy as you can, Ms. Crow." Frey handed back the Glock, and smiled. "And please don't run through the mall with that gun again. It tends to make the shoppers nervous."

The detectives left. Mary stuffed the gun in her purse and sat beside the now silent Ruth, trying to decide what they should do. It was almost three o'clock, but the thought of going back to the truck made her uneasy. She'd known from the moment she and Ruth got here that they were walking into a trap. Though it hadn't gone exactly as Logan had planned, he knew where they were. Before, he'd never known either their location or who was following him. Now he knew exactly that it was not the FBI, or the cops, or even Jonathan, but the oddball team of her and Ruth. Was he now lingering in the parking lot, just waiting for them to reemerge from the mall?

She walked into the outer office, where a bank of security monitors maintained constant views of strategic points of the huge shopping complex. Most scanned entrances, the food court, and a number of dimly lit hallways. Several, though, kept watch over the parking lot.

"Does someone monitor these twenty-four seven?" Mary asked the uniformed guard who sat there dipping french fries in a small cup of ketchup.

"Yes, ma'am. I take second shift, somebody else does the graveyard."

"And do they watch the parking lot at night?"

"Yes, ma'am," the guard said. "We pay close attention to the lot after the sun goes down. Haven't had an outdoor incident in nearly six months."

"Thanks," said Mary. She was beginning to formulate a strategy.

She walked back to the conference room, where Ruth sat like a zombie, staring at the floor.

"Come on, honey." Mary pulled her up by her elbow. "Let's get out of here."

"Where are we going?"

"Back to the truck. If we're lucky, Logan might be out there, waiting for us."

"Will he have Lily?"

Mary shook her head. "I doubt it."

"But won't we be walking back into his trap?"

"Yes," Mary said. "But we'll have the advantage. We already know he's out there waiting for us." She opened her purse, showing Ruth her gun. "It's risky, but we might be able to catch him at his own game."

Ruth blinked, as if processing what Mary had just said, then she grinned. "Okay," she said. "Let's go."

They thanked the secretary for her hospitality, then they left the office and strode down a long hall. They heard the mall before they saw it, the upbeat music playing, the low hum of shoppers as they busied around the concourse.

"Ready?" Mary asked Ruth, hesitating an instant before she pushed the door open.

"Yes." Ruth nodded.

I just hope I am, too, Mary thought, reaching in her purse to touch the handle of Gabe's gun as she pushed the door open and they walked together out into the bright bustle of people.

37

BIJAN HELD THE baby for over an hour. He sat capti-
vated by the child as she laughed and cooed, reaching
tiny, star-like hands up to touch his cheek. Kimberly had
never seen two human beings respond so to each other;
apparently neither had the two adoption counselors.

"You know, I bet she sees his pretty dark eyes and
thinks of her mother," croaked Mrs. Hatcher.

"Oh, Myrtle, she's much too young for that,"
snapped Mrs. Templeton, passing the sandwich tray to
her colleague.

"I don't know." Mrs. Hatcher grabbed two
cucumber-and-cream-cheese sandwiches from the silver
tray. "Like seeks its own. Blood knows blood."

Kimberly scooted closer to Bijan and put her arm
around his shoulders. She needed to be absolutely sure
of him before she gave the last remaining shred of her

heart to this baby. "You still think it's a go?" she whispered in his ear.

"Oh, yes," he said, not taking his gaze from the little girl's face. "This is our Jennifer Aziz."

Kimberly looked across the room, where Edwina Templeton sat riding her antique armchair like a gold brocade throne. "Well, Mrs. Templeton, what's the next step?"

"I'll need to fill out some forms, and you'll need to write a check." Mrs. Templeton smiled, but made no move toward any paperwork. Apparently, the wheels of adoption did not start turning until cash lay on the barrelhead.

"I'll go get my briefcase from the car," said Bijan, reluctantly handing the baby to Kimberly.

The two older women exchanged a glance as he left the room. They waited until the front door closed behind him, then Mrs. Hatcher leaned forward and spoke in a whisper.

"I've placed hundreds of children, dear, and I've never seen such a bond. And right off the bat! He's going to make a wonderful father."

Kimberly looked down at the little girl, who was now smiling up at her. "I knew he would be."

"I'll go get the papers." Mrs. Templeton rose from her chair. "In just a little while, you two will be parents."

The rest resembled a house closing. Edwina Templeton passed around various legal-sized documents that required everyone's signature—contracts with both adoption counselors, releases that absolved both her and Mrs. Hatcher of any legal malfeasance, should any be discovered.

"I'm not sure what this means," Kimberly said, her pen poised above the paper.

"It protects private adoption counselors from people who run baby scams," explained Mrs. Templeton.

"Someone brings a baby to us, says it's theirs, we find a parent, collect a fee, then the real parents show up with a lawyer and sue everyone for damages." She glanced at Mrs. Hatcher. "Latinos run that scam a lot in California."

"Forgive me, but how do we know that's not the case here?" Kimberly couldn't believe such distrustful words were coming out of her mouth, but Bijan was sitting next to her, besotted with the child, barely able to look up. Someone had to be practical.

"Well, you're doubly protected, because I'm licensed by the state and you've got an original birth certificate and a release from signed and notarized by the child's biological father." Mrs. Templeton handed three sheets of paper to Kimberly. "Read these closely. Tomorrow morning I'll file them with the Department of Human Services. The State of Tennessee will seal them, from there on out."

Kimberly studied the first sheet. Jennifer Aziz Khatar had been born Behbaha Jane McIntosh on July 24, in Sullivan County, Tennessee. Her father was John Winston McIntosh, her mother Mahvash Ankasa. The delivering physician was a signature she couldn't decipher, and Earlene Toomey was the official registrar. As her fingertips brushed the ridges of the official embossed seal, her tight little knot of hesitation loosened slightly. Little Behbaha seemed to be exactly who she was supposed to be.

The other papers made her sad. One was an account of Behbaha's mother. She'd been Iranian, a nurse, and had died accidentally, from drowning, at the age of twenty-five. The other was a lengthy document, mostly written in the arcane language of the courts. John Winston McIntosh had scrawled his name in blue ink at the bottom, printing in the word "deceased" in the space designated for the child's mother. The date indicated that McIntosh had signed away his daughter only three days ago.

That was probably the saddest day of his life,
Kimberly thought, picturing the young man walking
away from his baby, his wife, his life. Silently she
handed the papers back to Mrs. Templeton. *And this is
the happiest day of ours. Strange, how different two
sides of the same coin could be.*

"That does it for my end." Edwina Templeton col-
lected the papers. "Now I need a check from you, made
out to me, Edwina Scruggs Templeton."

"One hundred thousand dollars?" Kimberly looked
at Mrs. Hatcher as she pulled their checkbook from
Bijan's briefcase.

Mrs. Hatcher grinned smugly at Edwina Templeton.
"That's correct."

She turned to Bijan, who sat making faces at the
baby. "Do you want to write this or shall I?"

"You write it," he answered. "And we'll both sign it."

Her heart pounding, Kimberly filled out the check. It
was the largest she'd ever written in her life. She carefully wrote the "1," then an impressive line of five zeroes
behind it. With only the slightest tremble of her pen, she
signed her name and then passed the check to Bijan. He
barely shifted his position, just held the checkbook in his
left hand while he scribbled his name with his right.
Kimberly tore off the check and handed it to Mrs. Templeton, who took it with a smile.

"Congratulations," she said. "You've just become
parents."

"Oh, I'm so happy!" Mrs. Hatcher warbled as she
dabbed at her eyes with her napkin.

"We are, too." Bijan leaned over and gave Kimberly
a kiss. "I love you," he whispered.

"Love you, too," she murmured, kissing him back.

They sat there enjoying, for the first time in their
lives, the feeling of being three rather than two. Suddenly, more than anything, Kimberly wanted to take
their little girl back to Florida, so they could be a real

family in their own home, instead of in Edwina Templeton's antique-stuffed parlor.

"Honey, why don't I call and see if we can get a flight back tonight?" she asked.

Bijan grinned, understanding her need with that uncanny knack of his which made her wonder sometimes, if they hadn't been married before, in some other life. "That sounds terrific."

"Mrs. Hatcher, is going back tonight okay with you?" Kimberly dug in her purse for her cell phone.

"Whatever suits you suits me, dear."

While Kimberly called the airline, Mrs. Hatcher followed Edwina Templeton to her office, ostensibly to divide up the fee. Bijan sat there, still mesmerized by the baby. A skinny Latino man dressed in white peeked shyly into the parlor as Kimberly asked the travel agent to change their reservations.

"We got the last flight out," she told Bijan as she switched off the phone minutes later. "Nashville to Fort Lauderdale, seven P.M., on Delta." She looked down at the child in her husband's arms wishing she'd brought her camera, wishing she could somehow freeze this moment so she could go back to it, over and over again. Her Bijan. With their new little girl. "Just a few more hours, Jennifer Aziz, and you'll be home."

38

MARY AND RUTH sat in the truck. They'd walked back through the shopping mall conspicuously, stopping at several of the Tennessee Artisans' displays, hoping Logan would make some kind of move. Mary scanned the crowds for him, seeing older men, bearded men, a number of overweight men, but none resembling the battered, malevolent creature she'd seen in Atlanta. If Logan was still here at the mall, he was keeping himself hidden. When they reached the truck, Ruth handed Mary the keys, asking her to drive. Mary moved them to a different parking space, pulling up in a vacant slot well in range of a security camera. If Logan approached the truck here, he would at least get caught on video-tape. There was no point worrying about a long-range rifle attack. He could have killed them both a dozen times over since the moment they'd pulled up in the parking lot. Logan must have other plans for her—she only wished she knew what they were.

Now Ruth moaned amid troubled dreams while Mary studied the copy of the photo strip, desperately trying to glean clues about Lily.

She had to agree with Jane Frey: the skin tone and dress of the woman holding Lily in the photo did look Mexican, or perhaps Filipino. And the clerks at Kinko's had put a Mexican man with Logan, back when he was sending .jpg files over the Internet. But why would Mexicans get involved with a lame old man and a squalling baby? Her years at Deckard County had taught her that money was the prime motivator of most people, followed closely by the desire for power. Contrary to what the poets believed, love came in pretty far down on the motive list.

"So let's say money or power," Mary whispered. Either Logan held some kind of power over the Mexicans, or else he'd purchased their cooperation. Since he'd been on the lam for almost a year, she doubted he'd made enough money to put accomplices on his payroll. That left power, and Logan was an expert at wielding that. As the former sheriff of a county with a burgeoning Hispanic population, he would have knowledge of immigration law and might even speak some Spanish. If he'd bumped into two newly arrived Mexicans, he easily could have bullied them into doing exactly what he wanted. She jumped as a nearby horn gave an angry blast, jolting Ruth awake from her nap. "What's going on?" she muttered, half-asleep.

"Just a little road rage." Mary watched as a battered station wagon missed backing into an expensive SUV by inches. The wagon's driver, a grizzle-haired black man, nodded and waved apologetically at the vehicle behind him, but the man driving the SUV lifted his middle finger and leaned on his horn, blaring his rage to the world.

"Oh, cut him some slack," Mary said, as the old man rolled away, humbly ceding his parking place to the boxy SUV. The young man continued to honk, pulling into the space with an angry squeal of his tires.

"Asshole," muttered Mary, deciding that Tennessee drivers were no more polite than the ones in Georgia. She started to turn her attention back to the photo strip when she noticed the rear end of the SUV. Rampant anti-abortion stickers covered it, making a garish collage of conservative political sentiment. "Abortion Stops a Beating Heart!" "I'm Pro-Life and I Vote!" "Every Child Is a Gift From God!"

Though she'd seen them all a hundred times before, one bright red sticker caught her eye. "ADOPTION NOT ABORTION!"

"Adoption." She tested the word on her tongue as Ruth collapsed back into sleep. Why hadn't she thought of that? Could Logan have given Lily to the Mexicans to adopt? No, that couldn't be right. From what she knew of Logan, he never *gave* anything away. Or at least not unless his interests were served in the bargain. But maybe there was some other angle to adoption. . . . She leaned back in the seat and closed her eyes, trying to pull up the details of a case her old friend Frances Pratt had prosecuted. Frances had been an ADA in Suffolk County, New York, when she prosecuted a pair of French Canadians for running a baby scam—buying babies low from naive girls in eastern Canada and selling them high in New York. Frances had to brush up on her French, which she despised, and had gone to bed with a throbbing headache every night. *Avoid cases with children*, Frances had warned Mary afterward. *They never leave you alone.*

Suddenly it fell into place! If French Canadians could broker children in New York, why not Mexicans in Tennessee? Children were readily available, easily disguised, and could cross the border without identification papers.

And dark-skinned Lily would look like she belonged with Mexican parents. But how could Stump Logan have gotten involved in that? You couldn't just walk up and join illegal adoption rackets; you had to be connected, the players had to know you. When could Logan have made those kind of contacts?

She tried to come up with other reasons that Lily might be traveling in the care of Mexicans, but the idea of adoption kept niggling at her like a kettle left on the stove. She couldn't put it out of her mind and finally gave up trying to. What would it hurt to see how many local adoption agencies there were? Most likely it would be a waste of time, but until they heard from Logan again, they had nothing but time to waste. And at least she would be satisfied that she'd left no stone unturned in the search for Lily.

She shook Ruth's shoulder, hoping the good Ruth would open her eyes and leave demented Ruth in dreamland. Though the beleaguered woman startled at Mary's touch, she woke up and looked at Mary with a clear, rational gaze.

"Did we get another phone call?"

"No. But we need to go back inside the mall."

"Why?"

"I need to look up something in the phone book."

Ten minutes later they sat at an empty desk at the mall security office. With Ruth at her elbow, Mary turned to "Adoption Agencies" in the Yellow Pages. The directory listed fifteen—most in Nashville, with religious affiliations, a few sounding like state-run agencies. Picking up the receiver, she started at the top of the page. The calls went as she had feared; the people she spoke with were kind, concerned, and willing to help, but no one would admit to any recent knowledge of a baby fitting Lily's description. In half an hour she'd worked her way down to the last one on the list.

"Is that all of them?" Ruth sat listening to every call, twisting her shirt into yet another knot.

"One more to go," Mary said. Squinting at the last entry, something called the Tender Shepherd home, she dialed the number. The phone rang once, twice, then someone picked up. Mary heard rustling sounds, as if someone were juggling the receiver, then a high, breathy voice said, *"¡Diga!"*

Mary gasped. "Excuse me?"

"Por favor, llama después." A woman began speaking hurried Spanish, then switched to English. "Please call back later. No one can talk now!" She spoke with great agitation, then the line went dead.

"Holy shit!" cried Mary.

"What?" Ruth's eyes grew wild.

"Somebody at that adoption home speaks Spanish way too close for comfort!"

Quickly Mary rechecked the directory. The Tender Shepherd Home had a Franklin address! Suddenly she felt as if the phone had turned into a slot machine and all the coins were spilling into her hands. Could her wild hunch have actually played out? Stranger things have happened, she reminded herself, remembering that a cop stopped Timothy McVeigh on a traffic violation. Even her own pornographer Dwayne Pugh had originally been ticketed for vending food without a license. She grabbed Ruth by the arm.

"Come on," she said. "We're going to pay the Tender Shepherd Home a call."

39

NOT TOO MANY miles away, three people at the Tender Shepherd Home watched as Bijan Khatar fed his new daughter a bottle. The baby had just begun to suck down the chalky white liquid when, without warning, she spat the rubber nipple from her mouth and vomited all over Bijan's lap.

"What's the matter with her?" Bijan demanded, alarmed.

"Oh, she ate too fast." Edwina threw a linen napkin over her shoulder and scooped up the baby. "She needs to burp."

Laughing, she patted the baby on her back and turned to Kimberly. "Why don't I take care of her and you take care of your husband? There's a powder room tucked in beneath the staircase. Maybe you can help him clean up in there."

"Come on, Bijan." Kimberly took him by the hand

and led him, his dark trousers dotted with curds of milk, to where Mrs. Templeton had directed. As she opened the bathroom door, she noticed Mrs. Templeton's two servants huddling together in the shadowy hall, frowns on both their faces.

"*No se preocupe,*" Kimberly hastened to reassure them. "*Solo un accidente pequeño.*"

The young woman started to reply, but the man grabbed her arm. Nodding obsequiously, he smiled, saying, "*Sí, sí.*"

"What's with those two?" asked Bijan as he dampened a small hand towel.

Kimberly said, "What do you mean?"

"They've been lurking in the foyer the whole time we've been here."

"Lurking?"

"Yeah. Hiding in the shadows, watching. The girl keeps wiping her eyes, like she's crying. The man looks kind of, I don't know, ashamed."

"They must not want Jennifer to leave. They've probably gotten attached to her."

"Attached? In three days?"

Kimberly grinned. "You got attached in about thirty seconds, Mr. Let's-not-get-too-excited-about-this-baby."

"Yeah, I guess you're right," Bijan admitted as he hung up the towel and took his wife in his arms. "I am permanently attached to that little beauty. Just like I'm permanently attached to her mother."

"Oh, Bijan." Laughing, she kissed him, then wiped a rosy vestige of her lipstick from his mouth. "Come on. Let's go hold our daughter again."

Giggling like teenagers, they opened the door to find Mrs. Templeton standing by the front door, holding Jennifer in her arms.

"I might not have mentioned this," she called as the pair emerged from the powder room. "But the State of Tennessee requires that all infants be transported in a car seat. I know you didn't bring one with you, so I'll be happy to loan you one for your trip to the airport. What airline did you say you're on?"

"Delta," replied Kimberly.

"Then just leave it at their counter. I'll have Paz pick it up tomorrow."

"Thank you." Kimberly smiled. "That's very kind."

Mrs. Templeton handed the baby back to Bijan. "I know it seems early, but you three should probably leave now. Airports are crazy these days, and they're always doing construction on the Nashville interstates. I had Ruperta pack this bag for you. All your papers, plus the baby's records, are in here." She held up a white diaper bag embroidered with pink elephants. "You'll get an amended birth certificate from the state of Tennessee in a few weeks. You've also got formula, diapers, baby wipes, a binky, and an extra jumpsuit in case she soils the one she has on."

Mrs. Hatcher chuckled. "That should certainly get us to Fort Lauderdale."

Though Kimberly felt like they were being hustled out the door, she didn't mind. Mrs. Templeton could hustle them to China, for all she cared. They had their amazing, wonderful little daughter. Their family was now complete. That was all that mattered. "I can't tell you how grateful we are," Kimberly said. "You and Mrs. Hatcher have made our dream come true."

Mrs. Templeton smiled. "I'm just glad I was able to help out, dear." She hugged Kimberly, engulfing her in a wave of flowery perfume. "God blessed us with this one. It doesn't often happen this easily." She released Kimberly and nodded at Bijan. "Mr. Khatar, take the new Miss Khatar home to meet your family and friends. I know they'll find her just as enchanting as you."

"Thank you." Bijan knelt down and buckled the baby into the car seat. She seemed recovered from her bout of nausea, and gurgled up at him, her dark eyes once again bright.

"Come on, Jennifer Aziz," he whispered, grinning down at her. "It's time to go home."

Bijan lifted the car seat by its handle, then he gave Kimberly a quick kiss. With a final wave at Edwina Templeton, they buckled their new baby in the back of their rental car and with Mrs. Hatcher in tow, drove away from Tender Shepherd Home, eager to begin their life as a family of three.

"Holy Jesus!" hissed Edwina, watching as the white car disappeared down her driveway. "I thought they'd never leave!" She knew, from the sticky feel of her camisole, that she'd sweated through most of her under- wear, and that if she lifted her arms she would find fra- grant damp circles darkening the pale beige silk of her suit. Illegal adoptions always made her nervous, and with those Arabs and that babbling idiot Hatcher added to the mix, it was a miracle she hadn't jumped right out of her skin. And to top it all off, Ruperta had answered her telephone! She'd heard her wailing in Spanish just as the Khatars were leaving. Why had that moron chosen today, of all days, to break the first rule of her employ- ment?

"Ruperta!" Edwina locked the door and turned around. "Come here!"

She heard a soft scurrying in the hall, as if mice had been listening and were now fleeing her wrath. "Ru- perta!" she bellowed. "Right now!"

"*Sí*, Señora?" Soundlessly the young woman ap- peared in the doorway. Her eyes looked as if she'd been weeping, and she dabbed a wadded-up tissue at her nose.

"Did the phone ring while my guests were here?"

"*Sí*, Señora."

"Did the answering machine take the call?"

Visibly trembling, Ruperta backed up a step. "No, Señora."

"Then who did?"

Ruperta's chin quivered. "I'm sorry, Señora, but I did."

Edwina peered at her with narrowed eyes. "Don't you remember my first rule?"

"*Sí,* Señora. We are never to answer the telephone. But I was so upset about the baby, I just grabbed it without thinking!" Tears seeped from Ruperta's eyes. "She was just so little. And so sweet. And it just isn't fair to take her away—"

"From someone who doesn't want her? I think that's fair, Ruperta. I think that's more than fair." Edwina clenched her jaws together, furious. She expected this sentimental drivel from her teenage clients. She had no use for it in an employee. "Who was on the phone?"

"A woman. She did not say who she was. I told her no one could talk to her now and to please call back later."

"You told her no one could talk to her?" Edwina's outrage grew. What if it was one of the Christmas Tour ladies? What if one of them had called with an invitation to some nice tea or luncheon and Ruperta had rebuffed them with her babbling Spanish and sniveling tears? A fresh wave of anger engulfed Edwina. How dare these Mexicans show up at her house begging for work and then flagrantly disobey a simple rule that had been clearly stated, several different times? She had half a mind to fire both of them, right this very minute.

Edwina waggled her finger at Ruperta. "If I've told you once, I've told you a hundred times, let the answering machine pick up the phone," she said loud enough so Paz could hear. "Now go to your quarters! I don't want to see you until you bring my breakfast tomorrow morning!"

"*Sí*, Señora." Turning, Ruperta fled down the hall, her sobs echoing through the otherwise silent house.

"Jesus H. Christ," Edwina muttered, stomping down the hall to her office. "What a fat lot of trouble for one little bastard child." She should have known that anything connected with Duncan would mean trouble.

She stormed into her office and locked the door behind her. Sitting down at her desk, she began to twist the tumblers of the safe located in the wall behind her desk. As she ran through the familiar combination, her anger began to abate. She'd just made a nice amount of money for not a whole lot of work, and that bed would look amazing once she got it up here from New Orleans. If the lost caller had indeed been one of the Christmas Tour ladies, maybe she would forget about Ruperta's rudeness when she saw what a magnificent home this was. Maybe she would call back often, after that. Maybe they would become friends and have lunch together and one day laugh over the first day she called and a weeping Mexican house girl answered the phone, telling her no one was available to talk to her.

40

❦

MARY AND RUTH pulled into a brightly lit gas station across from the mall, where Mary bought a map of Franklin and left a message on Jane Frey's answering machine, telling her where they were going. Moments later they headed for Tender Shepherd Home for Girls, Mary driving as Ruth sat amazingly calm beside her. Thank God, thought Mary, her heart once again going out to the woman who'd endured so much.

"You don't think Lily might have already been adopted, do you?" Only the slightest tremor in Ruth's voice betrayed her fear.

"I don't know," Mary replied honestly. She didn't want to frighten Ruth, but neither did she want to give her any false hope. "I'm just guessing here, Ruth. Like most leads, it'll probably turn out to be a wild-goose chase."

"That's okay." Ruth spoke with a quiet resignation.

"Until I find Lily, I'll be going on a lot of wild-goose chases."

Aware that no less a fate awaited her, Mary sped down the highway. They drove with the map spread between them, Ruth reading the small print with a tiny flashlight as dusk deepened to darkness. She directed Mary first along a four-lane highway, then down a secondary road thick with commuter traffic. Finally they made a hard right turn at a green street sign that read "Hemlock Lane."

"Okay," Ruth said, peering at the mailboxes as they raced by. "We want three-forty." With every passing mile the landscape grew more rural, and houses became just small dots of light, set far back from the road. Suddenly a large black mailbox appeared around a curve.

"That's it!" Ruth cried. "Three-forty Hemlock Lane!"

Mary skidded into the driveway. They wound through several acres of rolling pastureland, crossed a narrow bridge, then a large white house loomed ahead of them. Columned and two-storied, it looked like it could have once had slaves picking cotton in the back fields.

"This is an adoption home?" Ruth eyed the structure, amazed.

"According to the telephone directory." Mary pulled up at an old hitching post, wondering if they'd truly stumbled onto something. All the adoption homes she'd ever seen were modest, unassuming places. This spread looked as if it could have a sign that read "Alternative Birth Options for the Rich and Famous."

Ruth drained her cup of tea. "So what's our plan?"

Mary gazed up at the house. No lights shone from any of the windows, and though it was just past six P.M., the whole place had a two-in-the-morning look about it—dark and silent and still. Wishing again that she'd been able to talk to Jane Frey in person, she turned to Ruth. "I'm going up there and find out as much as I can about what goes on here. I want you to stay in the truck."

"Stay in the truck?" The calmness left Ruth's voice. "Do you actually think I'm going to sit out here in this truck while you go search for my child?"

Again Mary's heart ached for the woman who had, for the last four days, been riding the lead car on the emotional roller coaster from hell. "I'm not sure what we might be walking into here, Ruth. And you haven't been totally yourself lately."

"You wouldn't be totally yourself either, if you'd lost your baby." Ruth's anger flared like a match. She unbuckled her seatbelt and grabbed her purse. "I'm not staying out here. Not if there's the slightest chance anybody in that house could have seen Lily."

Mary didn't know how to respond. If rational Ruth remained, they would have no problems. But if the Ruth who'd dumped her cousin on the interstate came back, she could easily blow whatever chance they might have of finding anything out. Nonetheless, she couldn't think of any way she could forbid the woman to leave her own truck.

"Okay." Reluctantly, Mary agreed. "But you've got to keep your mouth shut and let me do all the talking. You just look and listen."

"To what?"

"To everything. Try to remember every detail about whoever answers the door. Every detail about what they say. If we get inside, look around the house and see if everything squares with what they're saying."

Ruth gave a sardonic laugh. "So I'm to play Watson to your Holmes?"

"You got it," Mary said firmly.

"Terrific," muttered Ruth.

They got out of the truck, Mary again taking comfort in the fact that she still carried Gabe's gun. If they were indeed walking into a black market baby operation, things could get dicey, fast. A 9mm Glock had a nice way of calming the waters. She crossed in front of the truck and walked up the steps to the house, Ruth firmly in step beside her.

At the front door, Mary twisted an old-fashioned bell. The raspy sound reverberated through the house, but elicited no response. Ruth twisted it again, making it clear that they would not be ignored.

Once more, they waited. Mary started to turn the bell a third time when suddenly the whole house erupted in light. Porch lights, driveway lights, even a dazzling chandelier inside, all glittered to life. Blinking, Mary held her breath as locks turned and the door swung open.

A woman stood there. She had impossible auburn hair for someone her age, and wore it pulled back in a bun at the nape of her neck. Her lips looked as if smiling might entail some heavy lifting, and she was clad in a too-small beige suit accessorized with diamonds—two at her ears, a flashy solitaire on her right hand.

"May I help you?" The woman spoke as if she'd just bitten a lemon.

"Sorry to disturb you," Mary began, reaching in her purse for her IDs. "But we're with Deckard County Justice. We have information that a woman of Hispanic descent is working here." She flashed her IDs quickly in front of the woman's eyes, hoping she wouldn't notice that Deckard County was in Georgia and that her function in the Justice Department was assistant district attorney rather than cop. "May we come in?"

Without waiting for the woman to answer, she stepped into the dazzlingly bright foyer, Ruth at her heels. Inside, the house looked more like a showcase for an indulgent designer rather than a refuge for pregnant girls. A red oriental runner carpeted the wide staircase and an elegant Chippendale lowboy stood by the door.

To the right, Mary stared into a living room that could have served as the cover of *Architectural Digest*.

The woman's expression soured further as she was forced to close the door behind them. "I'm sorry, what county did you say you were from?"

"Deckard," Mary said briskly, trying to imitate the fast, aggressive questioning style of the Deckard County detectives. "We're looking for a girl who may have some immigration problems. Have you got any Latinos working here?"

The woman looked at both of them so long, Mary wondered if she wasn't going to ask to see her IDs again. Finally she answered the question, spitting out her words as if they were carpet tacks. "Two Mexicans."

"What are their names?"

"Paz and Ruperta Gonzalez." The woman gave up her employees without as much as an eye blink. "Paz takes care of the farm, Ruperta does housework and helps me with my girls."

"Your girls?"

"This is an adoption home, Detective—"

"Crow," Mary said, aware that she was breaking every code of ethics applicable to officers of the court. If this woman grew at all suspicious and pressed the case, it could easily result in her being disbarred. "Mary Crow. And you are?"

"Edwina Templeton. May I ask what kind of immigration trouble Ruperta's in?"

"A possible green card violation," Mary answered vaguely, aware of Ruth standing with increasing impatience beside her. "Is there any chance we might speak with her?"

"I'm afraid I gave them the night off just moments before you arrived." The woman gave a polite laugh. "I'm not sure if they're here or not."

"Oh, come on," said Ruth.

"Would you mind calling this Ruperta?" Mary over-rode Ruth firmly. "If we don't get this straightened out, INS will."

The woman pursed her lips tighter, but nodded for them to follow her into the splendid parlor, where she picked up and tinkled a small silver bell. "If she's here, that will bring her."

"Got her well trained, huh?" said Ruth, the manic gleam returning to her eyes.

Mary shot Ruth a warning look, then glanced around the ornate room. "You have anybody else working here, Mrs. Templeton?"

"A security man, but he's American. He's away, too, on personal leave."

"Any babies upstairs, waiting for new parents?" asked Ruth acidly as Mary gave an inward groan.

Edwina Templeton looked at Ruth and measured each word of her response as if it were gold. "No. My last adoption was six weeks ago." She rang the bell a second time. This time they waited in an icy silence, but no one answered the summons.

"I guess they've gone for the evening," Mrs. Templeton said, walking back toward the front door. "You'll have to come back tomorrow."

"I don't suppose you would show us Ruperta's room?" Mary pressed her luck, knowing she was taking a chance with Ruth's acerbic wisecracks.

"Don't you need a warrant to search my home?"

Mary gave her best cop smile. "If you'd prefer to do it that way, I can come back with one."

Again Templeton hesitated, as if deciding between the lesser of two evils—having her house searched now, in the dark of night, or tomorrow, when her friends and neighbors might drive up to see. Finally she made her choice.

"Not at all," she said, her eyes glittering like a cornered rat's. "Come this way."

She led them briskly down a long hall furnished just as elegantly as the living room, with another oriental runner and a tall case clock tocking away the hours. At the end of the hall they turned right and crossed a high-ceilinged kitchen, finally stopping at a closed door. With a smug nod at Mary, she knocked on the door.

"Ruperta? Paz? Open the door. Someone wants to see you."

No answer. Templeton knocked again, this time louder. "Paz! Ruperta! *Abra la puerta!*"

Again, no response. Edwina tried the knob. The door opened easily to reveal a small, neatly kept room. Though it held a bed covered in a bright patchwork quilt, a chest of drawers, and a small TV, it stood empty of its occupants. Just to make sure, Mary crossed the room and peeked into an equally empty bathroom.

"They aren't here," Edwina Templeton said, sounding surprised. "I wonder where they went?"

"Hard to tell," said Mary, exchanging a glance with Ruth. "People like that could be anywhere."

With no illegal aliens to be found, Edwina Templeton escorted them snappily out of Ruperta's room and back into the foyer. "Anything else I can help you with tonight?" she asked, opening the front door with a grand, exaggerated swoop.

Mary shook her head. "Please don't mention our visit to your employees. These people have a way of disappearing when they get wind of us."

"I understand completely. Good night." Edwina Templeton gave a tight smile as they stepped through the door, then she closed it with a resounding slam. An instant later, every light in the house went out just as quickly as they'd come on. Once again they stood in darkness.

"What the hell?" said Ruth.

"Come on," Mary whispered, her anger at Ruth forgotten. "We need to get out of here."

"Why?"

"Because Edwina Templeton was lying."

"What do you mean?" Ruth hurried after Mary, trying not to stumble down the stairs.

"There was a half-empty bottle of formula beside the living room sofa. If her last adoption was six weeks ago, why was that there?" She reached in her pocket for her cell phone. "We need to call Jane Frey, and we need to call her now!"

"It's much too late for that, Señorita," came a husky voice from the shadows as she felt a rough hand grab her shoulder. "It's too late for anything like that at all."

41

MARY SWUNG AROUND. A Latino couple stood in the shadows, ghost-like in the darkness. A small man who looked remarkably like the drawing of Joe Little Bear gripped Mary's shoulder while an equally petite woman stared at Ruth, her eyes big as an owl's.

"Take your hands off me," Mary snarled, hoping she sounded more threatening than she felt.

The man loosened his grasp. "We know where your baby is."

"You what?" Ruth lunged forward and grabbed the little man as if she might shake the words out of him.

"She got adopted," Joe Little Bear gasped, his forehead glistening with sweat. "Just a few hours ago."

"Adopted?" cried Ruth. "Who adopted her? And how do you know it was my baby who was adopted?"

"We saw you at the *manifestación*," the man explained breathlessly, "We hid in the bushes and watched

you leave your baby in the care of a young woman. You
told her to play music so the baby would not cry."

"You son of a bitch!" Ruth screeched.

Mary grabbed Ruth. The man's companion started
speaking Spanish, too rapidly for Mary to understand.
She did notice, however, that beneath the woman's
denim jacket, a crucifix dangled from her neck and
small turquoise earrings studded her ears. Finally Joe
Little Bear *shushed* her, and keeping well away from
Ruth, began talking to Mary.

"We need to leave here, Señorita. *Pronto!*" he said,
his gaze darting between her face and Ruth's. "If you
will take us with you, we will help you find your baby. I
swear it upon my mother's grave."

"But you took my baby in the first place!" cried Ruth.

As Joe Little Bear tried to formulate a response, the
woman stepped forward, her hands clasped in supplication.

"*Por favor*, Señoritas. It is not as it seems. We are not
secuestradors. Just let us come with you, and we will
explain."

Mary looked at the pair. Though they gave a good im-
pression of people in desperate trouble, she couldn't help
but wonder if they were true Latinos at all, or just ethnic-
looking con artists milking a lift. Both seemed suspiciously anxious to talk about the child they'd stolen.

"Señoritas, I beg you," the woman pleaded again.
"We must leave now. Men—bad men—are chasing us.
We have no more time!"

"Okay," Mary agreed, against her better judgment.
"But once we get inside that truck, you've got one
minute to tell us where the baby is."

"*Gracias,* Señorita. You will not regret this."

"You might, though," Ruth warned, her mouth a
snarl. "Because if you're lying, those bad men chasing
you are going to be the least of your worries."

The man introduced himself as Paz Gonzalez, the woman as his wife, Ruperta.

"Where's my baby? Why did you steal her?" Ruth faced backward, leaning against the dashboard, glaring at the two while Mary drove back to the more public area of the shopping mall.

"We work for Señora Templeton. Young girls who are *encinta* with no husbands come to her house. She finds their babies good homes."

"Lily had a good home."

"*Sí,* Señorita. But another man wanted your baby. He too works for Señora Templeton, as a guard. His name is Duncan, but we call him Gordo—the fat one. He has a limp, eats candy all the time."

Mary gasped, dumbfounded. Edwina Templeton's security guard! It was Logan! She listened as the man continued.

"Last week, Señora Templeton asked us to go with Gordo to pick up a baby. He told us the child was his, but Ruperta and I did not think so."

Ruperta began to cry again; Paz shushed her. "We drove to a campground far away, in Señora Templeton's van. Gordo told me he would turn us over to the cops if I didn't help him. He told me what to say and drove me to your campsite." Paz lowered his eyes in deference to Ruth. "The woman who tended your baby was with a man. She gave her . . . willingly."

Ruth's lips curled. "That was my former cousin," she said. "Go on."

The man shrugged. "After she gave me the baby, I walked back to the van and we drove away. Nobody said a word."

"*Dile lo demás!*" wailed Ruperta.

"I'm telling her, Ruperta! After we took the baby, Gordo began to do crazy things. He drove us to grave-yards, took pictures of the baby. We drove around and he took more pictures, of us holding the baby, as if she belonged to us."

"Like at the mall?" asked Ruth bitterly.

"*Sí,*" Paz replied, shamefaced. "But we took good care of your little one the whole time," he added softly. "Twice Gordo came close to killing her, but Ruperta talked him out of it."

"So where is Lily now?" asked Mary.

"A rich young couple came and adopted her this afternoon. They paid a lot of money for her, I think."

"What was their name?"

"I never heard their names, Señorita. The wife was a pretty blond Anglo. Ruperta thinks the husband was Arab."

"Oh, my God!" Ruth looked at Mary, panicked. "An Arab! What if they've taken her to Saudi Arabia? Or Iran? Once they take children over there, you can never get them back!"

"Hang on, Ruth. Let's hear the rest of the story." Mary asked Paz, "Do you know where they went? Did they live near here?"

Paz shook his head. "I listened when they called to change their airplane reservations. They asked for a flight to Fort Lauderdale, Florida."

"What time was that flight leaving?" asked Mary.

"I think they said seven."

Mary glanced at her watch. It was seven twenty-two. The flicker of hope she was beginning to feel died. If these two were telling the truth, the couple who'd adopted Lily were probably on their way to Florida. The jurisdictional squabbles involved in finding a North Carolina baby who was illegally adopted in Tennessee and then relocated to Florida would be a nightmare. Florida courts were notoriously erratic in their dispensation of child custody disputes, and Lily's affluent new parents would surely fight any action every step of the way. It wasn't quite Saudi Arabia, but Ruth's panic was justified. Lily could well be grown before her real parents ever saw her again.

Blinking away her own tears of frustration, Mary chanced one last question. "Do you know what airline they were on?"

"Pardon?" Paz frowned.

"Do you remember what airline they called?"

Paz put a protective arm around his wife. "I'm supposed to pick up Señora Templeton's car seat tomorrow morning at the Delta counter."

Delta! The airline that served the South! *The airline that routed nearly half its flights through Atlanta!* If this flight was like most Delta flights that originated south of Cincinnati, the couple who'd adopted Lily were probably at Hartsfield right now, bouncing their new baby girl and waiting to board the next plane to Florida.

She pulled off the road and screeched to a stop, throwing Ruth and the Mexicans hard against the dashboard. If she could get in touch with Danika before that plane took off, she might be able to stop the couple who adopted Lily before they reached Florida. If she could keep just them in Atlanta, they might be able to sort everything out! Grabbing her cell phone, she punched in Danika's number, knowing that this might well be their last chance to get Lily Walkingstick back home.

At that same moment, Danika Lyles was enduring yet another poke in her breast from her boss, Hobson T. Mott. As opposing centers in a pickup basketball game, Danika and Mott had battled each other for the better part of an hour. Danika was taller and faster, but not as strong. Hobson was a moderately good shot, playing the way a lot of men played against women, trying to intimidate them with bulk, then sneakily copping feels of their breasts and asses, all in the name of sport. Though Danika had long accepted it as the price of playing with

boys, tonight Mott's constant mauling of her left breast
was getting old. In the first place, it hurt. In the second
place, she loathed Hobson T. Mott. Never would she
forgive him for firing Mary Crow.

"This time, you're mine, boss man," she murmured,
loping into position as Mott's team brought the ball
down court. Hobson stood at the top of the key, waiting
for the pass. She stood in front of him, her long, spider-
like arms ruthlessly effective at keeping the ball away
from him. He rubbed up against her backside, his hand
on her ass. She moved up; he followed. The point guard
dribbled back and forth, ignoring Hobson, looking for
an opening under the basket. Suddenly he threw cross-
court, a line-drive that she could almost reach. She
leaped. Hobson leaped too, but too late. She grabbed
the ball and pulled it in, coming down with elbows out.
Immediately she pivoted on her left foot. She felt her elbow crack against some kind of bone, then watched as
Hobson crumpled to the floor, clutching his jaw.

"Sorry, Mr. Mott," she gushed as she began to dribble away. "Guess I forgot you were there."

As the horn sounded for the dazed Mott to leave the
court, Danika stood with her face lowered, trying to
hide her grin. She was still gazing at the midcourt line
when the cell phone that she kept stashed in her sock
rang. Tossing the ball to her point guard, she dug the little phone out and answered the call.

"Danika Lyles."

"Danika?" The voice was hard to hear in the cav-
ernous gym.

"Mary?" Danika frantically motioned her substitute
into the game as she hurried off the court, holding the
phone tight against her ear. She'd been desperate to talk
to Mary all day, but she'd only been able to reach
Mary's voice mail. "Girlfriend, what's going on? Have
you found that baby?"

"That's what I'm calling about, Danika."

Five minutes later Danika had the particulars. "A racially mixed couple with a baby traveling to Fort Lauderdale on Delta," she repeated back to Mary. "Any names? Flight numbers? ETAs?"

"Nope."

"How am I supposed to stop them? You gotta have a name to get a warrant."

"Call Hartsfield Airport Security as soon as we get off the phone. Call Diane Hart, the ADA in Clayton County. Tell them these people are suspects in an ongoing kidnapping investigation in Nikwase County, Tennessee."

"Okay." Danika scribbled notes on the back of a chewing gum wrapper. "Anything else?"

"I want you out there, too, Danika. Get a squad car. Tell whoever's driving that you needed to be there ten minutes ago."

"Where are you now?

"South of Nashville. I'm leaving right this minute. I'll meet you there in about five hours."

Danika switched off her phone. Collecting her gym bag, she hurried to the dressing room, ignoring the taunting, curled-finger summons from Mott to reenter the game.

"No more, you sorry-ass white boy," she muttered. "Tonight I'm working for Mary Crow."

In the locker room she placed a call to Security at Hartsfield. She was routed to one Arthur Stewart, a man who shot his words out like he was cracking a whip. She explained the situation as she tore off her gym clothes; she could almost see him salivating with excitement.

"Multiracial kidnappers?" Stewart's voice quavered. "Flying to Fort Lauderdale?"

"We think they're on Delta." Danika struggled to pull her trousers on. "But let me stress that they may not be the perpetrators of this crime. This couple could well be victims, too."

"What sort of racial mix are we talking here?"

"Our information indicates that the woman is white. The man is of Middle Eastern descent."

"Jesus! An Arab using a white girl for cover! You think they might be carrying explosives?"

Danika closed her eyes. Why, during the one chance she had to shine for the great Mary Crow, did she get stuck talking to a moron? "No, Mr. Stewart," she said forcefully, trying to put on her blouse and hang on to the cell phone at the same time. "We *do not* suspect them of any kind of terrorist activity. At this moment, we don't know if they're guilty of anything. We just want to keep them from going to Florida until we can get everything straightened out."

"I've heard they strap bombs to their babies' backs," Stewart continued to rave. "Don't even respect the lives of their own children as long as they can murder good Christians."

Danika envisioned foam frothing from Stewart's mouth. This idiot sounded ready to shut down the airport and shoot Mary's couple dead as they boarded their plane. "Mr. Stewart, could I speak to your superior?"

"I'm the officer in charge right now," Stewart replied, full of self-importance.

"Then please remember, sir, that all Deckard County is asking is that you detain these people until we get there. They have a three-month-old infant with them. You absolutely must *not* use excessive force."

"I'll be the judge of how much force to use, lady," Stewart growled. "I've got the second busiest airport in the country to protect. Up against that, your little A-rab baby doesn't mean squat."

"I'm leaving right now, Mr. Stewart." Danika tucked her pumps under her arm and ran out of the dressing room barefoot. "I'll see you in twenty minutes."

"It should be all over but the shouting by then," Stewart promised.

Dear God, prayed Danika, sprinting for the door. *Let that idiot shout all he wants, just don't let him hurt that child.*

42

MARY RACED BACK to the interstate highway that would lead them to Atlanta. If Danika could indeed stop this couple at Hartsfield, she would need several things from Ruth and she would need them fast—DNA tests, birth certificates, an incredibly detailed statement for the police. First, though, they had to get there, to see if the child in question even was Lily. As she sped along the dimly lit roads, she found her attitude toward the Gonzalezes softening as they revealed more about their troubles in Tennessee. Not only had Logan coerced them into snatching Lily, but they also claimed they were being stalked by members of a gang they called the Scorpions.

"That is why we agreed to go with Gordo in the first place," explained Paz. "The Scorpions were going to pour acid in Ruperta's eyes."

"Acid in her eyes?" Ruth shuddered. "Why?"

"To punish me. They think I stole drug money from them."

"Did you?" Mary asked.

"No, Señorita. They blame me for something Jorge Menendez did." Paz crossed himself. "They are true devils, spawn of the evil one himself."

Mary looked at the pair squeezed against the door. The man sat trembling, pathetic with fear, while the woman's eyes brimmed with tears. *If they're conning us, they're doing a hell of a job*, she decided with growing sympathy.

They finally reached the Cool Springs mall. Mary turned into the same high tech gas station where they'd bought their map and screeched up to one of the pumps. She turned to Ruth.

"Go in and get whatever you need to go to Atlanta. Food, Cokes, hot water for tea. I'll fill the tank. Once we get on the highway, I don't want to make any stops."

"What about them?" Ruth gestured at the pair crouched beside the door.

"I'll watch them," said Mary. "Hurry, Ruth. We can't waste any time."

Ruth ran into the gas station. Mary walked to the rear of the truck, zipped her credit card through the scanner, and started filling the tank. It had been an amazing night; her wild hunch had paid off big-time. If the couple who now huddled in the truck were telling the truth, they might be within hours of finding Lily.

Shrugging to release the tension from her neck, Mary leaned against the truck and watched the orange numbers of the pump. Tonight everybody had a devil nipping at their heels. For this couple, it was a Mexican drug gang; for her, it was Stump Logan. It seemed that whatever they did, however far they might run, their respective demons were always just half a step behind, their breath icy on the back of their necks. She sighed. Even if they did manage to rescue Lily tonight, Logan

would simply come at her again, through something else
or somebody else she loved, farther down the line.

She felt the truck wiggle. Logan's accomplices, no
doubt, moving around inside the cab. She knew she
should keep an eye on them, turn the pair over to Jane
Frey. But for some reason, she felt a kind of kinship with
the pair inside the truck. Though they were far from innocent, her instincts told her that their crime against
Lily had been born of circumstance rather than malice.
Everything they'd said about Logan rang with total
veracity, and their story of the Scorpions squared with
all she knew about Hispanic gangs. Some very bad men
probably did intend to dribble acid in the woman's eyes.
The image sent a shiver down her spine. Suddenly the
truck gave another, bigger bounce and she heard footsteps pattering across the concrete. Though she knew
exactly what was happening, she kept her eyes focused
on the gas pump.

"Since you came clean about Lily, you two get a free
pass tonight," she whispered softly. "Tomorrow, I will
not be so kind."

The pump switched off. Mary grabbed her receipt
and walked back to the driver's seat. Unsurprisingly, the
cab was empty. The Gonzalezes had taken their fate into
their own hands. As she stared into the shadowy darkness surrounding the gas station, she realized it was time
for her to do the same. Punching a number on her cell
phone, she fished in her purse for the small notepad she
carried and began jotting down numbers while she
waited for her call to connect. A moment later Ruth appeared at her elbow, thermos in hand.

"Are you ready? I've got some tea brewing, and I
bought us some snacks."

"We're good to go," replied Mary, moving aside so
Ruth could climb into the driver's seat.

Ruth stopped with one foot inside the cab.

77

"Where are Paz and what's-her-name?"

"They're gone," said Mary. "I let them go."

"Let them go?" Ruth's eyes widened in horror. "Are you crazy? They were the only leads we had to Lily!"

"Forget them, Ruth. Anything they can tell us, Edwina Templeton can tell us better." Mary clicked off her phone and handed Ruth the notepad she'd been scribbling on. "Listen carefully. I just called Danika Lyles, the ADA who's trying to stop Lily at Hartsfield. She doesn't answer her phone, so let's assume she's in the middle of something she can't break away from. If she does find Lily, I don't imagine her adoptive parents will give her up without a fight, so here are some numbers you'll need. You can stay at my house—there's a key under the big stone in the peony bed."

Ruth blinked, stunned. "Wait a minute. Aren't we going together?"

Mary shook her head. "I'm staying here."

"But why?"

"Because Stump Logan isn't going to quit just because we might have figured out where Lily is. He'll just come after me again, through some other innocent person I love, somewhere further down the road."

"But why not come to Atlanta with me, and then come back here with the cops?" Ruth looked as if she might cry.

"Logan's too clever, Ruth. He'd just go underground again. I need to end this now, tonight. I don't want to live the rest of my life looking over my shoulder, wondering when he's going to show up."

"But—"

Mary reached out and wrapped her arms around Ruth, holding her tight. "You go. Hurry to Hartsfield. I've got a real strong feeling that you're going to see Lily very soon."

"Are you sure?" Ruth's voice was choked with tears.

"Positive. Now get going! Just follow the signs, once

you get to Atlanta. The road's clearly marked." Mary released her friend. Ruth climbed into the truck, started the engine, and with a small, sad wave, left Mary standing alone in the night.

"Yank-ee Doodle went to town, riding on a po-ny; Da da dum dum da da dum dee da-da macaroni."

Bijan Khatar glanced around, hoping no adult was listening to him. Since he had spent the first decade of his life in Iran, his knowledge of American folk songs was sketchy, at best. He could sing most of the first lines, but the rest of the lyrics often eluded him, American enunciation being what it was. Though he'd finally figured out that the lyrics to "Jingle Bells" were not "dashing through the snow, with one whore, soap and sleigh," he'd thought he'd soon better ask Kimberly exactly who Yankee Doodle had been, and what Mr. Dandy had to do with pasta.

"We'll find out together, Jennifer Aziz." He grinned down at the little girl in his arms. She'd slept through most of the three-hour layover they'd had in Atlanta. Slept while he and Kimberly had taken turns holding her, slept through their discussion over what school she should attend, slept through whether she would grow up to sing at the Metropolitan Opera or captain the U.S. women's soccer team. Now the little diva-jock had woken up and Kimberly had fallen asleep, no doubt exhausted by all the possibilities that existed for their new baby girl.

"It's just you and me, kiddo," Bijan said as the child gave a mighty yawn. "You and your *Baba*."

Baba. The Persian word for Daddy. It sounded strange to his ears—an appellation meant for his father, rather than himself. He had never had any responsibilities for anyone other than Kimberly. Yet now, as of this afternoon, he did. The little girl who was waking up in his arms was his. For the next twenty years it would be his duty to keep her dry and well fed, safe and warm. Her *Baba*. Him.

He flexed the muscles in his shoulders, feeling both pride and terror. *My God,* he thought, gazing into the luminous brown eyes that looked up at him as if there were no one else on earth. *She is so tiny.* He'd never realized human beings started out so small. As he watched, her mouth curled down and her feathery little brows began to furrow. Suddenly he realized she was about to cry.

"No, no, no," he cooed, jumping up and jiggling her in his arms. "Let's not wake Mommy up. She's so tired."

And yet he almost hoped Kimberly would wake up. He wasn't quite sure of the protocol of babies. Did you change their diapers first and then feed them? That seemed odd, but the reverse seemed disgusting—who would want to eat their supper wearing wet underwear? Besides, he didn't think he could change a diaper here in the terminal. There wasn't much space and he needed room to maneuver—to see what went where, and how it all fastened together.

Nuts, he thought as Jennifer Aziz grew more fidgety in his arms. Just hours into this and you're already goofing it up. Some *Baba* you are.

He glanced around the waiting area, hoping they would announce their flight. Their plane from Nashville had arrived on time, but the connecting flight to Florida had been delayed. For hours, Delta agents had chatted away behind their desk, oblivious to the weary travelers waiting to fly south.

Shifting the baby gingerly to his shoulder, he turned toward the food court. If he could keep Jennifer Aziz from squalling for the next few minutes, Kimberly could get in a few more winks of sleep before a diaper change became critical. With the little girl warm against his cheek, he strolled past a newsstand, a Sbarro pizza, a man who would put a shine on your shoes for five dollars. People hurrying to other planes looked at him with hostile eyes, giving him the cold, distrustful stare he'd grown accustomed to since September 11. Suspicious looks, slurs directed at him in restaurants, once a strip-search in the Pittsburgh airport, he'd still had it easier than many of his Iraqi friends. In the heartland of America, anybody who looked even vaguely Semitic was a terrorist until proven otherwise. He smiled bitterly. He hoped Jennifer Aziz would have an easier time of it, but with a name like Khatar . . .

Sighing, he wandered toward the bar. Three businessmen were nursing drinks, idly watching Peyton Manning pick apart the Washington Redskin defense. He started to go in and order a beer, but as he stepped into the dimly lit space, he stopped. Somehow it didn't seem like the thing to do. He wanted his daughter's first solo excursion with her *Baba* to be church or the beach or even Disney World—not some lousy airport bar where men anesthetized themselves against the rigors of travel with overpriced drinks and endless replays on ESPN. With a small kiss on her ear, he turned and headed back out into the terminal.

They strolled over to their gate. He could see that Kimberly had woken up and was looking for him. He quickened his pace.

"Hi," he called.

"Where have you been? I was about to get worried. They're starting to board the plane."

"Really?" He looked at the counter, where the attendants were beginning to check the first-class passengers through. "I didn't hear them announce anything. Jennifer Aziz seemed restless, so I took her for a walk."

"Is she hungry?" asked Kimberly. "Has she cried?"

"No. I think she might need her diaper changed, though."

"Then let me have her. I'll change her and then we can get on the plane."

He handed his new daughter to his wife and watched as she carried her into the ladies' restroom. A few moments later they returned.

"There!" Kimberly said, smiling at him. "All fresh and clean. Now you can go back to your *Baba*!"

Bijan grinned. As Jennifer nestled down in his arms, Mrs. Hatcher came trundling over from the souvenir shop.

"How's it going, Mommy and Daddy?" she called loudly.

"Fine, Mrs. Hatcher," said Kimberly. "I think they're about to call us onboard. Have you got your pass?"

"Oh, yes." Mrs. Hatcher waved her card. "Right here."

"Good. Then let's go."

Hoisting the pink elephant diaper bag over her shoulder, Kimberly took Bijan's arm. "You and Jennifer just look so perfect together," she murmured as they walked to the gate. "We are the luckiest people in the world."

Bijan held his daughter tighter as Kimberly handed the diaper bag over for the gate attendant to search. As he breathed in her sweet baby smell, a feeling of utter happiness came over him. He had a wife who loved him and a beautiful new daughter whose eyes reflected the stars. Kimberly was right. Tonight they were the luckiest people in the world.

43

MARY STOOD AT the gas pump, watching the taillights on Ruth's truck grow smaller, wondering if she hadn't gone off the same deep end as Ruth had. She'd just allowed two possible felons to go free, and was sending an emotionally unstable woman on a five-hour drive on the outside chance she might find her baby. Even the greenest cop would groan at such ineptitude, but she figured the prospect of finding Lily would pull Ruth along like a homing beam, and the Mexicans were much like her—creatures who'd simply gotten caught in the web spun by Stump Logan.

"I hope to hell you've figured right, kiddo," she told herself, pulling out her cell phone. She needed to get in touch with Jane Frey.

A black van pulled up to the gas pump. A teenage boy in an orange jacket descended from the driver's seat, giving Mary an odd look. She supposed she did look strange, standing at a gas bay without a vehicle to fill, but she didn't care. Curiously, she felt safe outside—able to see everything around her and run, should the need arise. Inside, in the claustrophobic aisles of the gas station convenience store, Logan could sneak up on her, leaving her no way of escape.

She turned her back to the gas-pumping boy and punched in Jane Frey's number. This time Jane answered immediately. Mary asked if she'd had any luck finding Lily in Margaritaville, and smiled when Jane, unsurprisingly, said no.

"That's because its highly likely she's in Atlanta," said Mary.

"What do you mean?"

Mary filled her in on the Tender Shepherd Home, Edwina Templeton, and the pair of Mexicans who'd so willingly admitted their complicity.

"So where are the Mexicans now?" asked Jane.

"I'm not sure," Mary replied. "But they aren't important. Right now, I need your help. I want to set a trap for the man who started all this."

"You must be kidding."

"No, listen . . ."

"I am listening. I've no doubt you're hell on wheels in a Georgia courtroom, Ms. Crow. But this is Tennessee, and you are not a cop."

"But—"

"End of story. It's absolutely out of the question. You stay right where you are. I'm coming to get you. I'll be there in ten minutes." Jane clicked off, letting Mary know that as far as she was concerned, setting a trap for Logan was not an option.

Mary frowned. Now she would have to wait and talk Jane into this in person. Wary, she looked around. It was not the busiest of nights. Three pumps over, a tall, professorial-looking man was gassing up a Miata just like hers. Inside the station, the clerk watched a small television behind the counter. She saw nothing in the scraggly underbrush into which the Mexicans had fled. Nothing out of the ordinary at all except her—the lone car-less woman making phone calls at the pump.

She clicked on her phone and dialed the number of Vanderbilt Hospital. The phone started to connect when a flurry of static assailed her ears. She glanced behind her. Another van had just pulled up to the pump, this one white.

He must be interrupting my signal, she thought, moving a few feet away. Again she waited anxiously for Gabe to answer. How good it would be to hear his voice! She had so much she wanted to say, but as the phone began to ring, she felt a sharp sting on the side of her neck. Assuming it was some gnat or fly, she tried to brush the thing away, but instead, she was suddenly engulfed by a huge wave of weakness, as if every muscle in her body had turned to jelly. The phone slipped from her fingers as her knees collapsed. She dropped to the ground, the left side of her face landing in a shallow puddle of black motor oil. She tried to move both her arms and legs, but her muscles would not respond. Her mind reeled, frantic to regain control of her body, wondering if she'd had some kind of stroke. All at once, two boots appeared in front of her eyes.

"Hey, Mary," came the same deep voice who'd called her at the mall. "Glad we could finally get together."

She tried to speak, but her tongue would not move. She felt hands patting her down, lifting her purse from her shoulder, then arms hoisting her up, carrying her somewhere. She heard a door slide open, then she smelled a sour, stale odor as she was dropped on what felt like a plastic tarp. Suddenly she saw a face, one eye drooping, greasy, unkempt whiskers covering cheeks and chin.

"You know, it's never a good idea to hang around gas stations at night." Logan's breath was cloying and intimate on her face. "You never know what kind of trouble you might get into."

Desperately she tried to move, an arm, a leg, *an eyelash*, but her body would not respond. What had he done to her? Why couldn't she move? She watched, helpless, as Logan withdrew a plastic sandwich bag from his back pocket. Grinning, he opened the little bag and removed a white square of cloth no bigger than a deck of cards.

"This won't hurt a bit, Mary," he said, and clamped the cloth over her nose.

She tried to scream, then to hold her breath, but it was impossible. Soon she sucked in a noseful of air that smelled like fermenting pears. She held that breath until her eyes began to water, then she had to breathe again. With that breath the world began to spin. Then her third breath came easier, and with her last breath she felt as if she were dreaming, running down an endless hall on legs of air, with Logan's words reverberating in her ears.

"Just like I said before, Mary. You're as dumb a fuck as your dad."

Miles to the east, in Nikwase County, Tennessee, Jonathan Walkingstick also dreamed of running. In reality, he was walking, an endless circuit of his cell, ten strides down, four strides across, then repeating the process to the point that he'd driven his cell mate into a frenzy. As Jonathan crossed the top end of the grim little enclosure, Happy Lavalais bolted up on his cot and looked at Jonathan, wild-eyed. "So what is it with you, eh? You gonna walk all night and drive everybody crazy?"

"Everybody's only you, Lavalais," Jonathan replied. "And you're crazy already."

"So? Crazy people need sleep, too," Lavalais shot back. "Or else they grow crazier."

Jonathan snorted. He could tell Lavalais a lot about what drove people crazy, and it sure wasn't losing your eight hours of sack time. "Roll over, Lavalais. Put that pillow over your face and breathe deep."

"Fuck you," Lavalais muttered, flopping back down on his cot.

He wasn't intentionally trying to drive Lavalais nuts. He'd tried to sleep, last night, after Ruth left. Lay down on his cot, pulled the scratchy wool blanket over his shoulders, but every time he closed his eyes all he could see was Lily, in those pictures. The thought of someone stripping her naked and leaving her crying at a gravestone sent such a rage through him that he'd gotten up and started ramming his cot against the cell door. His third blow sent plaster dusting down from the ceiling; his fourth blow turned his cot to kindling; the next blow brought in his old buddies, Deputies Jenkins and Green. A few minutes later his cot was gone and he was lying in the corner, clutching two of the teeth they'd knocked from his jaw.

His fury, though, had raged on unabated. When he could get up without seeing double, he'd risen to his feet and started to walk. Up one side of the cell, down the other, stepping over Lavalais. Around and around. Every time he stopped, he felt that crazy rage start boiling through his veins all over again, so he'd continued his pacing. Though it got him no closer to Lily, at least it kept him marginally sane.

It had been twenty-four hours since he'd said goodbye to Ruth. He'd heard nothing from her or the lawyer she was supposed to have called. His only news came from Mrs. McClellan, the lady who brought their meals. She'd said Dula was still working on the case, but had nothing to report. He turned at one corner of the cell and began his miserable march to the other end. *Dear God*, he wondered. *How could everything have gone so wrong?*

His route took him toward Lavalais now, his tread as regular as the beat of a clock. Just as he reached the man's cot, Lavalais leapt to his feet.

"I tell you to quit walking, you crazy bastard!" Lavalais screamed, grabbing him by his collar. "You are like an animal in a cage!"

"Get your hands off me." Staring into Lavalais' bloodshot eyes, Jonathan shoved him backward. The angry Jamaican staggered, and fell against his cot. It wobbled, then broke under his weight, making a loud, splintering crash.

"You son of a bitch! You broke my bed!" Lavalais snarled, picking up one dismembered leg of the cot and swinging it at Jonathan's shin. When Jonathan kicked it from his hand, Lavalais threw himself at Jonathan's knees. Both men grappled on the floor, grunting and cursing.

They fought their way to the middle of the cell before a door opened and lights came on. Jonathan looked up to see Green and Jenkins standing there, grinning.

"Lookee there," said Green. "Rolling around like cats in heat. Did Happy try to put it to you, Walking-stick? Or are you missing your little wife and child so much you decided to bugger him?"

"Fuck you, Green," called Jonathan as Lavalais landed a painful jab on his broken ribs.

"Aw, don't get ugly, Tonto. I was just coming to give you some news about your kid."

"You what?" Jonathan looked at the whey-faced man.

"You heard me. We just got a call about her, not twenty minutes ago."

"What?" Jonathan disengaged himself from Lavalais, sorry that he'd paced, sorry that he'd broken his cot, sorry that he'd done anything that might keep him from hearing news of Lily. He grasped the bars. "What did you hear?"

"Oh, just that they'd found her." Green leaned against the door jamb and casually examined his manicure. "Down in Atlanta, wasn't it?" he added, looking at his partner.

"Yep." Jenkins nodded in agreement.

"Is she alright?" asked Jonathan.

"What was it they said?" Again Green turned to Jenkins for corroboration. "She got adopted. By a couple in Florida."

"Adopted?" Jonathan felt as if someone had plunged an ice pick into his gut. He wanted to cry, to scream. How had strangers adopted his Lily?

"Yeah." Green gave up looking at his nails and grinned at Jonathan. "The law down there tried to stop her, but they got there just a few minutes too late." The deputy chuckled. "Your little girl's gone, Walkingstick. Next time you see her again, she'll be wearing bikinis and fucking boys on some beach."

"Wait," Jonathan pleaded, the world spinning crazily as the two switched off the light and started to leave the room. "Those people can't just adopt a child who already has parents!"

Green shrugged. "I reckon if they got enough money, Walkingstick, they can pretty much do what they damn well please."

44

MARY AWOKE FEELING as if she'd been on a three-day drunk. Her head throbbed, her stomach churned, and she longed to do nothing more than drink gallons of cold, fresh water. Though she could not see, she could now move her body and she could feel that the same kind of tape that bound her wrists and ankles also sealed her eyelids shut. As time passed, her senses sharpened, and she became aware of a cold, mountain pine smell, then music. The rockabilly music her father loved. The Everly Brothers singing "Wake Up, Little Susie," to be exact.

Suddenly she sensed something else. Movement. Fast, then slowing down. The whine of an engine, then a bump as the back of her skull thudded against something hard. Golden spirals of light whorled before her, then everything stopped—the music, the motor, everything but the smell of evergreen trees.

She heard the squeaking of leather, then a different

smell assailed her nose. Something like burned chocolate and strong male sweat. Then that voice.

"Wake up, little Mary."

Every nerve in her body tensed as fingers teased around her temples, then ripped something from her skin. She opened her eyes to see Stump Logan, risen from the dead.

"Long time no see, Logan," Mary croaked.

He grinned, his scruffy beard and fish-scale eyes reminding her of the mad monk, Rasputin. "You're a hard girl to get ahold of."

"Really? You've seen me at the Deckard County Courthouse. Also in my grandmother's kitchen. Also in Atlanta, at Lenox Mall."

He leaned closer. "I mean really get ahold of. Up close and personal."

"Well, you pulled it off this time. What did you use?" She looked around to see that she lay in the back of a van. Crumpled candy and fast-food wrappers littered the floor, and several soiled plastic diapers had been rolled up and crammed under the driver's seat.

"I disabled you with this." He pulled something that looked like a garage door opener from his pocket. "Then I knocked you out with this." He held up a plastic sandwich bag containing a square of white gauze.

"First a Taser," she said, recognizing the electronic stun gun worn by a few Atlanta cops. "Then chloroform?"

He gave a modest nod. "An old trick, but effective. Just like me."

"Okay. The next question is why?"

"I'm taking you to a venue that you seem to have a real affinity for," he said proudly.

"And that would be?"

He chuckled. "A place in the mountains. Deep and dark and hidden away. There's a funny little spot up there with your name on it, Mary Crow. And that's where you're going. The only question now is, do you want to go there asleep or awake?" He held up his chloroform rag.

"Awake," she replied, trying to keep from trembling in front of him.

He returned to the driver's seat and restarted the engine. They drove along, Logan munching Krispy Kreme doughnuts from a green and white box, and humming a maddening tune that sounded like a polka played on slow speed. As she twisted her wrists against the tape that bound them, she wished she could wrap her hands around Logan's porcine neck and squeeze the life out of him.

She struggled to sit up and get a better view out the windshield. She had no idea whether they'd been traveling for hours or days, and all she could see were the beams of his headlights through thick woods. No stars, no streetlights, not even the smallest glimmer from a distant farmhouse. She closed her eyes, fighting tears, then a boiling surge of rage swept through her. If Logan was going to kill her and complete his trifecta on her family, it was going to cost him, and cost him dearly.

"So what is it with you, Logan? Payback? Are you just pissed because I sent you running off into the mountains, hiding from the Feds?" Getting him talking was an old cop trick that he probably knew better than she did, but it was worth a shot.

His gaze met hers in the mirror. "Actually, it's because you're Jack Bennefield's kid."

Mary frowned. "Why does that make me so special?"

"Remember when you came back to the mountains and tracked that nutcase who'd abducted your girlfriend?"

Mary would never forget that October, two years ago, when a pleasant autumn camping trip with her two best friends had turned monstrous, leaving one of them raped and another disfigured, and had nearly cost all of them their lives. "I do."

"You fucking amazed me that last day. You walked like Bennefield, laughed like Bennefield—hell, you even climbed into that chopper like Bennefield. But what scared the shit out of me was that you had his determination."

"So?"

He grabbed another doughnut. "Sugar, that kind of determination is a dangerous thing."

"What do you mean?"

"You want answers to your questions," he said flatly. "And you won't stop until you get them." He swallowed the doughnut in two bites, reached for another. "I know what you're like. I know you won't rest until you find out what happened the day your mother died. I want to live the rest of my life without looking over my shoulder, fretting about you."

She was amazed at how his words echoed her own, back at the gas station with Ruth. *The hunter and the hunted,* she thought. *Both equally obsessed.* "Okay. Since you're going to kill me anyway, tell me about my dad."

Logan was so quiet that she feared she'd spooked him, then abruptly he began to speak. "I met Jack Bennefield in boot camp, at Fort Benning. We'd both been drafted. Me because I was too poor to go to college, him because he'd flunked out of Georgia Tech. Not because he wasn't smart, he just didn't want to be an engineer. Rock 'n' roll was Bennefield's thing."

"*That's alright, Mama,*" Mary thought, remembering the wonderful old tape in her father's bedroom.

"We went through basic training together. I hated the water; Bennefield swam like a fish. He saved me from drowning once on a night exercise. Pulled me out of the drink, sixty-pound pack and all.

"A couple of months later, I took him home with me

on a three-day pass. We were going squirrel hunting.
That's when the trouble began."

"The trouble?"

He glanced at her in the mirror, his good eye wide
with surprise. "Did your mother never tell you this?"

"No."

He veered over to the side of the road. Unbuckling
his seat belt, he dug a small photo from his wallet,
switched on the overhead light, and held the picture in
front of her face.

It was a faded photo of a teenage couple at a dance.
The boy looked gawky, bony wrists protruding from a
suit too small, hair combed forward in an ersatz Beatle
haircut. The girl stood regal despite her slight stature,
smiling and wearing a simple pink gown with a modest
wrist corsage. It was easy to distinguish between the
lover and the loved; the boy was sorely smitten, the girl
was simply attending a dance. Then Mary caught her
breath. As she looked closer, she realized that the eyes
beneath those Beatle bangs were Logan's; the girl's
sweet smile belonged to none other than her mother.

"Senior prom," Logan told her. "Hartsville High,
1965."

She gazed at the photo, stunned. Her mother had
talked so little about her old boyfriends that Mary had
assumed that she hadn't gone out much until her father
came along. But there Martha stood with young Stump
Logan, eye-shadowed and coiffed in the stiff, bouffant
style of the day. Mary would have cherished the image,
were it not for the boy who stood at her mother's side.

"I played first-string quarterback on the football
team. Your mom played me like a short game of stud."

"She wouldn't do that," said Mary.

"I was just another patsy in that little game all you
gals play. Flirt with a boy, get his attention, make him
fall for you. Then spit him out like a wad of old gum
when somebody better comes along."

"You and my mother were in love?" She spoke haltingly, reluctant to even give the words voice.

"We were until your father came along," Logan said bluntly. "Then I made the mistake of bringing my good ol' Army buddy Jack Bennefield home with me. Took Jack up to Little Jump Off to meet my girl. That's when he turned my life to shit. Wasn't a thing I could do to stop it, either." Logan's voice grew dreamy as he drifted back in time. "Bennefield walked into the store, Martha looked up from the cash register, and bang! It kicked you like a mule—those two just gawked at each other like there wasn't anybody else in the world. You know how hard it was to stand there and watch that? *And know that they never would have even met if it hadn't been for me?*"

His mouth turned down in a bitter line. "Until that morning, I would have trusted Jack Bennefield with my life. Ten minutes after we walked into that store, he dragged me out on the porch and said, 'Say, if you two aren't engaged, do you mind if I ask her out?'"

"Why didn't you just tell him no?" Mary wondered how one simple word might have rewritten all their histories.

"I thought about it," Logan whispered. "But I'd seen the look on her face. I could have sent your mother fifty roses a day for the rest of her life. She still would have loved only Bennefield."

Mary squeezed her eyes shut. So the great mystery of her life was as old as the mountains themselves. Boy meets girl, boy loses girl. The third act should have been boy finds girl again, but this one had taken a lethal twist. In this one the spurned boy hunts down and kills everyone who's aggrieved him.

"Okay. My father stole your girl. That was wrong. But did you kill him for it? Was it just like Irene Hannah thought?"

Logan chuckled. "That old bird had it dead-on.

Bobby Wurth was in charge of clearing a minefield, just north of Song Be. I told him to leave a couple on the far edge and we'd fuck with Bennefield's head. Wurth hated Bennefield, too, because he smoked dope and gave candy to the kids who hung around the camp. It was a nice day, as I recall. Cool, by Vietnam standards. We started tossing a football around. I told Bennefield to go long, cut right. He ran out fast, turned, then leaped like he had wings on his feet." Logan shook his head. "When he came down, he didn't have any feet at all."

Mary pictured her father—the lanky Atlanta boy who sang like Elvis Presley—lying in a field in Indochina, bleeding his life away. She wanted to weep from the waste of it all. "How did you think this would help you with my mother?"

"With Bennefield gone, I could get Martha back. We would get married. I would raise you as my own."

The idea of this man as her stepfather made her want to vomit. How wise her mother had been! How much better to have no man at all than a monster like this!

Logan tossed the prom picture to the floor.

"For sixteen years, your mother was up at that store, all alone except for you. No man helping her during the day, no man loving her at night. You two lived like little nuns. Do you know how crazy that drove me?" His eyes flashed with anger.

"Every day I would stop by while you were in school, take her little presents—smelly soap from town, candy, flowers. Never made a bit of difference. She was always polite, but never anything more. Finally, that last afternoon, I took a diamond ring up there. I had it made special, up in Asheville. I asked her to marry me. I got down on one knee, took out that ring, and said 'Martha, I love you. Please be my wife.'"

Thank God she said no, Mary thought.

"She whipped out this letter she'd gotten. From some pussy I'd served with in Nam. He was asking the

Army to investigate Bennefield's death. Claimed I'd murdered him.

"Martha held up that letter and looked at me as if I were a cockroach. 'Marry you,' she told me, her mouth all twisted and sneering. 'I hope the next time I see you will be at your trial for Jack's murder.' "

"And so you killed her."

He nodded, his gaze turning inward, as if he were watching a movie playing inside his head. "I killed her. But not before I got what I wanted for so many years." His eyes slid back toward her. "You want to know what your mother was like, Mary Crow? Sweet. Tight. Clawed me like a wildcat, but it was worth every second. I finally took back what Bennefield had stolen from me."

Mary thought of the footsteps that had echoed in her head since that long-ago spring afternoon. An odd gait, she'd dutifully reported to Sheriff Logan, never realizing that she was talking to the killer himself. And the huge manhunt that had rendered nothing—Jonathan and Billy Swimmer, combing the deep forest for days. What fools they'd been!

"Zudugina," she whispered, the Cherokee word for devil bubbling up from her unconscious. She smiled a grim, ironic smile. The Mexicans' devil wore black and carried acid. Hers carried fifty pounds of fat and an old torch for her mother that licked at her heels tonight, thirty-five years since the tragic day it had been lit.

45

KIMBERLY KHATAR LOOKED up as two more claimants to Jennifer Aziz stumbled into the security room. She could hardly believe that their nightmare was still expanding. After the strike force of airport guards stopped them just as they were stepping onto the plane, they had been escorted at gunpoint into this room, to give statements to the airport security cops and a tall, bird-like black woman who claimed to be some kind of DA. After another DA from a different jurisdiction took the sputtering Mrs. Hatcher away, a bald man who flashed a GBI badge started asking them where they were going and what they intended to do with the child.

"Just raise her," Kimberly said, trying to explain the situation and quiet the squalling Jennifer Aziz at the same time. She had just begun to calm the fretful baby when a sour-faced woman from Child Protective Services came in, swooped the child from her arms, and took a seat in the far corner of the room. Later, when the tall black DA brought in a wild-looking woman who tried to grab the baby away from the welfare worker, Bijan demanded an attorney. Now they all sat across from each other, outrage and hostility hanging heavy as cigarette smoke in a back-street bar. On her side was her husband and Mark Thompson, a local attorney Bijan had contracted through his lawyer in Florida. Facing them was the tall DA, the GBI agent, two airport security guards, and Jennifer's supposed mother, the wild-looking woman who claimed to be a Cherokee Indian called Ruth Moon. Now two more people entered the fray. A snappily uniformed sher-iff who led in a tall, dark-haired man whose blackened eyes and swollen jaw looked as if his head had met up with the business end of a baseball bat. Though the man wore handcuffs and leg irons, he carried himself like a king.

"Who the fuck is that?" Bijan whispered bitterly.

"I don't know, honey," Kimberly replied. "Let's just wait and see."

Bijan glared at the newcomers. "This is such a pile of shit. We have papers proving who Jennifer's biological parents were."

Kimberly watched as the woman who claimed to be Jennifer's mother leaped to her feet and threw her arms around the handcuffed man, clinging to him as if she were surprised to find him still alive. They started talk-ing with each other in muted voices, every so often glancing over at her and Bijan with angry, accusing eyes. Each time, Kimberly felt her face grow hot with an inex-plicable shame.

Finally they sat down. A moment later yet another person entered the room—an older man with wire-brush eyebrows and a thick gray mustache. Suddenly the airport cops, the young DA, and even Ruth Moon became inconsequential. Kimberly realized instinctively that this was the person she truly needed to fear; this was the man who could take their Jennifer away. Frightened, she tapped their attorney's shoulder. "Who is that man who just came in?"

"Jim Falkner," Thompson replied in a whisper. "Used to be the best prosecutor in the State of Georgia. He retired last year."

"What's he got to do with Jennifer Aziz?" cried Kimberly.

"I wish I knew," replied Thompson glumly.

Kimberly slumped back in her chair. They had given all the statements they had to give, truthfully answered all the questions asked them. As Mark Thompson gathered his papers and got up to join the on going battle in the middle of the room, there was nothing left for them to do but watch.

"I can't believe this," Bijan whispered as he leaned forward and buried his face in his hands.

Kimberly put her arm around him and tried to comfort him. "Don't worry, honey," she whispered. "If this doesn't work out we can try again."

He lifted his head and glared at her with strange, hostile eyes. "That's Jennifer Aziz, Kimberly. I'm her *Baba*. I don't want to try again."

They sat for hours as everyone tried to figure out who the child belonged to. Mark Thompson would occasionally step over with updates, once happily informing them that he'd convinced the prosecutors that the Khatars had acted unwisely, but without "malice aforethought."

"That's fine," said Bijan. "But what about our baby?"

Thompson had no answer for that, so they sat and listened some more. Though Jonathan Walkingstick, the regal-looking man who claimed to be Jennifer's father, had been brought from the Nikwase County jail, they could hear Jim Falkner slowly and calmly explaining his various crimes away, then floating the words "lawsuit against Nikwase County" in the diminutive sheriff's direction. Mrs. Hatcher's colleague Edwina Templeton, whom Falkner was now calling a coconspirator, had been apprehended at the Nashville airport, trying to board a flight to New Orleans.

Please let them be mistaken, Kimberly prayed, her hands like ice. *Please let Jennifer Aziz still be ours.*

As more people began coming in and out of the room, a weariness came over Kimberly that extended down into her bones. She put her arm around Bijan again, wishing she could fix it all, wishing that they, too, could accomplish that most fundamental of things, having a child of their own. She leaned against him for a long time, reassured by his smell, the feel of his shirt against her cheek. She'd begun to nod off into a dream about the beach when she felt someone sit down beside her. She opened her eyes to see Mark Thompson.

"I'm afraid I've got some bad news," he told her softly. "Apparently, Edwina Templeton gave you a forged birth certificate. We can't find any Behbaha Jane McIntosh born in Sullivan County, Tennessee. Nor can we find any John Winston McIntosh enrolled in Vanderbilt Medical School or any drowning victim by the name of Mahvash Ankasa. Both the Georgia and Tennessee Bureaus of Investigation did independent searches of the relevant databases. Both came up with nothing."

Deep inside, Kimberly felt a door beginning to close.

"However, identifying footprints were never taken for this baby, nor is there a birth certificate. As full-blood Cherokee Indians, the Walkingsticks claim the baby was born at their home, and Cherokee tribal law applies fully to their child."

"But why doesn't anybody think they're lying?" Bijan demanded.

"They could well be. I just asked for and got a court order to do a DNA test on them. For it to be legally admissible in a custody case, the chain of evidence will have to be maintained. The police will take both the baby and the possible parents to Grady Hospital. They'll use buccal swabs on the inside of their cheeks."

"So we'll know in a few minutes?" asked Bijan.

Thompson shook his head wearily. "It'll take at least five days, and that's with Falkner rushing it through."

"But who's going to take care of Jennifer Aziz?" cried Kimberly. "Isn't she still legally ours?"

"I'm afraid not, Mrs. Khatar. Right now she's a ward of the state of Georgia. If she turns out not to be the natural child of the Walkingsticks, you can reapply to adopt her here."

"But there are thousands of Georgia couples ahead of us, aren't there?"

Thompson took off his glasses and rubbed his eyes. "Yes, ma'am. I'm afraid so."

Kimberly felt as if she were gazing through the wrong end of a telescope. Though no DNA tests had been performed, she knew that she would never hold Jennifer Aziz Khatar again. She closed her eyes, trying to hold back her tears. For an incredible half a day, she'd been a mother. Now she was childless once more.

Mark Thompson continued. "They've taken Myrtle Hatcher to the police station for further questioning. As long as you stay in touch with my office, you two are free to go. So far, Georgia has no case against you."

"But what about Jennifer Aziz?" asked Bijan. "Do the Cherokees get to take her home with them?"

"Until the lab reports prove they are her parents, she'll stay in foster care."

"But she's so little," Kimberly protested, her tears beginning to flow. "She's just three months old."

"I'm sorry." Mark Thompson offered her his handkerchief.

They watched as two airport guards escorted the Walkingsticks out of the room. The caseworker who held Jennifer Aziz followed, accompanied by the tall DA and the GBI agent.

"They're going to the hospital now," explained Thompson. "After they do the swab test, they'll take the baby to a foster home."

Kimberly stood up, panicked. "Can't we even hold her one last time?"

Mark Thompson shook his head as if embarrassed by his state and its legal code. "I'm afraid not."

Bijan reached up and pulled her back into her chair, putting his arms around her. She kept her eyes on the people who still stood in the doorway; the two Indians, the attorneys, and the little girl who had once been theirs.

"Good-bye, Jennifer Aziz," Kimberly whispered. "I know you'll have the most wonderful life." *And she will*, Kimberly thought, weeping as she lay her head on Bijan's shoulder. *I just wish I could say the same about ours.*

46

THEY DROVE FOR hours—Logan humming his bouncy polka while Mary's thoughts churned. She wondered about Gabe in the hospital, Ruth now in Atlanta. Had Danika gotten to the airport in time? Had Gabe recovered from his illness? And Jonathan—what had become of him? As she was pondering everything that might have happened to her friends, she noticed that the pavement was growing bumpier, gravel began to pop under their wheels. Abruptly even that sound stopped, and she felt the van slide. *Dirt road,* she thought. *Clay soil. Slick* mountain *soil. Logan had told her the truth. He was taking her home.*

Clumsily the van corkscrewed up what felt like a forest trail. Tree limbs thwacked against the windows as they bounced over rocks and deep ruts in the earth. When she thought they could go no higher, he made a

sharp right turn and continued on for another five minutes. Then he braked hard and turned off the engine.

He got out of the driver's seat and slid open the cargo
door. As she watched him, she found it hard to believe
that this sour-smelling old man had ever danced at a
prom or quarterbacked the Hartsville Rebels to a state
football championship. By the same token, though he
and her mother would have made an unlikely couple,
she could imagine her mother going out with him a few
times, then politely turning him down thereafter. Logan
emitted no light; such a grim plodder would never have
captured her mother's heart.

He pulled a small knife from his pocket, cut the tape
around her ankles, but left her wrists bound in front of
her. "Okay," he said, pulling her to her feet. "Jump
down here."

She did as he told her, her hips brushing against the
sleek little Smith & Wesson he carried in his belt. A
damp breeze cooled her face and carried the pine-cedar-
earth smell of the Appalachians. Though she had no
proof beyond her nose, she knew she was somewhere in
North Carolina.

"Come on," he said, pushing her toward a dark
stand of trees. "This way."

"What about Irene Hannah?" Mary resumed her
questioning, again hoping to distract him. "Why her?"

"That moron Wurth needed a judge to kill. I suggested Hannah because she and your mother were such
good friends. I figured Martha had probably shown her
copies of the letter from that bastard who nailed me for
your dad. In fact, it wouldn't surprise me at all if you
didn't have that letter now."

You're absolutely right, Mary thought, remembering
the pages she'd sneaked out of Irene's closet and stashed
in her lockbox in Atlanta.

She looked around, wondering if she might scurry
around the front of the van. She could probably hide in

the woods long before he could get a shot off. But as if
reading her mind, he drew his weapon and pointed the
stubby barrel of the gun at her.

"Over there." He nodded toward a narrow footpath
that led up the mountain "And for once, Mary, just co-
operate. I don't want to have put a bullet in that pretty
brain."

You and me both, you asshole, she thought.

He pushed her up a steep trail, full of switchbacks,
through trees that had recently shed their leaves. Above
her she could see stars twinkling in the sky, below her
nothing but blackness. They were high and climbing
higher.

By the time sweat began to dampen the back of her
sweater, they reached the top of the mountain. Logan
had to stop, to catch his breath. She looked over her
shoulder to find him bent double and gasping for
breath. A hope kindled that he might be having a heart
attack, but in a moment his wheezing stopped.

"Over to the right," he gasped, his voice sounding
like air escaping from a leaky tire.

They walked into a small meadow, bright in the
moonlight. Fighting the muzziness she still felt from the
chloroform, she struggled hard to stay alert.

He steered her through more pine trees, then the terrain began to slope downward. They came to a kind of
clearing between the rocky face of a mountain and a
mountain stream that was only a glistening ribbon in
the darkness.

"Where are we?"

"Madison County, North Carolina." He nodded at a
dark gap in the rock that seemed to crack the mountain
face in two. "After Russell Cave I ran north, mostly at
night, mostly in the shadow of the Appalachian Trail. I
got lost east of Hot Springs, but I also got lucky. Found
me quite a little hidey-hole up here, and put it to good
use, too."

"What do you mean?"

"I found me a cave with a hole so deep, I've never heard a rock hit the bottom. I pushed poor old Clootie Duncan down there some months ago. In just a few minutes, you're going to join him."

Mary's heart began to pound like a drum. Logan had hit upon the one fear neither Xanax nor Dr. Bittner had been able to help her overcome—her utter terror of tight spaces and total darkness. She would take a slug in her brain any day before she would die that way. Her mind raced, desperate for a plan. As she looked up to watch high clouds scudding across the moon, she had an idea. She turned to Logan. "Can I go to water in that creek first?"

He frowned. "Go to water?"

"Cherokees go to water," she said. "Before battle, before we marry, before we die."

"Your mother didn't."

"You didn't give her much of a chance, did you?"

A curious look of sadness passed over his face, then he nodded. "Go ahead. But I'll be pointing this at you the whole time. Try anything funny and I promise you'll die in a lot of pain."

With Logan on her heels, she walked toward the creek. They climbed down several layers of shale-like rock until they both stood on the bank. Ten feet wide, the dark water curled around smooth boulders, its voice a low rumble in the night.

She knelt and plunged her face into the stream trying hard to keep her balance with her wrists bound. The water was so cold, it made her skin burn. She held her breath and prayed for some way to kill Logan. She considered wrenching his pistol away, creasing his head with another rock, then she remembered what Czarnowski, her boxing coach, always told her. *Find the sweet spot and nail it!* She thought about that, then, when she could hold her breath no longer, she raised up, dripping and cold.

"Okay," Logan's voice came from behind her. "I think you've washed all your sins away."

She shook the water from her face and rose to her feet, stepping up close to him.

"I'm not going in any cave, Logan," she said calmly, staring into his ravaged face. "You're going to have to kill me here, and you're going to have to look me in the eye while you do it."

He shrugged. "Not a problem."

He raised his pistol, aiming it directly into her face. Just as his finger eased over the trigger, she lunged forward. She felt the bones of her left hand pop as she slammed both her fists into his jaw. The force of the blow thrust her sideways, but it took him totally by surprise. With rubbery legs, he collapsed on the ground, groaning as the wind whooshed out of him. She heard the gun clattering across the shale, rattling like bones in the night. Swiftly she lifted her right foot to punt his balls into the next county, when he rolled sideways and tangled his feet up with hers. She fell, her tailbone smacking hard against the rocky ground.

"You little bitch!" he gasped, scrambling for the gun.

She picked up a piece of shale and threw herself on top of him, smashing the rock into his skull. He roared with pain, then rolled toward the creek, desperate to shake her off. She scrambled up and started kicking. Kidneys, eyes, scrotum, whatever she could connect with. He rolled toward the water like a hewn log. In the darkness she heard him curse. Gasping for breath, she looked for the gun, but it was impossible to see. Now struggling to his feet, in the shadows he looked like some fat slug trying to crawl through salt.

With the bloody rock in both hands she flung herself at him again. This time he fell back into the water, thrashing and churning as he tried to regain his footing. She attached herself to him like a barnacle, holding him under the frigid water despite his blows to her stomach and breasts.

"Don't" he sputtered, bobbing to the surface, desperate for air. "I can't—"

"Is that what my mother said?" cried Mary. "Or was it my dad?"

"Swim—" he gurgled.

"I didn't know that, Logan. But then, I'm as dumb a fuck as my dad!" With those words she crashed the rock into his temple. He sank again; she pummeled him twice more, the blows making sick, wet whacks against his head.

She lost her grip on him, then he surfaced a few feet downstream, the current now carrying him along. Blood gushed down his face and his one good eye held the wide, shocked stare of death as he made a grab for the last boulder that would save him. Though she knew she was pushing the limits of her own strength, she awkwardly splashed forward. She brought the rock down again and again, smashing his face, his hands, trying to break his hold on anything that kept him breathing air instead of water.

"No!" he pleaded, choking and coughing.

"Don't like dying, huh?" She flailed at him like something gone mad. "Neither did Irene. Neither did Jack Bennefield. Neither did Martha Crow!"

He sank beneath the water for a moment, then rose again, blood covering his face, his fingers no longer able to find purchase on the boulder. "But she was mine!" he cried. "I loved her!"

For a second Mary almost pitied him, this singular monster for whom love had grown into a virulent cancer. Then she remembered that all the sorrows of her life had sprung from his heart, his hands, his sick brain. "But she never loved you back, Logan," she told him.

She never knew whether he heard her or not. His eyes rolled back in his head, his hands slid off the boulder, and he sank beneath the water. She listened for the sound of anyone thrashing farther downstream, but all she heard was the endless roar of the water on its millennia-long journey from the mountains to the sea.

Chest heaving, she hoisted herself upon the boulder. She sat, shivering, still gripping the bloody rock, then she began to cry great, gulping sobs. It was finished. Finally, and completely. She'd killed the man who'd killed her mother and ended a malevolent love that had begun back when young men brought their dates fat corsages and combed their hair like Paul McCartney. A long time by human standards, but not long at all for the stars. She looked up into the sky and found Jonathan's beloved Orion, Betelgeuse beaming centuries-old light down from the hunter's shoulder. Finally she'd found the answer to the great question of her life. For the first time ever she finally knew the *why*.

47

FOR A LONG time she sat there, listening to the water, her thoughts roiling, wondering what she should do with the rock she'd used to kill Logan. She knew she ought to save it as evidence for the cops, but then again, she wondered if she shouldn't take it and put it on her mother's grave. Let it serve as the capstone to the pile of seven she'd already left there. In a way, that seemed fitting; in another way, it seemed a sacrilege. Her mother had been good, kind. To top her grave with a stone rusty with her killer's blood would demean Martha's memory. Mary lifted the rock up, trying to embed its weight and heft forever in her memory, then she let it drop. It sank as profoundly into the water as Logan had, swept away forever.

Only then did she climb off the boulder and fight her way through the swift, neck-deep current to the bank. With her clothes heavy and dripping, she pushed through the pines and across the meadow, trembling under the caress of a cold night breeze. She located the van easily, its loaf-like shape looking out of place beneath the frilly, graceful pines. Logan had left the doors unlocked, but had taken the keys with him on his trip downriver. Mary rummaged around until she found a hunting knife under the passenger's seat and then managed, with some major contortions, to cut the duct tape that bound her wrists. With chattering teeth, she searched the vehicle for dry clothing. She found a pack rat's array of stuff—a laptop computer, her purse, Gabe's gun, three bottles of baby formula, and blessedly, in an old knapsack in the back of the van, a size XXX camouflage suit still in its plastic wrapper. As she stripped off her wet clothes and slipped the dry ones on, she spotted her mother's photograph on the floor where Logan had tossed it.

"I got him, Mama," she said. "He won't bother us anymore." She buttoned the photo in the breast pocket of the suit, deciding that when she got back to civilization she would have a copy made and slice Logan from the shot. Then it would be just her mother standing there at sixteen, with the whole of her life a great unwrapped present, one yet to be opened.

In the glove box she found a stash of sweets that put Jonathan's passion for Ding-Dongs to shame. Candy bars, jelly beans, a sticky, lint-covered jar of sourwood honey. Mary took one chocolate bar and closed the compartment, repulsed.

She found neither her Deckard County cell phone nor the one Logan had used to call with, so she stashed her candy in another pocket and stepped out of the van. If she could find her way back to the highway, she might be able to hitch a ride with somebody and bring the cops back up here at first light. Zipping Logan's giant-sized jumpsuit to her neck, she started walking back along the way they'd come, the moon now a hard white eye staring down upon her.

————

It was almost dawn before Bruce Clinedienst's pickup pulled up alongside her. "You been in a wreck?" The man eyed Mary curiously, his lower lip plump with a wad of tobacco.

"Kind of," she replied. "I need to get to a phone, or the nearest sheriff's office."

"I'm going into town to pick up my newspapers," said Clinedienst. "You could call from there."

"What town would that be?"

"Mars Hill, North Carolina." He frowned at her disapprovingly, no doubt wondering why a young woman would be wandering along this road in an oversized camouflage suit not even knowing where she was.

By the time the sun burned off the morning fog, Mary, Sheriff Jinx Jenkins of Madison County, two Carolina state troopers, one SBI agent, and two Feds were back at the crime scene. Though Sheriff Jenkins admitted once attending a convention in Raleigh with Stump Logan, he worked the scene with a chatty professionalism, scurrying back and forth between the federal and state officers. Mary sat in the backseat of a car with Federal Agent Lee Hoffman, watching as another agent took pictures of the van. She'd learned that both the Tennessee and Carolina highway patrols had been searching for the vehicle, registered to one Edwina Templeton, of Franklin, Tennessee.

"Everybody had a ten fifty-five on you," Hoffman informed her.

Mary frowned. "Who turned in the call? Nobody knew where I was."

Hoffman flipped through a small notebook. "The original ABP came from Officer Jane Frey of the Franklin, Tennessee, PD. She answered a call from two Hispanics at a gas station." Hoffman turned to her, puzzled. "That make any sense?"

Mary laughed. "Actually, it does. Do you know where they are now?"

He scanned another sheet of paper. "The Hispanics are in INS custody. Officer Frey continued her investigation with information they gave her. Looks like she busted one—"

"Edwina Templeton?" asked Mary.

"Yeah. DBA the Tender Shepherd Home. Frey nailed her for an immigration violation at the Nashville Airport, but the Mexicans are singing their own little tune about Templeton forging birth certificates and selling babies to the highest bidder."

"Will the INS send the Mexicans back across the border?" asked Mary.

"Not till after this goes to trial," said Hoffman. "Probably, though, after that."

Mary remembered the woman's luminous eyes, the man's protectiveness of her. She would call Chip Clifford about them when she got back home. He could make sure those two stayed safe from their tormenting Scorpions. "Do you have a cell phone I could borrow, Agent Hoffman?"

"Sure." He held out a government-issue model that lacked a video screen. "Help yourself."

She called Danika first. The tall black woman's voice bubbled with excitement.

"We got them, Mary! They were at the gate, about to board the plane, but we got them!"

Mary listened as Danika filled her in on the details— that the adoptive couple were nice people who'd been duped by some woman in Tennessee and another baby broker from Florida.

"When did the baby's mother get there?" asked Mary.

"About two A.M. Man, is she one weird chick. And then they brought the father in, right off the chain gang, apparently."

Mary frowned. "What do you mean?"

"Leg irons, handcuffs. The sheriff acted like he was leading in a grizzly bear. Plus, the poor guy had been roughed up pretty bad."

Mary didn't say anything. She was glad she hadn't been there. It would have broken her heart to see Jonathan led around in shackles.

Danika continued, "I gotta tell you, Mary. I had my doubts about the biological parents until Jim Falkner came along."

"What did Jim do?"

"Turned them into saints in buckskin. There wasn't a dry eye at that table when he got through. Then, when he suggested that the Walkingsticks had a damn good case of their own against Nikwase County, I thought that little sheriff was going to shit his pants!"

Mary laughed, imagining her old boss's bluster. "So what's going on now?"

"The baby's in protective custody. The parents are staying at your house, waiting for the DNA tests to come back. The woman said it would be okay, and they both knew where you kept your key."

"It's fine," said Mary. "They're both old friends of mine."

Mary listened as Danika went on about how cute Lily was and how heartbroken the Florida couple had been. She would have talked on for hours, but Mary interrupted her.

"Let me get back to you, Danika. There's another call I need to make."

She disconnected from Danika, then got the number of Vanderbilt Hospital. A moment later, a woman at the information desk answered.

"I'd like to speak to a patient," said Mary. "Gabriel Benge is the name."

"Just one moment."

The phone rang twice, then a woman said, "Room thirty-three seventeen."

"Could I speak to Gabe Benge, please?" Mary asked eagerly.

"He's gone. He done got released this morning," said the woman. "I came up here to clean his room and he was about to walk out the door."

"He was?" Mary tried to hide the disappointment in her voice. "Is he okay?"

"Well, I ain't no nurse, but he looked okay to me." The woman gave a raucous chuckle.

"I don't suppose he mentioned where he was going?"

"He said something about going to Peru. Don't that beat all? Get up from a hospital bed and head straight to South America?"

"Yes," said Mary. "That does beat all. Thanks just the same." With a sigh, she clicked off the phone. She'd hoped she and Gabe might have more to say to each other, but he apparently saw it differently. Probably a wise move, she decided. Digging up the dead was a lot safer than chasing after the living.

She left numbers where she could be reached with all the law enforcement agencies involved, then she got Agent Hoffman to give her a lift to Tremont. Her little Miata sat where she'd left it, like a dog waiting for its master to come home. Throwing her purse and Gabe's gun in the back, she revved the engine and pulled out onto the highway. With both the National Guard and the demonstrators gone, Tremont had regained its composure as a picturesque Tennessee mountain town, one that she sincerely hoped she would never see again.

She drove south, again passing through Chattanooga, again thinking of Gabe, and Nancy Ward's grave. A little after seven P.M., she pulled into her grandmother's driveway. The old house looked more like an old friend, with lights twinkling in the living room and Jonathan's truck parked outside. Wearily she pulled into the garage and trudged up the back stairs into the kitchen. Jonathan and Ruth sat in the breakfast nook, the Tiffany lamp that hung over the table casting their faces in a golden glow.

"Mary!" Ruth looked up, surprised.

"Hey!" Jonathan leapt from the table and threw his arms around her. Though he sported a black eye and a badly swollen jaw, he looked far from the handcuffed inmate Danika had described. "I'm so glad to see you!"

"I'm glad to see you, too." As she relaxed into his comfortable, familiar embrace, all that had happened suddenly grew real. "It was Logan," she told him, fighting tears. "Logan all along."

"What?" He looked down at her, incredulous.

The story of Logan and her parents came out in a gush. When she finished she felt drained, as if she'd emptied some long-buried cache of emotion.

"I figured it must be something like that when Ruth told me what you'd done," Jonathan said, holding her tight. "I wanted to come help you, but I couldn't. I don't know what I would have done if anything had—"

"Hush." Mary stopped him quickly. "It's over. Let's not talk about it anymore." She looked over at Ruth. "Let's talk about Lily."

Smiling, Jonathan grabbed her hand and pulled her over to the table. Ruth got up and made room for her between them. "Glad you're back, Mary," she said quietly.

"Hi, Ruth. How are you?" Mary couldn't help but check for the wild, erratic gleam that lately had appeared too often in Ruth's eyes. But tonight she seemed calm to the point of being subdued. Mary was delighted. Ruth deserved a rest after the great storm of losing Lily.

"I'm okay." Ruth rose from the table. "Would you like some soup?"

"No, thanks. I'm not hungry." Mary turned to Jonathan. "I talked to Danika earlier, so I know Jim

Falkner's representing you, but tell me what else is going on."

"Lily's in Child Protective Services right now," said Jonathan. "It'll take about a week to get the DNA tests back, although Falkner said he would have them rush it."

"So have you seen her at all?" Mary asked, foggy on her child custody procedures.

"No," snapped Ruth. "I haven't been allowed to even touch her."

"Well, a week will pass quickly," Mary promised. "What about the couple from Florida?"

"They're fighting it," Jonathan replied. "They hired an attorney and are staying here in Atlanta, waiting for the results of the test just like we are."

Mary tried to imagine two people cooped up in a hotel room, all their hopes pinned on a report that she knew would only bring them bad news. "That's sad."

"Not nearly as sad as if they'd flown off with Lily," said Ruth, stirring a pot on the stove.

"No, of course not," Mary agreed.

"So there's not much we can do but wait," Jonathan continued. "Is it okay if we stay here?"

"As long as you like," Mary said. "Maybe you ought to go over to Grady and have someone look at your jaw."

He started to reply, but Ruth returned to the table, carrying a steaming bowl.

"I know you must be hungry, Mary. Please try some of this soup."

"Thanks, Ruth, but I stopped on the way and ate a hamburger."

"Well, if you change your mind." She put the bowl of thick, orange-colored liquid down in front of Mary.

Mary shook her head. "I'm going upstairs. I need a long, hot shower and about a hundred hours of sleep." She stood, Jonathan and Ruth wavering before her eyes.

"You two make yourselves at home. I'll see you sometime tomorrow."

"Thanks, *Koga*." Jonathan smiled, his hawkish eyes kind. "I don't know how we'll ever repay you."

"No repayment needed, Udolanushdi." She gave his shoulder an affectionate squeeze. "You got Lily back. That's all that matters."

48

MARY TOOK THE longest shower of her life, then wrapped up in a towel and padded into her bedroom. Her old peony-grubbing jeans still lay on the floor, and piles of Jasmine Harris notes were strewn across her bed.

I wonder how Jasmine is doing, she thought as she moved the papers to her desk. *I wonder if Danika told her that she put the Popsicle Man away.* Mary sighed. Just last week she'd eaten, breathed, and slept Jasmine Harris and Dwayne Pugh—now the case seemed like something that had happened years ago; a postcard bought at a destination she could barely remember visiting.

She pulled on an old Emory sweatshirt and paused to look out her window. Outside, yellowish light from the kitchen spilled out on the lawn.

"Never again," she reminded herself aloud. "Will I

have to look out there and wonder if I'm going to see Logan."

She fell into bed, snuggling beneath the quilt she'd slept under since the first night Eugenia had brought her here. Again she thought of Gabe, hoping he was all right, wishing that he'd hung around long enough to say good-bye—then her body grew heavy and warm. The last thing she remembered was the luminous green numbers on her clock, glowing 8:27 P.M.

She dreamed then. Not of Logan, but jumbled snippets of her mother, Jonathan, her grandmother, and Gabe. One particularly long saga evolved where her father bounded up the stairs in his combat fatigues, grinning and full of life. Her grandmother held out her arms to hold him, weeping tears of joy. He kissed her on the cheek, then hurried to his bedroom, cranked up his electric guitar, and began singing "That's All Right, Mama."

Mary smiled in her sleep at the sound of her father's youthful voice. The dreamed changed then, segued into something about Eugenia and the flower beds, but the music went on. She stirred, rolled over, then finally opened her eyes. Though the clock now read 2:13 A.M., the music continued. She could still hear her father singing as if he were just down the hall.

"You're dreaming," she said aloud, sitting up in bed. She tried to wake herself up, counting five fingers on each hand, reacting sharply to being pinched, but still she heard the music. Throwing off her covers, she pulled on her old jeans and opened the bedroom door.

She crept out into the dark hall. Jonathan and Ruth had taken the small guest room downstairs, so she had the whole upper floor to herself. Though there was no need for her to be quiet, she felt an odd compulsion to tiptoe, like a child waking too early on Christmas morning. Her father's bedroom stood at the end of the hall, past her grandmother's room and a spare bedroom no one ever used. No light shone from beneath his door, yet his performance went on, just as if he'd come back from the dead. She felt the hair rise on the nape of her neck.

"Oh, come on," she chided herself. "It's just that crazy old tape deck." She started down the hall with intention, like someone about to fix a malfunctioning machine, but two steps later her bravado vanished and she started creeping toward the door like a mouse.

She reached her grandmother's room. The floorboard directly beneath the doorjamb gave a sudden loud pop, making her jump. She paused to collect herself, then she continued toward her father's old room. She'd just inched close enough to grab the doorknob when the music stopped, leaving her in a silence that seemed even eerier than the music itself. She stood like a statue, feeling vaguely foolish, wondering if she might have exchanged one hallucination for another one. Would she now start hearing her rockabilly father instead of seeing Stump Logan?

"Absolutely not," she told herself firmly. "Logan wasn't a hallucination to begin with."

Suddenly the music started again. Young Jack Bennefield sailed into the second verse of his song, jaunty as ever. Willing her hand steady, she turned the doorknob.

The door swung open. She gasped. Ruth was sitting in front of the tape deck, staring straight at her. She looked just like a case file photo Mary had once seen of a woman who'd hacked her family to pieces, convinced they were all demons from hell.

"Ruth?" Mary asked. "Are you okay?"

"I'm fine, Mary," Ruth replied, reaching to turn off the music. "I couldn't sleep. I thought I might poke around up here."

"Listening to my father sing?" Mary thought Ruth's choice of late-night diversions odd.

"Jonathan told me about how much your mother loved him. I guess I was just curious." She gave an apologetic shrug. "I hope I haven't intruded . . ."

"No, that's okay," Mary said guardedly. "I just couldn't imagine how that old tape deck had come on."

Ruth smiled. "Your father had a wonderful voice."

"Yes, he did."

"Was your mother musical, too?"

Mary shook her head. "My mother was a weaver. She painted some, too."

"A painter, huh?" Ruth bounded up from the chair as if struck by a brilliant idea. "Then come downstairs with me. I want to show you something."

"Right now?"

"It won't take a minute." She grabbed Mary's hand. "You'll appreciate this, especially if your mother was an artist."

Wondering what Ruth could possibly have in mind, Mary allowed her to pull her back out into the hall and down the stairs. They crossed the darkened foyer and the dining room, then Ruth began to tug her toward the guest room.

"Wait a minute, Ruth," said Mary. "Isn't Jonathan asleep in there?"

"It doesn't matter." Ruth turned to her with a malevolent little grin. "Come on in. You'll get a kick out of this."

She opened the door and pulled Mary inside. Jonathan lay on the bed, a sheet covering his nakedness. He slept so still that Mary wondered for an instant if he wasn't dead. She grabbed on to the door facing, unwilling to further intrude in the Walkingsticks' bedroom. "Ruth, this isn't—"

"You need to come over here, Mary." Ruth let go of her hand and walked over to switch on the bedside lamp. "It's important that you see this!"

Reluctantly Mary followed her, wondering what this woman was going to do. "Okay. What?"

Ruth smiled, then turned and looked down at Jonathan as if she were admiring some figure in a wax museum. "Isn't he beautiful? If your mother were here, she could paint him."

Mary nodded. This was getting more bizarre by the second. "Is he all right?"

"Just look at his shoulders, his arms." Ruth traced the straight line of Jonathan's clavicle with one finger.

"Stop, Ruth. You're going to wake him up," Mary warned, though Jonathan had not twitched an eyelash.

"No I won't." She looked up at Mary and grinned, sly as a mink. "Why don't you kiss him, Mary? I know how much you want to."

"Look, Ruth, I don't know what kind of game you're playing, but I'm going—"

"You don't have to worry about waking him up. I gave him some tea that will keep him sound asleep."

Mary watched, horrified, as Ruth reached under her sweater and pulled out Gabe's pistol. With her sly smile stretching into an obscene grin, she aimed it point-blank at Mary.

"I want to watch you kiss him, Mary. I want to watch you kiss him good-bye."

Mary froze, dumbstruck, certain she was sleepwalking through a nightmare. Then she saw the look in Ruth's eyes. Ruth Moon meant to kill her tonight. There was nothing dream-like about that.

She's out of her mind, Mary realized. *She's insane.*

"Okay, Ruth," she said as calmly as she could. "You put the gun down, then I'll kiss Jonathan."

For what seemed an eternity Ruth stared at her, keeping her finger on the trigger, the barrel pointed at Mary's chest. Mary held her breath, fearing that the slightest movement might set Ruth off. Time slowed to eternity, then Ruth slowly lowered the pistol. When she'd pointed at the floor, Mary took a deep breath and stepped toward Jonathan. He lay motionless, his face relaxed in slumber, unaware of all that was transpiring at his bedside. "Jonathan?" she said loudly, hoping that her voice might rouse him. "Can you hear me?"

He did not move. Ruth giggled. "See? I told you he wouldn't wake up. Now go ahead."

Mary could think of nothing else to do, so she leaned over and pressed her lips against Jonathan's. They felt warm, and his breath was soft and rhythmic upon her cheek. He was definitely alive, but way beyond her reach. Raising up, she turned toward the woman who held Gabe's gun.

"Okay. Now what?"

Ruth lifted the gun again. "Walk into the kitchen. You'll see."

Mary did as Ruth commanded, backing out of the bedroom and into the hall. She walked to the kitchen, Ruth two steps behind her. When they entered the kitchen, Mary saw that a single light burned over the stove, and the old telephone receiver dangled from its hook, bleating insistently. The bowl of soup Ruth had offered her earlier still sat on the table.

Suddenly it fell into place. Ever since she'd arrived in Tremont, Ruth had kept her tea thermos close at hand. She'd used tea to calm down, to perk up, to give the pretense of sanity. Ruth had served Gabe tea one night, and the next day he'd nearly died. Now Jonathan was in some kind of coma, victim of another of Ruth's brews. A sick reality pierced the very marrow of her bones as she turned to the woman she'd once considered a friend. "You're a poisoner, aren't you?"

Ruth's eyes glittered in the dim light. "I'm an herbalist. I use nature's medicines to suit my needs."

"And you need Gabe and Jonathan and me to die?"

"Gabe was just practice, and Jonathan will wake up in a few hours." She smiled a death's-head smile. "You're the only one I need to die."

"But why? I've never done anything to harm you."

"Because however close I hold my husband, you're always right there, between us."

Mary closed her eyes. Her long history with Jonathan—the vast, unspoken thing that had weighted every word between her and Ruth—had suddenly grown teeth and claws.

"Jonathan loved you before me; he prefers you even now," Ruth told her. "He will go to his grave loving you."

"That's not true, Ruth. Jonathan and I haven't—"

"Yes it is true!" Ruth poked the gun at Mary, as if that might shut her up. "Now it's worse. I thought he would be pleased that I called you when Logan took Lily, but he just blames me for losing her."

"Ruth—"

"But I thought we would get over that, you know? I thought eventually he would forgive me. But at the jail in Tremont, I finally realized how much he loved you. Oh, Jonathan wanted to find Lily, of course, but you were just as important. *You* go find *Mary,* Ruth. *Mary* needs your help. *Mary* can't do this all alone."

"That's not—"

"Logan and I had a lot in common, Mary. We both feared you. He because of his past; me because of my future."

Mary felt as if the air were being sucked from her lungs. Had she heard this right? Was Ruth admitting complicity with the man who'd kidnapped Lily? Had the whole thing been a setup? *No,* she told herself. *Ruth is raving, out of her mind. Nobody would do a thing like that.*

"Put the gun down, Ruth," she said. "You're not thinking straight right now."

"I'm thinking straight enough to succeed where Logan failed. I'm thinking straight enough to know that if I shoot you here, in this kitchen, I can make it look like I mistook you for an intruder long before the police get here."

Mary didn't know what to say. She felt as if she'd stepped outside of herself, risen sylph-like from her bed to act out this travesty with Ruth. She stood there, trying to think of what to do, when she noticed lights flickering, reflected in the windows over the sink. Was someone pulling into the driveway? Quickly she turned her attention back to Ruth and tried to keep her talking. "And how do you figure you can cover up a homicide, Ruth?"

"A stressed-out, exhausted woman in a strange house. Hears a noise, grabs a gun, and frantic to protect her family from yet another assailant, pulls the trigger."

"That's your story?" Mary laughed, but kept an eye on the light. "A first-year law student would rip you to shreds."

"They would try, sure. But think about it, Mary. What motive would I have to kill you? Who on earth would shoot the person who'd just saved their child?"

"Someone sick with jealousy," replied Mary. "It would take the cops about five minutes to figure that out."

"How? Who would tell them? Jonathan wouldn't. And nobody else knows."

"Ruth, a lot of people know about us. Jim Falkner, Alex Carter, Joan Marchetti. Gabe." Mary stared into the woman's haunted eyes. "You're going to need a whole lot more than laced tea to get away with this."

"Then I'll just plead insanity," said Ruth. "At least I'll still be alive. You'll be dead."

Suddenly noises erupted at the back door. Someone was knocking, yelling. Mary turned long enough to catch a glimpse of Gabe, then out of the corner of her eye she saw Ruth, pointing the pistol at him. In that instant, Mary took her chance. She leapt at Ruth, knocking her to the floor. She hoped to jar the gun from her hand, but Ruth managed to hold on to it. With the nine-millimeter barrel pressing against Mary's ribs, the two women grappled on the floor, knocking over one of the breakfast nook chairs, spilling the poisoned soup on the floor. For Mary, their struggle became a bizarre waltz of muscle and emotion. As she tried to wrest the gun from Ruth's hand, she heard Gabe banging on the door, the frantic rattle of the doorknob, then the distant whoop of a police siren. Ruth lowered the gun, now thrusting it hard into her belly. I'm going to die gut-shot, Mary thought, dreading the death that all cops fear. Loosening her grip on Ruth's hand, she grabbed the gun itself, trying to turn it away from her, toward the wall. Ruth gave a sudden twist backward, and Mary felt the gun slip. *One more good jerk,* she thought, *and I'll have it.* But before she could tighten her grip on the thing, Ruth's nails began to dig into her hand. She leaned to her left, then suddenly she heard a noise that sounded as if the roof was falling down around them. A hornet's nest seemed to envelope her right ear as she felt something warm and wet begin to dampen her chest. She thrust herself away from Ruth's grasp just as the woman flopped back under the table. Ruth lay with the gun still in her hand, her eyes wide with shock and fear, her blood already spreading toward the refrigerator, making a dark red finger just below Lily's christening photo, still hanging on the door.

49

W

One month later

"OH, WOW!" MARY paused to gaze out her bedroom window. Though it was only mid-November, a snow had fallen overnight, and the birdbath, the peony bed, and even her grandmother's cockeyed sundial stood covered in a dazzling blanket so white that it hurt her eyes. The sky was a clear ocean of crystal blue, and the only other color she saw was the bright red slash of a cardinal as it swooped over to the now-full bird feeder. She sat down on the window seat. Snow before Thanksgiving was almost unheard of in Atlanta, and already she could hear the delighted shrieks of the little boys next door, no doubt freed from a day of school. As she leaned against the windowsill, she saw a figure emerge from the kitchen below.

It was Jonathan, carrying Lily, bundled up in the little pink snowsuit Mary had bought her. He lifted the baby into the frosty air, pointing at the cardinal, then at the snow-covered magnolia, then up to the bright blue sky.

"Dotesuwa, looguhee, galuhlowee," Mary repeated softly, naming the things as Jonathan was, twenty feet below her. Since Ruth died, he'd revealed a far more extensive Cherokee vocabulary than Mary had ever known him to possess. He fed Lily breakfast, asking her *zayoshiha,* comforted her with *zasdizazoyihuh,* and rocked her to sleep with the old tales of how the Milky Way was made, and why the buzzard's head is bare. She couldn't figure out if he was working through his grief or trying to impart to his daughter some of those values her mother had so treasured. She supposed it didn't matter. Lily loved it, was growing bigger each day, and Jonathan was beginning to knit his life back together.

"Adahihi," Mary whispered as she watched Jonathan scoop up a tiny bit of snow and put it on the very end of Lily's nose. *Poisoner.* That was one word he would never teach Lily in Cherokee, or any other language. That word had etched such a sadness into his heart that she'd often feared he might die from it. It was still hard for any of them to believe, but the toxicology reports from Vanderbilt Hospital, and the results from the Georgia State forensics lab lay on top of her desk, along with all the other papers she'd cleared out of her office. Ruth had served Gabe a massive dose of *Lobelia inflata,* commonly known as pukeweed. He was on the verge of a coma when the paramedics had taken him; only atropine and a ventilator had saved him. Had Mary consumed the soup Ruth had laced with Carolina Jasmine, she would have taken her shower, gone to bed, and died of cardiac arrest. Both plants were easily gathered herbs that grew in the Appalachians; they'd discovered plenty of each in Ruth's medicine bag.

"But why?" For the hundredth time, Mary asked herself. "Why would she have done such a thing?"

At Jonathan's insistence, they had performed an autopsy. Mary knew Price Martin, the ME, well, and though he had been especially attentive, the results had come back inconclusive. Ruth had no brain lesions, no toxins in her bloodwork, no organic reason at all for her to try to poison the godmother of her child.

"If she was three months postpartum and her baby had been kidnapped, it might have pushed her over the edge," Price theorized, pulling off his latex gloves as Mary stood shivering in the autopsy room. "I'm no shrink, but I imagine that being pregnant, then lactating, then undergoing that kind of stress could shake up a pretty potent hormonal cocktail."

"Enough to make a normal emotion go off the charts?" Mary asked.

"Two drinks at a bar can make a normal emotion go off the charts," Price replied prissily. "You should know that."

Yes, Mary thought. *I do.* But had Ruth's jealousy gone so far out of control that she'd joined up with Logan? Once again Ruth's words echoed in her head as she watched Jonathan playing with Lily. *Logan and I had one thing in common, Mary. You.* She'd never told Jonathan what Ruth had said, but in the past month Mary had gone over those ten words ten thousand times, desperately searching for reason and motive. Some days, it actually seemed conceivable that Ruth had colluded with the former sheriff of Pisgah County; other days, Mary was ashamed to even consider such a thing. All she knew for sure was that she would ponder Ruth Moon until the day she died. Right now she preferred to think Logan acted alone. Who knew what she would think tomorrow? In a way, it didn't matter—the truth lay buried in a freshly dug grave in Tahlequah, Oklahoma. And there it would remain, forever.

She watched as Jonathan started carrying Lily toward the driveway. His breath was making plumes of smoke in the bright, cold air. Laughing, she tapped on the window. He looked up and grinned, and waved for her to join them.

"Coming!" she called. She rose from the window seat, closed the bulging suitcase that lay on her bed, and lugged it downstairs to the kitchen. Though the room had been professionally scoured after CSU had finished, they had not taken any of their meals there since the night Ruth died. Mary could not look at the kitchen door without seeing Gabe there that night, fresh from the hospital, frantic to warn her that Ruth Moon was a poisoner. He'd driven first to Tremont, then to Atlanta when Dula told him that the Walkingstick baby had been found. He'd gotten her home address from the suitcase that she'd left in his van and called the Atlanta cops to meet him here.

"Thank God for that," Mary whispered, closing her eyes against that awful night. Dropping her suitcase beside the door, she walked over to the telephone and looked at the list of numbers she'd left for Danika. Plumber, electrician, yardman, Walter and Pat Smith, her next-door neighbors. She thought she'd covered everything, but if she hadn't, Danika was a home girl. She had resources of her own in Atlanta. Her property would be in good hands.

As she turned to take a final walk-through of the house, the walls seemed to echo with seventy-five years of her family's history—Eugenia's wild parties, her father's guitar playing, her own addiction to figuring out the past. She would miss them, just as she would miss all her friends in Atlanta, but it was time for her to go. She glanced upstairs once, toward her father's old room, then she returned to the kitchen, threw on her coat, and lugged her suitcase outside, just as a white camper pulled into the driveway.

"Hi!" Gabe waved at her as he climbed down from the driver's seat, cloaked in a brightly striped Mexican serape. "How is everybody?"

"We're fine." Jonathan shifted Lily in his arms as the two men shook hands. "How about you?"

"Ready to head south," Gabe replied. "You two still going home?"

Jonathan nodded. "It's time for me to get back to real life. I don't think Aunt Little Tom can handle the Christmas mail rush all by herself."

"So Lily and her dad will have to help out," Mary said, walking over and taking Lily from Jonathan. The child grinned at Mary, once again making her funny little bird chirps. Though she immediately grabbed a lock of Mary's hair and gave it a painful tug, Mary held her close, enjoying the exquisite softness of Lily's cheek against her own. Smiling, she turned to Jonathan.

"Have you gotten everything from the house?"

He nodded. "I loaded up this morning. While you two were still asleep."

"That's your dad, Lily." Mary laughed. "The early bird, out catching all those worms. Come on. Let's go get in the truck."

She carried Lily over to the camper, Jonathan following. As their footsteps squeaked through the powdery snow, she could feel his gaze upon her, heavy as the now-white branches of the magnolia tree. When they reached his truck, he opened the passenger door, slipping a little in the process.

"I don't know what to say," he mumbled, suddenly awkward. "Except I love you."

She looked up at the face she'd held so dearly for so many years. "Me, too," she whispered. "But now I'll have to take a number. This brown-eyed girl snuck ahead of me in line."

"I have you to thank for that, too."

Mary shrugged. "I owed you one. Or maybe two. I lose count."

"Then let's just call it even."

"Suits me." Impulsively, she leaned over and kissed him. Even with the truck door between them, their old electricity zinged through her, just as intense as it had been way back in the seventh grade. For an instant she lost herself in the feel and taste of him, then Lily squawked, and she remembered that Gabe was standing there, not twenty feet away. She stepped back, embarrassed.

"You sure you won't change your mind about coming with us?" Jonathan gazed deeply into her eyes, his voice a husky whisper.

She shifted Lily in her arms, hugging the child's sweet warmth close. She loved Jonathan as no other, but so much lay tangled between them that she wasn't sure it could ever be sorted out.

"Thanks." She shook her head. "But I can't."

He looked at her for what felt like a lifetime, then his mouth curled in an ironic half-smile. "Maybe not now. But someday you will. We've come through too much to be apart."

His words took her by surprise. She leaned over quickly to tuck Lily into her car seat, trying to hide sudden tears. Jonathan was right—they had come through too much to be apart, but they'd also come through too much to stay together. For her, the best thing to do seemed to simply say farewell, and hope that all their wounds grew less tender with time. As she buckled Lily's seat belt, she whispered in her ear, "Take care of your *edoda*, Lily. He's mighty special."

With Lily secured, she wiped her eyes and straightened up. Jonathan was still looking at her, pointedly.

"I'm going to get you back, *Koga*," he said, closing Lily's door with finality. " I promise you that."

She wanted to tell him that no, he really needed to find someone else, but she couldn't make the words leave her mouth. Instead she just watched in silence as he walked around the front of the truck, got in, and started the engine. "Be careful" was the best thing she could finally come up with. "Take good care of Lily!"

He gave her that odd half-smile again, then drove slowly out of the driveway. With a plume of white smoke sputtering from the exhaust he turned right and disappeared down the road that would take him first to the interstate, then to the mountains, finally to the rambling country store beside the Little Tennessee River. There a new little Cherokee girl would spend her rainy days playing on the porch, and her starry nights watching Orion rise above the mountains in the eastern sky.

"*Dodadagohuhee,* Lily," she whispered. "Grow up as smart as your mother and as brave as your dad."

"Hey."

She jumped, unaware that Gabe had walked up beside her.

"I can catch him, you know. It's not too late to revise your travel plans."

She turned and looked up at the new man she'd grown to love. "Don't even think about it," she said, lifting her hand to stroke his cheek. "I was just saying good-bye to my oldest friend."

"You sure?" His deep blue eyes asked the unvoiced question. "Lima's pretty far away. I sure don't want to take you if you don't want to go."

"I want very much to go," she said, wrapping her arms around him. Though his kiss was different from Jonathan's, it elicited an equally compelling tingle deep inside her. "And I very much want you."

They stood there for a long time, then she grabbed his hand and pulled him toward the camper. "Now come on. You promised me a Peruvian Christmas—sixty five degrees, sunny, with the smell of jasmine in the air."

"You got it," he said, laughing. Suddenly he stopped. "Oops, I almost forgot. I brought you these."

He reached under his poncho and pulled out two bright blue sweet-potato looking things with a line of holes punched along the top.

"What are they?" asked Mary.

"Ocarinas—the national instrument of Peru. I figured we could learn to play them on the way down."

"You do realize that I've never played a duet with anybody in my life?" she asked as they walked to the camper together.

"Neither have I." He smiled, pulling her close. "That should make it interesting."

ABOUT THE AUTHOR

SALLIE BISSELL is a native of Nashville, Tennessee. She currently lives in Asheville, North Carolina, where she's at work on her fourth novel of suspense. Visit Sallie online at www.salliebissell.com.

DEAR READER:

I thought I was finished with Mary and Jonathan at the end of *Call the Devil by His Oldest Name,* but they kept tugging at my creative sleeve, even as I wrote another book—a novel about the Ani Zaguhi, Cherokee mystics who can assume the shape of bears. One evening last summer, I was biking down from the Blue Ridge Parkway when I came nose-to-nose with a bear! She was enormous and magnificent and before I could gather my scattered wits, she vanished without even rippling the leaves around her. Later, I began to wonder. Was it a real bear, or an Ani Zaguhi? Chance, or Cherokee magic, urging me to return to a story left unfinished?

That bear led me back to Mary and Jonathan and to *Legacy of Masks.* I hope you find it as exciting to read as I did to write!

Sallie Bissell

LEGACY
OF
MASKS
by Sallie Bissell

*Turn the page for an exciting preview
of Sallie Bissell's new thriller featuring
Cherokee prosecuter Mary Crow,
coming soon from Bantam Dell Books.*

LEGACY
OF
MASKS
Coming Soon

Hartsville, North Carolina
November 20, 1982

"GET A MOVE ON, Deke, we need to go help find that little girl." Harold Craig, assistant scout master of Boy Scout Troop 238, frowned at the skinny, redheaded boy who darted across the beams of his headlights.

"Coming, sir!" Deke Keener hurried to the rear of Mr. Craig's pickup truck. As he climbed into the back, Deke saw that all the other members of 238's wolf patrol sat shivering together, their eyes wide with the sudden urgency of their mission. Deke, however, was sweating with anticipation. No camping trip this; not even one of Mr. Craig's beloved forest fire drills. This was *real*. Eight-year-old Tracy Foster, daughter of the mayor and Deke's own across-the-street neighbor, had vanished from Beaver Moon Campground, a skinny finger of a picnic area between Tuckaseegee Creek and the 500,000 acres of the Nantahalah National Forest. Tracy had gone there on a cook-out with her own Brownie

Troop, and had not shown up when Mrs. Winston, the troop leader, took the final head count before leaving. Deke happened to be fishing right across from the campground when Mrs. Winston had started hollering like someone being skinned alive. He'd looked up to see the woman scurrying around, at first gathering the girls inside her station wagon, then ordering them back out to the edge of the woods to holler Tracy's name. All at once she spotted him on the other side of the creek, still holding his line calmly in the water.

"You, boy! Aren't you Joe Keener's son?"

Deke nodded, trying to pretend that he hadn't been watching them all along.

"Run home and call the sheriff. Tracy Foster's gotten lost in the woods!"

That was six hours ago. The bright autumn afternoon had turned into night, and Tracy had still not shown up. Deke smiled as a biting cold breeze brought the smell of dry leaves and far-off campfires.

Ten minutes later, Mr. Craig pulled his truck into the Beaver Moon parking area. Police cars, two fire trucks and an ambulance stood ready to receive the lost Tracy Foster. Deke's heart ratcheted up with the thrill of such commotion; his own father was out searching with the rescue squad while the mayor himself stood beside the creek, holding his weeping wife, both of them gazing fearfully into Tuckaseegee Creek.

"You boys stay put," Mr. Craig ordered. "I'll go talk to Sheriff Logan."

The boys watched as Mr. Craig walked over to a picnic shelter where Sheriff Logan and a Forest Ranger were shining flashlights on a map.

"What do you think they'll want us to do?" asked Jerry Cochran, a chubby, nervous boy who Deke knew hated the forest during the day, and feared it at night.

"Go on a snipe hunt." Randy Bradley stuck his tongue out at Jerry. "And you get to be the snipe, Cockroach."

"My Dad says a bear could've got her," offered Butch Messer, unwrapping a piece of pink bubblegum.

"Shoot, I bet she *drowned*. They'll probably find her down in Sley Holler, all swelled-up and *green*."

Ignoring the speculations of his troop-mates, Deke watched as Mr. Craig gave the sheriff a brisk nod and headed back toward their truck.

"Okay, boys," he called. "They want us to post a picket line at the entrance of the campground and keep any unauthorized vehicles from coming in."

"Will we have to go into the woods?" Jerry Cochran's voice wobbled like a girl's.

"No. We're going to stand in a line across a slab of asphalt." Mr. Craig, who often regaled them with tales of his adventures with General George Patton's Third Army, sounded slightly disappointed. "Bear patrol will spell us at 2200 hours, unless someone finds that poor little girl."

Oh, someone's gonna find her, Deke said to himself, his blood racing through his veins like fire. *Someone's gonna find her real soon.*

The Confederate soldier stood on the forty-sixth of the one hundred and five concrete steps that led from Main Street to the Pisgah County Courthouse. Rifle at his side, he'd kept a weather-beaten watch for any encroaching Yankees for as long as Mary Crow could remember. Passing him on her fourth grade Civics field trip, she'd found him impressively fierce. Six years later, as she'd rushed past to apply for her driver's license, she thought him quaintly embarrassing. Today, nearly twenty-five years after their first acquaintance, the old boy seemed comforting and familiar. No much else about Pisgah County did.

"Hey, Johnny Reb." She paused for a moment in the puddle of shade cast by the towering bronze figure. Already she was breathing heavily from her climb, and she still had fifty-nine steps to go. She'd forgotten how hot the early June sun could be in the Carolina mountains, and she'd foolishly worn her prosecutorial black suit, Deathwrap. Comfortable in the relentlessly air-conditioned courtrooms of Atlanta, on these steps Deathwrap felt like a portable sauna, buttoned in the front and zipped tight at the waist.

"Shoot," she hissed, leaning against the base of the statue. Already she'd torn her hose and sweated through her underwear. Pretty soon she'd have big damp circles under her arms. In her business it was never good to be visibly nervous; to be both nervous and sweating did not bode well at all.

Nonetheless, she had an appointment with DA George Turpin in four minutes, and she could not be late. Squaring her shoulders, she resumed her ascent to the courthouse. As her high heels clicked on the steps, she gave a rueful smile at the irony of her undertaking. When she was eighteen, she'd wanted to leave Pisgah County forever. Today, at thirty-five, she couldn't wait to come back home.

The past year had been her year of living danger-ously. She'd left her ADA job in Atlanta to go to Peru with archaeologist Gabe Benge. Though it seemed like a wonderful chance for a whole new life, eight months later she'd known she'd made a mistake. One day while riding in a *totora* boat in Lake Titicaca she'd been struck with such an ache for home that she almost wept. *Why are you here*, the lake itself seemed to whisper, *among mountains you don't know, Indians who will never regard you as anything more than a tourist*? At that instant she'd realized she had to go home. Not to Gabe in Lima or to her grandmother's house in Atlanta, but back to the mountains of North Carolina. Back to Jonathan Walkingstick. Somehow everything she didn't need at eighteen, she needed quite desperately now.

But coming home to Pisgah County required money, and to get that, she needed a job. To that end, she was seeing George Turpin. She'd called him two weeks ago, as soon as she stepped off the plane in Atlanta. George had sounded highly enthusiastic over the phone—Yes,

I'd love to talk to you, Love to have a woman of your experience on my staff. In fact, we have a man who's taking early retirement. When could you come up for a talk? They'd made their arrangements, and settled upon today, here, in about three minutes. If she hurried, she would be on time.

She finally reached the hundred and fifth step, and without pausing, strode into the vaulted lobby of the old courthouse. She passed a gaggle of secretaries clad in frothy print dresses, hurrying to begin the day's work. Suddenly she felt even more out of place in Deathwrap. Swathed in black among women clad in the colors of melting sherbet, she must look like the Grim Reaper, seeking her next victim. When she glanced over her shoulder and caught one of the secretaries casting a curious eye back at her, she knew without a doubt that she would be the gossip tidbit du jour. *Did y'all see that girl dressed in black? Who was she? You don't see clothes like that around here. She must be some fancy pants, over from Raleigh. Don't kid yourself, honey. Didn't you see that hair? She was pure Cherokee . . .*

Shrugging off the imaginary wags, Mary checked the building directory beside the elevator. Turpin's office was on the third floor. She punched the button, then rode up with two overweight men in seersucker suits, one of whom looked vaguely familiar. She considered introducing herself, but both men hurried out once they reached the second floor. She rode on, alone, to the third floor where, at the end of the hall was a frosted glass door with "George H. Turpin, District Attorney" lettered in gold.

She entered to find an older woman seated behind a desk. Gray hair curled all over her head like steel wool, and unlike her younger counterparts downstairs, she wore a beige linen suit with a simple white blouse. The woman looked up at Mary. At first she smiled; then, as if she found Mary somehow wanting, her mouth drew down in a severe line.

"May I help you?" she asked curtly.

"I have an appointment with Mr. Turpin at nine o'clock," Mary answered. "I'm Mary Crow."

For a moment, the secretary did not speak. Though Mary had no recollection of ever meeting this woman, she knew her name was not altogether unknown here. She had, three years ago, broken up a conspiracy that had put Pisgah County Sheriff Stump Logan on the FBI's most wanted list. Two years ago she had killed that same sheriff in Peter Cove creek. Although Logan had been proven to be a kidnapper, rapist and murderer, he had also been part of a powerful political organization, a man still fondly remembered by a certain number of people on the Pisgah County payroll. She would have to tread carefully in this courthouse.

Turpin's secretary began writing in some kind of logbook. "Mary C-r-o-w-e," she spelled aloud, using the traditional Cherokee spelling of the name.

"Just C-R-O-W," Mary corrected.

"Really? Most people around here spell it the other way."

Mary shrugged. She'd dropped the 'e' on the end of her name back when she'd gone to college and dropped most all of her Cherokee past. She wasn't sure there was any point in adding it now.

"Have a seat. Mr. Turpin'll see you in a moment."

Mary crossed the room to sit beside a window that afforded her a view of the Confederate soldier's bronze backside, with the town of Hartsville stretched out beyond him. Main Street ran straight as a ruler west, toward the hazy blue foothills of the Nantahala Forest. Though Hartsville had changed a lot in her seventeen-year absence, its chief industry had remained the same. As the county seat, all legal proceedings instigated by and against the 34,000 residents of Pisgah County took place here. The same small law offices that clustered around the courthouse when she was a child were still there, now headed by the descendants of their original founders.

"Ms. Crow?"

A man's voice interrupted her reverie. She turned to find a heavy-set, balding man dressed in the summer uniform of all Southern attorneys—khaki trousers, navy blazer, striped regimental tie. "George Turpin," he said, his smile revealing a chipped front tooth that gave him a boyish look. "I'm so glad to meet you."

Standing, she smiled and shook his hand.

"Come on back to my office," he said, leading her down a green carpeted hallway. "Would you like some coffee? A Coke?"

"No, thank you," she said, glancing once at the secretary, who watched them over her reading glasses.

Turpin led her to a corner office that boasted a now-empty fireplace. Where her former boss in Atlanta had decked his walls with basketball memorabilia, George Turpin celebrated himself. His person space was splattered with photographs of himself with the prominent and powerful. Turpin golfing with the governor of North Carolina, Turpin hewing down a tree with the local congressman, Turpin shaking hands with the chairman of the Cherokee gaming commission. Interspersed among the photos were a dozen shadow-box frames containing the kind of rosette ribbons won at horse shows and county fairs. Blues, mostly, with a few reds and yellows thrown in for a touch of humility.

"Do you show horses?" Mary stepped over to get a closer look at one of the displays.

"Honey, any horse I got on would keel over dead from the excess avoirdupois." Laughing, Turpin patted his rotund middle. "No, those ribbons are for barbecue."

"Barbecue?" Mary frowned. Had they made barbecue a contact sport while she was in Peru?

"Pisgah County DA's office has won the North Carolina Barbecue Championship for the past five years," Turpin explained proudly. "We compete in the vinegar-and-pepper category and the tomato-based group. Best durn stuff you'll ever put in your mouth. Here." Turpin sat behind his desk and pulled a bottle of orange-looking sauce from a drawer. "Take some of this home with you. Put it on anything—pork, chicken, ribs. Tofu, if you're a tree-hugger. You'll think you've died and gone to heaven."

"Thanks." Mary took the jar the man offered, then sat down across from him. "It looks wonderful."

"It is. I tell you, when I retire, I'm gonna open me up a little barbecue shack on 441. Catch all them tourists goin' into the Casino before they lose all their money." He laughed heartily, amused by his own future, then he returned to the present, pulling her resume from his drawer, and snapping it open.

"Let me say right off it's a real pleasure to meet you. I regarded your mentor, Judge Irene Hannah, as a great legal mind and a true friend." He tapped Mary's resume. "This record does her proud."

"Thank you." Mary smiled at the memory of the woman whose footsteps she'd followed, in whose home she now lived. "Irene was a wonderful person."

"She was indeed. Even though that Logan business caught us with our pants down, we owe you a debt of gratitude, for bringing her killer to justice."

Mary didn't know what to say. She hadn't intended to embarrass Pisgah County law, she'd simply killed a despicable man whose murderous history stretched back decades.

"So let's talk a little bit about this. Tell me why somebody with your record would want to work here?"

Mary's tongue felt stuck to the roof of her mouth. What should she say? That in the middle of Lake Titicaca she'd wanted to come home so bad she nearly wept? That as sweet as the jasmine-scented nights of Miraflores had been, she'd longed for the smell of cedar and pine?

"I want to come home," she said simply. "And I need a job. Criminal prosecution is what I do, and I'd like to do it here."

Turnpin smiled. "You're Cherokee, aren't you?"

"Half," replied Mary. "My mother grew up in Snowbird. My father was a Georgia boy."

"And you've lived away from here for how long?"

"Seventeen years. I went to live with my grandmother shortly after my mother was murdered."

"Well, I don't know how well you've kept up with things here, but this isn't Hot-lanta. We get one, maybe two murders a year, and most of those are somebody getting drunk and shooting whatever significant other gets in their way." Turpin sighed. "A trained monkey could put most of 'em away."

"That's okay," said Mary easily. "There's more to law than just convicting murderers."

Turpin frowned. "You say that now, but I bet if I put you on staff you'd be looking for a new job in six months. I don't mean to be discouraging, honey, but Pisgah County is for people like me—middle-of-the-class grads who want nice, quiet careers that allow them enough time to enter barbecue competitions or coach Little League." Again he tapped her resume. "These pages tells me that you eat, breathe and sleep felony prosecutions. Having you at Pisgah County would be like hitching Seabiscuit up to a plow."

"But I gave you my credentials when we talked on the phone. You seemed excited about the possibility of my joining your staff."

He sighed. "To be honest, Ms. Crow, I was very flattered that you'd called. And I'd love to put you in the office right next to mine. But the plain truth is, I just don't have room for you. There's not an opening on staff anymore."

Mary was stunned. Two weeks ago, Turpin had practically offered her a job over the phone.

He explained further. "When you called I had Pete Nicholson's resignation on my desk. Three days later, Pete came in and asked if he could stay on. His wife was just diagnosed with breast cancer, and they've still got a boy in college."

"I don't suppose you could give me a trial run? See how I fit in after six months?"

Turpin closed the folder that held Mary's resume. "I'm sorry. I just don't have the budget for that. Tell you what, though. Leave me a number where I can reach you. If and when I get a vacancy, you'll be the first person I call. I owe Irene Hannah that much."

Mary reached in her purse and handed him one of the business cards she'd made up last night, on her computer. Turpin's brows lifted as he read it.

"This is a local number. I thought you lived in Atlanta."

"Not anymore. I inherited Judge Hannah's farm. I'm a full-time resident of Pisgah County, as of a week ago."

"I see." A look of discomfort flitted across Turpin's face, then vanished. "Then welcome to the neighborhood. If anything opens up here, I'll be sure to call you right away."

Mary gathered up her bottle of barbecue sauce and her black leather briefcase. *I can't believe this,* she thought, trying to fight the blush of humiliation she felt spreading across her cheeks. She, with her dozen convictions, turned down by a man who could probably count all his murder indictments on one barbecue-sauce-stained hand.

"Thanks for seeing me, Mr. Turpin." She rose, smiling through clenched teeth. "It's been a pleasure."

"Thank you for coming, Ms. Crow." Turpin took her hand gently in his. "I promise I'll be in touch. It may be a while, but I won't forget you."

Moments later, Mary was trudging back down the hundred-and-five steps. She paused once again by the watchful Confederate.

"I crapped out, Johnny Reb," she told the silent statue, still incredulous at Turpin's complete about-face. "There's no place for me here."

Swallowing hard, she fought a second of panic. She'd left a man who loved her and a career she loved in Atlanta to come live in a rural mountain county that had no use for her or her skills. Had she totally lost her mind?

"No," she told the mute statue, looking into the bright blue bowl of the Carolina sky and the mountains rising high around her. "You've just come home to Pisgah County."

SARA PARETSKY

"Paretsky's name always makes the top of the list when people talk about the new female operatives." —*The New York Times Book Review*

___ Bitter Medicine	23476-X	$7.99/11.99
___ Blood Shot	20420-8	$7.99/11.99
___ Burn Marks	20845-9	$7.99/11.99
___ Indemnity Only	21069-0	$7.50/10.99
___ Guardian Angel	21399-1	$7.99/11.99
___ Hard Time	22470-5	$7.99/11.99
___ Killing Orders	21528-5	$7.99/11.99
___ Deadlock	21332-0	$7.99/11.99
___ Total Recall	22471-3	$7.99/11.99
___ Tunnel Vision	21752-0	$7.50/10.99
___ Windy City Blues	21873-X	$7.99/11.99
___ A Woman's Eye	21335-5	$6.99/8.99
___ Women on the Case	22325-3	$7.50/10.99

HARLAN COBEN

Winner of the Edgar, the Anthony, and the Shamus Awards

___ Deal Breaker	22044-0	$7.50/10.99
___ Dropshot	22049-5	$7.50/10.99
___ Fade Away	22268-0	$7.50/10.99
___ Back Spin	22270-2	$7.50/10.99
___ One False Move	22544-2	$7.99/11.99
___ The Final Detail	22545-0	$7.99/11.99
___ Darkest Fear	23539-1	$7.50/10.99
___ Tell No One	23670-3	$7.50/10.99
___ Gone for Good	23673-8	$6.99/10.99

RUTH RENDELL

Winner of the Grand Master Edgar Award from *Mystery Writers of America*

___ Road Rage	22602-3	$6.99
___ The Crocodile Bird	21865-9	$6.99
___ Simisola	22202-8	$6.99
___ Keys to the Street	22392-X	$6.99
___ A Sight for Sore Eyes	23544-8	$6.99

Ask for these titles wherever books are sold, or visit us online at
www.bantamdell.com for ordering information.

BANTAM MYSTERY COLLECTION

____57204-0 **KILLER PANCAKE** Davidson • • • • • • • • • • • • • • • • • $6.99

____56859-0 **A FAR AND DEADLY CRY** Holbrook • • • • • • • • • • $5.99

____57235-0 **MURDER AT MONTICELLO** Brown • • • • • • • • • • • $7.50

____58059-0 **CREATURE DISCOMFORTS** Conant • • • • • • • • • • • $6.99

____29684-1 **FEMMES FATAL** Cannell • • • • • • • • • • • • • • • • • $6.99

____58140-6 **A CLUE FOR THE PUZZLE LADY** Hall • • • • • • • • $6.50

____57192-3 **BREAKHEART HILL** Cook • • • • • • • • • • • • • • • $6.50

____56020-4 **THE LESSON OF HER DEATH** Deaver • • • • • • • • • $7.99

____56239-8 **REST IN PIECES** Brown • • • • • • • • • • • • • • • • • $7.50

____57456-6 **A MONSTROUS REGIMENT OF WOMEN** King • • • • • • $6.99

____57458-2 **WITH CHILD** King • • • • • • • • • • • • • • • • • • • $6.99

____57251-2 **PLAYING FOR THE ASHES** George • • • • • • • • • • $7.99

____57173-7 **UNDER THE BEETLE'S CELLAR** Walker • • • • • • • • • $6.50

____58172-4 **BURIED BONES** Haines • • • • • • • • • • • • • • • • $6.50

____57205-9 **THE MUSIC OF WHAT HAPPENS** Straley • • • • • • • • $5.99

____57477-9 **DEATH AT SANDRINGHAM HOUSE** Benison • • • • • • • $6.50

____56969-4 **THE KILLING OF MONDAY BROWN** Prowell • • • • • • • • $5.99

____57533-3 **REVISION OF JUSTICE** Wilson • • • • • • • • • • • • • $5.99

____57579-1 **SIMEON'S BRIDE** Taylor • • • • • • • • • • • • • • • $5.99

____58225-9 **REPAIR TO HER GRAVE** Graves • • • • • • • • • • • • • • $6.50

....

Please enclose check or money order only, no cash or CODs. Shipping & handling costs: $5.50 U.S. mail, $7.50 UPS. New York and Tennessee residents must remit applicable sales tax. Canadian residents must remit applicable GST and provincial taxes. Please allow 4 - 6 weeks for delivery. All orders are subject to availability. This offer subject to change without notice. Please call 1-800-726-0600 for further information.

Bantam Dell Publishing Group, Inc.	TOTAL AMT $_____
Attn: Customer Service	SHIPPING & HANDLING $_____
400 Hahn Road	SALES TAX (NY, TN) $_____
Westminster, MD 21157	
	TOTAL ENCLOSED $_____

Name _____

Address _____

City/State/Zip _____

Daytime Phone (_____) _____

MC 1 3/04